BIPOHL

Two Complete Novels

by

Frederik Pohl

A Del Rey Book

BALLANTINE BOOKS ● NEW YORK

A Del Rey Book
Published by Ballantine Books

Library of Congress Catalog Card Number: 81-22814

ISBN 0-345-30247-8

Manufactured in the United States of America

First Ballantine Books Edition: March 1982

Cover art by David B. Mattingly

A shorter version of "Drunkard's Walk" appeared in *Galaxy*
Magazine, © 1960 by Galaxy Publishing Corporation.

"The Age of the Pussyfoot" appeared in a shorter version in
Galaxy Magazine, © 1965, 1966 by Galaxy Publishing Corporation.

Contents

The Age of
the Pussyfoot

Foreword

I have two conflicting opinions. One is that any story should stand on its own feet—which means that, generally speaking, anything a writer has to say about his own story is better left unsaid. If it's worth saying, why didn't he say it in the story itself?

The other opinion, however, is equally firmly fixed in my mind, and at this moment it is in direct conflict with the first. That is, I think that more people should read science fiction than appear to be willing to do so; and I think the reason for this is that many people regard it as crazy, fantastic stuff with no basis in the real world and no relevance to their own lives.

I would like to hope that some people will read this book who normally don't read science fiction. If you are one of them, and if you begin to feel like those many others mentioned above, please pause in your reading and go on to look at the author's note included in the back of the book.

It seems to me that science fiction *can* have relevance to the real world and, yes, to your own life. And some of my reasons for thinking so are set forth here. . . .

Chapter One

Over everyone in the room, or perhaps it was a park, the lighting cast shapes and symbols of color. The girl in the filmy gown had at one moment glittering pink eyes and, at the next, an aura of silvery hair. The man next to Forrester had golden skin and a mask of shadow. Wisps of odor drifted past him, rosebuds following sage. There were snatches of a crystalline, far-off music.

"I'm rich!" he yelled. "And alive!"

No one seemed to mind. Forrester plucked one of the colorless grapes Hara had recommended to him, rose, patted the girl in the filmy dress, and walked unsteadily down to the pool where the revelers splashed and swam in a naked tangle. In spite of the long post-revival indoctrination that had given him so many new things and removed so much trash that was old, Forrester had not lost the habit of being a little dirty-minded, and he was interested in nakedness.

"It's Forrester the rich man!" one of them shouted. Forrester smiled and waved. A girl cried, "Sing him a song! A song!" And they all splashed at him and sang:

> *Oh, he died and he died and he died—*
> (SPLASH!)
> *And he cried and he cried and he cried—*
> (SPLASH!)
> *With his rages and his cholers he's a puzzle to
>   the scholars,*
> *And he's got a quarter of a million dollars!*
> *Forrester!*
> (SPLASH! SPLASH!)

Forrester ducked without thinking, then relaxed. He allowed them to drench him with the warm, scented water. "Enjoy, enjoy!" he cried, grinning at the bare bodies. Bronze and ivory, lean or soft, every body was beautiful. He knew that none of them would think the worse of him if he touched the two snaps at throat and waist and stepped out of his clothes to join them. But he also knew that his body would not compare well with those of the Adonises, would not impress the full-breasted Venuses, and so he stayed on the rim. "Drink and be merry, for yesterday we died," he called and squirted them at random with his joymaker. He didn't mind that he was not as beautiful as they. At least, not at this moment. He was happy. Nothing was troubling him. Not worry, not weariness, not fear. Not even his conscience; for, although he was wasting time, he had a right to waste time.

Hara had said so. "Relax," advised Hara. "Get acclimated. Go slow. You've been dead a long time."

Forrester was well content to follow his advice. In the morning he would take things seriously. In the morning he would go out into this new world and make a place for himself. With unassuming pride he thought that he would do this not because he really needed to, for he had that quarter of a million dollars, all right, but because it was proper that he should work and earn joy. He would be a good citizen.

Experimentally he shouted what he thought of as a friendly obscene suggestion to one of the girls (although Hara had said that the talk of this time contained no obscenities). In return she made a charming gesture which Forrester tried to think of as an obscene one, and her companion, stretched out at the edge of the pool, drowsily lifted his joymaker and drenched Forrester with a tingling spray that, startlingly, brought him to an instant thrill of sexual excitement and then left him replete and momentarily exhausted.

What a delightful way to live, Forrester thought. He turned and walked away, followed by more of the shouted song:

And he slept and he slept and he slept,
And he wept and he wept and he wept—
Is he damning? Is he dooming?
For that matter, is he human?
Forrester!

But he was too far away for them to splash him now and he had seen someone he wanted to talk to.

It was a girl. She had just come in and was still rather sober. She was alone. And she was not quite as tall as Forrester himself.

Hara would introduce him to her if asked, Forrester knew, since this was more or less Hara's party. But he did not at that moment see Hara. Didn't need Hara, either, he decided. He walked up to the girl and touched her on the arm.

"I am Charles D. Forrester," he said. "I am five hundred and ninety-six years old. I have a quarter of a million dollars. This is my first day out of the sleep-freeze, and I would appreciate it if you would sit down and talk to me for a while, or kiss me."

"Certainly," she said, taking his hand. "Let's lie down here on the violets. Careful of my joymaker; it's loaded with something special."

Half an hour later Hara came by and found them, lying on their backs, each with an arm under the other, heads inclined toward each other.

Forrester noticed him at once, but went on talking to the girl. They had been plucking and eating the glass-clear grapes from a vine over their heads. The intoxicating fruit, the occasion, and his general sense of well-being combined to erase social obligations from his mind. Anyway, Hara would understand and forgive any offense. "Don't mind him, dear," Forrester said to the girl. "You were telling me not to sign up as a donor."

"Or as game. A lot of greenhorns fall for that, because the money's good. But the way they get you is that you don't figure what it will cost in the long run."

"That's very interesting," said Forrester, then sighed,

looked away from the girl, and nodded up at Hara. "You know, Hara," he said, "you're a drag."

"And you're a drunk," said Hara. "Hello, Tip. You two seem to be getting on well enough."

"He's nice," the girl said. "Of course, you're nice too, Tip. Is it time for the champagne wine yet?"

"Well past. That's why I came looking for you. I went to a lot of trouble to get this champagne wine for the party, and Forrester will damn well get up and drink some to show the rest of us how it's done."

"You tilt," said Forrester, "and you pour."

Hara looked at him more carefully, then shook his head and fingered his joymaker. "Don't you remember anything I tell you?" he chided, spraying Forrester with what felt for a moment like an invigorating, and not at all shocking, ice-cold shower. "Not too drunk tonight. Get adjusted. Don't forget you were dead. Do what I tell you, will you? And now let's see about this champagne wine."

Forrester got up like an obedient child and trailed after Hara toward the dispensing tables, one arm around the girl. She had pale hair, up in a fluffy crown, and the tricks of the lighting made it look as though fireflies nested in it.

In the event that he ever saw his once and potentially future wife Dorothy again, Forrester thought, he might have to give this sort of thing up. But for the time being it was very pleasant. And reassuring. It was hard for him to remember, when he had an arm around a pretty girl, that ninety days before his body had been a cryogenic crystal in an ambience of liquid helium, with his heart stopped and his brain still and his lungs a clot of destroyed scar tissue.

He popped the cork of the champagne like a good fellow, toasted, and drank. He had never seen the label before, but it was champagne, all right. At Hara's request he roared the verses of "The Bastard King of England," amid much applause, and would not let anyone sober him although he knew he was beginning again to reel and stammer. "You decadent sods," he bellowed amiably, "you know so much! But you don't know how to get drunk."

They were dancing, a linked circle of all twenty-odd of them, with foot-stamping and sudden changes of direction, a little like a morris dance, a little like a Paul Jones, to music like pizzicato cello and the piping of flutes. The girl cried, "Oh, Charles! Charles Forrester! You almost make an Arcadian of me!" He nodded and grinned, clinging to her on his right and to a huge creature in orange tights on his left, a man who, someone said, had just returned from Mars and was stumbling and straining in Earth's gravity. But he was laughing. Everyone was laughing. A lot of them seemed to be laughing at Forrester, perhaps at his clumsy attempts to follow the step, but no one laughed louder than he.

That was almost the last he remembered. There was some shouting about what to do with him, a proposal to sober him up, a veto, a long giggling debate while he nodded and nodded happily like a pottery head on a spring. He did not know when the party ended. He had a dreamlike memory of the girl leading him across an empty way between tall dark structures like monuments, while he shouted and sang to the echoes. He remembered kissing the girl, and that some vagrant aphrodisiac wisp from her joymaker had filled him with a confused emotion of mingled desire and fear. But he did not remember returning to his room or going to sleep.

And when he awoke in the morning he was buoyant, rested, vigorous, and alone.

Chapter Two

The bed in which Forrester awoke was oval, springy, and gently warm. It woke him by purring faintly at him, soothingly and cheerfully. Then as he began to stir the purring sound stopped, and the surface beneath his body gently began to knead his muscles. Lights came on. There was a distant sound of lively music, like a Gypsy trio. Forrester stretched, yawned, explored his teeth with his tongue, and sat up.

"Good morning, Man Forrester," said the bed. "It is eight-fifty hours, and you have an appointment at nine seventy-five. Would you like me to tell you your calls?"

"Not now," said Forrester at once. Hara had told him about the talking bed. It did not startle him. It was a convenience, not a threat. It was one more comfortable part of this very amiable world.

Forrester, who had been thirty-seven years old when he was burned to death and still considered that to be his age, lit a cigarette, considered his situation carefully, and decided that it was a state unmatched by any other thirty-seven-year-old man in the history of the world. He had it made. Life. Health. Good company. And a quarter of a million dollars.

He was not, of course, as unique as he thought. But as he had not yet fully accepted the fact that he had himself been dead and was now returned to life, much less that there were millions upon millions like him, it *felt* unique. It felt very good.

"I have just received another message for you, Man Forrester," said the bed.

"Save it," said Forrester. "After I have a cup of coffee."

"Do you wish me to send you a cup of coffee, Man Forrester?"

"You're a nag, you know that? I'll tell you what I want and when I want it."

What Forrester really wanted, although he had not articulated it even to himself, was to go on enjoying for a moment the sensation of being uncommitted. It was like a liberation. It was like that first week of basic training, in the Army, when he realized that there was a hard way to get through his hitch and an easy one, and that the easy one, which entailed making no decisions of his own and taking no initiative, but merely doing what he was told, was like nothing so much as a rather prolonged holiday in a somewhat poorly equipped summer camp for adults.

Here the accommodations were in fact sumptuous. But the principle was the same. He did not have to concern himself with obligations. He had no obligations. He didn't have to worry about making sure the kids got up for school, because he no longer had any children. He didn't have to think about whether his wife had enough money to get through the day, because he didn't now have a wife. If he wanted to, he could now lie back, pull the covers over his head, and go to sleep. No one would stop him, no one would be aggrieved. If he chose, he could get drunk, attempt the seduction of a girl, or write a poem. All of his debts were paid—or forgiven, centuries since. Every promise was redeemed—or had passed beyond the chance of redemption. The lie he had told Dorothy about that weekend in 1962 need trouble him no longer. If the truth came out, no one would care; and it was all but impossible that the truth should ever come out.

He had, in short, a blank check on life.

More than that, he had a pretty substantially underwritten guarantee of continuing life itself. He wasn't sick. He wasn't even threatened; even the lump on his leg, which he had once or twice gazed on with some worry in the days before his death, could not be malignant or threatening; if it had been, the doctors at the dormer would have fixed it. He need not even worry about being run over by a car—if there were cars—since at worst that might mean only another few centuries in the bath of liquid helium, and then back to life—better than ever!

He had, in fact, everything he had ever wished for.

The only things he didn't have were those he had not wished for because he already had them. . . . Family. Friends. Position in the community.

In this life of the year 2527 A.D., Charles Forrester was entirely free. But he was not so joyous as to be blinded to the fact that this coin of his treasure had two sides. Another way of looking at it was that he was entirely superfluous.

"Man Forrester," said the bed, "I must insist. I have both an urgent-class message and a personal-visit notice." And the mattress curled under him, humped itself, and deposited him on the floor of the room.

Staggering, Forrester growled, "What's urgent?"

"A hunting license has been taken out on you, Man Forrester. The licensee is Heinzlichen Jura de Syrtis Major, male, dipara-Zen, Utopian, eighty-six elapsed, six feet four inches, import-export. He is extraterrestrial-human. No reason declared. Bonds and guaranties have been posted. Would you like your coffee now?"

While the bed was speaking it had been rolling itself into the wall. It disappeared into a sphincter that closed and left no trace. This was disconcerting, but Forrester remembered Hara's instructions, searched for and found his joymaker, and said to it, "I would like my breakfast now. Ham and eggs. Toast and orange juice. Coffee. And a pack of cigarettes."

"They will be delivered in five minutes, Man Forrester," said the joymaker. "May I give you the rest of your messages?"

"Wait a minute. I thought it was the bed that was giving me messages."

"We are all the same, Man Forrester. Your messages follow. Notice of personal visit: Taiko Hironibi will join you for breakfast. Dr. Hara has prescribed a euphoric in case of need, which will be delivered with your breakfast. Adne Bensen sends you a kiss. First Merchants Audit and Trust invites your patronage. Society of Ancients states you have been approved for membership and relocation benefits. Ziegler, Durant and Colfax, Attorneys—"

"You can skip the commercials. What was that about a hunting license?"

"A hunting license has been taken out on you, Man Forrester. The licensee is Heinzlichen Jura de—"

"You said that. Wait a minute." Forrester regarded his joymaker thoughtfully. The principle of it was clear enough. It was a remote input-output station for a shared-time computer program, with certain attachments that functioned as pocket flask, first-aid kit, cosmetic bag, and so on. It looked something like a mace or a jester's scepter. Forrester told himself that it was really no less natural to talk to something like a mace than it was to talk into something like a telephone. But at the other end of a telephone had been a human being . . . or at least, he reminded himself, the taped voice of what at one time had been a human being. . . . Anyway, it didn't *feel* natural. He said guardedly, "I don't understand all this. I don't know who these people are who are calling me up, either."

"Man Forrester, the personal callers are as follows. Taiko Hironibi: male, dendritic Confucian, Arcadian, fifty-one elapsed, six feet one inch, organizer, business political. He will bring his own breakfast. Adne Bensen: female, Universalist, Arcadian-Trimmer, twenty-three declared, five feet seven inches, experiencer-homeswoman, no business stated. Her kiss follows."

Forrester did not know what to expect but was pleasantly ready for anything.

What he got was indeed a kiss. It was disconcerting. No kissing lips were visible. There was a hint of perfumed breath, then a pressure on his lips—warm and soft, moist and sweet.

Startled, he touched his mouth. "How the devil did you do that?" he shouted.

"Sensory stimulation through the tactile net, Man Forrester. Will you receive Taiko Hironibi?"

"Well," said Forrester, "frankly, I don't know. Oh, hell. I guess so. Send him in. . . . Wait a minute. Shouldn't I get dressed first?"

"Do you wish other clothing, Man Forrester?"

"Don't confuse me. Just hold on a minute," he said, rattled and angry. He thought for a minute. "I don't know who this Hirowatsis is—"

"Taiko Hironibi, Man Forrester. Male, dendritic Confucian—"

"Cut that out!" Forrester was breathing hard. Abruptly the joymaker in his hand hissed and sprayed him with something that felt damp for a second, then dissipated.

Forrester felt himself relaxing. He appreciated the tranquilizing spray, without quite liking the idea of having a machine prescribe and dispense it.

"Oh, *God*," he said, "what do I care who he is? Go ahead. Send him in. And get a move on with my breakfast, will you?"

"You'll do!" cried Taiko Hironibi. "The greatest! What a cranial index! You look—cripes, I don't know what to call it—you look like a brain. But a swinger."

Charles Forrester, gravely and cheerfully, indicated a seat with his hand. "Sit down. I don't know what you want but I'm willing to talk about it. You're the damnedest looking Japanese I ever saw."

"Really?" The man looked disconcerted. He also looked quite non-Japanese: crew-cut golden hair, blue eyes. "They change you around so," he said apologetically. "Maybe I used to look different. Say! Did I get here first?"

"You got here before my breakfast, even."

"Great! That's really great. Now, here's the thing. We're all messed up here, you have to get that straight right away. The people are sheep. They know they're being expropriated, but do they do anything about it? Sweat, no, they sit back and enjoy it. That's what we're for in the Ned Lud Society. I don't know your politics, Charley—"

"I used to be a Democrat, mostly."

"—Well, you can forget that. It doesn't matter. I'm registered Arcadian myself, of course, but a lot of the guys are Trimmers, maybe—" he winked —"maybe even something a little worse, you know? We're all in this together. Affects everybody. If you raise your kids with machines you're bound to have machine-lovers growing up, right? Now—"

"Hey!" said Forrester, looking at his wall. At a point as near as he could remember to be just about where the bed had disappeared, a sphincter was opening again. It disgorged a table set for two, one side bearing his breakfast, the other a complete setting but no food.

"Ah, breakfast," said Taiko Hironibi. He opened a pouch in the kiltlike affair he wore and took out a small capped bowl, a plastic box that turned out to contain something like crackers, and a globe, which, when squeezed, poured a hot, watery, greenish tea into the cup at his place. "Care for a pickled plum?" he asked politely, removing the cap from the bowl.

Forrester shook his head. Chairs had appeared beside the table, and he slid into the one placed before the ham and eggs.

Next to the steaming plate was a small crystal tray containing a capsule and a scrap of golden paper on which was written:

I don't know much about that champagne wine. Take this if you have a hungover.

Hara

To the best of Forrester's knowledge he didn't have a hangover, but the capsule looked too good to waste. He swallowed it with some of the orange juice and at once felt even more relaxed. If that were possible. He felt positively affectionate toward the blond Japanese, now decorously nibbling at a dark, withered object.

It crossed Forrester's mind that the capsule, plus what the joymaker had sprayed him with, might add up to something larger than he was ready for. He felt almost giddy. Better guard against that, he thought, and demanded as unpleasantly as he could, "Who sent you here?"

"Why—the contact was Adne Bensen."

"Don't know her," snapped Forrester, trying not to grin.

"You don't?" Taiko stopped eating, dismayed. "Sweat, man, she told me you'd be—"

"Doesn't matter," cried Forrester, and prepared for the

killing question he had been saving. "Just tell me this. What's the advantage of my joining your society?"

The blond man was clearly disgruntled. "Listen, I'm not *begging* you. We got something good here. You want in, come in. You want out, go—"

"No, don't give me an argument. Just answer the question." Forrester managed to light a cigarette, puffed smoke in Taiko's face. "For instance," he said, "would it be money that's involved?"

"Well, sure. Everybody needs money, right? But that's not the only thing—"

Forrester said, politely but severely, restraining the impulse to giggle, "You know, I had an idea it would be like that." His two tranquilizers, plus what was still in his system from the previous night, were adding up to something very close to a roaring drunk, he noticed. With some pride. How manly of him, he thought, to keep his wits so clear when he was so smashed.

"You act like I'm trying to take advantage of you," Taiko said angrily. "What's the matter with you? Don't you see that the machines are depriving us of our natural human birthright? to be miserable if we want to, to make mistakes, to forget things? Don't you see that we Luddites want to smash the machines and give the world back to *people?* I mean, not counting the *necessary* machines, of course."

"Sure I see," agreed Forrester, standing up and swaying slightly. "Well, thanks. You better be going now, Hironibi. I'll think over what you said, and maybe we can get together sometime. But don't you call me. Let me call you." And he bowed Taiko to the door and watched it close behind him, keeping his face relaxed until the Japanese was gone.

Then Forrester bent over and howled with laughter. "Con man!" he shouted. "He thinks I'm an easy mark! Ah, the troubles of the rich—always somebody trying to swindle you out of it!"

"I do not understand, Man Forrester," said the joymaker. "Are you addressing me?"

"Not in this life," Forrester told the machine, still chuckling. He was filled with a growing pride. He might look like a country cousin, he thought, but there went one sharper who had got no farther than first base.

He wondered who this Adne Bensen was who had fingered him for the swindler and sent him an electronic kiss. If she kissed in person the way she kissed through sensory stimulation of the tactile net, she might be worth knowing. And no problem, either. If Taiko was the worst this century could turn up, Forrester thought with pleasure and joy, his quarter of a million dollars was safe!

Twenty minutes later he found his way to the street level of the building, not without arguments from his joymaker. "Man Forrester," it said, sounding almost aggrieved, "it is better to take a taxi! Do not walk. The guaranties do not apply to provocation and contributory negligence."

"Shut up for a minute, will you?" Forrester managed to get the door open and looked out.

The city of 2527 A.D. was very large, very fast-moving, and very noisy. Forrester was standing in a sort of driveway. A clump of ethereal, thirty-foot-high ferns in front of him partially masked a twelve-lane highway packed to its margins with high-speed traffic moving in both directions. Occasionally a vehicle would cut in to the entrance to his building, pause before him for a moment, and then move on. Taxis? Forrester wondered. If so, he was giving them no encouragement.

"Man Forrester," said the joymaker, "I have summoned death-reversal equipment, but it will not arrive for several minutes. I must warn you, the costs may be challenged under the bonding regulations."

"Oh, shut up." It seemed to be a warm day, and Forrester was perhaps still slightly befuddled; the temptation to walk was irresistible. All questions could be deferred. Should be deferred, he told himself. Obviously his first task was to get himself oriented. And—he prided himself on this—he had been something of a cosmopolitan, back in those days before his death, equally at home in San Francisco or Rome as in New York or Chicago. And he had always made time to stroll around a city.

He would stroll through this one now. Joymakers be damned, thought Charles Forrester; he right-faced, hooked the joymaker to his belt, and set off along a narrow pedestrian walk.

There were very few walkers. It didn't do to make snap judgments, Forrester thought, but these people seemed soft. Perhaps they could afford to be. No doubt someone like himself, he mused soberly, seemed like a hairy troglodyte, crude, savage, flint-axed.

"Man Forrester!" cried the joymaker from his belt. "I must inform you that Heinzlichen Jura de Syrtis Major has waived protest of the bonding regulations. The death-reversal equipment is on its way." He slapped it, and it was quiet, or else its continued bleating was drowned out by the sound of the clamoring traffic. Whatever drove these cars, it was not gasoline. There were no fumes. There was only a roar of air and singing tires, multiplied a hundredfold and unending. The trafficway lay between tall bright buildings, one a soft, flowing orange, one the crystalline, blue-gray color of fractured steel. In the court of a building across the trafficway he could see, dimly through the glass and the momentary gaps in the traffic, a riot of plant growth with enormous scarlet fruits. On a balcony above him scented fountains played.

The joymaker was addressing him again, but he could catch only part of it. ". . . On station now, Man Forrester." A shadow passed over him, and he looked up.

Overhead a white aircraft of some sort—it had no wings—was sliding diagonally down toward him. It bore a glittering ruby insigne like the serpent staff of Aesculapius on its side. The nearer end of it was all glass and exposed, and inside a young woman in crisply tailored blue was drowsily watching something on a screen invisible to Forrester. She looked up, gazed at him, spoke into a microphone, then glanced at him again, and went back to watching her screen. The vehicle took position over his head and waited, following with him as he walked.

"That's funny," said Forrester aloud.

"It's a funny world," said somebody quite near him.

He turned around. Four men were standing there, looking at him with pleasant, open expressions. One of them was very tall and very heavy. In fact, he was gross. He leaned on a cane, studying Forrester, his expression alert and interested.

Forrester realized that he was the one who had spoken and, in the same moment, realized that he knew him. "Oh, sure," he said, "The Martian in orange tights."

"Very good," said the Martian, nodding. He was not in orange tights now; he wore a loose white tunic and slate-gray shorts. He wasn't really a Martian, Forrester remembered; at least, his ancestors had come from Earth.

One of the other men took Forrester's hand and shook it. "You're the one with the quarter of a million dollars," he said. "Look me up when this is all over. I'd like to know what a fellow like you thinks of our world."

He brought his knee up and kicked Forrester in the groin. Hard.

Forrester felt the world explode, starting inside him. He saw that the man was stepping back, looking at him with interest and pleasure; but it was hard to watch him because the city was moving. It tilted up at an angle, and the sidewalk struck him on the forehead. He rolled, clutching at his testicles, and found himself looking upward.

The man from Mars said conversationally, "Don't hurry. Plenty of time for everybody." He lifted his cane and limped forward. Moving was quite an effort for him in Earth's gravity, after Mars, Forrester saw. The cane came down on his shoulder and upper arm, was lifted and came down again, regularly, slowly, and strongly. It must have been weighted. It felt like a baseball bat.

The pain in Forrester's gut was like death. His arm was numb.

All in all, though, he realized quite clearly—unable to move, watching as they passed the cane from hand to hand and the white aircraft hovered overhead, the woman's face peering patiently down—all in all, it was hurting rather less than he might have expected. Perhaps it was Hara's hungover medicine. Perhaps it was just shock.

"You were warned, Man Forrester," said the joymaker sadly from where it lay beside his head.

He tried to speak, but his lungs were not working.

He could not quite lose consciousness, either, though he wanted to very much. Perhaps that was another result of Hara's euphoric pill. Then he felt that he was succeeding. The pain in his belly grew alarmingly and began to recede again, and then he felt nothing at all, or nothing physical.

But there was something painful in his mind, something that whimpered, *Why? Why me?*

Chapter Three

Howls of laughter rolled over Forrester. A girl was screaming, "He's spinning it! He's spinning it! Gee, I think I saw the cartridge!"

Forrester opened his eyes. He was in something that lurched and hummed. A girl in a tailored blue suit, her back to him, was staring at what seemed to be a television screen showing a sort of arena, where the screaming girl, face flushed and happy, stamping with excitement, was standing over a blind-folded man who held a gun.

Forrester's aches and bruises reminded him at once of what had happened. He was surprised that he was still alive. He croaked, "Hey!"

The girl in tailored blue looked over her shoulder at him. "You're all right," she said. "Just take it easy. We'll be there in a minute."

"Where?"

Impatiently she moved her hand. The arena with the man and girl disappeared—just as the man seemed to be raising the gun—and Forrester found himself looking at blue sky and clouds. "Lift up a little," the girl in blue said. "You'll see it. There."

Forrester tried to raise himself on an elbow, caught a glimpse of trees and rambling pastel buildings, and fell back. "I can't lift myself up! Damn it, I've been half killed." He became aware that he was on a sort of a stretcher and that there was another one beside him. The other one was also occupied, by someone with a sheet over him. "Who's that?" he cried.

"How would I know? I just bring them in, I don't write

their life stories. Now relax, or I'll have to put you to sleep."

"You silly bitch," said Forrester precisely. "I'm not going to stand for this. I demand that you— Wait a minute! What are you doing?"

The girl had turned around, and she was holding something very like his own joymaker, pointed at him. "Are you going to shut up and lie still?"

"I warn you! Don't you dare—"

She sighed, and something cool touched his face.

Forrester gathered all his strength to tell her what he thought of her, her probable sex life, and this world of hers, in which arbitrary and unpleasant things were done to well-to-do men like himself. He couldn't. All that came out was, "Arr, a-r-r-r." He was not unconscious, but he was very weak.

The girl said, "You sweat me, greenie. You are a greenhorn, aren't you? I can always tell. You people wake up in the dormer and you think you're God's own sweat. Mother! Sure you're alive. Sure you've had the biggest break you can imagine. But do you think *we* care?"

All this time the aircraft was slipping and turning, coming in for a landing. The girl, who one would have thought to be the pilot, paid no attention. She was very cross. She said, "Now, I know my job, and my job is to keep you alive—or keep you safely dead till they can take care of you. I don't have to talk to you. I especially don't have to listen to you."

Forrester said, "A-r-r-r."

"I don't even like you," she said with vexation, "and you've made me miss my favorite program. Oh, go to sleep."

And, just as Forrester felt the aircraft touch ground, she raised the joymaker again, and he did.

At the temperature of liquid helium, chemistry stops.

On this fact, and on one reasonable hope, the largest industry of the late twentieth century had been built.

The reasonable hope was that the progress of medicine

in past years would be matched by similar progress in the future—so that, no matter what a person might die of, at some future time a way would be found to cure it, to repair it, or at least to make it irrelevant to continuing life and activity (including a method of repairing the damage done by freezing a body to that temperature).

The fact was that freezing stopped time.

And the industry was Immortality, Inc.

In the city of Shoggo in which Forrester had awakened, a city that was nearly eight hundred years old and enormous, a thousand acres of park along a lake front had humped themselves into a hill. All around was flat. The hill itself was an artifact. It was, as a matter of fact, the freezing center for that part of the world.

A hundred and fifty million cubic yards of earth had been eaten out of the ground to make a cold-storage locker for people. After the locker was built, most of the dirt was heaped back on top of it for insulation.

The differential in temperature between ground level and the heart of the frozen hill was nearly five hundred degrees, Fahrenheit, or three hundred and more in the Kelvin scale on which the dormer operated.

When Forrester realized where the white aircraft had taken him, he was instantly submerged in a terror he could not express. Beginning to awaken, he was still terribly weak, as though one of those sprays from the girl's joymaker had shorted out ninety percent of his volitional muscle control. (As in fact it had.) When he saw the bright featureless ceiling overhead and heard the moan and click of the thousand frightening instruments that brought people back to life, he fugued into a terrifying certainty that they were going to freeze him again. He lay there, groaning inarticulately, while things were done to him.

But they were not freezing him.

They were just patching him up. The blood was washed away. The bruises were scrubbed with something metallic, then touched with a transparent stiff jelly from a long silvery tube that looked something like a large lipstick. His left thigh was pressed for a moment between two glowing screens, which he knew to be a sort of X-ray device, and a fine wash of something that glistened wet and dark was painted over his heart.

This last treatment made him feel better, whatever it was. He found that he was able to speak.

"Thank you," he said.

The young-looking, red-faced man who was working over him at that moment nodded casually and touched Forrester's navel with the end of a silvery probe. He glanced at it and said, "All right, I guess we're through with you. Get up, and let's see if you can walk to Hara's office."

Forrester swung his legs out of the sort of low-walled crib he was lying in and found he could walk as well as ever. Even his bruises didn't hurt, or not much, although he could detect what seemed to be the beginning return of pain.

The red-faced man said, "You're fine. Stay out of here for a while, will you? And don't forget to see Hara, because you're in some kind of trouble." He turned away as Forrester started to question him. "How would I know what kind? Just go see Hara."

Although a slim green arrowhead of light skipped along the floor ahead of him, guiding him to Hara's office, Forrester thought he could have found it without the arrowhead. Once he left the emergency rooms he was in the part of the dormer he remembered. Here he had awakened out of a frozen sleep lasting half a millennium. There, every day for a week, he had gone bathing in some sort of light, warm oil that had vibrated and tingled, making him feel drowsy but stronger each day. It was on the level below this that he had done his exercises and in the building across the bed of poinsettias (except that these poinsettias were bright gold) that he had slept.

He wondered what had become of the rest of what he thought of as his graduating class. The thawed Lazaruses were processed in batches—fifty at a clip in his group— and, although he had not spent much time with any of them, there was something about this shared experience that had made him know them quickly.

But when they were discharged, they all went in separate directions, apparently for policy reasons. Forrester regretted they had lost touch.

Then he laughed out loud. A blue-jacketed woman, walking toward him along the hall and talking into an instrument on her wrist, looked up at him with curiosity and faint contempt. "Sorry," he said to her, still chuckling, as the green beacon of light turned a corner and he followed. He didn't doubt he looked peculiar. He felt peculiar. He was amused that he was missing these fellow graduates of the freezatorium with the fond, distant detachment he had felt for his high school class. Yet it was less than forty-eight hours since he had been with them.

A busy forty-eight hours, he thought. A bit frightening, too. Even wealth was not as secure a buffer against this world as he had thought.

The flickering green light led him into Hara's office and disappeared.

Hara was standing at the door, waiting for him. "Damned kamikaze," he said amiably. "Can't I trust you out of my sight for a minute?"

Forrester, who had never been a demonstrative man, seized his hand and shook it. "Jesus, I'm glad to see you! I'm mixed up. I don't know what the hell is going on, and—"

"Just stay out of trouble, will you? Sit down." Hara made a seat come out of the wall and a bottle out of his desk. He thumbed the cork expertly and poured a drink for Forrester, saying, "I expected you under your own power this morning, you know. Not in a DR cart. Didn't the center warn you somebody was after you?"

"Positively not!" Forrester was both startled and indignant. "What do you mean, somebody was after me? I had no idea—"

Then, tardily, recognition dawned. "Unless," he finished thoughtfully, "that's what the joymaker was mumbling about. It was all about bonds and guaranties and somebody named Heinz something of Syrtis Major. That's on Mars, isn't it? Say!"

"Heinzlichen Jura de Syrtis Major," Hara supplied,

toasting Forrester with his glass and taking a tiny sip of the drink. Forrester followed suit; it was champagne again. Hara sighed and said, "I don't know, Charles, but I don't think I'll acquire a taste for this stuff after all."

"Never mind that! The Martian! The fellow in orange tights! He's the one who beat me up, he and his gang!"

Hara looked faintly puzzled. "Why, of course."

Forrester tipped up his ruby crystal glass and drained the champagne. It was not very good champagne—heaven knew where Hara had found it, after Forrester had mentioned it as being one of the great goods of the past—and it was by no means appropriate to the occasion. It tickled his nose. But at least it contained alcohol, which Forrester felt he needed.

He said, humbly, "Please explain what happened."

"Sweat, Charles, where do I start? What did you do to Heinzie?"

"Nothing! I mean—well, nothing, really. I might have stepped on his feet when we were dancing."

Hara said angrily, "A *Marsman?* You stepped on his *feet?*"

"What's so bad about that? I mean, even if I did. I'm not sure I did. Would you blow your stack about something like that?"

"Mars isn't Shoggo," Hara said patiently, "and, anyway, maybe I would. Depends. Did you read your orientation book?"

"Huh?"

"The book of information about the year 2527. You got it when you were discharged here."

Forrester searched his memory. "Oh, that. Maybe I left it at the party."

"Well, that adds," Hara said with some disgust. "Will you please try to bear in mind, first, that you're sort of my responsibility; second, that you don't know your way around? I'll see you get another copy of the book. Read it! Come back and see me tomorrow; I've got work to do now. On your way out, stop at the discharge office and pick up your stuff."

He escorted Forrester to the door, turned, then paused. "Oh. Adne Bensen sends regards. Nice girl. She likes you," he said, closed the door, and was gone.

Forrester completed his processing and was released by the medical section, receiving as he left a neat white folder with his name imprinted in gold.

It contained four sets of documents. One was a sheaf of medical records; the second was the book Hara had mentioned, slim and bronze-bound, with the title printed in luminous letters:

YOUR GUIDE TO THE 26TH CENTURY
[1970-1990 EDITION]

The third document seemed to be a legal paper of some kind. At least, it was backed with a sheet of stiff blue material that gave it the look of a subpoena. Forrester remembered that the doctor who had patched him up had spoken of trouble. This looked like the trouble, though the words were either unfamiliar in context or totally meaningless to him:

You, Charles Dalgleish Forrester, uncommitted, undeclared, elapsed thirty-seven years, unemployed-pending, take greeting and are directed. Requirement: To be present at Congruency Hearing, hours 1075, days 15, months 9 . . .

It had the authentic feel of legalese, he saw with dismay. Much of the face of the single sheet of paper that the blue material enclosed was covered with a sort of angular, almost readable lettering—something like the machine script they used to put on checks, Forrester thought, and then realized that that was no doubt what it was.

But the paper had a date on it, and since that date appeared to be a week or more away, as near as Forrester could figure, he tabled it with some relief and turned to the next and last item in the folder.

This was a financial statement. Attached to it was a crisp metallic slip with the same angular printing on it, which Forrester recognized as a check.

He fingered it lovingly and puzzled out the amount.

It was made out to him, and it was for $231,057.56.

Forrester attempted to fold it—it sprang back like spring steel—and then put it away flat in his pocket. It felt good there.

He was faintly puzzled by the fact that it was some twenty thousand dollars less than he had expected. But in terms of percentage the amount didn't seem very significant, and he was cheerfully reconciled to the opinion that this society, like all societies, would no doubt have some sort of taxes. Twenty grand was, after all, an amount he could well afford as a sort of initiation fee.

Feeling much more secure, he emerged into the sunlight and looked about him.

It was late afternoon. The sun was to his right. Slate-blue water stretched to his left. He was looking southward over the great pinnacled mass of the city.

Aircraft moved above it. Things crawled in its valleys. The sun picked out reflections from glass and metal, and, although it was still daylight, the city already exuded a developing glow of neon and fluorescence.

There were at least ten million people in Shoggo, Forrester knew. There were theaters and card parties and homes, places where he might find a friend or a lover. Or even an enemy. Down there was the girl who had kissed him last night—Tip?—and the crazy Martian and his gang, who had tried to kill him.

But where?

Forrester did not know where to begin.

Alive, healthy, with almost a quarter of a million dollars in his pocket, he felt left out of things. Standing on a planet with a population of seventeen billion active human beings, and at least twice that number dreaming in the slow cold of the helium baths, he felt entirely alone.

From his belt the voice of the joymaker spoke up. "Man Forrester. Will you take your messages?"

"Yes," said Forrester, disconcerted. "No. Wait a minute."

He took the last cigarette out of the pack he had got that morning, lit it, then crumpled the pack and threw it away. He thought.

Owning a joymaker was a little like having a genie with three wishes. The thing's promptness and precision disconcerted him; he felt that it demanded equal certitude from himself and he did not feel up to it.

He grinned to himself ruefully, admitting that he was being made self-conscious by what he really knew to be nothing but a radio connection with some distant lash-up of cold-state transistors and ferrite cores. Finally he said, "Look. You. I think what I ought to do is go back to my room and start over again from home base. What's the best way to get there?"

"Man Forrester," said the joymaker, "the best way to get to the room you occupied is by cab, which I can summon for you. However, the room is no longer yours. Will you accept your messages?"

"No. Wait a minute! What do you mean, no longer mine? I didn't check out."

"Not necessary, Man Forrester. It is automatic on departure."

He paused and thought, and on consideration it didn't seem to matter much. He had left nothing there. No bag, no baggage. No personal possessions, not even a shaving brush: he wouldn't have to shave for a week or two anyway, Hara had told him.

All of himself that he had left in the room was the garments he had worn last night. And those, he remembered, were disposable . . . and so had no doubt been disposed of.

"What about the bill?" he asked.

"The charge was paid by the West Annex Discharge Center. It is entered on your financial statement, Man Forrester. Your messages include one urgent, two personal, one notice of legal, seven commercial—"

"I don't want to hear right now. Wait a minute."

Once again Forrester tried to frame the right question.

He abandoned the effort. Whatever his skills, he was not a computer programmer, and it was no good trying to talk like one. It seemed absurd to ask a machine for value judgments, but—

"Cripes," he said, "tell me something. What would you do, *right now*, if you were me?"

The joymaker answered without hesitation, as though that sort of question were coming up every day. "If I were you, Man Forrester, which is to say, if I were human, just unfrozen, without accommodations, lacking major social contacts, unemployed, unskilled—"

"That's the picture, all right," Forrester agreed. "So answer the question." Something was crawling underfoot. He stepped aside, out of its way, a glittering metal thing.

"I would go to a tea shop, Man Forrester. I would then read my orientation book while enjoying a light meal. I would then think things over. I would then—"

"That's far enough."

The metal thing, apparently espying Forrester's discarded cigarette pack, scuttled over to it and gobbled it down. Forrester watched it for a second, then nodded.

"You've got some good ideas, machine," he said. "Take me to a tea shop!"

Chapter Four

The joymaker procured a cab for Forrester, a wingless vehicle like the death-reversal conveyance that had brought him in for repair, but orange and black instead of white; it looked like Hallowe'en. And the cab took him to the joymaker's recommended tea shop.

The shop was curious. It was located in an interior hall of a great spidery building in the heart of the city. The cab flew under a pierced-steel buttress, actually into a sort of vaulted opening that could have served only birds and angels, or men in aircraft, since it was at least fifty feet above ground. It halted and hovered before a balcony planted with climbing roses, and Forrester had to step over a knife edge of empty space. The cab did not quiver, not even when his weight left it.

A girl with hair like transparent cellophane greeted him. "I have your reservation, Man Forrester. Will you follow me, please?"

He did, walking behind her across a quartz-pebbled court and into the hall that was the tea room, admiring the swing of her hips and wondering just what it was that she did to her hair to make it stand out like a sculptured puffball and rob it of opacity.

She seated him beside a reflecting pool, with silvery fish swimming slowly about. Even with the peculiar hairdo, she was a pretty girl. She had dimples and dark, amused eyes.

He said, "I don't know what I want, actually. Anyway, who do I order from?"

"We are all the same, Man Forrester," she said. "May I choose for you? Some tea and cakes?"

Numbly, he nodded and, as she turned and left, watched

the sway of her hips with an entirely different kind of interest.

He sighed. This was a confusing world!

He took the book out of the folder he had been given at the West Annex Discharge Center and placed it on the table. Its cover was simple and direct:

YOUR GUIDE TO THE 26TH CENTURY
[1970-1990 EDITION]
Where to Go
How to Live
Managing Your Money
Laws, Customs, Folkways

It was edge-indexed with helpful headings: MAKING FRIENDS, LIVING ON A BUDGET, HOW TO GET THE MOST OUT OF YOUR JOYMAKER, JOB OPPORTUNITIES, WHERE TO GET NEEDED TRAINING . . . it went on and on. Forrester, flipping through the pages, was astonished to find how many of them there were.

He had a good week's reading here, he estimated. Obviously the first thing for him to do was to decide what was the first thing to do.

Making friends could wait a bit. He seemed already to have made more friends—and enemies!—than he could assimilate.

Living on a budget? He smiled to himself and patted the pocket that held his check.

How to get the most out of your joymaker, though. That was a good place to start, thought Forrester, then opened the book to the right page and began to read.

The remote-access computer transponder called the "joymaker" is your most valuable single possession in your new life. If you can imagine a combination of telephone, credit card, alarm clock, pocket bar, reference library, and full-time secretary, you will have sketched some of the functions provided by your joymaker.

Essentially it is a transponder connecting you with the central computing facilities of the city in which you reside on a shared-time, self-programming basis. "Shared-time" means that many other joymakers use the same central computer—in Shoggo, something like ten million of them. If you go to another city your joymaker will continue to serve you, but it must be reset to a new frequency and pulse-code. This will be done automatically when you travel by public transportation. However, if you use private means, or if for any reason you spend any time in the agricultural areas, you must notify the joymaker of your intentions. It will inform you of any steps you must take.

"Self-programming" means that the programmed software includes . . .

The self-programming, shared-time girl with the dark, grave eyes brought Forrester his tea and cakes. "Thank you," he said, staring at her. He was still not quite sure of his deductions about her. He tried an experiment. "Can you give me my messages?" he asked.

"Certainly, Man Forrester, if you wish," she said promptly. "Alfred Guysman wishes to see you on political business. Adne Bensen asks you to return her message of this morning. The Nineteenth Chromatic Trust informs you that arrangements have been made for you to establish banking facilities with them—"

"That's enough," he said, marveling at how nicely a shared-time transponder could be packaged. "I'll take the rest later."

There was no sugar for the tea, but it was physically hot and chemically cool at the same time—rather like a mentholated cigarette, except that there was no particular taste associated with it. Forrester returned to his book.

"Self-programming" means that the programmed software includes procedures for translating most normal variations of voice, idiom, accent, and other variable modalities into a computer-oriented simscript and thence into the mathematical expressions on which the computers operate. As long as your personal joymaker is within reception range of your voice, you may communicate via other shared-time transponders if you wish. Appropriate modulation will be established automatically. However, do not attempt to use another individual's joymaker when yours is not within range. Proper coding cannot be assured. In the event that your joymaker is lost or damaged . . .

Forrester sighed and ate one of the cakes. It was rich with flavors like butter and cinnamon and with others he could not identify. Pleasant but strange.

Very much like this world that had been given him.

"Man Forrester," said the joymaker at his belt, its tones muffled by his coat and the tablecloth, "it is necessary for you to accept some messages. I have a notice of personal visit and—"

Forrester said, "Look, I'm doing what you said, right? I'm reading my book. Let me figure it out a little before you throw messages at me. Unless," he said as an afterthought, "there's some matter of life or death."

"There are no messages involving life or death, Man Forrester."

"Then wait awhile." He was aware—he didn't know how long it had been going on—that a distant wind instrument was hooting faintly. Pleasant but strange. Spiced cool breezes blew from the paneled walls, also pleasant but strange.

He said hesitantly, "Joymaker, answer me a question. Why did what's-his-name, Heinzie, beat me up?"

"I cannot identify the individual, Man Forrester. You were beaten up by four persons in the one recorded incident of attack. Their names were Shlomo Cassavetes Heinzlichen Jura de Syrtis Major, Edwardino—"

"That one. Heinzlichen Jura de Syrtis Major. Or, for that matter, all of them—why did they rumble me?"

"I have a priority message regarding Heinzlichen Jura de Syrtis Major, Man Forrester. Perhaps it will be informative. May I give it to you?"

"Oh, hell. Why not?"

"Heinzlichen Jura de Syrtis Major is protesting enforcement of guaranties and has enjoined disbursements under his bond. You are notified, Man Forrester."

Forrester said hotly, "That's what you call informative? Look, skip the damned messages and answer the question. What was that scene all about?"

"You have asked three questions, Man Forrester. May I offer a synoptic reply?"

"Please do, old friend.

"Heinzlichen Jura de Syrtis Major, a guest in the rep-rooms utilized by Alin Hara, conceived a grievance against you, cause unstated. He called into association Shlomo Cassavetes, Edwardino Wry, and Edwardeto Wry; they formed an ad hoc club and filed appropriate conformance in regard to bonds and guaranties. The intention was stated as murder, first phase, ad lib. The motivation was stated as grievance as to de Syrtis Major, practical joke as to the others. Conformances were recorded, and the subject—that is, yourself, Man Forrester—was notified. Does that answer your three questions, Man Forrester?"

"What do you think?" Forrester snapped. "Well, maybe it does. Sort of. You mean those other three finks lumped me for a *joke?*"

"They so stated, yes, Man Forrester."

"And they're still running around loose?"

"Do you wish me to ascertain their present whereabouts, Man Forrester?"

"No—I mean, aren't they in jail or something?"

"No, Man Forrester."

Forrester said, "Joymaker, leave me alone for awhile. I better get back to my orientation book. I see I don't know as much as I thought I did."

Forrester drank the rest of his tea, ate the rest of his cakes, and plowed back into his book.

To use your joymaker as telephone: You must know the ortho-name and identification spectrum of the person you wish to reach. Once you have given this information to the joymaker it will be remembered, and you can then refer to the person in later calls by a reciprocal name or any other personal identification programmed into your joymaker. If you have been called by any person, the joymaker will have recorded the necessary ortho-name and identification spectrum. Simply ask the joymaker to call the person you wish to speak to. If you wish to establish a priority rating with any person, that person must so inform his joymaker. Otherwise your calls may be deferred or canceled as directed by the called person.

To use your joymaker as credit card: You must know the institutional designation and account spectrum. . . .

A belated thought percolated to the surface of Forrester's mind. Messages. Financial institutions. One of the messages had been from something that sounded like that.

He sighed and looked around the room. Most of the tables were empty. But it was a large room, and there were perhaps fifty other people in it, all of them seated at tables in twos and threes and larger groups. Through some effect of the sound-conditioning, he could not hear their voices, only the distant hooting flute and a faint splashing from the giant fish in the reflecting pools.

He wondered if any of these fifty people would mind if he got up and walked over to them.

Touching the faintly sore spots on his shoulders and neck he decided against trying it. But it gave him an idea, and he turned to the section of the book called MAKING FRIENDS.

"I have an *urgent* notice of personal visit, Man Forrester," grumbled the joymaker from his waist.

"Just save it," said Forrester, preoccupied. He was startled at the length of the list of ways of making friends. Above all, there were clubs. Clubs in such profusion that he wondered that even seventeen billion people could fill their rolls. Social clubs, gymnastic clubs, professional clubs. Political groups, religious groups, therapeutic groups. There was a Society of First Families of Mars, and a Loyal Order of Descendants of Barsoom Fans. There were forty-eight bird-watching groups in Shoggo alone. There were stamp collectors and coin collectors and tax-token collectors and jet-car-transfer collectors.

There was something called the Society of Ancients that looked interesting, as it appeared to be an organization of persons like Forrester himself, revived from the dead heart of the freezers. Yet it was listed along with such curiosities as the B.P.O.E. and the Industrial Workers of the World (Memorial Association) in small type at the end of the section.

Puzzling. If it existed at all, should it not have a membership in the billions?

Evidently it did not, but . . .

"Man Forrester," shrilled the joymaker. "I must inform you of a personal visitation by—"

"Wait a minute," said Forrester, suddenly looking up, startled.

There was a hint of perfume in the air.

Forrester put down his book, frowning. The scent was familiar. What was it. Another tactile-tape message from Adne Bensen, whoever she might be?

He felt a touch on his shoulder, then warm arms around him, a hug.

These tactile tapes were certainly convincing, he thought momentarily, then realized this was not a tape. He was not merely feeling and smelling the presence of the embracing arms. He saw them, from the corner of his eye and, awkwardly, like a wrestler struggling to break a hold, he turned inside them.

He saw the face of the girl from the party, very near to his.

"Tip!" he cried. "My God, I'm glad to see you!"

When you came right down to it, Forrester hardly knew the girl, barring a little friendly kissing at a party, but at this moment she was very dear to him. It was like a chance meeting in Taiwan with somebody who had sat at the far end of the same commuter train for years. Not a friend, hardly even an acquaintance; but promoted by the accident of unexpected meeting to the status of near and dear. Half rising from his seat, he hugged her tight. She laughed breathlessly and shook free. "Dear Charles," she gasped, "not so *hard*."

"I'm sorry." She sat down opposite him, and he sank back in his chair, admiring her dark hair and pale skin, her cheerful, pretty face, and her figure. The others in the tea room, some of whom had turned to look at them, were losing interest and returning to their own affairs. Forrester said, "It's just that I'm so glad to see you, Tip."

She looked startled, then faintly reproving. "My name is Adne Bensen, dear Charles. Call me Adne."

"But last night Hara called you—oh!" he said, remembering. "Then you're the girl who has been sending me the messages."

She nodded.

"Very nice messages they were," he said. "Would you like some tea?"

She said, "Oh, I think not. I mean, not here, anyway. I came to see if you'd like to come to my place for dinner."

"*Yes!*"

She laughed. "You are such an impetuous man, Charles. Is that why they call you the kamikaze people? I mean, your century and all."

"As to that, Adne, I don't know," he said. "Because, when you come right down to it, I don't know who calls me what. I am, you might say, confused. One of the many reasons why I am pleased to see you is that I need somebody to talk to."

She leaned back in her chair, smiling, and said she would take some tea, after all. It came without being asked for; apparently the joymaker had monitored their conversation and drawn the inferences any good waiter would draw. She threw back her filmy, puffy wrap—it had floated around her shoulders like a cloud, but now it lay back against the chair quite inconspicuously, Forrester noticed— to reveal a deep-cut, tight-fitting, flesh-colored vest or jerkin of some sort, which was startling at first glance.

At the second, it was still startling.

She said, "Dear Charles. Don't you ask your joymaker things?"

"I would, except I don't know what to ask."

"Oh, anything! What do you want? Have you filed an interests profile?"

"I don't think so."

"Oh, do! Then it will tell you what programs are on, what parties you will be welcomed at, who you would wish to know. It's terrible to go on impulse, Charles," she said earnestly. "Let the joymaker help you."

He discovered that his own teacup had been replenished and he took a sip. "I don't understand," he said. "You mean I should let the joymaker decide what I'm going to do for fun?"

"Of course. There's so *much*. How could you know what you would like?"

He shook his head. . . .

But that was all of that conversation, all for then. His joymaker said suddenly, its voice curiously tinny, "*Priority urgent! This is a drill! Take cover! Take cover! Take cover!*"

"Oh, dear," said Adne, pouting. "Well, let's go."

"*Take cover!*" blared the joymaker again, and Forrester discovered the reason for its metallic sound. Not only his but the girl's, those of patrons at other tables, all the joymakers at once were repeating the same message. "*Take cover! Countdown starts now! One hundred seconds. Ninety-nine. Ninety-eight.*"

"Where are you going?" Forrester asked, rising with her.

"To the shelter, of course! Hurry it up, Charles, will you? I hate it when I'm out in a public place in one of these things."

". . . *Ninety-one. Ninety. Eighty-nine. . . .*"

He asked, swallowing hard, "Air raid? A *war?*"

She held his hand and was tugging him along toward an exit at the rear of the tea room, through which the other patrons were already beginning to stream out. "Not exactly, Charles dear. Don't you know *anything?*"

"Then what?"

"Aliens. Monsters. That's all. Now, hurry, or we'll never get a seat."

Chapter Five

A walk, an elevator ride, a short stretch through a light-walled corridor, and they came out into a great shadowy auditorium. There was just enough light to find their way to seats. It was filling rapidly, and behind them Forrester heard heavy doors slamming.

When about three quarters of the seats were filled, a man in black climbed onto the stage and said, "Thank you all for your cooperation. I'm pleased to be able to tell you that this building has achieved four-nines compliance in exactly one hundred and forty-one seconds."

There was a stir of interest from the audience. Forrester craned his neck to find the source of the PA system—it seemed to murmur from all over the hall—and located it at last as the man spoke again. It was his joymaker, and all the joymakers, repeating what the man said.

"This is one of the best showings we've ever had," he said warmly, "and I appreciate it. You may leave."

"You mean that's all there is to it?" Forrester asked the girl.

"That's all. Are you coming up to my place?"

"But," he went on, "if there's going to be a raid, or any chance of one, shouldn't we wait and see—"

"See what, Charles dear? There's no need to grovel in the ground like *moles*. It's just a test."

"Yes, but—" He hesitated, and then followed her out of the auditorium thoughtfully.

It was confusing. No one had mentioned war to him.

But when he said as much to Adne, she laughed. "*War?* Oh, Charles! You're so *funny*, you kamikazes! Now, we've wasted enough time—are you coming to my place for dinner or not?"

He sighed.

"Oh, sure," he said. As brightly as he could.

In the life that had begun with his birth in 1932 and ended with the inhalation of a lungful of flame thirty-seven years later, Forrester had been a successful, self-sufficient, and substantial man.

He had had a wife—her name was Dorothy—small, blonde, a little younger than himself. He had had three sons, and a job as copy chief of a technical writing service, and a reputation among his friends as a fine poker player and useful companion.

Although he had missed combat participation in a war, he had been a Boy Scout during World War Two, participating in scrap-metal drives and Slap the Jap waste-fat collections. As a young adult he had lived through the H-bomb hysteria of the early fifties, when every city street blossomed out with signs directing the nearest way to a bomb shelter. He had seen enough movies and television shows to know what air raid drills meant.

He was not very satisfied with the one he had just seen. He tried to phrase his dissatisfaction to Adne as she changed clothes behind a screen, but she was not very interested. Drills were an annoyance to her, it was clear, but not a very serious one.

She came out from behind the screen, wearing something filmy and pale and not at all practical for cooking dinner. On the other hand, Forrester thought, who knew how these people cooked their dinners? She rustled over to him, lifted his hand, kissed his fingers, and sat down beside him, pulling her joymaker from the place by the arm of the chair where she had left it. "Excuse me, Charles dear," she said; and, to the joymaker, "Receiving messages."

Forrester could not hear what the joymaker said to her, because she was holding it close to her ear and had evidently somehow turned the volume down—which he resolved to learn how to do. But he heard what she said to it, although the words were mostly incomprehensible. "Cancel. Hold Three. Commissary four, two as programmed, two A-varied." And, "That takes care of that," she said to him. "Would you like a drink?"

"All right." She lifted glasses out of the well of the—Forrester would have called it a cocktail table, and perhaps it was. He noticed her eyes were on a stack of parcels on a low table across the room. "Excuse me," she said, pouring a glass of minty liquid for him and one for herself. "I just have to look at these things." She took a small sip of her drink, rose, walked over to the table.

Forrester decided he liked his drink, which was not sweet and made his nose tingle. He stood up and crossed over to her. "Been shopping?" he asked. Adne was taking out clothes, small packets that might have been cosmetics, some things like appliances.

"Oh, no, Charles dear. It's my job." She was preoccupied with a soft, billowy green thing, stroking it against her cheek thoughtfully. With a twist of her arms she threw it around her shoulders and it became a sort of Elizabethan ruff. "Like it, dear?"

"Sure. I mean, I guess I do."

"It's soft. Feel." She drew it over his face. It felt like fur, although its points thrust out again the moment they left his skin, looking starched and thorny. "Or this," she said, taking it off and replacing it with something that had looked like oiled silk in the box it came in, but which, on her shoulders, disappeared entirely, except that it gave luster and color to her skin. "Or—"

"They're all beautiful," he said. "What do you mean, it's your job?"

"I'm a reacter," she said proudly. "Weighted at nearly fifty million, with two-nines reliability."

"Which means?"

"Oh, you know. If I like a thing, chances are ninety-nine out of a hundred that the others will, too."

"Fifty million others?"

She nodded, flushed and pleased.

"And this is how you make your living?"

"It's how I get rich," she corrected him. "Say!" She looked at him thoughtfully. "I wonder. Do you have any idea how many others like you have come out of the dormers? Maybe you could get a job doing the same thing. I could ask—"

He patted her hand indulgently, amused. "No, thanks," he said, careful not to mention the fact that he was rich—although, he remembered dimly, he had been far less reticent about it at the party the night before. Well, he had made a lot of mistakes at that party—as witness his troubles with the Martian.

"I never asked," said Adne, putting the things away. "How did you die, Charles?"

"Why," he said, sitting down again and waiting for her to join him, "I died in a fire. As a matter of fact, I understand I was a hero."

"Really!" She was impressed.

"I was a volunteer fireman, you know, and there was an apartment fire one night—it was January, very cold, if you stood in the puddles of water you'd freeze to the ground in two minutes—and there was a child in the upper part of the building. And I was the nearest one to the ladder."

He sipped his drink, admiring its milky golden color. "I forgot my Air-Pak," he admitted. "The smoke got me. Or the combination did—smoke and heat. And maybe booze, because I'd just come from a party. Hara said I must have inhaled pure flame, because my lungs were burned. My face must have been, too, of course. I mean, you wouldn't know, but I don't think I look quite the same as I used to. A little leaner now, and maybe a little younger. And I don't think my eyes were quite as bright blue."

She giggled. "Hara can't help editing. Most people don't mind a few improvements."

Dinner arrived as his breakfast had that morning, through a serving door in the wall. Adne excused herself for a moment while the table was setting itself up.

She was gone more than a moment and came back looking amused. "That's that," she said without explaining. "Let's eat."

Forrester was able to identify few if any of the foods served him. The textures were sort of Oriental, with crisp things like water chestnuts and gummy things like sukiyaki lending variety to the crunch of lettuce and the plasticity of starches. The flavors were queer but palatable. While they ate he told her about himself—his life as a tech writer, his children, the manner of his death.

"You must have been one of the first to be frozen," she commented. "1969? That's only a few years after it began."

"First on the block," he agreed. "It was because of the fire company, I guess. We'd just got the new death-reversal truck—gift of our local millionaire, who wanted it around. I didn't think I'd be the one to christen it."

He ate a forkful of something like creamed onions in pastry crust and said, "It must have been confusing for Dorothy."

"Your wife?"

He nodded. "I wonder if there's any way I can find out about her. What she did. How the children made out. She was young when I was killed. . . . Let's see. Thirty-three, about. I don't know if having a husband dead but frozen . . . if she would marry again. . . . Hope she did. I mean—" He broke off, wondering what he did mean.

"Anyway," he said, "Hara had some records. She lived nearly fifty more years, died in her eighties of the third massive stroke. She'd been partly paralyzed for some time." He shook his head, trying to visualize small, blonde Dorothy as an ancient, bedridden beldame.

"Had enough?" asked Adne.

He came back to present time, faintly startled. "Dinner? Why, I guess so. It was delicious." She did something that caused the table to retract itself and stood up. "Come over here and have your coffee. I ordered it specially for you. Would you like some music?"

He started to say, "Not particularly," but she had already turned on some remote recording equipment. He paused to listen, braced for almost anything, with visions of Bartók and *musique concrète*. But it turned out to be something very like violins, playing something very like detached, introspective Tchaikovsky.

She sank back against him and she was very warm and fragrant. "We'll have to find you a place to live," she said.

He put his arm around her.

"This is a condominium building," she said thoughtfully, "but I think there might be something. Do you have any preferences?"

"I don't know enough to have preferences." He caressed her soft hair.

She said drowsily, "That's nice." And in the same tone, a moment later, "But I think I should warn you I'm natural-flow. And this is about M day minus four, so all I want is to be cuddled." She yawned and touched her mouth with her hand. "Oh! Excuse me."

Then she caught a glimpse of his face. "You don't mind, do you?" she asked, sitting up. "I mean, I could take a pill—Charles, why are you that color?"

"Nothing. Nothing at all."

She said apologetically, "I'm sorry, but I don't know much about kamikaze ways. If there's a ritual taboo . . . I'm sorry."

"No taboo. Just a misunderstanding." He picked up his glass and held it out to her. "Any more of this stuff around?"

"Charles dear," she said, stretching, "there's all you want. And I have an idea."

"Shoot."

"I'm going to find you a place to live!" she cried. "You just stay here. Order what you want." She touched something that he could not see and added, "If you don't know how, the children will show you while they're keeping you company."

What had seemed to be a floor-length mural opened it-self and became a doorway. Forrester found himself look-ing into a bright, gay room where two small children were racing each other around a sort of climbable maze.

"We ate our dinner, Mim," cried one of them, then saw Forrester and nudged the other. The two looked at him with calm appraisal.

"You don't mind this, either, do you, Charles dear?" Adne asked. "That's another thing about being a natural-flow."

There were two of them, a boy and a girl, about seven

and five, Forrester guessed. They accepted him without question. . . .

Or not exactly that, thought Forrester ruefully. There were questions.

"Charles! Did people really *smell bad* in the old days?"

"Oh, Charles! You rode in *automobiles*?"

"When the little children had to work in the coal mines, Charles, didn't they get anything to *eat*?"

"But what did they *play* with, Charles? Dolls that didn't *talk*?"

He tried his best to answer. "Well, the child-labor time was over when I lived, or almost. And dolls did talk, sort of. Not very intelligently—"

"When *did* you live, Charles?"

"I was burned to death in 1969—"

The little girl shrieked, "For *witchcraft*?"

"Oh, no. No, that was hundreds of years earlier, too." Charles tried not to laugh. "You see, houses used to catch on fire in those days—"

"The Shoggo fire!" shouted the boy. "Mrs. Leary's cow and the earthquake!"

"Well—something like that. Anyway, there were men whose job it was to put the fires out, and I was one of them. Only then I got caught and died there."

"Mim drowned once," the little girl bragged. *"We* haven't died at all."

"You were sick once, though," said the boy seriously. "You could have died. I heard Mim talking to the medoc."

Forrester said, "Are you children in school?"

They looked at him, then at each other.

"I mean, are you old enough to start lessons?"

The boy said, "Well, *sure*, Charles. Tunt ought to be doing hers right now, as a matter of fact."

"So should you! Mim said—"

"We have to be polite to the guest, Tunt!" The boy said to Charles, "Is there anything we can get you? Something to eat? Drink? Watch a program? Sex-stim? Although I guess you ought to know," he said apologetically, "that Mim's natural-flow and—"

"Yes, yes, I know about that," Forrester said hastily, and thought, Sweet God!

But when in Rome, he thought, it was what the Romans did that counted, and he resolved to do his best. He resolved it earnestly.

It was like being at a party. You got there at ten o'clock, with your collar too tight, and a little grouchy at being rushed and your starched shirt front still damp where the kids had splashed it as you supervised their bedtime toothbrushing. And your host was old Sam, who'd been such a drag; and his wife Myra was in one of her nouveau-riche moods, showing off the new dishwasher; and the conversation started out about politics, which was Sam's most offensive side. . . .

But then you had the second drink. And then the third. Faces grew brighter. You began to feel more at ease. The whole bunch laughed at one of your jokes. The music on the stack of records changed to something you could dance to. You began to catch the rhythm of the party. . . .

Oh, I'll try, vowed Forrester, joining the children in a sort of board game played against their own joymakers. I'll catch the mood of this age if it kills me. Again.

Chapter Six

Up betimes, and set out to conquer a world.

The home that Adne found for him was fascinating—walls that made closets as he needed them, windows that were not windows but something like television screens—but Forrester resolutely spent no time exploring its marvels. After a disturbed night's sleep he was up and out, testing his new world and learning to cope with it. The children were marvelous. He begged the loan of them from Adne, and they were his guides. They took him to the offices of the Nineteenth Chromatic Trust, where a portly old Ebenezer Scrooge gravely examined Forrester's check, painstakingly showed him how to draw against it, severely supervised his signing the necessary documents to open an account, and only at the end revealed himself by saying, "Man Forrester, good day." They took him to a Titanian restaurant for lunch, a lark for them, but for him a shattering test of nerve, since the Titanians ate only live food, and he was barely able to cope with an aspic that writhed and rustled in his spoon. They showed him their playschool, where for three hours a week they competed and plotted with their peers (their lessons were learned at home, via their child-modified joymakers), and Forrester found himself playing London Bridge Is Falling Down with fourteen children and one other adult, symbolically acting out the ritual murder and entombment in the bridge's foundations that the nursery rhyme celebrated. They took him to where the poor people lived, with half-fearful giggles and injunctions against speaking to *anyone*, and Forrester found himself out of pocket change, having given it all away to pale, mumbling creatures with hard-luck stories about Solburn

46

on Mercury and freezer insurance firms that had gone bankrupt. They took him to a park—indoors, underground—where the landscaping was topologically grotesque and a purling stream flowed through a hill's base and up the other side, and where ducks and frogs and a feathery sort of Venusian fish ate morsels of food the children tossed them. They took him to a museum where animated, enlarged cells underwent mitosis with a *plop* like a cow lifting her foot from a bog, and a re-created Tyrannosaurus rex coughed and barked and thumped its feet clangorously, its orange eyes glaring straight at Forrester. They showed him all their treasures and pleasures. But they did not show him a factory, or an office building, or a store of any size. For it did not seem that any of these existed any more. They showed him all around Shoggo until their joymakers chided them, and Forrester's own said severely, "Man Forrester! The children must be returned for their naps. And you really must receive your messages."

The children looked at him with woe. "Ah, well," said Forrester, "we'll do it again another day. How do we get home from here?"

"A cab," said the girl doubtfully, but the boy shouted, "Walk! We can walk! I know where we are—ten minutes will do it. Ask your joymaker if you don't believe me."

"I believe you," said Forrester.

"Then this way, Charles. Come on, Tunt." And the boy led off between two towering buildings on the margin of a grassy strip, where huge hovercraft swished by at enormous speeds.

The joymaker complained, "Man Forrester, I have dichotomous instructions. Please resolve them."

"Oh, God," said Forrester, tired and irritable. "What's your trouble now?"

"You have instructed me to hold messages, but I have several that are high priority and urgent. Please reaffirm holding order, stipulating a time limit if possible, or receive them now."

The boy giggled. "You know why, Charles?" he demanded. "It tickles them when they're holding messages. It's like if you have to go to the bathroom."

The joymaker said, "The analogue is inexact, Man Forrester. However, please allow me to discharge my message load."

Forrester sighed and prepared to contemplate reality again. But something distracted him.

Besides the steady *whush, whush* of the passing hovercraft, besides the distant chant of a choir—they were passing some sort of church—there was another sound. Forrester looked up.

A faint tweeting sound of communications equipment was coming from a white aircraft, glass-fronted, hanging overhead. It bore the shining ruby caduceus, and behind the glass a dark-skinned man in blue was regarding Forrester gravely.

Forrester swallowed.

"Joymaker," he demanded, "is that a death-reversal vehicle overhead?"

"Yes, Man Forrester."

"Does that mean—" He cleared his throat. "Does that mean that crazy Martian is after me again?"

"Man Forrester," said the joymaker primly, "among your urgent priority messages is a legal notice. The twenty-four-hour hold period having expired, and appropriate notices and action having been filed and taken, the man Heinzlichen Jura de—"

"Cut it out! Is he *after* me?"

"Man Forrester," said the joymaker, "yes. As of seventeen minutes ago, the hold period having expired then, he is."

At least the crazy Martian wasn't in sight, thought Forrester, scanning the few visible pedestrians. But the presence of the death-reversal aircraft was a poor omen.

"Kids," he said, "we got troubles. I'm being chased."

"Oh, Charles!" breathed the boy, fascinated. "Will you get *killed?*"

"Not if I can help it. Look. Do you know any short cuts from here? Any secret ways—through cellars, over rooftops—you know."

The boy looked at the girl. The girl's eyes got very big.

"Tunt," she whispered, "Charles wants to *hide*."

"That's it," said Forrester. "What about it, son? You must know some special way. Any kid would."

The boy said, "Charles. I know a way, all right. But are you sure—"

"I'm sure, I'm sure!" snapped Charles Forrester. "Come on! Where?"

The boy surrendered. "Follow me. You too, Tunt."

They turned and dived into one of the buildings. Forrester took a last look around for Heinzlichen whatever-his-name-was. He was not in sight. Only the hovercraft thrumming past, and the few uncaring pedestrians . . . and overhead the man in blue in the death-reversal vehicle, staring down at him, his expression both surprised and angry.

When he was safely back in the condominium building, the children returned to their own home to await the arrival of their mother. Forrester hurried to his apartment, closed the door, and locked it.

"Joymaker," he said, "you were right. I admit it. So now let's have all those messages. And take it slow, so I can understand what they're about."

The joymaker said serenely, "Man Forrester, your messages follow. Vincenzo d'Angostura states that he is still available for legal representation, but will not call again under Bar Association rules. Taiko Hironibi feels there was some misunderstanding and would like to discuss it with you. Adne Bensen sends you an embrace. A document package is in your receiving chute. Will you receive the embrace?"

"Hold it a minute. Gives me something to look forward to. Is any of the other stuff important?"

"As to that, Man Forrester, I have no parameters."

"You're a big help," said Forrester bitterly. "Get me a drink while I'm thinking. Uh, gin and tonic." He waited for it to appear and took a long pull.

His nerves began to feel less like tangled barbed wire. "All right," he said. "Now, what was that about a package?"

"You have a document package in your receiving chute,

Man Forrester. Envelope. Approximately nine centimeters by twenty-five centimeters, less than one half centimeter in thickness, weighing approximately eleven grams. Inscription: 'Mr. Charles Dalgleish Forrester, Social Security Number 145-10-3088, last address while living 252 Dulcimer Drive, Evanston, Illinois. Died of burns received 16 October 1969. To be delivered upon revival.' Contents unknown."

"Hum. Is that all it says?"

"No, Man Forrester. There are machine-script handling instructions on the document. I will phonemize them as closely as possible: 'Sigma triphase ooty-poot trip toe, baker tare sugar aleph, paraphase—' "

"Yeah, well, that's enough of that. I mean, is there anything in English? Anything I could understand?"

"No, Man Forrester. Faint carbonization marks are visible where the envelope has been creased. There are several minor discolorations, which may represent latent human skinprints. At some time a mild corrosive liquid was spilled—"

"Say, joymaker," said Forrester, "I've got an idea. Why don't I open it up? Where'd you say it was?"

Retrieved from his receiving chute, the envelope turned out to be a letter from his wife.

He stared at it and felt something tingling in the corners of his eyes. The handwriting was very strange to him. The signature was "Still with affection, Dorothy" . . . but the hand that had formed those letters scrawled and shook. She had even abandoned her little finishing-school affectations of penmanship, the open-circle dots over the *i*'s, the flowing crosses on the *t*'s. He could read it only with difficulty.

Dear Charles,
   This is, I think, the tenth or eleventh time I have written this letter to you. I seem to do it every time there is a death or bad news, as though the only gossip I have that is worth the effort to pass on for what may be another century—or more!—is that which has to do with trou-

bles. Not your troubles, of course. Not any more.
Usually the troubles are mine.

Although I must say that really my life has not been a
burden to me. I remember that you made me happy,
Charles. I must tell you that I missed you terribly. But I
must also tell you that I got over it.

To begin with: You will want to know what you died
of, I know, and perhaps the people who bring you back
to life will not be able to tell you. (I am assuming that
you will be brought back to life. I didn't believe it at the
time—but since then I've seen it happen.)

You were burned to death in a house fire on Christie
Street on October 16th, 1969. Dr. Ten Eyck, who was
with the first aid squad, pronounced you dead and, with
some difficulty, persuaded them to use their death-
reversal equipment to freeze you. There was some trouble about lacking glycerol for perfusion, but the whole
fire company, you will be glad to know, dug into their
liquor closets and came up with several bottles of bour-
bon . . . and it was that which was used as a buffer.
(If you woke up with a hangover, you now know why!)

There was some question as to whether too much time
had elapsed, too. They thought you might have spoiled
during the discussion, you see. But as it was cold
weather for October they decided to take a chance, and
you were ultimately consigned to a freeze-dormer at liquid helium temperatures. Where, as I write this, you
now lie . . . and where, or in one like it, I expect to be
myself before long.

I should tell you that I didn't pay for any of this. Your
fire company insurance, it turned out, was adequate to
cover all the costs and was in fact earmarked for that
purpose. If it had been up to me I don't think I would
have gone to the expense, Charles, because after all
there were the children to bring up.

What can I tell you about them? They missed you
very much.

Vance, in particular, played truant from school for the
best part of a month, forging notes to his teacher, persuading some adult—I suspected our cleaning woman at

*the time—to phone the principal to explain his absence,
before I found out about it. But then he joined a Boy
Scout troop and, as they say, developed other interests.*

*David didn't say much. But I don't think he ever got
over it. At least not during his lifetime. He joined the
Peace Corps four years later and was executed by insur-
gents during the Huk uprising in* VTGD. *Since his body
was mutilated before being found he could not be frozen.
So he, at least, we will never see again.*

*Vance is now married, and is in fact a grandfather. It
was his second marriage; the first was annulled. His present wife was a schoolteacher before their marriage
. . . and they have been happy. And I really can think
of nothing else to tell you about your son Vance that
does not involve attempting to explain what broke up his
first marriage and why his second wife could not stay in
the United States. I suppose you may meet him some
day. You can ask him yourself.*

*Billy, you will be astonished to learn, is now a Great
Man.*

*Let me see. He was two when you died. Now he's our
senator from Hawaii, and they say he will be President
one day. But you will find out more about him in the
history books than I can tell you, I think. Let me only
say, what I know will interest you, that his first cam-
paign was on a platform of free freezing for everyone,
paid for out of Social Security funds, and you were mentioned in every speech. He won easily.*

And I . . . am seventy-nine years old.

*Since you died forty years ago I cannot now remem-
ber you well enough, my Charles, to know if you will
mind what I have to say next. Three years after your
death I remarried. My husband—my other husband—
was a doctor. Still is, though he is out of practice now.
We have been very happy, too. We had two other children. Both girls. You never met him, but he is a good
man, barring the fact that at one time he drank too
much. He gave it up. He looks a little like you. . . .*

If I remember correctly, he does.

And I am now in brittle health and I think this is the

*last time I will write you this letter. Perhaps we will
meet again. I wonder what it will be like.*

Still with affection,
Dorothy

Forrester put down the letter and cried, "Joymaker! Was
there ever a President named Forrester?"

"President of what, Man Forrester?"

"President of the United States!"

"Which United States is that, Man Forrester?"

"Oh, for God's sakes! The United States of America.
Wait a minute. First off, do you know the Presidents of
the United States of America?"

"Yes, Man Forrester. Washington, George. Adams,
John. Jefferson, Thomas—"

"Later on! starting with the middle of the twentieth century."

"Yes, Man Forrester. Truman, Harry S. Eisenhower,
Dwight D. Kennedy—"

"Move it up! Start with around 1990."

"Yes, Man Forrester. Williams, Harrison E. Knapp,
Leonard Stanchion, Karen P. Forrester, Wilton N.
Tschirky, Leon—"

"Well, my God," said Forrester softly, and sat marveling
while the joymaker droned on to the end of the twenty-first
century and stopped.

Little two-year-old Willy. Baby Bill. A senator . . . and
President. It was an unsettling idea.

The joymaker said, "Man Forrester! Notice of physical
visit. Adne Bensen is to see you, purpose unstated, time of
arrival less than one minute."

"Oh," said Forrester, "good. Let her right in." And he
rehearsed what he would tell her, but not to any effect.
Genealogy was not what was on her mind. She was angry.

"You," she cried, "what the sweat do you think you're
doing to my kids?"

"Why, nothing. I don't know what you're talking about."

"Dog sweat!" The door crashed closed behind her.
"Twitching kamikaze!" She flung her cape against the
wall; it dropped to a chair and arranged itself in neat

square folds. "Pervert creep, you get a kick out of this, don't you? Want to make my kids like you! Want to change them into chatter-toothed, hand-working, dog-sweaty, *cowardly*—"

Forrester guided her to a chair. "Honey," he said, attempting to get her a drink, "shut up a minute."

"Oh, sweat! Give me that—" She quickly produced drinks for them, without a pause in her talking. "My kids! You want to *ruin* them? You hid from a challenge!"

"Look, I'm sorry, but I didn't mean to get them in a dangerous—"

"Dangerous! Go crawl! I'm not talking about *danger*."

"I didn't let them get hurt—"

"Sweat!"

"Well, it isn't my fault if some crazy Martian—"

"*Dog* sweat!" She was wearing a skintight coverall that seemed to be made of parallel strands of fabric running top to bottom, held together God knew how; with every movement as she turned, as her breast rose and fell, tiny slivers of skin showed disturbingly. "You're not even a man! What do you know about—"

"I *said* I was sorry. Listen, I don't know what I did wrong, but I'll make it up to them."

She sneered.

"No, I *will!* . . . I know. There must be something they want. I've got plenty of money, so—"

"Charles, you're pathetic! You haven't got money enough to feed a sick pup—or character enough to make him a dog. Go rot!"

"Now, wait a minute! We're not married. You can't talk to me like that!" He got up and stood over her, the glass unheeded in his hand. Now he was getting angry, too. He opened his mouth to speak, gesticulating.

Six ounces of icy, sticky fluid slopped into her face.

She stared up at him and began to laugh.

"Oh, Charles!" She put down her own glass and tried to wipe her face. "You know you're an idiot, don't you?" But the way she said it was almost affectionate.

"I'm sorry," he said. "Times, let's see, times three, anyway. For spilling the drink on you, for getting the kids in trouble, for yelling back at you—"

She stood up and kissed him swiftly. As she lifted her arms, the strands of fabric parted provocatively. She turned and disappeared into the protean cubicle of the lavatory.

Forrester picked up the rest of his drink, drank it, drank hers, and carefully ordered two more from the dispenser. His brow was furrowed with thought.

When she came back he said, "Honey, one thing. What did you mean when you said I didn't have a lot of money?"

She fluffed her hair, looking abstracted.

He said persistently, "No, I mean it. I mean, I thought you knew Hara pretty well. He must have told you about me."

"Oh, yes. Of course."

"Well, then. I had this insurance thing when I died, you see. They banked the money or something, and it's had six hundred years to grow. Like John Jones's Dollar, if you know what that was. I didn't have much to begin with, but by the time they took me out of the cooler it was over a quarter of a million dollars."

She picked up her new drink, hesitated, then took a sip of it. She said, "As a matter of fact, Charles dear, it was a lot more than that. Two million seven hundred thousand, Hara said. Didn't you ever look at your statement?"

Forrester stared. "Two million sev— Two mill—"

"Oh, yes." She nodded. "Look it up. You had the papers with you in the tea room yesterday."

"But—but, Adne! Somebody must've—I mean, your kids were with me when I deposited the check! It was only two hundred and some thousand."

"Dear Charles. Will you please look it up in your statement?" She stood up, looking somewhat annoyed and, he thought, somewhat embarrassed. "Oh, where the devil did you put it? It was a silly joke anyway, and I'm tired of it."

Numbly he stood up with her, numbly found the folder from the West Annex Discharge Center, and placed it in her hands. What joke? If there was a joke, he didn't know what it was. But already he didn't like it.

She fished out the sheaf of glossy sheets in the financial report, glanced at them, began handing them to him. The first was entitled CRYOTHERAPY, MAINTENANCE, SCHEDULE 1. It bore a list of charges under headings like Annual Rental, Biotesting, Cell Retrieval and Detoxification, as well as a dozen or more recurring items with names that meant nothing to him—Schlick-Tolhaus Procedures, Homiletics, and so on. On the second sheet was a list of charges for what appeared to be financial services, presumably investing and supervising his capital. The third sheet covered diagnostic procedures; there were several for what seemed to be separate surgeries, sheets for nursing care and for pharmaceuticals used. . . . There were in all nearly thirty sheets, and the totals at the bottom of each of them were impressive, but the last sheet of all took Forrester's breath away.

It was a simple arithmetical statement:

AGGREGATE OF CONVERTED ASSETS		$2 706 884.72
AGGREGATE OF SCHEDULES	1–27	2 443 182.09
NET DUE PATIENT ON DISCHARGE		$ 263 702.63

Forrester gasped and coughed and cried, half strangled, "Two and half million *dollars* for medical—Sweet Jesus God!" He swallowed and looked up unbelievingly. "Holy AMA! Who can afford that kind of money?"

Adne said, "Why, you can, for one. Otherwise you'd still be frozen."

"Christ! And—" A thought struck him— "Look at this! Even so they're cheating me! It says two hundred and sixty thousand, and they only gave me two thirty!"

Adne was beginning to look faintly angry again. "Well, after all, Charles. You did go back there for extra treatment. You might get some of that back from Heinzie, I don't know. . . . Of course, he's protesting it because you messed things up."

He looked at her blankly, then back at the statement. He groaned.

"Reach me my drink," he said and took a long pull of it. He announced, "The whole thing's crazy. Millions of dollars for doctors! People just can't *have* that much money."

"You did," she pointed out. "Given time, people can. At compound interest, they can."

"But it's—it's medical profiteering! I don't know what they did to me, but surely there should be *some* attempt to control fees!"

Adne took his arm and drew him down again on the couch beside her. She said with patience, but not very much patience, "Dear Charles, I wish you would learn a little something about the world before you tell us all what's wrong with it. Do you know what they had to do to you?"

"Well— Not exactly, no. But I know something about what medical treatment costs." He frowned. "Or used to cost, anyway. I suppose there's inflation."

"I don't think so. I—I think that's the wrong word," she said. "I mean, that means things cost more because the money is worth less, right? But that isn't what happened. Those operations would have cost you just as much in the nineteenth century, but—"

"Twentieth!"

"Oh, what's the difference! Twentieth, then. That is, they would have cost just as much if anybody had been able to do them. Of course, nobody was."

Forrester nodded unwillingly. "All right, I admit I'm alive and I shouldn't kick. But still—"

Impatiently the girl selected another document from the sheaf, glanced at it, and handed it to him. Forrester looked, and he was very nearly sick. Full color, nearly life size, he thought at first that it was Lon Chaney made up as the Phantom of the Opera.

But there was no makeup. It was a face. Or what was left of one.

He gagged. "What— What—"

"Do you see, Charles? You were in bad shape."

"Me?"

"Oh yes, dear. You really must read your report. See here . . . evidently you fell forward into the flames. Besides your being killed, the whole anterior section of the head was destroyed. At least, the soft parts. Mm . . .

lucky your brains weren't cooked, at that." He saw with
incredulity that this tender, charming girl was studying the
photograph with as little passion as though the charred
meat it represented were a lamb chop. She went on,
"Didn't you say you noticed your eyes were different?
New eyes."

Forrester croaked, "Put that thing away."

He took a swallow of his drink and immediately regretted it, then fished one of the remaining cigarettes out of his
second pack and lit it. "I see what you mean," he said at
last.

"Do you, dear? Good. You know, I bet four or five
hundred people worked on you. All sorts of specialists.
All their helpers. Using all their equipment. They get a
case like yours, it's like one of those great big enormous
jigsaw puzzles. They have to put it all back together, piece
by piece—only they don't have all the pieces, so they have
to get or make new ones . . . and of course the stuff spoils
so. They have to—"

"Quit it!"

"You're awfully jumpy, Charles."

"All right! I'm jumpy." He took a deep drag on the cigarette and asked the question that had been developing in
his mind for ten minutes now. "Look. At a normal rate of
expenditure—oh, you know; the way you see me living—
roughly how long is my quarter of a million dollars going
to last?"

She looked into space and tapped her fingernails against
her teeth. "There are those custom items of yours," she
said thoughtfully. "They come high—those things you
smoke, and fowl eggs, and—what was that other thing?
The oransh juice—"

"Leaving out that kind of stuff! How long?"

She pursed her lips. "Well, it depends—"

"Roughly! How long?"

She said, "Well, maybe the rest of this week."

He goggled at her. He repressed a laugh that sounded
almost like a sob.

The end of the *week*?

He had been building himself up to hear an answer he

wouldn't like, but this exceeded his expectations. He said wretchedly, "Adne—what am I supposed to do?"

"Well," she said, "you could always get a job."

"Sure," he said bitterly. "Got one up your sleeve? One that pays a million dollars a week?"

To his surprise, she seemed to take him seriously. "Oh, Charles! Not that much. I mean, you're not skilled. Twenty, twenty-five thousand a day—I don't think you can really expect more."

He said, "You can find me a job like *that?*"

"Well, what do you think Taiko would have paid?"

"Wait a minute! You mean Taiko would have given me a *job?* But I thought— I mean, he said it was his club. What did he call it, the Ned Lud Society?"

"Yes, that's right." She nodded. "What do you think a club's for, Charles?"

"Why—so that people with like interests can, well, get together and work on their interests."

"And what did you used to so quaintly call a business company?"

"Why . . . Yeah, but look, a company produces something of *value.* Something you can *sell.*"

She sniffed. "We've got beyond that sort of consideration. Anything that any reasonably competent people agree is worth doing is worth a salary in exchange for doing it."

"Gosh," said Charles Forrester.

"But Taiko was quite astonished at the way you acted, Charles. I don't know whether he's angry or not. But I wouldn't count on the offer still being open."

"Figures," said Forrester gloomily, musing over lost possibilities.

"Man Forrester!"

The sound of the joymaker was almost like an alarm wakening him from sleep. It took him a few moments to realize what it was, as he emerged from his bemused state. Then he said, "In a minute, machine. Adne, let me get this straight—"

But she was looking urgent and abashed. "Charles dear, you'd better take this message."

"Man Forrester! I have a priority notice of personal visit!"

"Yeah, but Adne—"

"Charles," she said, "please take it. Or—never mind. I'll tell you myself." She looked down at her hands, avoiding his eyes. "I guess I should have told you before. I think that's Heinzie coming now."

"Heinzie? The *Martian?* The one—"

She said apologetically, "I told him to come, Charles dear. You'd really better let him in."

Chapter Seven

As Forrester faced the man named Heinzlichen Jura de Syrtis Major, he felt he was in the state described as "ready for anything." What this actually meant was that he was totally unready. He did not know what to expect. He could feel his heart pounding; he sensed that his hands were beginning to shake. Even Adne seemed stimulated; she was watching them, her small face intensely interested, and she was fumbling something out of her joymaker. A tranquilizer? No, more likely something to pep her up, thought Forrester. Whatever it was, she popped it in her mouth and swallowed before she said, "Hello, Heinzie. Come on in. I think you and Charles have met."

Forrester gave her a look, then returned to Heinzlichen. He started to put out his hand, then stopped, balancing on the balls of his feet, half ready to shake hands, half in a stance resembling the attack position of karate. "We've met, all right. Too damned often, if you ask me."

Heinzlichen came in, allowed the door to close behind him, and stood still, studying Forrester as if he were a specimen in a museum. Adne had been playing with the lights again, and mottled reds and yellows flecked his face. They suited his personal color scheme. He was a tall, fat man. His hair was red, and he wore a close-cut red beard that covered all of his face except for nose, lips, and eyes, like the mask of a chimpanzee. He rubbed his beard thoughtfully while he examined Forrester's face with attention, glanced appraisingly at his arms and body, stared down at the position of his feet, and finally nodded. He returned his gaze to a point on Forrester's chest and stabbed at it with a finger. He said, "Dat is where I will kill you. Dere. In de heart."

Forrester exhaled sharply through his nose. It tingled. He felt the flush of adrenalin through his bloodstream. He opened his mouth; but Adne cut in swiftly before he could speak.

"Heinze dear! You promised."

"Promised? What promised? I promised to talk, dat's all. So let's talk."

"But Charles doesn't understand how things are, Heinzie. Sit down. Have a drink."

"Oh, sure I'll have a drink. You pick me out something nice. But make it fast, because I have only a couple of minutes." He returned to Forrester. "Well? You want to talk?"

Forrester said belligerently, "You're damned right I want to talk. And, no, Adne, I don't want a drink. Now, look here, you—" He hesitated, finding it hard to think of the right thing to say. "Well, what I want to know is, why the devil do you want to kill me?"

The Martian looked baffled. He glanced at Adne helplessly, then back to Forrester. "Sweat, I don't know," he said. "Up dere at de party you stomped my foot. . . . But I guess I just didn't like you anyway. What do you want to ask a question like dat for?"

"Why? It's my life!"

The Martian growled, "I knew dis was a bad idea. Honey, I'm going. De more I see of dis guy, de less I like him."

But Adne had her hand on his arm. "Please, Heinzie. Here." She handed him a fizzy orange drink in a thing like a brandy inhaler with a hollow stem. "You know Charles is just out of the sleep-freeze. He's kind of a slow learner, I'm afraid."

"Dat's his business. Killing him, dat's my business." But the Martian grumpily accepted the drink. The girl pressed her advantage.

"Yes, but Heinzie—dead—what's the fun of it if he doesn't know what it's all about?"

"Trimmer!" Heinzlichen growled. "Maybe it's more fun dat way. I can't help dinking we lose some of de important values when killing's all so cut and dried."

"All right, Heinzie, maybe you're right, but there's such a thing as fair play, too. Why, I don't even think Charles really knows what his rights are."

The Martian shook his head. "Dat's not my business eider. Dere's his joymaker; let him call up and find out."

Adne winked reassuringly at Forrester, who was not in the least reassured. But she seemed more confident and relaxed now. She leaned back, sipping her drink, and said silkily, "Wouldn't it be nicer for you to talk to him about it? Tell Charles what you want to do, exactly?"

"Oh, dat part's all right." The Martian put down his drink, scratched his beard thoughtfully, and said, "Well, it's like dis. I want to beat him up good, and den I will stomp on his chest cage until it breaks and ruptures de heart. De reason I like to do it dat way is it hurts a lot, and you don't get near de brain. Of course," he mused, "I got to pay a little more, but de best pleasures are de ones you pay for. Cheap's cheap." Then his expression lightened—or seemed to: the beard hid most of his transient looks. "Anyway," he added, "maybe I can get off paying de bill. I talked to de lawyer, and he said Forrester hasn't touched all de bases, law-wise, so maybe we can fight de costs. But dat doesn't matter in de long run. What de hell, if it costs it costs."

Forrester nodded thoughtfully and sat down. "I believe I'll have that drink now, Adne," he said. He realized, with a certain amount of pride, that he was perfectly calm.

The reason was that Forrester had come to a decision while Heinzlichen was talking: he had decided to go along with the gag. True, it wasn't really a gag. True, when this man said he intended to cause Forrester a lot of pain and bring about his ultimate death, he meant every word of it. But you could not spend your life in weighing consequences. You had to pretend that the chips were only plastic and did not represent real currency of any sort, otherwise you would lose the game out of nerves and panic.

The very fact that the stakes were so important to Forrester was a good reason for pretending they were only make-believe.

He accepted a glass from Adne and said reasonably, "Now, let's get this straight. Did I understand you right? You talked to a lawyer before you tried to kill me?"

"Nah! Wake up, will you? All I did den was file de papers."

"But you just said—"

"Listen, why don't you? De *papers* was so I could kill you—all de usual stuff, bonds to cover de DR business, guaranties against damaging de brain, and like dat. Den de *lawyer* was just yesterday, when I got de idea maybe I could kill you and save all de bond and guaranty money."

"Excuse me. I didn't understand that part." Forrester nodded pleasantly, thinking hard. It began to make a certain amount of sense. The thing you had to remember was that death, to these people, was not a terminal event but only an intermission.

He said, "As I understand it—I mean, if I understand it—the legal part of this business means you have to guarantee to pay my freezer costs if you kill me."

"Nah! Not 'if.' Odderwise you got it."

"So I don't have anything to say about it. The law lets you kill me, and I'm stuck with it."

"Dat's right."

Forrester said thoughtfully, "But it doesn't sound fair to me, everything considered."

"Fair? Of course it's fair! Dat's de whole idea of de guaranties."

"Yes, of course—if the circumstances are normal. But in this case, with death-reversal out of the question . . ."

The Martian snorted angrily. "Are you crazy?"

"No, really," Forrester persisted. "You said you were going to try to get out of paying my expenses. You know more about it than I do. Suppose you succeed?"

"Oh, boy! Den you have to pay dem yourself."

Forrester said politely, "But you see, I can't. I don't have any money to pay them with. Ask Adne."

The Martian turned to Adne with a look of unbelieving

anger, but she said, "As a matter of fact, Heinzie, Charles is telling you the truth. I didn't think of it, but it's so. I mean, I haven't checked his balance . . . but it can't be much."

"De hell with his balance! What de sweat do I care about his balance? I just want to kill him!"

"You see, Jura, if you kill me—"

"Shut up, you!"

"But the way things are—"

"Dog sweat!" The Martian's face was working angrily under the mask of beard. He was confused, and that made him mad. "What's de matter with you, Forrester? Why didn't you get a job?"

"Well, I will. As soon as I can."

"Sweat! You want to chicken out, dat's all!"

"I simply didn't understand my money situation. I didn't *plan* it this way. I'm sorry, Jura, I really am, but—"

"Shut up!" barked the Martian. "Look, I got no more time for dis talk. I have to go to de rehearsal hall; we're doing de Schumann *lieder*, and I'm de soloist. Answer de question. Do you want to chicken out?"

"Well," said Forrester, fiddling with his glass and casting a sidelong glance at Adne, "yes."

"Fink! Dog-sweat fink!"

"I know how you feel. I guess I'd feel the same way."

"De hell with how you'd feel. All right, look. I'm not promising anything, but I'll talk to de lawyer again and see where de hell we stand. Meanwhile, you get a job, hear?"

Forrester showed the Martian out. For some reason that he could not quite analyze, he was feeling elated.

He stood thoughtfully at the door, testing the feeling. For a man who had just discovered he was a pauper, who had reinforced the dislike of an enemy who proposed to kill him, Forrester was feeling pretty good. Probably it was all an illusion, he thought fatalistically.

Adne was curled up on the couch, studying him. She had been doing something with the lights again; now they were misty blue, and her skin gleamed through the lacy strands of her coverall. Perhaps she had been doing something with that, too; it seemed to be showing more of Adne than it had earlier. Forrester excused himself and went into the little lavatory room to splash cold water on his face. And then he realized the cause of his elation.

He had managed to win a point.

He was not a bit sure it was a worthwhile point; he wasn't even quite sure of what he had won. But, for better or for worse, he had gained a small victory over Hein-zlichen Jura de Syrtis Major. For days Forrester had been a cork bobbing to the thrust of every passerby; now he was thrusting back. He came smiling back into the room and cried, "I want a drink!"

Adne was still on the couch, murmuring into her joy-maker. "—And be sure you're locked up," she was saying. "Don't forget your prophylaxis and say good night, Mim." She put it down and looked up at him. Her expression was sulky but entertained.

"The kids?" She nodded. "My God, is it that late?" He had forgotten the passage of time. "I'm sorry. I mean, what about their dinners and all?"

She looked slightly less sulky, slightly more entertained. "Oh, Charles! You weren't thinking I had to boil oatmeal or peel potatoes? They've had their dinners, of course."

"Oh. Well. I guess we should be thinking about ours. . . ."

"Not yet."

Forrester said, reorienting his thinking very quickly, "All right. Then what about that drink?"

"I'm not thirsty, you fool. Sit down." She lifted her joy-maker, looked him over with narrowed eyes, kissed the soft spot at the base of his throat, and touched it with the joy-maker.

Forrester felt a sudden surge inside him. It was like a mild electric shock, like a whiff of mingled oxygen and musk.

Adne studied him critically, then leaned forward and kissed him on the lips.

A moment later he said, "Do that again."

She did. Then she lay back against him with her head on his shoulder.

"Dear Charles," she said, "you're such a nut."

He stroked her and kissed her hair. The parallel-strand fabric did not feel coarse or wiry; he could hardly tell it was there.

"I don't know if you did the right thing with Heinzie," she said meditatively. "It's kind of—you know. Almost chicken . . ." Then she turned inside his arm and kissed his ear. "I know it embarrasses you when I talk biology, but—well, the reason I'm natural-flow, you see, is that I'm a natural type of girl. Do you understand?"

"Sure," he lied, only vaguely hearing her.

"I mean, if you want to you can take the pills and use the chemosimulants, and it's just *about* the same. But I don't do that, because, if you're going to do that, you might just as well go all the way and use the joy machine."

"I can see that, all right," he said, but she fended him off and added, "Still, one doesn't have to be *rigid*. Sometimes you're at a low point, and something special happens, and you'd like to be at a high point. Then you can take a pill if you want to, do you see?"

"Oh, yes! Say!" said Forrester, pleasantly excited, "I wonder! How would you feel about taking a pill now?"

She sat up, stretched, and put her arms around him. "Don't have to," she said, resting her cheek against his. "I took one when you let Heinzie in."

With two victories in one day, thought Forrester in a mood of pleasant triumph and lassitude, this world had come pretty close to his first hopes for it, after all. After the girl had gone, he slept for ten good hours and woke with the conviction that everything would turn out right. The father of a President and the lover of Adne Bensen was, at least in his own eyes, a figure of much mana. There were problems. But he would cope with them.

He ordered breakfast and added, "Machine! How do I go about getting a job?"

"If you will state parameters, Man Forrester, I will inform you as to openings that may be suitable."

"You mean, what kind of job? I don't know what kind. Just so it pays—" he coughed before he could get the figure out—"around ten million bucks a year."

But the joymaker took it in stride. "Yes, Man Forrester. Please inform me further as to working conditions: home or external; mode of payment—straight cash or fringed; if fringe, nature permitted—profit-sharing, stock issue, allocated earnings bonus, or other; categories not to be considered; religious, moral or political objections, not stated in your record profile, which may debar classes of employ—"

"Slow down a minute, machine. Let me think."

"Certainly, Man Forrester. Will you receive your messages now?"

"No. I mean," he added cautiously, "not unless there are some life-or-death ones, like that Martian being out to kill me again." But there weren't. That, too, thought Forrester with pleasure, set this day off from other days.

He ate thoughtfully and economically, bathed, put on clean clothes, and allowed himself an extremely expensive cigarette before he tackled the joymaker again. Then he said, "Tell you what you do, machine. Just give me an idea of what jobs are open."

"I cannot sort them unless you give me parameters, Man Forrester."

"That's right. Don't sort them. Just give me an idea of what's going."

"Very well, Man Forrester. I will give you direct crude readout of new listings as received in real time. Marking. Mark! Item, curvilinear phase-analysis major, seventy-five hundred. Item, chef, full manual, Cordon Bleu experience, eighteen thousand. Item, poll subjects, detergents and stress-control appliances, no experience required, six thousand. Item, childcare domestics—but, Man Forrester," the joymaker broke in on itself, "that clearly specifies female employment. Shall I eliminate the obviously inappropriate listings?"

"No. I mean, yes. Eliminate the whole thing for now. I get the idea." But it was confusing, thought Forrester uncomfortably; the salaries mentioned were hardly higher than twentieth-century scale. They would not support a Pekingese pup in this era of joyful extravagance. "I think I'll go see Adne," he said suddenly, and aloud.

The joymaker chose to reply. "Very well, Man Forrester,

but I must inform you as to a Class Gamma alert. Transit outside your own dwelling will be interrupted for drill purposes."

"Oh, God. You mean like an air raid."

"A drill, Man Forrester."

"Sure. Well, how long is that going to go on?"

"Perhaps five minutes, Man Forrester."

"Oh, well, that's not so bad. I tell you what, why don't you give me my messages while I'm waiting."

"Yes, Man Forrester. There are one personal and nine commercial. The personal message is from Adne Bensen and follows." Forrester felt the light touch of Adne's hand, then the soft sound of Adne's voice. "Dear Charles," her voice whispered, "see me again soon, you dragon! And you know we have to think about something, don't you? We have to decide on a name."

Chapter Eight

When he reached Adne's apartment, the children let him in. "Hello, Tunt," he said. "Hello, Mim."

They stared at him curiously, then at each other. Blew it again, he thought in resignation; it must be the girl that's Tunt, the boy that's Mim. But he had long since decided that if he tried to track down all his little errors he would have time for nothing else, and he was determined not to be derailed. "Where's your mother?" he asked.

"Out."

"Do you know where?"

"Uh-huh."

Forrester said patiently, "Would you like to tell me where?"

The boy and girl looked at each other thoughtfully. Then the boy said, "Well, not particularly, Charles. We're kind of busy."

Forrester had always thought of himself as a man who liked children, but, although he smiled at these two, the smile was becoming forced. "I guess I can call her up on the joymaker," he said.

The boy looked scandalized. *"Now?* While she's *crawling?"*

Forrester sighed. "Look, fellows, I want to talk to your mother about something. How do you recommend I go about it?"

"You could wait here, I guess," the boy said reluctantly.

"If you *have* to," added the girl.

"I get the impression you don't want me around. What are you kids doing?"

"Well—" The boy overruled his sister with a look and said sheepishly, "We're having a meeting."

"But please don't tell Taiko!" cried the girl.

"He doesn't like our club," the boy finished.

"Just the two of you?"

"Sweet sweat, no!" laughed the boy. "Let's see. There are eleven of us."

"Twelve!" the girl crowed. "I bet you forgot the robot again."

"Maybe I did. You and me, Tunt. Four boys. Three girls. A grown-up. A Martian . . . and the robot. Yeah, twelve."

"You mean a Martian like Heinzlichen what's-his-name?"

"Oh, no, Charles! Heinzie's a dope, but he's people. This is one of the big green ones with four arms."

Forrester did a double take, then said, "You mean like in Edgar Rice Burroughs? But—but I didn't think those were real."

The boy looked politely interested. "Yes? What about it?"

"What do you mean by 'real,' Charles?" asked the girl.

In the old days, before Forrester died, he had been a science-lover. It had always seemed to him wonderful and exciting that he should be living in an age when electricity came from wall sockets and living pictures from a box on a bench. He had thought sometimes, with irony and pity, of how laughably incompetent some great mind of the past, a Newton or an Archimedes, would have been to follow his own six-year-old's instructions about tuning a television set or operating his electric trains. So here I am, he thought wryly, the bushman in Times Square. It's not much fun.

But by careful and single-minded questioning he got some glimpse of what the children were talking about. Their playmates were not "real," but they were a lot realer than, say, a Betsy-Wetsy doll. They were analogues, simulacra; the children, when pressed, called them "simulogs." The little girl said proudly that they were very good at de-

veloping interpersonal relationships. "Got that much," said
Charles, "or, anyway, I think I do. So what does Taiko
have to do with it?"

"Oh, *him!*"

"He doesn't like anything that's *fun.*"

"He says we're losing the will to cope with—with what
you said, Charles. Reality."

"And all that sweat," added the girl. "Say! Would you
like to hear him?"

She glanced toward the view-wall, now showing a placid
background scene of woody glades and small furry animals. "You mean on the television?" Forrester asked.

"The what, Charles?"

"On that."

"That's right, Charles."

"Well," said Forrester. . . .

And thought that, after all, he might as well. If worst
came to worst, he could take up Taiko's offer of a job,
assuming it was still open; and before he came to that
worst he would be better off knowing something about it.
"Display away," he said. "What have I got to lose?"

The viewing wall, obedient to the little girl's orders,
washed out the forest glade and replaced it with a stage.
On it a man in a fright wig was bounding about and howl-
ing.

With difficulty Forrester recognized the blond, crew-cut
visitor he had so unceremoniously got rid of—when? Was
it only a couple of days ago? Taiko was doing a sort of
ceremonial step dance: a couple of paces in one direction
and a stomp, a couple of paces away and another stomp.
And what he was shouting seemed like gibberish to Forrester.

"Lud, lords, led nobly!" (*Stomp!*) "Let Lud lead, lords,"
(*stomp!*) "lest lone, lorn lads lapse loosely" (*stomp!*) "into
limbo!" (*Stomp!*) He faced forward and threw his arms
wide. The camera zoomed in on his impassioned, tortured
face. "Jeez, kids! You want to get your goddamn brains
scrambled? You want to be a juiceless jellyfish? If you
don't, then—let Lud lead!" (*Stomp!*) "Let Lud lead!"
(*Stomp!*) "Let Lud lead—"

The boy cried over the noise from the view-walls, "Now he's going to ask for comments from the viewers. This is where we usually send in things to make him mad, like 'Go back in the freezer, you old icy cube' and 'Taiko's a dirty old Utopian!' Of course, we don't give our names."

"Today I was going to send in, 'If it was up to people like you we'd still be swinging from our tails like apes,' " said the girl thoughtfully, "but it probably wouldn't make him very mad."

Forrester coughed. "Actually, I'd just as soon not make him mad. I may have to go to work for him."

The children stared at him, dismayed. The boy extinguished Taiko's image on the view-wall and cried, "Please, Charles, don't do that! Mim said you turned him down."

"I did, but I may have to reconsider; I have to get some kind of a job. Matter of fact, that's why I'm here."

"Oh, good," said the girl. "Mim'll get you a job. Won't she, Tunt?"

"If she can," the boy said uncertainly. "Say, what can you do, Charles?"

"That's one of my problems. But there has to be something; I'm running out of money."

They did not respond to that, merely looked at him wide-eyed. They not only looked astonished, they looked embarrassed.

At length the little girl sighed and said, "Charles, you're so sweaty ignorant I could freeze. I never heard of anybody being out of money, 'cept the Forgotten Men. Don't you know how to get a job?"

"Not very well."

"You use the joymaker," the boy said patiently.

"Sure. I tried that."

The boy looked excited. "You mean— Look, Charles, you want me to help you? Cause I will. I mean, we had that last year in Phase Five. All you have to do is—"

His expression suddenly became crafty. "Oh, sweat, Charles," he said carelessly, "let me do it for you. Just, uh, tell it to listen to me."

Forrester didn't need the girl's look of thrilled shock to

warn him. "Nope," he said firmly. "I'll wait for your mother to come home."

The boy grinned and surrendered. "All right, Charles. I just wanted to ask it something about Mim's other— Well, here's what you do. Tell it you want to be tested for an employability profile and then you want recommendations."

"I don't exactly know what that involves," Forrester said cautiously.

The boy sighed. "You don't have to understand it, Charles. Just do it. What the sweat do you think the joymaker's *for?*"

And, actually, it turned out to be pretty easy, although the employability profile testing involved some rather weird questions. . . .

What is "God"?

Are your stools black and tarry?

If you happened to be a girl, would you wish you were a boy?

Assume there are Plutonians. Assume there are elves. If elves attacked Pluto without warning, whose side would you be on?

Why are you better than anyone else?

Most of the questions were like that. Some were worse— either totally incomprehensible to Forrester or touching on matters that made him blush and glance uneasily at the children. But the children seemed to take it as a matter of course, and indeed grew bored before long and wandered back to their own view-wall, where they watched what seemed to be a news broadcast. Forrester growled out the answers as best he could, having come to the conclusion that the machine knew what it was doing even if he didn't. The answers, of course, made no more sense than the questions; tardily he realized that the joymaker was undoubtedly monitoring his nervous system and learning more from the impulses that raced through his brain than from his words, anyway. Which was confirmed when, at the end of the questions, the joymaker said, "Man Forrester, we

will now observe you until you return to rest state. I will
then inform you as to employability."

Forrester stood up, stretched, and looked around the
room. He could not help feeling that he had been through
an ordeal. Being reborn was nearly as much trouble as
being born in the first place.

The children were discussing the scene on the view-wall,
which seemed to show a crashed airliner surrounded by
emergency equipment, on what appeared to be a mountain
top somewhere. Men and machines were dousing it with
chemical sprays and carrying out injured and dead—if
they made that distinction!—on litters, to what Forrester
recognized by the ruby caduceus as death-reversal vehicles.
The mountainside was dotted with what looked like pleasure craft—tiny, bright-colored aircraft that had no visible
business there, and that seemed to be occupied by sight-
seers. No doubt they were, thought Forrester—
remembering the crowds that had stood by the night he
was burned to death, heedless of icy spray, icy winds and
irritated police trying to push them back.

"Old Hap's never going to make it," said the boy to the
girl, then looked up as he saw Forrester. "Oh, you're
done?"

Forrester nodded. A drone from the view-wall was saying, ". . . Made it again, with a total to this minute of
thirty-one and fifty-five out of a possible ninety-eight. Not
bad for the Old Master! Yet Hap still trails the rookie
Maori from Port Moresby—"

"What are you watching?" he asked.

"Just the semifinals," said the boy. "How'd you make
out on your tests?"

"I don't have the results yet." The screen flickered and
showed a new picture, a sort of stylized star map with arrows and dots of green and gold. Forrester said, "Is ten
million a year too much to ask for?"

"Sweat, Charles! How would we know?" The boy was
clearly more interested in the view-wall than in Forrester,
but he was polite enough to add, "Tunt's projected life average is about twelve million a year. Mine's fifteen. But of

course we've got, uh, more advantages," he said delicately.

Forrester sat down and resigned himself to waiting for the results. The arrows and circles were moving about the star map, and a voice was saying, "Probe reports from 61 Cygni, Proxima Centauri, Epsilon Indi, and Cordoba 31353 show no sign of artifactual activity and no change in net systemic energy levels."

"Dopes!" shrilled the little girl. "They couldn't find a Martian in a mattress."

"At Groombridge One, eight, three, oh, however, the unidentified object monitored six days ago shows no sign of emission and has been tentatively identified as a large comet, although its anecliptic orbit marks this large and massive intruder as a potential trouble spot. Needless to say, it is being carefully watched, and SEPF headquarters in Federal City announce that they are phasing two additional monitors out of their passive orbits. . . ."

"What are they talking about?" Forrester asked the boy.

"The war, of course. Shut up, won't you?"

". . . Well, there's good news tonight from 22H Camelopardis! A late bulletin just received from sortie-control headquarters states that the difficult task of replacing the damaged probe has been completed! The first of the replacements rushed out from BO 7899 has achieved stellar orbit in a near-perfect, almost circular orbit, and all systems are go. Seven backup replacements—"

"Sweat," said the girl. "What a tedious war! Charles, you used to do things better, didn't you?"

"In what way?"

The girl looked puzzled. "More *killing*, of course."

"If you call that better, maybe we did. World War Two killed twenty million people, I think."

"*Weep.* Twenty *million*," breathed the girl. "And so far we've killed, what is it, Tunt? Twenty-two?"

"Twenty-two million?" asked Forrester.

The boy shook his head disgustedly. "Twenty-two individual Sirians. Isn't that rotten?"

But before Forrester could answer, his joymaker spoke up.

"Man Forrester! Your tests have been integrated and assayed. May I display the transcript on Bensen children equipment?"

"Go ahead," the boy said sullenly. "Can't be any worse than *that*."

The star map disappeared from the wall and was replaced by shimmering sine waves, punctuated with numbers that were quite meaningless to Forrester. "You may apply for reevaluation on any element of the profile, if you wish. Do you wish to do this, Man Forrester?"

"Hell, no." The numbers and graphs were not only meaningless but disturbing. Forrester had a flash of memory, which he identified as dating from the last time a government agency had concerned itself with finding him a job—after his discharge from his post-Korean peacetime army service, when he joined the long lines of unemployables telling their lies to a bored State Employment Service clerk. He could almost see the squares of linoleum on the floor, the queues of those who, like himself, wanted only to collect unemployment insurance for a while, in the hope that during that time the world would clarify itself for them.

But the joymaker was talking.

"Your profile, Man Forrester, indicates relatively high employability in personal-service and advocative categories. I have selected ninety-three possible openings. Shall I give you the list?"

"My God, no. Just give me the one you like best."

"Your optimum choice, Man Forrester, is as follows: Salary, seventeen thousand five hundred. This is rather less than your stated requirements, but an expense—"

"Hold on a minute! I'll say it's less! I was asking for ten million!"

"Yes, Man Forrester. You stated ten million per year. This is seventeen thousand five hundred per day. At four-day-week norm, allowing for projected overtime as against health losses, three million eight hundred thousand dollars per year. Expenses are also included, however, optimized at five million plus in addition to salary."

"Wait a minute." The numbers were so large as to be

dizzying. He turned to the children. "That's almost nine million a year. Can I live on that?"

"Sweat, Charles, sure, if you want to."

Forrester took a deep breath.

"I'll take it," he said.

The joymaker did not seem particularly concerned. "Very well, Man Forrester. Your duties are as follows: Conversation. Briefing. Discussion. The orientation is timeless, so your status as a recent disfreezee will not be a handicap. You will be expected to answer questions and be available for discussions, usually remote due to habitat considerations. Some travel is indicated."

"*Sweat*." The Bensen children were showing signs of interest; the boy sat up, and his sister stared wide-eyed at Forrester.

"Supplementary information, Man Forrester: This employer has rejected automated services for heuristic reasons. His desideratum is subjectivity rather than accuracy of data. The employer is relatively unfamiliar with human history, culture, and customs—"

"It *is!*" cried the girl.

"—And will supplement your services with TIC data as needed."

Forrester cut in, "Never mind that. Where do I go for my interview?"

"Man Forrester, you have had it."

"You mean I've got the job? But—but what do I do next?"

"Man Forrester, I was outlining the procedure. Please note the following signal." There was a mellow, booming chime. "This will indicate a message from your employer. Under the terms of your employment contract, you may not decline to accept these messages during the hours of ten hundred to fourteen hundred on working days. You are further required to receive such messages with no more than twelve hours' delay even on nonworking days. Thank you, Man Forrester."

And that, thought Forrester, was that.

Except for trying to find out what was bugging the kids. He said, "All right. What's eating you?"

They were whispering together, their eyes on him. The boy stopped long enough to ask, "Eating us, Charles?"

"Why are you acting like that?" Forrester amended.

"Oh, nothing."

"Nothing *important*," corrected the girl.

"Come on!"

The little girl said, "It's just that we never knew anybody who'd work for *them* before."

"Work for who?"

"The joymaker told you, Charles! Don't you listen?" said the boy, and the girl chimed in, "Sweat, Charles! Don't you know who you're working for?"

Forrester took a deep breath and glared at them. He told himself that they were only children and that in fact he was rather fond of them; but they seemed on this particular morning to be determined to drive him mad. He sat down and picked up his joymaker. Carefully he scanned the cluster of buttons until he found the crystal-clear, rounded one he was looking for, turned the joymaker until its spray nozzle was pointing at the exposed flesh of his arm, and pressed the button.

Happily it was the right button. What the fine mist that danced into his wrist might be he did not know, but it achieved the expected effect. It was like a supertranquilizer; it cleared his mind, quieted his pulse, and enabled him to say, quite calmly, "Machine! Just who the hell have you got me working for?"

"Do you wish me to display a picture of your employer, Man Forrester?"

"You damn bet I wish!"

"Please observe the view-wall, Man Forrester."

And observe it Forrester did; and he swallowed hard, stunned.

In all justice to the joymaker, Forrester was forced to admit that he had placed no restrictions on its choice of an employer for him. He had been willing to accept almost anything, but all the same he was surprised.

He hadn't expected his employer to have bright green fur, or a diadem of tiny eyes peering out of a ruff around a pointed head, or tentacles. He had not, in fact, expected it to be one of the enemy, the race whose presence in space had scared mankind into a vast series of raid drills, weapons programs, and space probes . . . in short, a Sirian.

Chapter Nine

Forrester could have carried on his new duties anywhere. But he didn't want to, he wanted to return to the nest; and there in his room he wrestled with the joymaker and the view-wall and emerged with some sort of picture of what the Sirians were and what they were doing on Earth.

There were eleven of them, as it turned out. They were neither tourists nor diplomats. They were prisoners.

Some thirty years earlier, the first human vessels had made contact with the outposts of the Sirian civilization—a civilization much like the human in the quality of its technology, quite inhuman in terms of the appearance of its members and in their social organization. The human exploring party, investigating an extrasolarian planet, had encountered a Sirian ship nosing about a ringlike structure orbiting that planet.

Forrester, having learned that much, had already discovered some enormous gaps in his knowledge. Why hadn't somebody said something to him about men exploring extrasolar space? Where was this system? And what was the orbital ring? It puzzled and confused Forrester; evidently it was not a Sirian structure and it certainly was not man's. But he avoided the proliferation of questions in his mind and stuck to the straight line of the first encounter with the Sirians.

The Earth ship was loaded for bear. Having found bear, it pushed all the buttons. The commander may or may not have been given discretion about the chances of alien contact and what to do when and if it happened. But he wasted no time in contemplating choices. Everything the Earth ship owned lashed out at the squat, uneven Sirian

vessel—lasers and shells, rockets and energy-emitting de-
coys to confuse and disrupt its instruments. The Sirians
didn't have a chance. Except for a few who were found
still alive in space tanks—their equivalent of suits—they all
died with their ship.

The Earthmen brought them warily aboard, then turned
tail and fled for home. (Years later, remote-operated
probes cautiously returned to look at the scene. They discovered that even the wreckage of the Sirian ship was
gone, apparently retrieved by . . . someone. Whereupon
the probes fled, too.)

Fourteen Sirians had survived the attack. Eleven of them
were still alive and on Earth.

Forrester, watching the picture-story of the Sirians
spread across his view-wall while the joymaker stolidly recited the facts of their exile, could not help feeling a twinge
of sympathy. Thirty years of imprisonment! They must be
getting old now. Did they hope? Did they despair? Were
their wives and kiddies waiting back in the nest, or hatch-
ing pond, or burrow?

The joymaker did not say; it said only that the Sirians
had been thoroughly studied, endlessly debated—and released. Released to house arrest.

The Parliament of Ridings had passed laws about the
Sirians. First, it was, from that moment, cardinal policy to
avoid contact with their home planet. It was possible that
the Sirians would not attack even if they discovered
Earth—but it was certain that they wouldn't if they didn't.
Second, the Sirians now in captivity could never go home.
Third—mankind prepared for the attack it hoped would
not come.

So the Sirians were spread across the face of the earth,
one to a city. They were provided with large subsidies,
good living quarters, everything they could want except the
freedom to leave and the company of their kind. Every one
of them was monitored—not with a mere joymaker. Transponders linked to the central computing nets were
surgically built into their very nervous systems. The whereabouts of each was on record at every moment. They were
informed as to the areas forbidden to them—rocket landing

grounds, nuclear power stations, a dozen other classes of installations. If they ignored the warning, they were reminded. If they failed to heed the reminder, they got a searing jolt of pain in the central nervous system to emphasize it. If that did not stop them, or if for any reason their transponders lost contact with the central computer, they would be destroyed at once. Three of them already had been.

At that moment the mellow chime sounded, the viewwall flickered and changed its picture, and Forrester was face to face with his employer.

It was just like the picture he had seen before. Maybe it was the same Sirian. But it was looking at him now, or seemed to be, although it was hard to tell from the dozens of tiny eyes that rimmed its upper parts, and it spoke to him.

"Your name," it said in hollow, unaccented English, "is Charles Dalgleish Forrester, and you work for me and you call me S Four."

It sounded like a robot talking. More like a robot than the joymaker itself.

"Right, S Four," said Forrester.

"You tell me about yourself."

It sounded like a reasonable request. "All right, S Four. Where do you want me to begin?"

"You tell me about yourself." The tentacles were rippling slowly, the circlet of tiny eyes winking at random like the lights on a computer. He had been wrong about its sound, Forrester decided. It was more like a dubbed-in voice in a foreign film on the Late Show—back when there were foreign films and Late Shows.

"Well," said Forrester ruminatively, "I guess I can start with when I was born. It was the nineteenth of March, nineteen thirty-two. My father was an architect, but at that time he was unemployed. Later he worked as a project supervisor for the WPA. My mother—"

"You will tell me about WPA," interrupted the Sirian.

"It was a government agency designed to relieve unemployment during the Depression. You see, at that time there were periodic cyclic imbalances in the economy—"

"You will not lecture me," interrupted the Sirian, "and will explain terms for which letters WPA are function of entity."

Dashed, Forrester tried to put in concrete terms the business of the New Deal's work relief program. Only concrete terms would do. The Sirian was distinctly not interested in Forrester's digressions into economic theory. Probably he liked his own theories better. But he seemed interested in, or at least did not interrupt, a couple of jokes about leaf-raking and about a WPA worker falling down when someone kicked the broom he was leaning on. The Sirian listened impassively, the girdle of eyes twinkling, for half an hour by the clock; then it said, cutting through Forrester's description of his high school graduation, "You will tell me more at another time," and was gone.

And Forrester was well enough pleased. He had never talked to a Sirian before.

Although the children were romantically thrilled, Adne did not approve when she heard about it. Not in the least. "Dear Charles," she said patiently, "they're the *enemy*. People will say you are doing an evil thing."

"If they're so dangerous, why aren't they in concentration camps?"

"Charles! You're acting kamikaze again!"

"Or why isn't there a law against working for them?"

She sighed and nibbled what looked like a candied orchid, regarding him with fond concern. "Oh, Charles. Human society is not merely a matter of *law*. You have to remember *principle*. There are certain standards of what is good and what is bad, and civilized people comply with them."

Forrester grumbled, "Yes, I understand that. It's good when anybody jumps on me. It's bad when I try to do anything about it."

"Kamikaze, Charles! I'm *simply* trying to point *out* to you that Taiko—for instance—would pay you at least as much as this filthy Sirian for a socially *useful* job—"

"Sweat Taiko!" shouted Forrester, making her laugh with his malaprop anger. "I'm going to do this by myself!"

So Adne left him there on friendly terms, but she left him nonetheless; an engagement in connection with her employment, she said, and Forrester did not know enough about her job to question it. He hadn't found an opportunity to ask what her "crawling" date had been, nor did he see a chance to bring up her suggestion about picking a name. She volunteered nothing, and he was just as well pleased.

Besides, he wanted to talk more with the children.

With their help he was learning more about the Sirian than the Sirian would be able to learn about him. The kids frothed with information. It wasn't difficult to master all the facts they had on tap, for there were not many real facts about Sirians to learn. All the hostages on Earth were of the same sex, for example, but there was a good deal of argument about what that sex was. Nor was their family structure at all clear. Whatever their relationships may have been on the planet from which they came, none of them had ever given any signs of being particularly depressed over being separated from their near and dear. Forrester took in the information grudgingly; he could not help thinking there should have been more of it. He said, "Do you mean to tell me that the only time we've ever seen them is this one time when we wiped out their exploring party?"

"Oh, no, Charles!" The boy was indulgent with him. "We long-range spied their home planet once, too. But that's dangerous. Anyway, that's what they say; so they stopped it. If it was up to me I would have kept it up."

"And like in the chromosphere of Mira Ceti," added the girl brightly.

"The what?"

The boy chortled. "Oh, yeah. That was a fun one! We had it on our class evaluation trip."

"Sweat!" cried the girl excitedly. "Say! Maybe Forrester would like to go with us if we do it again. *I'd* like to!"

Forrester felt a sensation of committing himself to more than he liked. He said uncertainly, "Well, sure. But I don't have much time right now. I mean, these are my working hours—"

"Oh, sweat, Charles," said the boy impatiently, "it doesn't take *time*. I mean, you don't go anywhere in *space*. It's a construct."

"Only it was kind of real, too," added the girl.

"But it's all just tapes now," explained the boy helpfully.

"Show him!" crowed the girl excitedly. "Mira Ceti! Please, Tunt, you *promised!*"

The boy shrugged, cocked an eye thoughtfully at Forrester, then leaned forward. He spoke into his junior joymaker and touched a button on his teaching desk.

At once the cluttered children's room disappeared, and they were surrounded by a wall of hot swirling gray and incandescent orange. It cleared. . . .

And at once Forrester and the two children were seated in the bridge of a spaceship. The toys were gone, the furnishings replaced by bright metal instruments and flickering, whistling gauges. And outside crystal panels surged the devastating chromosphere of a sun.

Forrester shrank back instinctively from the heat before he realized that there was none. It was illusion. But it was perfect.

"By God!" he cried admiringly. "How does that work?"

"Sweat, *I* don't know," scoffed the boy. "That's ninth-phase stuff. Ask your joymaker."

"Well, machine? How about it?"

The calm voice of the joymaker replied at once. "The phenomenon you are currently inspecting, Man Forrester, is a photic projection on a vibratory curtain. An interference effect produces a virtual image on the surface of an optical sphere with the nexus of yourself and your companions as its geometric center. This particular construct is an edited and simplified reproduction of scansion of a Sirian exploration vessel in a stellar atmosphere, to wit—"

"That's enough," interrupted Forrester. "I liked the kid's answer better."

But the boy said tautly, "Knock it off, Charles. We're starting! See, there's this Sirian high-thermal scout vessel, and we're about to run into it."

A harsh male voice rasped, "Tractor ship Gimmel! Your

wingmate has an engine dysfunction! Prepare to lock, grapple, and evacuate crew!"

"Are!" cried the boy. "Start search procedures, Tunt! Keep a watch, Charles!" His hands flashed over the keyboard—it had not been there a moment before, but it was operative; when he energized a circuit, their make-believe ship responded. He put it through a turn; the "virtual" sunship heeled sharply and sped through fountains of flaming gas.

Forrester could not repress his admiration at the perfection of the illusion. Everything was there, everything but the heat and the feeling of motion—and, gazing at the images around him, Forrester could almost feel the surge and shudder of their ship as it responded to the boy's touch at the controls. Clearly, they were part of a squadron on some adventurous, unspecified mission. Forrester saw nothing that resembled a Sirian; he saw nothing at all, in fact, but the serpents and coils of gas through which they hurtled. But he was conscious of illusory vessels around them. A spatter of command signals came through the speaker as other "ships" talked back and forth. A panel showed their position in plan and elevation as they swam through the stripped-atom gases of Mira Ceti's ocean of fire. Forrester ventured to say, "Uh, Tunt. What am I supposed to be doing again?"

"Just use your eyes!" the boy hissed, his attention riveted to the controls. "Don't mix me up, man!" But his sister was shrieking, "I see it! I see it, Tunt! Look over there!"

"Oh, sweat," he groaned in despair. "Will you *ever* learn to make a report?"

She gulped. "I mean, wingmate sighted, vector oh, seven, oh, I guess. Depression—um—not much."

"Prepare to grapple!" roared the boy.

Through the incandescent swirl a fat slug of a ship appeared, vanished, and appeared again. It was black against the blinding brilliance of its surroundings. Black on its metal skin, black in its ports, black even at the tail where a rocket exhaust discharged dark gases into the brightness around them. The rocket cut off as a labored voice gasped through the speaker, "Hurry it up, Gimmel! We can't hold out much longer!"

They jockeyed close to the stranded "ship," buffeted this way and that by the force of the flaming gas. Forrester stared open-mouthed. There was the ship, derelict and helpless. And beyond it, swimming faintly toward them through the chromosphere, something that was bright even in this explosion of radiation, something that loomed enormous and fearsome. . . .

"Holy God," he cried, "it's a Sirian!"

And the whole picture shivered and winked away.

They were back in the children's room. For a moment Forrester was almost blind; then his strained optic centers began to register again. He saw the view-walls, the furnishings, the children's familiar faces. The expedition was over.

"Fun?" demanded the girl, jumping up and down. "Wasn't it, Charles? Wasn't it fun?"

But her brother was staring disgustedly at a readout on his desk. "Tunt," he grumbled, "*you* should know better. Don't you see the tally? We were late locking up. There was a crew of three there, and two of them are scored dead . . . and we never even got to see the Sirian at all. Just *him*."

"I'm sorry, Tunt. I'll look better next time," the little girl said repentantly.

"Oh, it's not you." He glared past her at Forrester and said bitterly, "They set the norms for a three-person mission. As if *he* was any help."

Thoughtfully Forrester picked up the mace of his joymaker, selected a button, pointed it at the base of his skull just behind the ear, and squirted. He was not sure he had picked the right joy-juice for the occasion; what he wanted was something that would make him tranquil, happy, and smart. What he got was more like a euphoric, but it would serve.

He said humbly, "I'm sorry I messed it up for you."

"Not your fault. Should have known better than to take you, anyway."

"But I wish we'd seen the Sirian," said the little girl wistfully.

"I think I did. A big bright ship? Coming toward us?"

The boy revived. "Really? Well, maybe that's not so bad, then. You hear that, monitor?" He listened to what was, to Forrester, an inaudible voice from his teaching machine, then grinned. "We got a tentative conditional," he said happily. "Take it again next week, Tunt. For record."

"Oh, wonderful!"

Forrester cleared his throat. "Would you mind telling me exactly what it was we just did?" he asked.

The boy put on his patient expression. "It was a simulated mission against the Sirian exploring party in the chromosphere of Mira Ceti. I thought you knew that. Basically a real observation, but with the contact between our ships and theirs variably emended."

"Oh. Uh-huh."

The boy looked quizzically at him. He said, "The thing is, Charles, we get graded on these simulations. But it's all right; it didn't hurt us."

"Sure." Forrester could feel the beginnings of an idea asserting themselves. No doubt it was the spray from the joymaker, but . . . "Could you do the same trick with some other things about the Sirians? So I could get a better look at them? Maybe the original encounter, for instance?"

"Neg." The boy glared at his sister. "It's Tunt's fault, of course. She cried when the Sirians got killed. We have to wait to take the prebriefing over when we're older."

The little girl hung her head. "I was sad," she said defensively. "But there's other things we can do, Charles. Would you like to see the coconut on the Moon?"

"The what?"

"Oh, sweat. We'll just show you." The boy scratched his ear thoughtfully, then spoke to his junior joymaker. The view-walls clouded again.

"It's supposed to be another artifact like the one the Sirians were searching for in Mira Ceti's atmosphere," he said over his shoulder, manipulating his teaching machine as he spoke. "Don't know much about it, really. It's not Sirian. It's also not ours. Nobody knows whose they are, really, but there are lots of them around—and the Sirians don't seem to know any more about them than we do. They're *old*. And this is the nearest one."

The view-walls cleared to show the lunar Farside. They were near the terminator line, with crystalline white peaks and craters before them, the jet black of a lunar night to one side. They were looking down into the shallow cup of a crater, where figures were moving.

"This is just tape," the boy said. "No participation. Just look as long's you want to."

There was a clump of pressure huts in the crater. Perhaps they were laboratories, perhaps housing for the scientists or for those who were studying the "artifact" in the center of the screen—or who had been studying it once, perhaps, and had given it up.

It did indeed look like a coconut. As much as it looked like anything.

It was shaggy and rather egg-shaped. Its tendrils of—whatever they were—were not organic, Forrester thought. They were almost glassy in their brightness, reflecting and refracting the sunlight in a spray of color. By the scale of the huts, the thing appeared to be about the size of a locomotive.

"It's empty, Charles," volunteered the girl. "They all are."

"But what *are* they?"

The girl giggled. "If you find out, tell us. They'll make us twelfth-phase for sure!"

But the boy said kindly, "Now you know as much as anybody does."

"But the Sirians must—"

"Oh, no, Charles. The Sirians are late arrivals. Like us. And that thing's been there, just the way it is now, for no less than a couple gigayears." He switched off the scene. "Well," he said brightly. "Anything else you want to know?"

There was indeed. But Forrester had grasped the fact that the more he got to know, the more he was going to realize how little that knowledge was.

Astonishingly enough, it has not really occurred to him before this that a lot of things had been happening to the human race while he was lying deep in the liquid-helium baths of the West Annex Facility. It was like a story in a magazine. You turn a page. Ten years have passed; but you know perfectly well that they weren't *important*; if they were, the author would have told you about them.

But far more than ten years had passed. And they were important, all right. And there was no Author to fill in the gaps in his knowledge.

Chapter Ten

On the third day of his job, Forrester had been six days out of the freezer. He felt as though it had been a million.

But he was learning. Yes, he told himself—gravely gratulatory—he was doing all his homework, and it was only a question of time until all answers were revealed to him and he took his proper place in this freemasonry of heroes.

Meanwhile, working for the Sirian was not at all disagreeable. The social pressure against his job came only from Adne, and he had seen very little of her since that first day. He missed her; but he had other things on his mind. The Sirian—it had agreed to allow Forrester to think of it as a male, although it did not concur in the diagnosis and would not explain further—was curious, insatiable but patient. When Forrester could not answer questions, it permitted him to take time to look them up. Its orientation, surprisingly enough, was all to the past. It volunteered an explanation for this—well, a sort of explanation. In its view, it said, the present state of any phenomenon was a mere obvious derivative of some prior state; and it was the prior states of mankind that it wanted to know about.

It crossed Forrester's mind that if *he* were a war captive on a planet of alien enemies, the sort of knowledge that he would try to acquire would have more to do with arms and defense strategies. But he was not a Sirian, and he had decided not to bother trying to think like one. That was obviously beyond his powers. So he answered questions about Madison Avenue ad agencies and the *angst* that surrounded a World Series, and every day called up his bank to verify that his day's salary had been deposited.

It had finally penetrated to Forrester that money was

still money. His quarter of a million dollars would have bought him—and in fact *had* bought him—something very like a quarter of a million dollars' worth of goods and services, even by twentieth-century standards. It was not the dollar that had been inflated. It was the standard of living.

There were so many things that a dollar could now buy. . . . And he had been buying quantities of them.

He could even, he discovered, have managed to live out his life on that quarter of a million dollars—just as he could have in 1969—provided he had lived at a 1969 level. No robot servants. No extensive medical services—above all, no use of the freezer facilities and their concomitant organ banks, prostheses, antientropic chemical flushings and so forth. If he had eaten no costly, custom-prepared natural foods, had not traveled, had acquired no expensive gadgets . . . if he had, to be exact, lived exactly the life of a twentieth-century suburban peasant, he could have made it last.

But not now. It was gone now. All gone, except for a few tens of thousands left in the account at the Nineteenth Chromatic, plus what the Sirian paid to his account every day. It was about enough to pay his standard joymaker fees for a couple of weeks, maybe. If he was careful.

But Forrester was resigned to the situation. He didn't mind it particularly—at least, he didn't mind his bankruptcy, since it lay within his power to work and make more money than he had ever dreamed of anyway. What he minded very much was the fact that he had been a joke—he and his quarter of a million dollars. And he minded most of all the fact that Adne had shared in that joke.

Because dimly, like a faint, predawn glow in the desert, he could see the foretaste of a time when Adne could be very important to him.

Was already very important to him, he thought wryly. At least in a potential sort of way. He wondered again what she had meant about that business of choosing a name . . . and why, he suddenly thought, had she not called him?

But what was important to him, Forrester realized, was not necessarily important to anyone else. For now, he was a sort of apprentice to life. For now, he would wait, and work, and learn. For now he would not push his luck.

Forrester had learned modesty, if he had learned nothing else.

Forrester had not yet discovered that, in one particular and quite unpleasant way, he was on his way to becoming the most important man in the world.

What mostly confused Forrester about his Sirian employer was that the creature seemed preoccupied. Forrester even asked his joymaker about it.

"Can you clarify your question, Man Forrester? What is there about the behavior of Alphard Four Zero-zero Trimate that puzzles you?"

"Just call him 'the Sirian,' will you? Anyway, he has a funny way of talking."

"Perhaps that lies in my computation, Man Forrester. The Sirian language is tenseless and quasi-Boolean. I have taken the liberty of translating it into approximately twentieth-century English modes of speech, but if you wish I can give you a more literal rendering or—"

"No, it's not that. He seems to have something on his mind."

There was a pause of a second or two. Even Forrester knew enough to remark this occurrence; for the computer facilities to hesitate or search for an answer meant that the problem was something remarkable. But all the joymaker said was, "Can you give me an instance, Man Forrester?"

"Not really. Well, he has me doing some odd things. Is it right for him to want to hypnotize me?"

A pause again. Then the joymaker said, "I cannot say, Man Forrester. But I advise you to be cautious."

Well, cautious he was, Forrester reflected. But he was also puzzled.

The Sirian did not repeat its suggestion about hypnotizing Forrester—"to secure in-depth referents, plus buried traumas of former time"—but it remained hard to figure out. It capriciously had him talking about the twentieth century at one moment, explaining the Arian-Athanasian wars of nearly two millennia before that at another. (Forrester had had to beg time out to research the heresies revolving around the distinction between the words "homo-ousian" and "homoiousian"; even so, he never really did get the problem straight.) It kindly volunteered to assume his joymaker costs as part of his expenses. It refused to allow him to charge as travel expenses a trip to the deepest vaults of Shoggo, where he had been looking up records of the abandoned pressure-dome settlements on Saturn. "Capricious" was the word.

It occurred to Forrester that the Sirian might simply be lonesome. But it rejected his offer to come visit it in its quarters. And, as far as he was able to tell, it showed no interest in the fate of its ten compatriots also in exile on Earth.

"You explain common-law marriage." And, gamely, Forrester tried to describe to a Sirian the drives of sexual impulse and family needs, which had brought about a formal institution to regularize irregular conduct. "There exist trading stamps!" boomed the hollow, empty voice; and Forrester did his best to clarify the complexities of retail supermarket sales. "You have or have not violated legislative compulsion programs," stated the Sirian; and that was the most prolonged session of all. Try as he would, Forrester could not seem to get across the idea of a personal ethic—of laws that one did not violate, because they were morally right, and of laws that everyone violated if they possibly could, because they were morally irrelevant.

He found himself feeling sorry for the Sirian. Its homework was even more arduous than his own.

But Forrester's homework could not be neglected. He ordered his joymaker to display the records of the long-range reconnaissance of the Sirian planet.

He had been thinking of the Sirians as a paper tiger, but now he saw fangs. Englobed by fortresses, with fast and mighty vessels of war flitting about like wasps, the whole Sirian system was a vast network of armament. There were a dozen planets in all, two of them in Trojan orbit with Sirius B, the rest normal satellites of the great white star. All were inhabited. All were defended.

Earth's reconnaissance drones had been lucky enough—
or unlucky enough—to find themselves observing and tap-
ing what seemed to be war games. The Sirians took their
war games seriously. Edited and compressed, the records
showed a waste of creature and armament that only a massive war effort could justify. A hundred of the great ships
were damaged, some destroyed. A fleet of them converged
on an icy satellite of one of the outlying planets . . . and
the satellite was melted into glowing slag before Forrester's
eyes.

There was no more after that. Clearly, the operators of
the drones had felt that enough was enough; it was less
dangerous to leave the Sirians unwatched than to run the
risk of attracting attention with the drones.

Forrester did not again offer to visit the Sirian in its
quarters.

On the fifth day of his new life, Forrester arose to the
promptings of his bed, ordered a standard low-cost breakfast (it was, as a matter of fact, far tastier than his hand-
hewn specials), checked his messages, and started to work.

With some pride in his expertise, he commanded the joymaker to select and mark a course to the buried vastnesses
of the American Documentation Institute. The green-
glowing arrows sprang to life at his feet. He followed them
out the door, into a sort of elevator cab (but one that
moved laterally as well as up and down), out of the cab,
into another building, through a foyer clattering with old-
fashioned punchcard sorters, into a vault containing some
centuries-old records in which his employer had shown a
certain interest.

His joymaker said abruptly, "You will inform me about
the term 'space race.' "

Forrester took his eyes from the old microfilm viewer.
"Hello, Sirian Four," he said. "I'm busy looking up the beginnings of the Ned Lud Society, as you asked me. It's
pretty interesting, too. Did you know they used to break up
computers and—"

"You will discontinue Ned Lud Society research and

state motives that led two areas of this planet to compete in reaching the Moon."

"All right. In a minute. Just let me finish what I'm doing."

There was no answer. Forrester shrugged and returned to the viewer. The Luddites appeared to have taken themselves a great deal more seriously when they first started: where Taiko postured and coaxed, his predecessors had done the Carrie Nation bit with the axes, chopping up computing machines with the war cry, "Men for men's jobs! Machines for bookkeeping!"

As he read he forgot about the call from his employer. Then—

"Man Forrester!" cried his joymaker. "I have two urgent notices of intention for you!"

It was the master computing center this time, not the deep, remote, echoless voice of the Sirian. Forrester groaned. "Not again!"

"Heinzlichen Jura de Syrtis Major—"

"I knew it," Forrester muttered.

"—states that he has reactivated his hunting permit. You are notified, Man Forrester, so please be guided accordingly."

"I'm guided, I'm guided. What's the other one?"

"Man Forrester, it is from Alphard Four Zero-zero Trimate," said the joymaker; then, unbending slightly, "or, as you call him, Sirian Four. A notice to terminate employment. Guarantees are met, and notice paid. Reason: failure to comply with reasonable request of employer, to wit, research questions concerning early U.S. and U.S.S.R. space probe motivation."

Forrester squawked, "Wait a minute! That sounds like— you mean—hey! I'm fired!"

"Man Forrester," said the joymaker, "that is correct. You are fired."

After the first shock had worn off, Forrester was not particularly sorry, although his feelings were hurt. He had thought he was doing as good a job as could be done. Considering the job. Considering the employer.

Nevertheless, it had had its disadvantages, including the barely polite remarks Adne and the children had been passing about working for the enemy. So with a light heart Forrester dismissed the Sirian from his mind and informed the joymaker he wanted another job.

Quite rapidly he had one: standby machine monitor for the great sublake fusion generating station under Lake Michigan. It paid very well, and the work was easy.

Not for twenty-four hours did Forrester discover that the premium pay was due to the fact that, at unpredictable intervals, severe radiation damage was encountered. His predecessor in the job—in fact, all of his predecessors—were now blocks of low-temperature matter in the great lakeside freezers, awaiting discovery of a better technique for flushing the radioactive poisons out of their cells; and the joymaker candidly informed him that their probable wait for thawing and restoration, which depended on the pace at which certain basic biophysical discoveries were likely to be made, was estimated to be of the order of magnitude of two thousand years.

Forrester blew his top. "Thanks!" he grated. "I quit! What the devil do they need a human being down here for anyway?"

"In the event of cybernetic failure," said the machine promptly, "an organic overseer may retain the potential of voice connection with the central computing facility, providing an emergency capability—"

"It was only a rhetorical question. Forget it. Say," said Forrester, punching the elevator button that would bring him up to the breather platform at the lake's surface and thence back to the city, "why didn't you tell me this job would kill me?"

"Man Forrester," said the machine gravely, "you did not ask me. Excuse me, Man Forrester, but you have summoned an elevator. Your relief is not due for three hours. You should not leave your station unattended."

"No, I shouldn't. But I'm going to."

"Man Forrester! I must warn you—"

"Look. If I read the plaque on the surface right, this particular installation has been in service for like a hundred and eighty years. I bet the cybernetic controls haven't failed once in all that time. Right?"

"You are quite correct, Man Forrester. Nevertheless—"

"Nevertheless my foot. I'm going." The elevator door opened; he entered; it closed behind him.

"Man Forrester! You are endangering—"

"Oh, shut up. There's no danger. Worst that would happen would be that it might stop working for a while. So power from the city would come from the other generators until it got fixed, right?"

"Yes, Man Forrester, but the danger—"

"You argue too much. Over and out," said Forrester. "Oh, except one thing. Find me another job."

But the joymaker didn't.

Time passed, and it still didn't. It didn't speak to him at all.

Back in his room, Forrester demanded of the joymaker, "Come on, what's the matter? You computers don't have human emotions, do you? If I hurt your feelings I'm sorry."

But there was no answer. The joymaker did not speak. The view-walls would not light up. The dinner he ordered did not appear.

The room was dead.

Forrester conquered his pride and went to Adne Bensen's apartment. She was not there, but the children let him in. He said, "Kids, I've got a problem. I seem to have blown a fuse or something in my joymaker."

They were staring at him, bemused. After a moment Forrester realized he had blundered in on something. "What is it, Tunt? Another club meeting? How about it, Mim?"

They burst out laughing. Forrester said angrily, "All right. I didn't come here for laughs, but what's the joke?"

"You called me Tunt!" the boy laughed.

His sister giggled with him. "And that's not the worst, Tunt. He called me Mim! Charles, don't you know *anything*?"

"I know I'm in trouble," Forrester said stiffly. "My joy-maker doesn't work any more."

Now their stares were round-eyed and open-mouthed. "Oh, *Charles!*" Obviously the magnitude of the catastrophe had overwhelmed their defenses. Whatever it was that had been occupying their minds when he came in, they were giving him their whole attention now.

He said uncomfortably, "So what I want to know is, what went wrong?"

"Find out!" cried Mim. "Hurry, Tunt! Poor Charles!" She gazed at him with a compassion and horror, as at a leper.

The boy knew what practical steps to take—at least, he knew enough to be able to find out what Forrester had done wrong. Through his pedagogical joymaker, the boy queried the central computing facilities, listening with eyes wide to the inaudible response, and turned to stare again at Forrester.

"Charles! Great sweat! You quit your job without notice!"

"Well, sure I did," said Forrester. He shifted uneasily in his seat. "All right," he said, to break the silence. "I did the wrong thing, huh? I guess I was hasty."

"Hasty!"

"Stupid," Forrester amended. "I'm sorry."

"Sorry!"

"If you just keep repeating everything I say," said Forrester, "you might drive me crazy, but you won't be exactly helping me. I goofed. All right. I admit it."

The boy said, "Yes, Charles, but didn't you know you forfeited your salary? And you didn't have anything much else, you know. A couple K-bucks sequestrated for the freezers, but not much loose cash. And so you're—" The boy hesitated, forming the words with his lips. "You're *broke*," he whispered.

If those were not the most frightening words Forrester had ever heard, they certainly were well up in the running. Broke? In this age of incredible plenty and high-velocity spending? He might as well be dead, again. He sank back in his chair, and the little girl sprang helpfully forward and

ordered him a drink. Forrester took a grateful swallow and
waited for it to hit him.

It didn't hit him. It was, of course, the best the girl could
get for him on her own joymaker, but it had about as much
kick as lemon pop.

He put it down carefully and said; "See if I've got this
straight. I didn't pay my bills, so they turned off the joymaker. Right?"

"Well, I guess you could say that."

"All right."- Forrester nodded. "So the first thing I have
to do is reestablish my credit. Get some money."

"Right, Charles!" cried the girl. "That'll fix everything
up!"

"So how do I do that?"

The two children looked at each other helplessly.

"Isn't there anything I can do?"

"Well, sure, Charles. Sweat, there's got to be! Get another job, I guess."

"But the joymaker wouldn't get me one."

"Sweat!" The boy gazed thoughtfully at his joymaker,
picked it up, shook it, then put it down again. "That's bad.
Maybe when Mim comes home she can help you."

"Really? Do you think she'll help?"

"Well, no. I mean, I don't think she'd know how."

"Then what do I *do?*"

The boy looked worried and a little scared. Forrester was
pretty sure he looked the same way himself. Certainly that
was how he felt.

Of course, he told himself, Hara might help him once
more; certainly he'd had the practice. Or Taiko might be
sportsman enough to get over his snub and reopen the invi-
tation to work for the Luddites.

But he was pretty sure that neither of these possibilities
represented any very hopeful facts.

The little girl wandered thoughtfully away, not looking
at Forrester, and began muttering into her joymaker—back
to the game he had interrupted, Forrester thought with totally unjustified bitterness. He knew it was unjustified.
These were only children, and he had no right to expect
them to handle adult problems that at least one adult—

himself—couldn't handle at all. The boy said suddenly, "Oh, one other thing, Charles. Mim says Heinzie's out after you again."

"Don't I know it." But it didn't seem such a threat, compared with the disaster of insolvency.

"Well, you see, you've got a problem there," the boy said. "If you don't have your joymaker you won't have any warning when he's around. And also there's something about the DR equipment you might not know. You have to have *some* credit rating or they won't freeze you at all if you're killed. You know. There's always the chance that you'll do something that annuls the bonds, so Heinzie, or whoever, might protest payment—then they'd be in trouble. I mean, they don't want to get stuck with a stiff that can't pay up."

"I appreciate their difficulty."

"I just thought you'd like to know."

"Oh, you were right." Forrester's glance wandered. "Mim—whatever your name is. You! What are you doing?"

The girl looked up from her joymaker, her face flushed with excitement. "Me, Charles?"

"Yeah. Didn't I hear you mention my name just now?"

"Sure, Charles. I was proposing you for membership in our club. You know, we told you about it."

"Nice of you," said Forrester bitterly. "Has it got a dining room?"

"Oh, it's not that kind of a club, Charles. You don't understand. The club will *help* you. Already they've made a suggestion."

He looked skeptical. "Is that going to help?"

"Sweat, yes! Listen. Tars Tarkas just said, 'Let him seek in the dead sea bottoms and the ancient cities. Let him join the haunted hosts of old Jasoom.' "

Forrester puzzled over the message drearily. "It doesn't mean anything to me," he said.

"Of course it does! Clear as the crawlers on the Farside coconut, don't you see? He thinks you ought to hide out with the Forgotten Men!"

Chapter Eleven

It was only ten minutes walking from the children's home to the great underbuilding plazas and warrens where the Forgotten Men lived. But Forrester had no guide this time, nor was there a joymaker to display green arrows to guide him, and it took him an hour. He dodged across an avenue of grass between roaring hovercraft, his life in his hands, and emerged under a hundred-story tower where a man came humbly toward him. He looked vaguely familiar.

"Stranger," the man said, softly pleading, "Ah've had a turrible lahf. It all started when the mahns closed and my wahf Murry got sick—"

"Buddy," said Forrester, "have *you* got a wrong number."

The man stepped back a pace and looked him up and down. He was tall, lean, and dark, his face patient and intelligent. "Aren't you the fellah Ah panhandled with those two little kids?" he said accusingly. "Gave me fifty bucks, Ah think."

"You remember good. But that was when I had money; now I'm broke." Forrester looked around at the tall buildings and the greensward. They did not seem hospitable. "I'd be obliged to you," he added, "if you'd tell me where I can sleep tonight."

The man glanced warily around, as if suspicious of some kind of a trick, then grinned and stuck his hand out. "Welcome to the club," he said. "Name's Whitlow. Jurry Whitlow. What happened?"

"I got fired," said Forrester simply, introducing himself. Jerry Whitlow commiserated. "Could happen to anybody, Ah guess. You know, Ah noticed you didn't have a joymaker, but Ah didn't think much about it. Figured, sweat, he's just a damn greenhorn, prob'ly forgot to take it with him. But you got to get yourself one raht away."

"Why?"

"Whah? Sweat, man! Don't you know you're fur game for anybody on the hunt? They come down here, take one look around, and they see you're busted—hell, man, you wouldn't last out the day." He unclipped his own joymaker—or what Forrester had taken to be a joymaker—and proudly handed it over. "Fake, see? But it looks lahk the real thing. Fool anybody. Fooled you, Ah bet."

It had, as a matter of fact. But actually, Forrester saw with surprise, it wouldn't fool anyone at all, not at close range. It was far too light to be a joymaker, apparently whittled out of some organic plastic and painted in the pale patterns of a joymaker. "Of course, it don't *work*," Whitlow grinned. "But on the other hand Ah don't have to pay rent on it. Keeps 'em off pretty good. Didn't have that, one of these preverts that get they kicks from total death'd come down here and tag me first thing."

Gently he pulled it out of Forrester's hand and looked at him calculatingly. "Now, you got to get one just lahk it and, damn, you hit lucky first tahm. Theah's a fellow two houses over makes them to sell. Friend o' mahn. Ah bet he'll give you one for—hell! Maybe little as a hundred dollars!" Forrester started to open his mouth. "Maybe even eighty! . . . Seventy-fahv?"

"Whit," said Forrester simply, "I haven't got a dime."

"Sweat!" Whitlow was awed. Then he shrugged. "Well, hell, Ah guess we can't let you get killed for a lousy fifteen bucks. Ah'll get you fixed up on spec."

"Fifteen?"

Whitlow grinned. "That's without mah commission. Come on with me, boy. You got some ropes to learn!"

The Forgotten Men lived on the castoffs of the great world overhead, but it did not seem to Forrester that they lived badly. Jerry Whitlow was not fat, but he was obviously not starving, either. His clothes were clean and in good repair, his attitude relaxed. Why, thought Forrester, it might even turn out that I'll like it here, once I learn my way around. . . .

Whitlow was a first-rate teacher, even though he never stopped talking. He conducted Forrester through under-building mazes and footbridges Forrester had not even seen, his mouth going all the while. Mostly it was the story of his life.

". . . Laid off at the mahns when Ah was sixteen. Out of work, Chuck, and me with a family to support. Well, we made out, kahnd of, until mah wahf Murry got sick and we had to go on the relief. So a gov'ment man came around and put me on the Aydult Retraining and gave me tests and, Chrahst, Chuck, you know Ah scored so hah Ah just about broke the scales. So then Ah went back to school and—"

He stopped and glanced apprehensively overhead. They were between buildings, under a tiny square of open sky. He grabbed Forrester and dragged him swiftly back into the cellar where the joymaker-maker had kept his shop.

"Watch out!" he whispered fiercely. "They's a reporter up there!"

The word meant nothing to Forrester, but the tone carried the message. He ran one way, Whitlow the other. The joymaker-maker's shop had been in a sort of vermiform appendix to the plumbing of an apartment complex, in an area where some installation had been designed into the plans, then was outmoded and removed, and the space left vacant. The little man who sold the joymakers occupied a sort of triplex apartment—three rooms on three levels—and out of it and around it ran, for some reason, a net of empty, four-foot-wide tunnels. Down one of them Whitlow fled. Down another ran Forrester.

It was dark. The footing was uneven. But Forrester hurried down it, stooped over to avoid banging his head, until the blackness was total and he fell to the rough floor, gasping.

He still did not know what he had been running from, but Whitlow's fear was contagious. And it reawakened a hundred old pains; until this moment he had almost forgotten the beating he had taken the first day out of the freezer, but the exertion made every dwindling ache start up again. His sides pounded, his head throbbed.

He had now been a Forgotten Man for exactly two hours.

Time passed, and the silence was as total as the darkness. Whatever it was that Whitlow had feared, it did not seem to be pursuing here. It would take a human stoat to pursue a human rabbit in this warren, he thought; and in the darkness maybe even the rabbit would develop claws. It had been bad enough when all he had to fear was the crazy Martian. Now. . . .

He sighed, and turned over on the rough, cast-stone floor.

He wondered wistfully what had become of all the furnishings and gadgets he had bought so recklessly for the apartment he no longer owned. Shouldn't there be some sort of trade-in allowance?

But if there was, he did not have the skill to claim it. Nor did he own a working joymaker to help him with instructions. He wondered if Hara would help him out at this last juncture and resolved to go looking for the doctor. After all, it was in a way Hara's responsibility that he was in this predicament. . . .

"No," said Forrester in the darkness, aloud and very clearly.

It wasn't Hara's responsibility at all. It was his own.

If there was one thing that he had learned in his two hours as a Forgotten Man, it was that there were no responsibilities any more that were not his own. This was not a world where a protective state provided for its people. It was a world of the individual; he was the captain of his fate, the master of his soul—

And the prisoner of his failings.

By the time he heard Whitlow cautiously calling his name, Forrester had come to terms with the fact that he was all alone in a cold and uncaring world.

Cautiously they tiptoed out of the pipes, across a hoverway, and under a huge building that was supported on a thousand elliptical pillars, set in beds of grass. What light kept the grass growing came from concealed fixtures in the ten acres of roof over their heads.

Whitlow, regaining the appearance of confidence, led the way to one particular pillar that held a door, marked in glittering red letters EMERGENCY EXIT. He pushed it open, shoved Forrester inside, and closed it behind them.

"Whew," he said cheerfully. "That was close, but we're all raht now. You beginning to get hungry?"

Forrester had been about to ask questions, but that totally diverted his attention. *"Yes!"*

Whitlow grinned. "Figured," he said. "Well, Ah've got just the thing for you, prob'ly. Ah've got a steady clah'nt in this building, fellow who used to work with me at the labs, back before. He's on diet programming now, see, and he always manages to slip me something out of the expurimental allowance. So let's see——"

He rummaged in a cupboard and emerged with a pair of thermal-covered hot dishes. They opened at a touch and displayed a steaming, fragrant dinner for two. "Damn, he done better than ever! Looks lahk smoked oysters Milanese! Sink your teeth in this, Chuck: Ah guarantee you won't do better at the Senate of the Twelve Apostles!"

While he wolfed down the food, Forrester glanced about him to discover what sort of place he was in. It seemed to be an air-raid access to the underground park from the building above, no longer used because, since the beginning of the Sirian threat, complete new facilities had been excavated at the five-hundred-foot subterranean level. But this little forgotten vestige of a completely stocked shelter remained, and, as no one else had any use for it, Whitlow had taken it for his own. It was temperature controlled; it had lights and plumbing; and, as Forrester had already seen, it was provided with food storage facilities. All Whitlow had to do was furnish the food. Forrester leaned back, relaxed, trying to summon up the energy to eat a chocolate mousse and half listening to Whitlow's stream of talk. ". . . So then when Ah got out of M. Ah. T. they weren't vurry many jobs open for coal-mahning engineers, of course. So Ah went back and took mah master's in solid-state electronics. Then Bell Labs sent they recruiter up to scout out prospects and he made me this offer, and Ah went into the labs at nahn thousand to start. Sweat, man, things looked *good*. Murry was puttin' on weight, and the kids were fahn. But Ah'd had this little cough for some tahm, and—"

"Whit," said Forrester, "hold off on that a minute, will you? I want to ask you something. Why did we hide from that reporter?"

Whitlow looked startled. "Ah'm sorry," he apologized after a minute. "Ah keep forgetting what a greenhorn you are. You don't know about these reporters."

"No, I don't."

"Well, all you have to know is seeing one of them's *poison*. Whah, that lahk a vulture hovering over a hill. You just know they's going to be a corpse down below. See, they've got this Freedom of the Press thing, so when anybody takes out a killing lahcense he got to tell the reporters raht away. And he's got to fahl a complete plan of action, see, so the reporters can be raht there when the blood starts flahing, because they tape it all and they put it on the viewwalls. Specially if the killer's in one of the tournaments. Fella from the National Open was here last week and, God, they was reporters hanging out of every cloud."

"I think I understand," said Forrester. "You mean if you can keep out of the way of the reporters, you can probably keep out of the way of the assassins, too."

"Stands to reason, don't it?"

"I don't know what stands to reason," Forrester said humbly. He was beginning to wish he had not been so quick to follow the advice of Adne's children, so reluctant to wait and expose himself to more of Adne's gentle scorn. He felt a quick surge of anger. How dare this world treat *his* life so lightly!

But if it had not been for this world he would not have a life at all; would have stayed dead with a lungful of smoke and fire, centuries before, his body now no more than a soft place in the ground. He leaned back and let himself be lulled by Whitlow's continuing story of his own adventures.

"So then Ah went to the comp'ny doctor and he told me

Ah had it, all rhat. The Big C. Well! Scared? But we had this comp'ny freezer plan at the labs, and Ah reported in to the medics. 'Sheeoot,' they said. 'Lung cancer, hey? Well, you lay raht down here and we'll freeze your bones—' "

Relaxing, half listening, Forrester found himself getting drowsy. It had been a very strange day, he thought; but then he stopped thinking and fell asleep.

In order to live successfully as a panhandler, you had to exercise special care in picking your "clients," Whitlow said. The worst thing you could do was guess wrong. There was always the chance that you might sidle up to somebody and hit him for a touch—and then find out that he was some jet-set happy-boy looking for an economical murder to commit, one that might get him out of the problem of paying for the victim's repairs, and one with double thrills, since there was always the chance that the victim would stay dead.

To avoid that, you had to study each prospective mark carefully. No one came down here on business. The best ones were the rubberneck tourists. They usually came in pairs; and, of any two, the one who was being shown around could safely be figured for a greenhorn—himself too fresh out of the freezers, or back from the starways, to be eager for murder as yet. The problem there was to make an accurate assessment of the one who was doing the showing. "That's whah Ah picked you, Chuck. Ah wasn't worried about the little boy. Though you can be vurry surprised sometahms."

And, of course, everything they did was more or less illegal, so you had to watch out for the coppers.

The coppers would not trouble you unless they saw you actually breaking the law—or unless you were wanted for something. Then they would trouble you a lot. Forrester's first contact with one of the coppers came as he was on the point of bracing a woman alone, Whitlow hiding behind a flowering lilac bush and coaching him in whispers. "See thur, Chuck, what she did? Threw away a cigarette butt. Well, that's ten to one she's from nahnteen eighty or earlier, so go get 'er, boy!" But Forrester had taken no more than a single step before Whitlow's piercing whisper stopped him. *"Copper!"*

The copper was seven feet tall, uniformed in blue, swinging what looked like a nightstick but was not. Forrester had been warned: it was a sort of joymaker, full of anesthetic sprays and projectile weapons. And the copper had seen him.

It strolled right up to them, swinging the stick. It stopped and looked Whitlow in the eyes, right through the lilac blooms. "Good morning, Man Whitlow," it said courteously and moved on to Forrester. It stared silently into his eyes. Then, "Nice day, Man Forrester," it said, and moved away.

"How'd he know?" gasped Forrester.

"Retina pattern. Don't worry about it; if he wanted you for anything he'd have you by now. Just give him a minute to get out of saht."

The woman prospect was gone then. But there were plenty of others.

Keeping out of the way of coppers, trying to learn Whitlow's skill at estimating the potentials of a mark, Forrester found that the time passed. Nor was it the most disagreeable way he had ever spent a day. The weather was warm and dry, the growing plants were scented, the people he hit up were no worse than the average run. Forrester took five dollars from a pretty girl in a sort of mirror-bright bikini, then fifty from a man who had brought his pet animal—it was a little silk-furred monkey—down to the underbuilding park to run free, and who seemed to accept Forrester's touch as a form of rent for the use of the premises. Forrester paid back Whitlow's outlay for the fake joymaker and found himself with cash money in his pocket. As he could see no particular need for spending much of it, he began to feel solvent again.

Then Whitlow's hawk eyes brightened, and he whispered tautly, "Eeow! Look over thur, will you? We've got ourselfs a lahv one now!"

On the fringe of a bed of tall gladioli a man had stepped out of a hovercar and dismissed it. He seemed young, although you couldn't really tell. He moved idly across the grass, like a sightseer. His gait was peculiar, and he wore an expression of grave joy as he minced toward them.

"Look how he walks!" exulted Whitlow.

"I am looking. What about it?"

"Whah, Chuck, he's out of low-gee! Thur's a fella just back from a long trip if Ah ever saw one, and prob'ly loaded with pay. Sic 'im!"

Forrester accepted Whitlow's diagnosis unquestioningly. He marched up to the spaceman and said clearly, "My name is Charles D. Forrester, and due to my ignorance of the customs of this time I've lost all my money and have no work. If you could possibly spare me some cash, I would be deeply indebted to you."

Whitlow appeared magically at his elbow. "That goes for me, too, boss," he said sorrowfully. "We both in pretty bad trouble. If you could be kahnd enough to help us now, we'd be eternally grateful."

The man stopped, his hands in his pockets, neither surprised nor disturbed. He turned to face them with grave interest. "Sorry to hear that, gentlemen," he said. "What seems to be your problem, sir?"

"Mahn? Well, it's just about lahk Forrester here. Mah name's Whitlow, Jurry Whitlow. It starts way back when Ah was first born, working in the mahns in West Virginia. They closed down, and—"

The spaceman was not only polite but patient. He listened attentively through all of Whitlow's long story, and to as much of Forrester's as Forrester thought worth telling. He commiserated with them, wrote their names down, and promised to look for them again if he ever came back this way. He was, in short, an ideal prospect—not only a spaceman, but a member of one of the rotating crews who manned the right-angle communications satellites that whirled out around the sun at ninety degrees to the ecliptic, furnishing interference-free relay facilities for the whole solar system. The job paid well, but that was only part of it. Because of the energy budget for matching orbits with the right-angle satellites, the crews were relieved only at six-month intervals, and they came back with a fortune in their pockets and a mad hunger for company; and Whitlow and Forrester walked away from him with two thousand dollars apiece.

That night they ate their dinner in a restaurant. Over Whitlow's protests, Forrester insisted on standing treat.

The restaurant was a hangout for Forgotten Men—and Forgotten Women. It was something like a private home, something like an Automat. You had full joymaker service in it, but in order to make it work you had to feed money into a slot. The prices caused Forrester's scalp to prickle, but he reassured himself that he was just learning the ropes and experience was worth paying for; so at Whitlow's suggestion they started with a squirt of joy apiece (fifty dollars a shot), then cocktails (forty), then a clear, filling soup (twenty-five), then more drinks, and about then Forrester began to lose count. He remembered something that looked like meat but wasn't—it seemed to be coated with a sort of vanilla fudge, although it was bloody inside—and then they began drinking in earnest.

They were not alone. The place was crowded. Whitlow seemed to know everyone there, an assembly that hailed from six centuries, seven continents, and one or two extraterrestrial planets and moons.

There was a huge red-faced man named Kevin O'Rourke na Solis Lacis, who gave Forrester a shock until they exchanged names, for he resembled Heinzie the Assassin. The reason was good, when Forrester found it out: they were both Martians. O'Rourke, however, was a poet. As a matter of principle, he refused to accept the bribes of what he called the iron-headed state. Probing, Forrester discovered that he was talking about foundation grants, which were available to poets in almost any quantity; but O'Rourke spurned them all. He had been briefly involved with the Ned Lud Society—but they were as bad as the ironheads, he declared. All Earth was a disaster area. Let the Sirians take it away! "So why don't you go back to Mars?" Forrester inquired, politely enough; but the Martian took it as an insult, glowered, and lumbered away across the room.

"Don' worry 'bout heem," said the pretty little dark girl who had somehow come to be leaning against Forrester's shoulder, helping him drink his drink. "He be back. *Certainement.*"

There was a certain United Nations quality to the gathering, Forrester was discovering. Apart from a few oddballs like the Martian poet, the bulk of the Forgotten Men seemed to come from nearly his own time. Had the hardest time fitting in, he supposed—and the hardest time earning money.

But it was not always that. The tiny dark girl, for instance, had originally been a ballet dancer from Czechoslovakia, shot as a Chinese Bolshevik counter-revolutionary in 1991, frozen at great peril by the Khrushchevite underground, revived, killed seven times since in one way or another, and revived each time. Her reasons for hiding out with the Forgotten Men had nothing to do with money—she was loaded, Whitlow whispered; had made a collection of gold and gems from admirers in a dozen countries, over the centuries, and owned them with their pyramiding value now. But one of her assassinations had produced some cell changes in the brain, and now she awoke each time convinced that Stalinist agents lurked abroad, waiting for her. She did not exactly fear them. She objected to the idea of being killed somewhat as Forrester, in the old days, had objected to going to the dentist: you didn't really *worry* about it, but you were pretty sure it would be unpleasant. As someone who had seen each of seven centuries, Forrester found her fascinating—and she was beautiful as well. But she quickly became so drunk that her reminiscences stopped making sense.

He got up for another drink and found himself lurching slightly. Only slightly, he was sure, but somehow, when he got the drink, it spilled all over a lean, old, nearly bald man, who grinned and nodded and said, *"Tenga dura, signore! E precioso!"*

"You're right," said Forrester, and sat down beside him. Whitlow had pointed him out as they entered, as a sort of curiosity; he had actually been born before Forrester himself. He had been a hundred and seven years old when, in 1988, he had died of an embolism. The embolism could have been repaired at once, but the ravages of age could not. Not then. After six centuries in the dreamless, liquid-helium sleep, his original stake had multiplied to the point where the trustees of the freezer had decided to revive him; but there had been only money enough to give him operational youth. Not much had been done cosmetically; and it had taken everything he had. "I bet you've had an interesting life," Forrester told him solemnly, finishing what remained in his glass.

The man gave him a grave nod. "*Signore,*" he said, "*durante la vita mia prima del morte, era un uomo grande! Nel tempo del Duce—ah! Un maggiore del esercito, io, e dappertutto non mi dispiacciono le donne!*"

Whitlow patted the old man on the shoulder and led Forrester away. "Forebrain damage," he whispered.

"But he was talking in Italian."

"Sure, Chuck. He can't learn raht, that's what he's doing here. You know, they ain't many jobs for a fella that can't talk lahk the rest of us."

The Martian lurched past them, his head twisted sidewise toward them. Whether he had been listening or not Forrester could not say, but he was declaiming, "Talk like de rest. Live like de rest. Live for de state, for de state knows what's best."

The whole party was coming to life, thought Forrester, flushed and happy. A small man in a green ruff—it seemed to be an imitation of the Sirian coloration—cried, "And what's best? Adolf Berle asked it half a millennium ago: 'What does a corporation want?' And the state has become a corporation!"

The ballet dancer hiccoughed and opened glazed and angry eyes. "Stalinist!" she hissed, then returned to sleep; and Forrester dug deep for hundred-dollar bills and fed them to the joymaker slots for more drinks all around.

Forrester was perfectly aware that he was rapidly depleting his last thousand dollars. In a way, it pleased him. He was drunk enough, euphoric enough, to let tomorrow face tomorrow's fears. However badly the next day began, it could not be worse than this one had been. He saw advantages even in being a Forgotten Man: you could spend yourself into pennilessness, but not into bankruptcy; you could never go into debt, since you had no credit to begin with. Wise Tars Tarkas! Excellent kids, to have found him such fine advice. "Eat!" he cried, shaking off Whitlow's cautionary whisper. "Drink! Be merry! For tomorrow we die, again!"

"*Domani morire!*" shrilled the old Italian, uptilting his glass of heaven-knows-how-costly grappa that Forrester had provided for him, and Forrester returned the toast.

"Listen, Chuck," said Whitlow uneasily. "You better take it slow. We don't get a mark lahk that space fella every day."

"Whit, shut up. Don't be a grandma, will you?"

"Well, it's your money. But don't blame me if you're broke again tomorrow."

Forrester smiled and said clearly, "You make me sick."

"Now, cut it out raht there!" blazed Whitlow. "Whur'd you be if it wasn't for me? God damn, Ah don't have to take this kind of—"

But the Martian with the Irish name interrupted them. "Hey, you fellows! Dat's enough, dere. You got to buy drinks yet." As Whitlow cooled off, Forrester turned to inspect him; something had been on his mind.

"You," he said. "How come you talk like that?"

"Like what, 'like dat'? You tink dere's someting funny about de way I talk?"

"Yeah, matter of fact. Why?"

But something had occurred to the Martian. He snapped his fingers. "Wait a minute! Forrester, is dat what you said your name was?"

"That's right. But we're talking about you—"

"You should learn not to interrupt dat way," reproved Kevin O'Rourke na Solis Lacis. "What I want to tell you is dis. Dere's a Sirian been around looking for you."

"Sirian? One of the green fellows?" Fuzzily Forrester tried to concentrate, but it was not much fun. "You mean S Four?"

"How de hell would I know his number? He came around in one of dem pressure-cloaks, but I could tell he was a Sirian. I saw plenty of dem."

"Probably wants to sue me for breach of contract,"

Forrester said bitterly. "He's welcome; there's plenty of others."

"No, I don't tink so, because—"

"Cut it out," interrupted Forrester. "You know, I hate the way you Martians keep changing the subject. What I want to know is why you all talk like that. This other one that wants to kill me, he had the same kraut accent, but in his case it figured, because he had a kraut name. But you talk the same way and you're Irish, right?"

Kevin O'Rourke stared at him disapprovingly. "Forrester, you're drunk. What de hell's 'Irish'?"

How long the party lasted Forrester did not know. He remembered a long harangue in which the drunken ballet dancer was trying to explain to him that the accent was Martian, not German; something to do with six-hundred-millibar oxyhelium air, which got them out of the habit of hearing certain frequencies. He had a clear memory of reaching into his pocket one time and coming up empty; and a fuzzy, frightening recollection of something bad that had happened.

But it was all hazy and distant and it came back to him only in random patches.

What he knew for sure was that when he woke up the next morning he was back in the rough-hewn tunnel next to the joymaker shop. How he had gotten there he had no idea. And he was alone.

Except, that is, for the granddaddy of all hangovers.

He dimly remembered that Whitlow had warned him about that, too. There were no autonomic monitoring circuits on the public joymakers, Whitlow had said. He would have to decide for himself when he had had enough, because the joymaker would not stop service at the point of no return—not as long as the money held out.

Apparently it had held out too long.

He shook his head miserably. The movement sent cascades of pain down the back of his skull.

Something bad had happened. He tried half-heartedly to recall it, but all that would come to his memory was a mosaic of mass terror. *Something* had broken up the party with drunken men and women racing around in terror, even the Italian and the ballerina rousing themselves enough to flee. But what?

He was not sure; and he suspected that he would rather not remember, not just now.

He lurched to the end of the tunnel, climbed down metal steps, and pushed a door ajar. He stood gazing out over the plantings, touched by a warm breeze in which he took no pleasure at all. It was daylight, and, except for a distant swish of hovercar traffic, there was no sound of anyone around.

It was too soon to judge, on the basis of less than twenty-four hours' experience. And no doubt his troubles were all his own fault. But Forrester was ready to concede that life with the Forgotten Men was not his place in this new world, either.

If he had any place at all.

By the time Whitlow showed up, looking fat and happy and as though hangovers had never existed in the world, Forrester had come to the conclusion that, since he was alive, he would have to go on living.

"Ev'thing all raht this morning?" Whitlow asked cheerfully. "Man! You were flahing hah when we parted."

"I'm aware of that," said Forrester glumly. "I guess I'll have to take your word for the details. Whitlow, how do I go about getting a job again?"

"What for?"

"I think it's about time I grew up," said Forrester abjectly. "I'm not knocking you. But I don't want to live this way."

"You better start with some money," Whitlow offered. "Won't anybody hah'r you if you come in this way."

"All right. So the first step is to panhandle a stake?"

"Raht!" cried Whitlow. "And that's whut Ah came to tell you, Chuck! The flah-boy's around again. Whahn't you see if you can score again with him?"

They moved out across the broad green belt under the pylons, looking for open sky. Whitlow had seen the space pilot in a one-man flier, cruising aimlessly around; according to Whitlow, the man had looked as though he were

about to land and stroll among the Forgotten Men again,
but there was no sign of him. "Sorry," Whitlow apologized.
"But Ah'm sure he's around somewhere."

Forrester shrugged. Truth to tell, he was thinking, he
wasn't sure he wanted to panhandle anybody. When you
came right down to it, he had been living off this society
without contributing anything in return. Not even anything
in terms of the peculiar values of the society itself; something that, it appeared, could be as little as a membership
in Taiko's revolutionary society dedicated to its overthrow.
With the endless flexibility of employment available,
Forrester thought, surely there was *something* he could
do—something that he would enjoy, and think worth his
while to do. . . .

"Told you, Chuck!" Whitlow yelled. "See 'im? There!"

Forrester looked upward, and Whitlow was right. A face
looked down from the flier; it looked like the astronaut's
face, the eyes regarding them thoughtfully.

The figure picked up a joymaker and whispered into it.
The flier dipped and slid away toward a landing.

"He's landing," said Forrester unnecessarily.

Whitlow was rubbing his chin, watching the flier de-
scend toward the ground. He said abstractedly, "Uh-huh."
His eyes looked worried.

"What's the matter?" Forrester asked.

"Huh?" Whitlow frowned at him, then back at the flier.
"Oh, nothing, Chuck. Only Ah have a bad feeling raht
now."

"What about?"

"Well . . . Nothing, Chuck. Only you never know what
these flah-boys will want to do for fun, an'—Listen,
Chuck. Ah believe Ah want to get out of here." And he
turned briskly, catching Forrester's arm to pull him along.

Alarmed only because Whitlow seemed to be alarmed,
not yet comprehending what it was all about, Forrester
went along. If he thought at all, he only thought that it was
rather cowardly of Whitlow to be so fearful, and not untyp-
ical of this cowardly age, where the very hope of immortality had produced exaggerated fear of permanent death. It

was not until he felt the rush of air overhead that fear struck him personally and acutely.

The flier had taken off again, was now circling over them.

"It's him!" Forrester cried. "You're right, he is after us!"

He turned and ran, Whitlow dodging away in another direction, the two of them scattering as the flier dipped and turned overhead. . . .

It was funny, Forrester realized tardily, but he hadn't seen the man's face looking out of the flier this time.

At that moment he heard Whitlow's yell. The man hadn't been looking out of the flier. He hadn't even been in it; had sent the thing on its autonomic circuits into a hovering pattern, while he himself waited on the ground. And he stood there now, holding something that looked like a whip, directly in Whitlow's path, under the skirt of a tapering yellow building.

Whitlow tried to turn again and run, but he never had a chance. The thing that looked like a whip was a whip. The spaceman seemed only to shake it gently, and its tip hissed out to touch Whitlow, then curled around his neck and threw him to the ground.

Forrester turned and ran. Directly behind him was the hoverway, with its hissing, rocketing, ground-effect cars following each other like tracer rounds out of a machine gun. If one of them struck him, he would die as surely as at the hands of any assassin; but he did not wait, he flung himself across the broad strip and miraculously missed them. A copper was standing, regarding him curiously, as Forrester turned to look back.

The spaceman was lifting the whip again, an expression of alert pleasure on his face. Over the *whush* of the hovercars Forrester could hear Whitlow's scream. Their benefactor from space reached out again with the whip as Whitlow tried to rise; he was slashed back to earth again; he tried to get up once more, and his body shook as the whip flicked blood from the side of his head. He tried again, and was thrown down. And stopped trying.

Forrester turned away and found he was sobbing.

I have a *right* to be scared, he told himself, half crazed. No one could watch a friend whipped to death unmoved. Not when the death was so vicious and so pointless. Especially not when the victim could so easily have been himself.

Could still be himself.

Forrester started to run and blundered into the ruddy metal arms of the copper. "Man Forrester," it said, staring into his eyes, "I have a message for you and good morning."

"Let go!" shouted Forrester.

"The message is as follows," said the copper inexorably. "Man Forrester, will you care to accept reemployment? It is from the one you know as Sirian Four."

"Let go of me, damn you!" cried Forrester. "No. Or, yes—I don't know! I just want to get out of here!"

"Your wishful prospective employer, Man Forrester," said the copper, releasing him, "is nearby. He will see you now if you wish."

"He will go plumb to hell," snarled Forrester, shaking himself. He trotted away, only coincidentally in the direction in which the copper had faced him; but it turned out that no coincidence was involved. The copper had pointed him toward the Sirian's waiting aircar. Forrester saw the aircar first, and outside of it something he did not immediately recognize. It looked a little like a glittering mushroom, a little like a chromium ice cream cone. It rested on ducted jets that swept it across a bed of storm-tossed poppies toward Forrester. It moved toward him very fast, so fast that recognition was tardy; he did not realize it was a pressure suit until he was close enough to see within the bulge of the mushroom, behind an inset band of crystal, a ring of bright green eyes.

It was his Sirian. And it was reaching out to touch him with something that glittered and stung.

Forrester found himself lying on the ground, staring up at the suit that rode beside him on its jets.

"I never said I'd go back to work for you," he said. It hung there unresponding, the long tendril that had stung him now dangling slackly by its side.

"I don't need a job that bad," he babbled, squeezing his eyes closed. He thought that whatever the Sirian had stabbed him with was something very peculiar indeed. For he could not move. And the Sirian seemed to be changing shape.

It no longer looked like a Sirian at all.

Chapter Twelve

At some later time Forrester realized that he could move again, and he found that he was in a flier, laughing to himself over something he had forgotten, staring down at a bright golden farm scene below.

A voice from behind him said, "Dear Charles, you are all right, it is true?"

He turned, grinning. "Sure. Only I've forgotten some things."

"You will say what those things are, dear Charles?"

He laughed, "Oh, what happened to the Sirian. Last I remember, he did something to me—it felt as though he were giving me a hypospray of something. And where we're going—would you believe it, I don't even remember getting into this thing with you. And another thing, I don't remember why you're wearing that funny-looking suit, Adne."

Adne said nothing, only regarded him roguishly through her circlet of green eyes.

He was no longer laughing. "It's confusing," he apologized. "I'm sorry if I've messed things up again."

She still did not speak, although she was busy enough. With others of her eyes she was apparently studying the instrument board of the flier, which was marked off in terrain segments, showing their flight plan as they moved.

"Dear Charles," she said suddenly, "you are ready to perform your programmed tasks?"

"What programmed tasks?"

But the question was a mistake. An explosion of pain formed under his skull and burst through his body to the tips of fingers and toes, where it recoiled and surged back and forth through his nervous system in dwindling echoes. He cried out. It was not the first time he had felt that pain; he remembered now. And he remembered his programmed tasks.

"You are Adne Bensen. As a joke you want me to smuggle you onto a starship. I must carry you aboard and plug in the command unit you have given me to the starship's circuits and tell no one, or it will spoil the joke. And hurt me."

"Dear Charles," boomed the hollow, resonant voice, "you are ready to perform your programmed tasks."

The pain was receding. Forrester leaned back, dizzy, sick, extremely confused. He wondered if his mind were breaking down. Certainly it would be no wonder if it were, after what he had been through.

It did not seem to him that Adne's joke was very *funny*. But Forrester recognized that his mind was not very sharp at that moment, and perhaps it was his judgment that was at fault, not the joke. He felt as though he were crazy. He felt both unbearably sleepy and keyed up, like an insomniac glaring hatefully at the slowly brightening window of his room. His eyes were gritty and sore, but when he closed them they sprang open again. It was frightening.

And he was disoriented in space and time. He had no idea where they were. He realized with dismay that it was dark night outside the flier. When had that happened? Time passed that he did not mark in any way; he would look up to see Adne regarding him with her strangely bright green eyes, look again, and she was somewhere else; but he had not seen her move. Delusions. Had he not thought that Adne had stabbed him with something like a hypodermic? What possible motive would she have for that? Had he not seemed to remember her *telling* him who she was over and over? (As though he couldn't recognize her!) Wasn't there a memory of the girl, looking so strangely unlike herself in that Sirian spacesuit, repeating and endlessly repeating instructions on what he was to do at some later time, emphasizing them with jabs of that explosive pain?

He closed his eyes, groaning.

They flew open again, but curiously he was not in the flier any more. Dizzy and sick, he saw only in flashes, but the flashes told him that he was standing on hot, baked, dead grass; there was the whir of the flier's idling rotors behind him, ahead of him a metallic whining of gears as a port opened, beside him a hiss of ducted gas. He found himself pushing the bobbing, silent figure in the cone-shaped spacesuit through the opening port; found himself connecting something flat and shiny to jacks on an instrument board. And then he was outside again, and under stars, and getting back into the flier.

But where was Adne?

He flung himself petulantly down on the seat. His head was splitting with pain. "Damn you," he whispered, and slept.

When he woke up, the flier was standing at the side of the hoverway, across from the tapering yellow spire. The engines were stopped and silent. As best he could tell, it was at the exact spot where the Sirian had reached out for him with the thing that stung.

He staggered out and breathed deep. *Whush* of vehicles from the hoverway, scream of tires from another, more distant road. There was no other sound. It appeared to be morning.

He called tentatively, "Adne?"

There was no answer. In a way, he had not expected one, only hoped.

Twenty-four hours had disappeared out of his life, and he was very hungry. He searched his pockets, to see what might be left of the handout from his friend, the whip-murderer. Nothing. He had expected that, of course. His resources were dwindling all the time. His money was gone. His credit was destroyed. Whitlow, his mentor among the Forgotten Men, was dead—irrevocably dead, Forrester thought, making the distinction in his mind that this age made out of instinct.

He had only Adne left—if he had Adne. So he did what he had known all along he was going to do; he headed for Adne's condominium.

He knew perfectly well, as he skulked through the underways and dodged passing fliers, that he had no real claim on her. She might not be home; she might not admit him if she was.

But she was home and did admit him, without much enthusiasm. "You look a mess," she said, averting her face. "All right, come in."

He sat down, ill at ease. The two children were there, staring with total interest at something on the view-wall. They barely glanced his way, then returned to their show. For that matter, Adne's attention was on the wall as well.

Forrester cleared his throat. He was aware that, besides being hungry and broke, he was also far from clean. He cast about in his mind for some conversational gambit that would give Adne a chance to invite him to eat, or at least to wash up. "I, uh, had a funny experience," he said tentatively.

She grunted over her shoulder, "Hold it, will you, Charles?" She seemed very upset over something, he thought, watching her as she fingered her joymaker and stared at the changing patterns on the view-wall.

He said desperately, "I thought you were with me yesterday. It was all dreamlike and crazy, and I'm worried. It wasn't you, was it?"

"Charles, will you shut up a minute?" Her attention was on the wall. Forrester glanced at it. . . .

And saw a scene that he recognized. It was dried, seared grass on an open plain. There was a mark where something heavy had ground into the earth. A man's voice was saying, in tones of sonorous mourning, "The liftship appears to have evaded orbital patrols, and so it must be assumed to be on its way to Sirius itself. Radar-net surveillance detected it at launch, and appropriate challenges were issued. But there was no response. . . ."

Forrester swallowed a lump in his throat. "Did—did a Sirian—did one of them escape?"

The boy snapped, "Sweat, Charles! Where've you been? Happened hours ago!"

Forrester let his eyes close on his interior agony. The organ voice of the man narrating from the view-wall continued.

"Meanwhile, there is much concern at every level of authority. There can be no doubt that there must have been human complicity in the escape. Yet no joymaker monitors have registered any such event, nor can any motive be found. The Alliance for Solar-Sirian Amity has voluntarily offered all of its members for mind-probing; eight registered nihilist-obliterative organizations have been questioned about statements of policy suggesting that, in one formulation or another, all of humanity should destroy itself. No information suggesting complicity has emerged.

"But transcending any question of guilt are the considerations of consequence. One fact is beyond argument: a Sirian has managed to begin the long trip back to his home planet, undoubtedly carrying with him the information that Earth is the culprit in the destruction of a Sirian spacecraft. Experts in Sirian psychology declare that the result will be war. All over the world at this hour—"

"He's looping it, Mim," grumbled the boy. "We heard this part twice already. Can I shut it off?"

Adne nodded and sank back, her face tense and almost expressionless as the wall relapsed into a decorative jungle scene.

Forrester coughed.

"Oh," said Adne. "I almost forgot you were here. Did you want to ask me something?"

"Well," said Forrester, "I did, but it isn't important now."

"Not compared to *this*," she agreed. "What was it?"

"Nothing. It was just something about whether you were with me yesterday, but I don't have to ask you any more. I know who was with me now."

Chapter Thirteen

Once, many years before (it was actually several centuries, counting the deep-freeze time), little Chuck Forrester had caused a three-car auto smash that put two people in the hospital.

He had done it with his little slingshot, lying out in the tall grass next to his house in Evanston, taking shots at the cars on the highway. His aim was too good. He hit one. He got a state policeman in the eye. The cop had lost control, jumped into the opposite lane, sideswiped a convertible, and skidded into a station wagon.

Nobody died; the policeman didn't even lose his eye, although it was close for a while; and, as it happened, they didn't think to look around the neighborhood for kids with slingshots. The accident went down on the books as having been caused by a pebble thrown up by a passing car. But Chuck didn't know that, and for a solid year afterward he woke up in a sweat of fear every night, and all his days were horrors of anticipating being caught.

It was just so now.

It was perfectly clear to Forrester that he was the one who had helped the Sirian circumvent the electronic defenses that kept the alien bound to Earth. He could work it out step by step in his mind. The Sirian had shopped around until it found a human being ignorant enough, and pliable enough, to be unsuspicious. It had contrived to inject him with some hypnotic drug; it had made him believe it was Adne Bensen, then induced him to fly it to the site of an obsolete, but still workable, spaceship—unconscious, or in whatever state in a Sirian passed for unconsciousness, so that the electronic alarms would register nothing. It had commanded him to load it aboard the ship and launch it into space, and he had done as he was commanded, in the fuzzy-minded suggestibility it had doped him into.

Perfectly clear! He could see every step. And, if he could, certainly others could. All they had to do was take the trouble to think it through. And certainly all the world was thinking hard about the Sirians. The view-wall was full of news: special investigating teams ransacking the site of the take-off for clues, a hundred new probes launched to guard the perimeter of the solar system, Condition Yellow alert declared, and everyone cautioned to remain within easy distance of a raid shelter at all times.

Forrester kept waiting for the hand to fall on his shoulder and the voice to cry, "You, Forrester! You are the man!"

But it did not come. . . .

Meanwhile, the flap over the escape of Sirian Four had had one good effect, and that was that Adne was so interested in the excitement that she became much more friendly to Forrester again. She even fed him, let him clean himself up in her bath, and, as the children were off on some emergency drill with their age-peers, gave him their room to sleep in when it became obvious he was near collapse.

Voices woke him—Adne's and a man's.

". . . Mostly for the kids, of course. I'm not so worried for myself."

"Natch, honey. God! At a time like this! Just when the society's ready to swing."

"It wouldn't be so bad, but it makes you wonder about a lot of other things. I mean, really, how could they *let* that thing escape?"

A masculine growl: "Hah! How? Haven't I been telling you how? It's letting machines do men's work! We've put our destiny in the hands of solid-state components, so what do you expect? Don't you remember my White Paper last year? I said, 'Guarding men's liberties is a post of honor, and only the honored should hold it.' "

Forrester sat up, recognizing the voice: Taiko Hironibi. The Luddite.

"I thought you were talking about the coppers," said Adne's voice.

"Same thing! Machines should do machine work, men should do men's—Hey, what's that?"

Forrester realized he had made a noise. He stood up, feeling ancient and worn, but somewhat better than before he had slept, and was coming out toward them even before Adne answered Taiko. "It's only Charles. Come in here, Charles, why don't you?"

Taiko was standing before the view-wall, joymaker in his hand; his thumb was on one of the studs, and apparently he had just been giving himself a shot of one brand or another of euphoria. Even so, he glowered at Forrester.

"Oh, don't be like that," said Adne.

"Huh," said Taiko.

"If I can forgive him, you can forgive him. You have to make allowances for the kamikaze ages."

"Hah," said Taiko. But the euphoria prevailed—either the spray from the joymaker, or the spice of danger that was sweeping them all. Taiko clipped the joymaker to his belt, rubbed his chin, then grinned. "Well, why not? All us human beings have to stand together now, right? Put 'er there."

Gravely they shook hands. Forrester felt altogether ridiculous doing it; he was not sure just what he had done to offend Taiko in the first place, and was not particularly anxious to be forgiven by him now. Still, he reminded himself, Taiko had once offered him a job. A job was something he needed. Although, with the Sirian threat so urgent and imminent now, it was at least an open question whether the Ned Lud Society would need any more workers. . . .

It could not hurt to find out. Before he could change his mind, Forrester said rapidly, "I want you to know, Taiko, that I've been thinking a lot about what you said. You were right, of course."

Taiko's eyes opened. "About what?"

"About the danger of the machines, I mean. What I think is, men should do men's work and machines should do machine work."

"There's only one computer you can trust." Forrester tapped his skull with a forefinger. "The one up here."

"Sure, but—"

"It just burns me up," said Forrester angrily, "to think that they left the safeguarding of our planet to solid-state components! If only they'd listened to you!"

With part of his attention, Forrester could hear a smothered giggle from Adne, but he ignored it. "I want you to know," he cried, "that I've come to some conclusions over the last few days and I'm for the Ned Lud Society a hundred percent. Let me help, Taiko! Call on me for anything!"

Taiko gave the girl a look of absent-minded puzzlement, then returned to Forrester. "Well," he said, "I'm glad to hear that. I'll keep that in mind, if anything comes up."

It took all of Forrester's self-control to keep his expression friendly and eager; why was Taiko being so *slow?* But Adne rescued him. Suppressing her giggles, she said excitedly, "Say, Taiko! Why don't you let Charles in the Society? I mean, if he'd be willing."

Taiko frowned and hesitated, but Forrester didn't give him a chance. "I'm willing," he said nobly. "I meant what I said. Glad to help."

Taiko shrugged after a second and said, "Well, fine, then, Forrester. Of course, the money's not much."

"Doesn't matter a bit!" cried Forrester. "It's what I want to do! Uh, how much?"

"Well, basic scale is twenty-six thousand."

"A day?"

"Sure, Forrester."

"It doesn't matter," said Forrester largely. "I only want to serve any way I can." And, exultant, he allowed himself to be given a drink to celebrate, which he enlarged to be a meal. Adne was tolerantly amused.

And all the while the view-wall was displaying scenes of alarm and panic, unheeded.

Forrester had not forgotten that he had betrayed Earth

to the Sirians; he had only submerged that large and unpleasant thought in the smaller, but more immediate, pleasure of having escaped from the Forgotten Men. He drank a warm, minty froth and ate nutlike little spheres that tasted like crisp pork; he accepted a spray of a pinkly evanescent cloud from Adne's joymaker that made him feel about seventeen again—briefly. Tomorrow would be time enough to worry about what he had done to the world, he thought. For today it was enough to be eating well and to have a place in the scheme of mankind.

But all his worries came back to him when he heard his name spoken. It was Taiko's joymaker that spoke it, and it said, "Man Hironibi! Permit an interruption, please. Are you in the company of Man Forrester, Charles Dalgleish?"

"Yes, sure," said Taiko, a beat before Forrester opened his mouth to plead with him to deny it.

"Will you ask Man Forrester to speak his name, Man Hironibi?"

"Go ahead, Forrester. It's to identify you, see?"

Forrester put down the cup of frothed mint and took a deep breath. The pink cloud of joy might as well never have been. He felt every year of his age, even the centuries in the freezer. He said, because he could think of no excuse for not saying it, "Oh, all right. Charles Dalgleish Forrester. Is that what you want?"

Promptly the joymaker said, "Thank you, Man Forrester. Your acoustic pattern is confirmed. Will you accept a message of fiscal change?"

That was quick, thought Forrester, clutching at a feeling of relief; the thing only wanted to acknowledge his new job! "Sure."

"Man Forrester," said Taiko's joymaker, "your late employer, now permanently removed from this ecology, left instructions to disburse his entire residual estate as follows: to the League for Interspacial Amity, one million dollars; to the Shoggo Central Gilbert and Sullivan Guild, one million dollars; to the United Fraternity of Peace Clubs, five million dollars; the balance, amounting to ninety-one million, seven hundred sixty-three thousand, one hundred forty-two dollars, estimated as of this moment—mark!—to be transferred to the account of his last recorded employee as of date of removal, to wit, yourself. I am now so transferring this sum, Man Forrester. You may draw on it as you wish."

Forrester sank weakly back against the cushions of Adne's bright, billowy couch. He could not think of anything to say.

"God bless," cried Adne, "you're rich again, Charles! Why, you lucky creature!"

"Sure are," echoed Taiko, grasping his hand warmly. Forrester could only nod.

But he was not really sure that he was so lucky as he seemed. Ninety-one million dollars! It was a lot of money, even in this age of large numbers. It would keep him in comfort for a long time, surely; it would finance all sorts of pleasures and pursuits; it would remove him from the whim of Taiko's pleasure and insure him against a relapse to the Forgotten Men. But what would happen, Forrester thought painfully, when somebody asked, first, who that late employer happened to be—and why that employer, before returning to his native planet circling around the star Sirius, had so lavishly rewarded Charles Forrester?

The news from the view-wall kept coming in, in a mounting torrent of apprehension and excitement. Forrester, watching Adne and Taiko as they responded to the news reports, could hardly tell when they were reacting with fear and when with a sense of stimulation. Did they really expect Earth to be destroyed by the retaliation of the Sirians? And what were they going to do about it?

When he tried to ask them, Taiko laughed. "Get rid of the machines," he said largely. "Then we'll take 'em on—any snake or octopus from anywhere in the galaxy! But first we've got to clean house at home."

Adne only said, "Why don't you come with us—and relax?"

"Come along and see," she said.

Considering his own guilt in that area, Forrester did not want to attract attention by seeming *specially* concerned about the Sirians. But he insisted, "Shouldn't somebody be doing something?"

"Somebody will be," said Taiko. "Don't worry so, boy! There'll be a run on the freezers—people chickening out, you see. You know. 'Leave it to George.' Then, by and by, the Sirians'll come nosing around, and the appropriate people will deal with them. Or they won't."

"Meanwhile, Taiko and I have a date to crawl," said Adne, "and you might as well come along. It'll rest you."

"Crawl?"

"It's everybody's duty to keep fit—now more than ever," Taiko urged.

"You're being very good to me," Forrester said gratefully. But what he really wanted was to sit in that room and watch the view-wall. One by one the remote monitoring stations of Earth's defense screen were reporting in, and although the report from each one of them so far was the same—"No sign of the escaped Sirian"—Forrester wanted to stay with it, stay right in that room watching that view-wall, until there was some other report. To make sure that Earth was safe, of course. But also to find out, at the earliest possible moment, if the (hopefully) recaptured Sirian would give out any information about his accomplice. . . .

"Well, we're going crawling," said Adne. "And we really ought to take off right now."

Forrester said irritably, "Wait a minute. What did they just say about Groombridge 1830?"

"They said what they've been saying for a week, *dear* Charles. That thing they spotted is only a comet. Are we going to crawl or aren't we?"

Taiko said humorously, "Charles is still a little dazed about his new loot. But look, old buddy, some of us have got things to do."

Forrester took his eyes from the view-wall's star map and looked at Taiko, who winked and added, "Now that you're on the team, you ought to learn the ropes."

"Team?" said Forrester. "Ropes?"

"I have to do a communication for the society," Taiko explained. "You know. What you used to call a widecast. And as you're on the payroll now you ought to come along and see how it's done, because frankly—" he nudged

Charles— "it won't be too long before you're doing them yourself."

"But first we crawl," said Adne. "So shall we the sweat get *going?*"

They hustled Forrester along, muttering and abstracted as he was, until he realized that he was attracting attention to himself, and he didn't want to do *that.*

It might be, thought Forrester, that the right and proper thing for him to do was to go to someone in authority—if he ever found anyone in authority in this world, except maybe the joymaker—and say, frankly and openly, "Look, sir. I seem to have done something wrong and I wish to make a statement about it. Under what I guess was hypnosis I made it possible for that Sirian to escape, thus blowing the whole security of the human race forever." Confess the whole thing and take his medicine.

Yes, he thought, some time I probably had better do just that; but not right now.

Meanwhile, he tried to look as much like everybody else as he possibly could, and if this required him to be thrilled but casual about the danger of an invasion fleet of Sirians appearing in the sky at any moment to crush the Earth, then he would do his best to seem thrilled but casual.

"Well," he cried gaily, "we sure had a good run for our money! Best little old masters of the planet *I* ever saw! But may the best race win, right?"

Adne looked at him, then at Taiko, who shrugged and said, "I guess he's still a little shook."

Dampened, Forrester concentrated on observing what was going on around him. Taiko and the girl were bringing him to a part of Shoggo he had not previously visited, south along the shore to what looked like a leftover World's Fair. Their cab landed and let them out in a midway, bustling with groups and couples in holiday mood, surrounded by buildings with a queer playtime flavor. Nor was the flavor confined to the buildings. The place was a carnival of joy and of what Forrester at once recognized as concupiscence. The aphrodisiac spray that individual joymakers dispensed in microgram jolts was here a mist hanging in the air. The booths and displays were shocking to Forrester, at first, until he had taken a few deep breaths of the tonic, the invigorating air. Then he began at last to enjoy himself.

"That's better," cried Adne, patting him. "Down this way, past the Joy Machine!"

Forrester followed along, observing his surroundings with increasing relaxation and pleasure. In addition to its other attractions, the place was a horticultural triumph. Flowers and grasses grew out of the ground he walked on and along the margins at his sides; out of elevated beds that leaned out to the midway, heavy with emerald grapes and bright red luminous berries; out of geometrical plantings that hung on the sides of the buildings. Even on the walk itself, among the happy humans, there were what looked like shrubs bearing clusters of peach- and orange-colored fruits—but they moved, walked, stumped clumsily and slowly about on rootlike legs.

"In here," said Adne, clutching at his arm.

"Hurry up!" cried Taiko, shoving him.

They entered a building like a fort and went down a ramp surrounded by twinkling patterns of light. The concentration of joymaker spray was a dozen times stronger here than in the open air. Forrester, feeling lightheaded, began to look at Adne with more interest than he would have believed himself able to show in anything but Sirians. Adne leaned close to nibble his ear; Taiko laughed in pleasure. They were not alone, for there was a steady stream of people going down the ramp with them, fore and aft, all with flushed faces and excited.

Forrester abandoned himself to the holiday. "After all," he shouted to Adne, "what does it matter if we're going to be wiped out?"

"Dear Charles," she answered, "shut up and take your clothes off."

Surprised, but not very, Forrester saw that the whole procession was beginning to shed its outer garments. Shaggy vests and film-and-net briefs, they were tossed on the floor, where busy glittering little cleaning creatures tugged them away into disposal units. "Why not?" he laughed, and kicked his slipper at one of the cleaners, which reared back on its wheels like a kitten and caught it in midair. The crowd rolled down the ramp, shedding clothes at every step, until they were in a sort of high-vaulted lounge and the noise of laughter and talk was loud as a lynching.

And then a door behind them closed. The cloying joy-maker scent whisked away. Streams of a harsher, colder essence poured in upon them, and at once they were all standing there, nearly nude and cold sober.

Charles Forrester had had something less than four de-cades of actual life—that is to say, of elapsed time measured by lungs that breathed and a heart that beat. The first part of that life, measured in decades, had taken place in the twentieth century. The second part, measured in days, had taken place after more than half a millennium in the freez-ing tanks.

Although those centuries had sped by tracelessly for Forrester, they represented real time to the world of men: each century a hundred years, every year 365 days of twenty-four hours each.

Of all that had happened during those centuries, Forres-ter had managed to learn only the smallest smattering. He had not learned, even yet, what powers this century could pack into a wisp of gas. Playing with the studs of his joy-maker or submitting to the whims of his friends, Forrester had tasted a variety of intoxicants and euphorics, wake-up jolts and sleepy jolts. But he had never before tasted the jolt that drugged no senses but sharpened them all. Now he stood in this room, Taiko on one side of him and Adne in the circle of his arm, surrounded by half a hundred other men and women; and he was fully awake and *sensing* for the first time in his life.

He turned to look at Adne. Her face was scrubbed bare, her eyes were looking at him unwinkingly. "You're nasty in-side," she said.

What she said was the exact equivalent of a slap in the face; and Forrester accepted it as such. A cleansing anger filled his mind. He growled, "You're a trollop. I think your children are illegitimate, too." He had not intended to say anything of the sort.

Taiko said, "Shut up and crawl."

Over his shoulder and without passion, Forrester said, "You're a two-bit phony without an ounce of principle or a thought in your head. Butt out, will you?"

To his surprise, Adne was nodding in agreement; but she said, "Pure kamikaze, just like the trash you come from. Vulgar and a fool." He hesitated, and she said impatiently, "Come on, kamikaze. Let it out. You're jealous too, right?"

Theirs was not the only argument going on; there was a bitter rumble of insult and vituperation all around them. Forrester was only marginally aware of it; his whole attention was concentrated on Adne, on the girl he had thought he might be in love with, and his best efforts were devoted to trying to hurt her. He snapped, "I bet you're not even pregnant!"

She looked startled. "What?"

"All that talk about picking a name! You probably just wanted to trick me into marrying you."

She stared at him blankly, then with revulsion. "Sweat! I meant our *reciprocal* name. Charles, you talk like an idiot."

Taiko shrilled, "You're both idiots! *Crawl.*"

Forrester spared him a glance. Curiously, Taiko was down on his knees and for the first time Forrester realized that the floor was damp—not damp, muddy. A thin gruel of softly oozing mud was pouring in from apertures in the wall. Others were getting down into the mud, too; and, for possibly the thousandth time since being taken from the freezer, Forrester found himself torn between two choices of puzzles to try to solve. What was going on here, exactly? And what the devil did Adne mean by "our" name?

But she tugged at him impatiently, slipping down to wallow in the porridgy substance. "Come on," she cried. "You're not doing it right, but come on, you sweaty kamikaze."

All the while the air was being recharged with the stimulant, if it was a stimulant, that had opened the gates of his senses for Forrester. It was like LSD, he thought, or a super-Benzedrine: he was seeing a whole new spectrum; hearing bat shrieks and subsonic roars; smelling, tasting, feeling things that had been out of his reach before. He perceived clearly that this was some sort of organized ritual he was in, understood that its purpose was to allow the release of tensions by saying whatever the inner mind had wanted to say and the outer censor in the brain had forbidden. Allow it? He could not stop it! He listened to the things he was saying to Adne and realized that, at a later time, in an undrugged moment, he would be appalled. But he said them.

And she nodded gravely and replied in kind. "Jealous!" she shrieked. "Typical manipulative ownership! Filthy inside, trashy!"

"Why shouldn't I be jealous? I *loved* you."

"Harem love!" sneered Taiko from beside him. The man was lying full length in the mud now—it had reached a depth of several inches and seemed to have stopped there. "She's a brainless blot of passions, but she's human, and how *dare* you try to own her?"

"Fake!" howled Forrester. "Go pretend you're a man! Bust up some machines!" He was furious, but in one part of his mind he was alert enough and analytical enough to be surprised that he wasn't impelled to hit Taiko. Or Adne, for that matter. What he was impelled to do was to say wounding things, as true and hurtful as he could make them. He looked around him and saw that he was the only one still on his feet. The others were all full-length in the mud, writhing and creeping. Forrester dropped to his knees. "What's this damn foolishness all about?" he demanded.

"Shut up and crawl," grunted Taiko. "Get some of the animal out of you." And Adne chimed in, "You're spoiling it for all of us if you don't crawl! You have to crawl before you can walk."

Forrester leaned down to her. "I don't *want* to crawl!"

"Have to. Helps you get out the rot. The secrets that fester . . . Of course, you kamikazes like to decay."

"But I don't have—"

And Forrester paused, not because he had voluntarily chosen to stop talking just then, but because what he had been about to say was not true, and he simply could not say it. He had been about to say that he had no secrets.

He had, in fact, more secrets than he could count; and

one very large one that appalled him, because his mouth wanted to blurt it out even while his brain screamed *No!*

If he stayed in this room one more moment, Forrester knew, he would shout at the top of his voice the fact that he had been the one to help the Sirian escape and thus had made it a good gambling bet that the whole world of men would be destroyed. Dripping mud, panting, mumbling to himself, Forrester climbed to his feet and forced himself to run—a staggering, broken-field run that dodged flailing limbs and leaped over writhing bodies, that carried him through the angry rumble of the crawlers and out into a dressing chamber, where he was sluiced down with fragrant spray, dried with warm blasts of air, and bathed in hot light. Fresh garments appeared before him, but he took no pleasure in them. He had forgotten for a moment, but now he remembered again.

He was the man who had destroyed Earth. At any moment he would be found out. . . . And what his punishment might be, he dared not think.

"Man Forrester," cried the voice of a joymaker, "during the period of interrupted service, a number of messages accumulated for you, of which the following three priority calls are urgent."

"Wait up," said Forrester, startled. But there it was. Rummaging through the nearly folded heap of T-shirt and Turkish pants, he came upon the macelike shape of a joymaker. "Ho," he said. "I've got you again, eh?"

"Yes, Man Forrester," the joymaker agreed. "Will you receive your messages?"

"Um," said Forrester. Then, cautiously, "Well, I will if any of them are of great urgency at this very moment. I mean, I don't want somebody coming in here and blowing my brains out while I'm talking to you."

"No such probability is evident," said the joymaker primly. "Nevertheless, Man Forrester, there are a number of highly important messages."

Forrester sat down on a warmed bench and sighed. He said meditatively, "The thing is this, joymaker. I never seem to get to the end of a question, because two new questions pop up while I'm still trying to find the answer to the first one. So what I would like to do right now, I would like you to get me a cup of black coffee and a pack of cigarettes, right here in this nice, warm, safe room, and then I would like to drink the coffee and smoke a cigarette and ask you some questions. Now, can I do that without dying for it?"

"Yes, Man Forrester. However, it will take several minutes for the coffee and cigarettes to be delivered, as they are not stock items in this facility and must be secured from remote inventories."

"I understand all that. Just get them. Now." Forrester stood up and drew the baggy pants over his legs, thinking. At last he nodded to himself.

"First question," he said. "I just came out of a place where Adne Bensen and a bunch of other people were wallowing in mud. What was that all about?—I mean," he added hastily, "in a few words, what is it called, and why do people do it?"

"The function is called a 'crawl session,' Man Forrester, or simply 'crawling.' Its purpose is the release of tensions and inhibitions for therapeutic purposes. Two major therapies are employed. First, there is a chemical additive in the air that suppresses inhibitors of all varieties, thus making it possible to articulate, and thus to relieve, many kinds of tensions. Second, the mere act of learning to crawl all over again is thought to provide benefits. I have on immediate access, Man Forrester, some thirty-eight papers on various aspects of the crawl session. Would you care to have me list them?"

"Not in the least," said Forrester. "That's fine; I understand that perfectly. Now, second question."

There was a *thunk*; a receptacle opened beside him; Forrester reached in and took out a steaming and very large cup of coffee covered with a plastic lid. He worried the lid off, sought and found the cigarettes and lighter that accompanied the coffee, lit up, took a sip of the coffee, and said, "Adne Bensen said something to me about choosing a name. I interpreted this to mean that she was, uh, well, pregnant. I mean, I thought she meant a name for a baby; but actually it was something else. Reciprocal names? What are reciprocal names?"

"Reciprocal names, Man Forrester," lectured the joy-maker, "are chosen, usually by two individuals, less typically by larger groups, as private designations. A comparable institution from your original time, Man Forrester, might be the 'pet' name or nickname by which a person addressed his or her spouse, child, or close friend; however, the reciprocal name is used by each of the persons in addressing the other."

"Give me a for instance," Forrester interrupted.

"For instance," said the joymaker obediently, "in the universe of Adne Bensen and her two children, the reciprocal names are 'Tunt'—a form of address from one child to the other—or 'Mim,' when Miss Bensen addresses or is addressed by a child. As mentioned, this situation is not typical, since more than two persons are involved. A better example from the same demesne would be the relationship of Adne Bensen and Dr. Hara, where the reciprocal designation between them is 'Tip.' Are those adequate for instances, Man Forrester?"

"Yeah, but what's this about Hara? You mean he and Adne have a pet name?"

"Yes, Man Forrester."

"Yeah, but— Well, skip it." Forrester glumly put down his coffee; it didn't taste as good as he had thought it would. "Sounds confusing," he muttered.

"Confusing, Man Forrester?"

"Yeah. I mean, if you and I have the same name, how do we know which one— Oh, wait a minute. I see. If you and I have a name, then if *you* use it, obviously you mean me. And if I use it, I have to mean you."

"That is correct, Man Forrester. In practice it does not appear that much confusion arises."

"All right, the hell with that, too. Let's see." Forrester frowned at his cigarette; it didn't taste particularly good, either. He was unable to decide whether the reason was that he had lost the taste for coffee and cigarettes, or whether these were simply miserable examples of their kind, or whether what tasted bad was his mood. He dropped the cigarette into the rest of the coffee and said irritably, "Question three. Now that I have you again, and plenty of money, is there some way I can keep from foolishly losing it all again? Can we like work out a budget?"

"Certainly, Man Forrester. One moment. Yes. Thank you for waiting. I have obtained a preliminary investment schedule and prospectus of probable returns. By investing a major fraction of your holdings in the Sea of Soup, with diversification in power, computation, and euphoric utilities, you should have a firm annual income in excess of eleven million, four hundred thousand dollars. This can be prorated by week or by day, if you wish, and automatic limits placed on the amounts you can spend or hypothecate. In this way it will be possible—*Man Forrester!*"

Forrester was startled. "What the devil's the matter with you?"

"Your instructions, Man Forrester! Urgent priority override: statement made earlier that you are in no immediate danger of death is no longer true. Man Heinzlichen Jura de Syrtis Major, having filed appropriate bonds and guaranties—"

"Oh, no!" cried Forrester. "Not that crazy Martian again!"

"Yes, Man Forrester! Coming through the crawl chamber right now, armed, armored, and looking for you!"

Chapter Fourteen

Forrester snapped tight the baggy trousers, tucked in the pullover, slipped his feet into sandals, and hooked the joymaker to his belt. "Out!" he barked. "Which way?"

"This way, Man Forrester." An opening in the wall widened like a pair of parentheses, and Forrester bolted through it. A lounge, a ramp, an open double door, and he was out into the midway again, with the bright sun pounding down on him, the gay crowds staring at him casually.

He glanced around: yes, there was the DR vehicle, shining white overhead, its attendant with chin on hand gazing into space. "Where's Heinzie?" he cried.

"Following, Man Forrester. Do you wish to fight him here?"

"Hell, no!"

"Where would you prefer, Man Forrester?"

"You idiot, I don't want to fight him at all. I want to get away from him."

He was attracting attention from the crowd, he saw. Their expressions were no longer vacant, but puzzled, and beginning to be hostile.

The joymaker said hesitantly, "Man Forrester, I must ask you to be specific. Do you wish to avoid combat with Man Heinzlichen *permanently?*"

"That's the idea," Forrester said bitterly. "But I see it's a little late for that now." Because the Martian was churning out of the double doors of the crawling building and heading straight for him. "Oh, well," said Forrester. "Easy come, easy go."

The Martian planted himself in front of Forrester, puffing. He said, "Hello, dere. Sorry I kept you waiting so long."

"You didn't have to hurry on my account," said Forrester cautiously. He was scanning the Martian carefully for weapons, but there didn't seem to be anything. He was wearing what looked like a wig, close blond curls that hugged his scalp, surrounded his ears and jawline, and went down in back to the nape of his neck, but otherwise he was unchanged in appearance from the last time Forrester had seen him. And he did not even carry a stick. His joymaker was clipped to his belt; his hands were empty and hung loosely at his sides.

"Vell," said the Martian, "you were with de Forgotten Men, you know, and den I had other things to do. Anyway, here we are, so let's get it over with. O.K.?"

Forrester said honestly, "I don't know what I'm supposed to do."

"Fight, you fool!" cried the Martian. "What de hell do you think you're supposed to do?"

"But I'm not even mad," Forrester objected.

"Dog sweat!" roared the Martian. "I am! Come on, fight, will you?" But his hands still hung at his sides.

Forrester shifted position cautiously, sparing the time for a glance around. The crowd was definitely interested now, forming a neat ring around them; Forrester thought he could see bets being made on the outcome. The DR man overhead was watching them carefully. At least, Forrester thought, if I let him kill me, they'll just freeze me up again. And then they'll put me back together later on. And maybe the freezer isn't such a bad place to be for a while, until this business with the Sirians get straightened out. . . .

"Are you going to fight or not?" the Martian demanded.

Forrester said, "Uh, one question."

"Vell?"

"The way you talk. I had an argument about that the other day—"

"What's de matter with de way I talk?"

"It's a sort of German accent, I thought, but this other Martian was Irish, and he talked the same way—"

"Irish? German?" Heinzlichen looked baffled. "Look,

Forrester, on Mars we got six-hundred-millibar pressure, you understand? You lose some of de high frequencies, dat's all. I don't know what 'German' or 'Irish' is."

"Say, that's interesting!" Forrester cried. "You mean it's not an accent, really?"

"I mean you wasted too much of my time already!" the Martian cried and leaped for his throat. And right there, in the bright midway with the ambulatory plants jolting past him and the crowds cheering and shouting, Forrester found himself fighting for his life. The Martian was not only bigger than he was, the damned skunk was stronger! Fleetingly Forrester blazed with anger: how dare the Martian be stronger? What about the supposition that light-gravity inhabitants would lose their muscle tone? Why was he not able to crush this flimsy, light-G creature with a single blow?

But he could not; the Martian was on top of him, systematically thudding his head against the paving of the midway. It was Forrester's good fortune that the flooring was a resilient, rubber-like substance, not concrete; all the same, he was developing a headache, and his senses were spinning. And now the Martian added insult to injury. "Get up and fight!" he bawled. "Dis is no fun!"

That marked the limit of Forrester's civilized control. He screamed in rage and surged up; the Martian went flying. Forrester was up and after him, flinging himself on top of him, a knee in the Martian's throat; he saw the Martian's joymaker loose by his side and caught it up—grabbed it like a club, smashed the macelike large end against the Martian's skull. It rang like bronze. Even in his rage Forrester felt a moment's astonishment; but clearly the close-cropped blond wig was not merely hair, it was a protective armor skullpiece. "Louse!" roared Forrester, enraged all over again; the Martian had prepared himself for this battle by wearing a helmet! He shortened his stroke and clubbed the Martian across the face. Blood spurted; teeth broke. Again and again, and the Martian tried to cry out but could not; again, again—

Behind him the voice of the attendant from the DR cart

said, "All right, all right, that's enough. I'll take care of him now."

Forrester rocked back on his haunches, panting hoarsely, staring at the terrible ruin he had made of the Martian's face. He managed to gasp, "Is—is he dead?"

"They don't come any deader," said the DR man. "Would you move a little bit?—Thanks. All right, he's mine now. Wait here for the copper, please; he'll take care of filling out a report."

What happened next for Forrester was hazy. He had a confused memory of returning to the lavatory facilities of the crawl room and getting cleaned up again, a shower, fresh clothes, a steam of reviving gases that woke him up and cleared his head. But when he was out of the room the fog returned; it was not the drain resulting from his efforts that muddled his thinking, or the aching pain in his head where Heinzie had bashed it against the pavement. It was pure psychic shock.

He had destroyed a human life.

Not really, he told himself at once. Not now. A short rest in the freezer and then he's good as new!

But it didn't register with him; he was still in shock—and puzzled. He could not decide: had he imagined it, or had the Martian not been fighting back?

Adne was waiting for him, with Taiko; they had seen the fight and had stayed to help him get straightened out afterward. Help him or help the Martian, Forrester thought bitterly. It probably didn't matter to them which. Nevertheless, he was grateful for their help. Adne took him to her own home, left him there a minute, returned with the news that his apartment was ready for him again, and escorted him there. And left him with Taiko, who wanted to talk. "Nice fight, Charles. Shook you up, of course—hell, I remember my own first killing. Nothing to be ashamed of. But, listen, if you're going to come to work for the society you've got to pull yourself together."

Forrester sat up and looked at Taiko. "What the devil makes you think I want to work for the Luddites?"

"Come on, Charles. Look, take a shot of bracer, will you? That green stud, there on the handle—"

"Will you get out of here and leave me alone?"

"Oh, for sweat's sake," cried Taiko impatiently. "Look, you said you wanted to help out with the society's program, right? Well, there's no time to waste! This is the chance we've been waiting for, man! Everybody's got the Sirians on their minds; they'll be diving into the freezers so fast the teams won't be able to handle them, and that's when those of us who can face the world realistically will have a chance to take action. We can get rid of the machine menace once and for all if we—" Taiko hesitated and gave Forrester a thoughtful look. Then he said, "Well, never mind that part of it just yet. Are you with us or against us?"

Forrester contemplated the problem of trying to explain to Taiko that his interest in the Ned Lud Society had been only an interest in making enough money to live on, and that, when the Sirian had left him ninety-three million dollars, that interest had evaporated. It did not seem worth the effort, so he said, "I guess I'm against you."

"Charles," said Taiko, "you make me sick! You of all people! You, who have suffered so much from this age. Don't you want to try to cure the evils of machine domination? Don't you want—"

"I'll tell you what I want," said Forrester, rousing himself. "I want you to go away—fast!"

"You're not yourself," said Taiko. "Look, when you get straightened out, give me a call. I'll be hard to reach, because— Well, never mind why. But I'll leave a special channel for you. Because I know you, Charles, and I know that you'll have to decide you want to end these cowardly times and give man back his— All right! I'm going!"

When the door had closed behind him, Forrester stared into space for more than an hour. Then he rolled over and went to sleep. His only regret was that sooner or later he would wake up.

Chapter Fifteen

What Forrester could not understand was why it was taking them so long to arrest him.

He began to see just why a criminal might give himself up. The waiting was hard to endure. Ten times an hour he reached for the joymaker to say, "I am the one who helped the Sirian escape. Report me to the police," and ten times each hour he stopped himself. Not now, he said. Tomorrow, no doubt, or maybe even a few minutes from now; but not just now.

From time to time the joymaker informed him of messages—forty-five of them the first day alone. Forrester refused to accept them all. He didn't want to see anyone until—until— Well, he didn't want to see anyone at the moment. (He could not make up his mind at just what moment the world would so clarify itself to him that he would be willing to start living in it again; but he always knew that that time was certainly not yet.) He explored the resources of his apartment, the joymaker, and his own mind. He ate fantastic meals and drank odd foaming beverages that tasted like stale beer or celery-flavored malted milks. He listened to music and watched canned plays. He wished desperately for a deck of cards, but the joymaker did not seem to understand his description of them, and so solitaire was denied him; but he found almost the same anesthesia in reading and reading over again what scraps of written matter he had on hand. His late wife's letter he practically memorized; his briefing manual for this century he studied until his fingers were weary from turning the pages.

On the second day there were nearly seventy messages. Forrester refused them all.

At his direction the joymaker displayed for him selected news pictures on the view-wall. The only subject Forrester would allow himself an interest in was the progress of the trouble with the Sirians. There was strangely little news after the first day—negative reports from drone patrols in every quadrant of the heavens, a diminishing flow of projections and estimates as to when an attack might be expected. The consensus seemed to be: not for several weeks at least. Forrester could not understand that at all. He remembered quite distinctly that Sirius was something like fifty light-years away, and the joymaker confirmed that no way had been found to exceed the speed of light. Finally he gathered that the Sirians were thought to have some sort of faster-than-light message capability, as did Earth for that matter; so that, even if the fleeing Sirian did not make it back to his own planet, he might send a message. And it was a possibility, at least, that some wandering Sirian war patrol might be near Sol.

But none made itself evident; and on the third day there were only a dozen messages for Forrester; and he refused them all.

What he did with most of his time was sleep.

He had ninety-three million dollars and perfect health. He could think of no better way to spend either of them.

"Joymaker! Tell me what I did wrong with Adne."

"Wrong in what sense, Man Forrester? I have no record of antisocial acts."

"Don't split hairs with me. I mean, why didn't she like me after the first few days?"

The joymaker began to answer with statements about hormone balances, imprinting, and the ineluctable components of emotions, but Forrester was having none of it. "Get me a beer," he ordered, "and give me specific answers. You hear everything that happens, right?"

"Right, Man Forrester. Except when instructed otherwise."

"All right. I offended her. How?"

"I cannot evaluate the magnitude of the offenses, Man Forrester, but I can list certain acts that would appear to be of greater significance than others. Item, you refused her offer of a reciprocal name."

"That was bad?"

"It is offensive by social convention, Man Forrester, yes." The glass of beer appeared by Forrester's couch; he tasted it and made a face.

"No, not that," he said. "What was that other thing, the beer with some kind of raspberry sauce?"

"*Berlinerweisse*, Man Forrester?"

"Yeah, get me one of those. Go on with the list."

"Item, your actions when Man Heinzlichen Jura de Syrtis Major filed intent to kill you were considered contemptible in certain lights."

"Didn't she understand that I just wasn't used to the way things go now?"

"Yes, Man Forrester, she did. Nevertheless, she considered your behavior contemptible. Item, you allowed yourself to become improverished. Item, you criticized her for a relationship with other males."

The large goblet of pale beer appeared along with a little flask of dark red syrup; Forrester decanted the syrup into the beer and sipped it. It too tasted terrible, but he had run out of things to ask for and he drank it. "It was only that I loved her," he said irritably.

"There are ineluctable aspects to the syndrome 'love,' which we cannot distinguish, Man Forrester."

"Hell, I don't expect you to. You're a machine. But I thought Adne was a woman."

"I can only surmise from the evidence of her responses that she did not comprehend or accept your behavior either, Man Forrester."

"I have to admit you've got a point there," sighed Forrester, putting down the goblet and getting up to roam around. "Well, never mind." He rubbed his chin thoughtfully, then waved a hand; a mirror appeared, and he studied his face in it. He looked like a bum. Hair unkempt, beard beginning to grow again. "Oh, hell," he said.

The joymaker made no answer.

What Forrester really wanted to know—whether anyone had come to suspect him of being the one who had let the Sirian escape—he dared not ask. The questions he did ask, on the other hand, turned out to have answers as confusing as the questions were. Even simple questions. He had asked after his friend among the Forgotten Men, Jerry Whitlow, for example. He had not been surprised to find out that Whitlow was dead—he had seen that happen; or to learn that his revival was problematical; but he still did not know what the joymaker meant by saying that Whitlow was "returned to reserve." It *seemed* to mean that Whitlow's body had been used as raw material, perhaps in one of the organic lakes like the "Sea of Soup," from which the world's food supplies came; but Forrester was too repelled by that notion to follow it any further, and even so he could not understand why Whitlow's revival would then be "problematical."

"How many messages today, joymaker?" he asked idly.

"There are no messages for you today, Man Forrester."

Forrester turned to look at the thing. That was a welcome surprise—any change was welcome—but it was worrisome, too. Had everyone forgotten him?

"No messages?"

"None that you have not already refused, Man Forrester."

"Doesn't anyone want to talk to me?"

"As far as indicated by the message log, Man Forrester, only Man Hironibi wishes to talk to you. He left special instructions in regard to forwarding of communications. But that was six days ago."

Forrester was startled. "How the devil long have I been here?"

"Nineteen days, Man Forrester."

He took a deep breath.

Nineteen days! How little his so-called friends cared for him! he told himself with self-pity. If they *really* liked him they would have broken the door down, if necessary.

But it was not all bad. Nineteen days? But surely, if he were going to be arrested for helping the Sirian escape, it

would not have taken this long. Was it safe to assume the
heat was off? Did he dare go back into the world of men?

He made up his mind rapidly and, before he could
change it, acted at once. "Joymaker! Get me cleaned up.
Shave, bath, new clothes. I'm going outside!"

His resolve lasted him through the cleaning-up process
and into the condominium hall, but then it began to dissi-
pate.

No one was in the hall; there were no sounds. But to
Forrester it seemed like a jungle trail with unknown dangers on every side. He ordered an elevator cab to take him
to slideway level, and when the door opened he entered it
cautiously, as though an enemy might be lurking inside.

But it too was empty. And so—he found a moment later—was the wide hoverway. There was simply nothing
there.

Forrester stared around, unable to believe what he saw.
No pedestrians—well, that was understandable. There were
seldom very many, and he had no idea what time of day it
was. No hovercraft? That was harder to accept. Even if for
a moment none were in sight, he should be able to hear the
hissing roar of their passage somewhere in the city. But to
see no aircraft, no sign of life at all—that was flatly unbelievable.

Where was everybody?

He said, with a quaver in his voice, "Get me a cab."

"One will arrive in two minutes, Man Forrester." And it
did—a standard automated aircab; and Forrester still had
not seen a human being. He climbed in quickly, closed the
door, and ordered it to take him up—not up to any place in
particular, just up, so that he could see farther in all directions.

But no matter how far he looked, no one was there.

Words forced themselves out. "Joymaker! What's happened?"

"In what respect, Man Forrester?" the machine benignly
asked.

"Where did everybody go? Adne? The kids?"

"Adne Bensen and her children, Man Forrester, at present are being processed for storage in Sublake Emergency Facility Nine. However, it is not as yet known whether space will be available for them there on a permanent basis, and so the location must be considered tentative pending the completion of additional facilities—"

"You mean they're *dead?*"

"Clinically dead, Man Forrester. Yes."

"How about—" Forrester cast about in his mind—"let's see, that Martian. Not Heinzie, the one with the Irish name, Kevin O'Rourke; is he dead, too?"

"Yes, Man Forrester."

"And the Italian ballerina I met at the restaurant where the Forgotten Men hung out?"

"Also dead, Man Forrester."

"What the hell *happened?*" he shouted.

The joymaker replied carefully, "Speaking objectively, Man Forrester, there has been an unforecast increase in the number of commitments to freezing facilities. More than ninety-eight point one percent of the human race is now in cryogenic storage. In subjective terms, the causes are not well established but appear to relate to the probability of invasion by extra-Solarian living creatures, probably Sirian."

"You mean everybody committed suicide?"

"No, Man Forrester. Many preferred to be killed by others; for example, Man Heinzlichen Jura de Syrtis Major. He, you will recall, elected to be killed by you."

Forrester sank back against the seat. "Holy sweet heaven," he muttered to himself. Dead! Nearly the whole human race, dead! It was more than he could take in at once. He sat staring into space until the joymaker said apologetically, "Man Forrester, do you wish to select a destination?"

"No—wait a minute, yes! Maybe I do. You said ninety-eight percent of the human race is dead."

"Ninety-eight point one, yes, Man Forrester."

"But that means there are some who are still alive, right? Are there any I know?"

"Yes, Man Forrester. Certain classes are still in vital state in large proportion because of special requests made for their services—e.g., medical specialists working in the freezer stations. Also, there are others. One you know is Man Hironibi. He is not only in vital state but has, as you know, given special instructions in regard to receiving messages from you."

"Fine!" cried Forrester. "Just take me to Taiko, right away! I want to see someone who's alive!"

Because—went the unspoken corollary—he didn't want to see the ruins left by the dead. Not as long as he was so completely convinced that it was he himself who had killed them.

Chapter Sixteen

But, as it turned out, the cab did not take him to see Taiko after all.

It did what it could. The joymaker programmed it properly enough, and Forrester found himself high in a building of bright ruby crystal, in front of a door inscribed THE NED LUD SOCIETY. Inside was what he supposed was the latter-day equivalent of an office—although it was warm and damp and a fountain played among ferns. But no one was inside.

"What the devil's the matter with you, joymaker?" he demanded. "Where's Taiko?"

"Man Forrester," said the joymaker, "there is an anomaly here. My records indicate Man Hironibi's presence at this place, but clearly they are wrong. My records have never been wrong before."

"Well, let me talk to him. You said he'd left special instructions about that."

"Yes, Man Forrester." Pause. Then Taiko's voice came on. "That you, Charles? Glad to hear from you. I'm busy now, but I'll be in touch when I get a chance—only don't refuse my message this time, will you?"

That was all. "Wait a minute," cried Forrester. "Taiko!"

The joymaker interrupted him. "Man Forrester, that was a recording."

Forrester growled profanely. He walked around the office, examining it, but without finding anything that would help him locate Taiko. "Well, hell," he said. "Let's see. Is anybody else I know still alive?"

"Man Forrester, Edwardino Wry is also ambient. Do you consider that he is known to you?"

"I doubt it, because I never heard of the son—Wait a minute. Was he one of the ones that beat me up?"

"Yes, Man Forrester."

"Well, I don't want to see *him*. Forget it, joymaker," said Forrester. "I guess I'll just wait for Taiko."

Three or four times he thought he saw people, but he was only able to get close to one of them, and it said civilly, "We are not human, Man Forrester. We are merely a special-purpose service unit diverted to aid at the cryogenic facilities." It had looked like a pretty young blonde in a bikini, perhaps a barmaid somewhere, Forrester thought; but was too dispirited to inquire further. Apart from those, there was no one in sight in Shoggo.

He walked aimlessly, shaking his head.

His long days of self-imposed exile had let most of the guilt evaporate from him. He no longer felt either fearful of discovery or humiliated; the Sirian had used him as a tool, true, but if it had not been him, it would have been someone else. Anyway, he was more concerned about this world. The year 2527 was a great disappointment to him. He could think of no other age when the response of the populace to a threat of death would have been such universal suicide. It was simply crazy. . . .

Of course, he reminded himself, death was not the same to these people as it had been to his contemporaries. Death was no longer necessarily permanent. It was like fleeing to a neutral country to sit out a war, and heaven knew there were lots of twentieth-century examples of that.

Nevertheless, in Charles Forrester's opinion the world of 2527 A.D. was chicken.

Forrester filled his lungs and shouted, "You are all cowards! The world's better off without you!" His voice echoed emptily among the tall, hard building faces.

"Man Forrester," said the joymaker, "were you addressing me?"

"I was not. Shut up," said Forrester. "No, cancel that. Get me a cab." And, when it came, he took it back to the broad hovercraft way where he and Jerry Whitlow had hidden out as two of the Forgotten Men. But there were no more Forgotten Men in evidence, not wherever he looked, no matter how loudly he called out. "Take me to Adne Bensen's home," he commanded, and the cab flew him into the entrance port at the midtower level of the building they had shared, but there was no one visible there, either. Not in the streets, not in the halls, not even in the apartment, after Forrester had commanded the joymaker to let him in.

He ordered himself a meal and sat on the edge of a sort of couch in the children's room, feeling put-upon and sad. When he had finished eating he said, "Joymaker, try getting Taiko for me again."

"Yes, Man Forrester. . . . There is no new message, Man Forrester."

"Don't give me that! Say it's priority, like you're always doing to me."

"You do not have the authority to classify a message priority, Man Forrester."

"I do if I say I'm planning to kill him," Forrester said cunningly. "You have to notify him of my intentions, right?"

"I do indeed, Man Forrester, but not until you have filed appropriate bonds and guaranties. Until you have done so, your notice cannot be effective. Do you wish to file, Man Forrester?"

"Well," said Forrester, thinking about filling out forms and signing documents, "I guess not, no. Isn't there *any* way I can get through to him?"

The joymaker said, "I have a taped message from him, which I can display on the view-wall if you wish, Man Forrester. It is not, however, directly addressed to you."

"Display the son of a gun then," ordered Forrester. "And make it snappy!"

"Yes, Man Forrester."

The view-wall lighted up, obediently; but what appeared on it was not Taiko Hironibi. It was a tall, largely built woman with a commanding presence, who said, "Girl Goldilocks and Terror of Bears!"

The joymaker said apologetically, "There is a malfunction, Man Forrester. I am investigating."

Forrester was startled. "What the devil!" he cried. The voice went on. "Bears! Think of bears. Great biting creatures, shaggy-haired, smell of animal sweat and rot. A bear can kill a man—*crunch*, crush his head; *smash*, crash his spine; *zip*, rip his heart." At every word the woman's image acted out crunching, smashing, ripping.

"Hey," said Forrester, "I didn't order any bedtime stories!"

The joymaker said, in the same tone of apology, "Man Forrester, the technical difficulty is being analyzed. I suggest you permit this tape to finish."

And meanwhile the woman was orating. "A girl child, little as you. Littler. Little as you used to be when you were little. Call the girl . . . give her a name. . . . Let her be called, oh, Goldilocks. Golden hair; locks of gold. Sweet, small, defenseless girl."

Forrester snarled, "Will you turn this damn thing *off?*"

"Man Forrester," admitted the joymaker, "I can't. Please be patient."

"Imagine this girl doing a naughty thing!" cried the woman. "Imagine her going where she should not go, where her mother/father told her not to go. Imagine her rejecting their wise counsel!"

Forrester sank back on the couch and said glumly, "If you can't turn it off, at least get me a drink while I'm waiting. Scotch and water."

"Yes, Man Forrester."

The view-wall was showing real bears now, large and ferocious grizzlies, while the woman chanted, "And Goldilocks goes to the bear lair—roaring, biting, slashing bears! But they are not home.

"They are not home, and she eats their food. She sits where they sit, lies where they lie, and sleeps.

"She sleeps, and the bears come home!"

Forrester's drink appeared; he tasted it and glowered, for it was not Scotch. As best as he could tell from the flavor, it was a sort of salty applejack.

"The bears come home! The bears come home, and their muzzles foam; the bears come back ready to attack, the bears come in with their jaws agrin!

"Red eyes glowing! (She sleeps, unknowing.)

"Claws that rend (is this the end?), paws that break (she starts to wake), teeth that bite—

"And Goldilocks opens her eyes, screams loudly, leaps to her feet and takes flight."

The woman on the view-wall paused, staring sorrowfully straight into Forrester's eyes. Her oratorial stance relaxed; her eyes seemed to lose their dramatic glow, and she said conversationally, "Now, you see? What a terrible thing to happen to a little girl, and all because she rejected her parents. She ran and ran and ran and ran, a long, long time, and then she got back to her father/mother and promised never to reject them again, and made a good adjustment. Now please prepare to answer questions on the theme: 'Is it wise to take chances on going to places your father/mother do not approve?'" She smiled, bowed, and vanished.

The joymaker said, "Man Forrester, thank you for waiting. There are certain nexial recursions malfunctioning at the present time, and we regret any inconvenience."

"What was that? One of Adne's kids' bedtime stories?"

"Exactly, Man Forrester. Our apologies. Shall I attempt to display the Taiko tape again?"

"I think," said Forrester, with a sense of foreboding, "that I am beginning to feel kind of lonesome."

"That is not due to any malfunction on our part, Man Forrester," said the joymaker with dignity. "That is due to—"

Silence.

"What did you say?" demanded Forrester.

"That is due to— That is due to—*Awk*," said the joymaker, as though it were strangling. "That is due to the flight of many persons to freezing facilities."

"You sound as though you're breaking down, machine," said Forrester apprehensively.

"No, Man Forrester! Certain nexial recursions are not operative, and some algorithms are looping. It is a minor technical difficulty."

The machine paused, then said in a different tone, "Another minor technical difficulty is that certain priority programs have not been executed on schedule. My apologies, Man Forrester."

"For what?"

"For not delivering a priority notice regarding your imminent arrest."

Forrester was jolted. "The devil you say!"

"No, Man Forrester. It is a true message. The coppers are coming for you now."

Chapter Seventeen

The door opened with a *thwack*, and two coppers plunged into the room. One of them grabbed him, rather roughly, Forrester thought, and glared into his eyes. "Man Forrester!" it cried. "You are arrested on sufficient charges and need make no statement!"

As if he could, thought Forrester, whirled off his feet as the coppers flanked him, one on each side, and half carried him out into the corridor and down to the fly-in, where a police flier was waiting for him. He shouted to them, "Wait! What's it all about?"

They did not answer, merely thrust him in and slammed the door. It must be the Sirian business, he thought sickly, staring back at them as they watched the flier bear him away. But why now? "I didn't *do* anything!" he cried, knowing that he lied.

"That is to be determined, Man Forrester," said a voice from a speaker grille over his head. "Meanwhile, please come with us."

The "please" was totally sense-free, of course; Forrester had no choice. "But what did I *do?*" he begged.

"Your arrest has been ordered, Man Forrester," said the quiet, unemotional voice of the central computation facility. "Do you wish a precis of the charge against you?"

"You bet!" Forrester stared around fearfully. There was no one at the controls, but there didn't seem to be a need for anyone; the car was sliding rapidly through the air toward the lake front.

"Your arrest has been ordered, Man Forrester," repeated the computer voice. "Do you wish a precis of the charge against you?"

"Damn it, I just said I did!" They were over blue water and moving fast. Forrester hammered the fleshy part of his fist against a window experimentally, but naturally enough the glass did not break. It was just as well, of course; there was no place for him to go.

"Your arrest," said the computer voice calmly, "has been ordered, Man Forrester. Do you wish a precis of the charge against you?"

Forrester swore furiously and hopelessly. They were approaching a metal island in the lake, and the aircraft was dropping toward it. "All I want," he said, "is to know what the devil's going on. Joymaker! Can you tell me what this is all about?" But the mace clipped to his belt only said, "We are all the same, Man Forrester. Do you wish a precis of the charge against you?"

By the time the aircraft landed, Forrester had regained control of himself. Obviously something was wrong with the central computation facilities, but equally obviously there was nothing much he could do about it now. When two more coppers, waiting on the hardstand for the police car to alight, seized his arms and pulled him out of the door, he did not resist. The coppers' grip was quite unbreakable, their strength far greater than his own.

He saw no human being and no other automata, while he was herded like livestock down through underground passages, under the lake waters, until finally he was pushed into a door that locked behind him.

He was in a cell. It held a bed, a chair, and a table, nothing else. Or nothing that was visible; its walls were mined with the usual electronic maze, however, because a voice said at once, "Man Forrester, message."

"Drop sick," said Forrester. "No, I don't want a precis of the charge against me."

But the message that followed was not the repetitious drone of the faulty machines. It was Taiko's voice, and a wall of the cell sprang into light to show his face. "Hi, there, Chuck," he said. "You said you wanted to see me."

Forrester exhaled sharply. "Thank God," he said. "Look, Taiko, something's gone wrong with the machines, and I'm in jail!"

Taiko's bland face creased in a smile. "Number one," he said, "there's nothing wrong with the machines—in fact, something's going right with them! And, number two, of course you're in jail. Who do you think brought you here?"

"Here? You mean you're—"

Taiko grinned and nodded. "Not more'n fifty meters away, pal. Considering how messed up the computers are, the easiest way to get you here was to have you arrested. So I did. So now we come right down to it. Are you with the Ned Lud Society or are you against it? Because this is our chance. Everything's so stirred up for fear of a Sirian invasion that we can straighten things out the *right* way. Know what I mean by the right way?"

"Smash the machines?" Forrester guessed. "You mean, you and I are going to break up the central computers?"

"Oh, not just you and I," said Taiko triumphantly. "We've got a lot of help we didn't have before. Would you like to see them?"

Taiko touched his joymaker, and the field of the viewscreen widened. Forrester was looking into a fairly large room and a rather heavily populated one.

Taiko did indeed have a lot of help. There were perhaps a dozen of them, Forrester saw, but he did not count them very accurately. He was too shocked to count when he discovered that only one or two of the dozen "helpers" in the room were human.

The rest were not. They looked out at Forrester through eyes that were circlets of gleaming green dots. They were Sirians.

"You see, pal," said Taiko easily, "it's a matter of loyalties. Our friends here are kind of funny-looking, I admit. But they're *organic*."

Forrester goggled. The Sirians in their cone-shaped pressure suits looked exactly like his late friend and benefactor, S Four. The idea of making allies of them was hard to accept. Not only because they were potentially dangerous enemies, but because his own contact with S Four had left him with an unshakable conviction that men and Sirians were far from being able to communicate on any meaningful level.

Taiko laughed. "Takes you aback, eh? But it was obvious—only it took somebody like me to see how to make it work. These guys are *geniuses* on the electronic stuff, absolute geniuses. They've given us a chance to put the ideals of the Ned Lud Society into practice, once and for all. . . . Look, are you interested or not? Because I can send you back where you came from as easily as I brought you here."

"I'm interested, all right," said Forrester.

Taiko was sharp enough to catch a hint of double meaning. "Interested to work with us? Or to try to mess us up?" But he didn't wait for an answer. He chuckled. "Makes no difference in the long run," he said merrily. "What can you do? Come on up and talk it over, anyway. . . ."

And there was a faint click, and the door of Forrester's cell sprang open, and a line of pale glowing green arrowheads appeared to point the way for him to walk.

I wish, he thought, that Adne were here to talk to.

But Adne was deep in the liquid-helium sleep of death, with her children, with nearly everyone else Forrester had met in this century. There was no one to tell him what to do.

He followed the tick of the arrowheads appearing before him as precisely as though they were the measures of a dance. It could not possibly be right, he told himself, to change the ways of the world with the aid of creatures from another star. It violated every principle of equity and human rights.

On the other hand, what Taiko was after made sense. Was it right to submit the destinies of the world to a cluster of computers?

For that matter, thought Forrester, tardily realizing how little of his homework he had done, was the premise right in that statement? *Were* the computers masters of the world? Who *did* make fundamental decisions?

Was it possible that a state had been reached in which fundamental decisions made themselves—not by the acts of a legislature, but by the actions of sovereign individuals, viewed en masse?

He shook his head. It was rather pointless to be considering these large questions, in view of his circumstances. He was several hundred meters under the surface of a lake, he reminded himself, in a world that had rejected him several times and was now dissolving around him.

The arrowheads ended at a door, which wheeled itself open as he approached, and he entered the room he had seen in the view-screen.

"About time!" cried Taiko, advancing toward him and clapping him on the shoulder. "You know, Charles, you should have confided in me. If it hadn't been for my friends here—" he gestured at the Sirians in their conical suits—"I'd never have known how much you had to do with our success. Haw! You *said* you'd help the society if I'd let you join. I just had no idea how much!"

"So you know how S Four tricked me," said Forrester.

"Don't be modest! It was a noble deed—even if he had to, well, lean on you a little to make you do it. I can only wonder," Taiko went on modestly, "why I didn't think of it myself. Obviously, the way to make Ned Lud ideals real is to get enough people so chicken-scared that they light out for the freezers, leaving the rest of the world to take care of whatever happens next. Only there isn't enough rest of the world still alive to matter. And while things are messed up, we *move*."

One of the Sirians moved restlessly. Its circlet of green eyes winked like gems, dimmed only faintly by the sheen of the crystal band that kept it from the corrosive attack of Earth's air. It did not speak, but Taiko seemed to understand what it was thinking.

"They don't exactly want you here," he said, turning a thumb toward the Sirian. "Not that they're not grateful. Well, whatever a Sirian would be that you might call grateful. But there's a lot riding on all this for them, and they don't like to take chances."

"Do you want me to promise not to interfere?" asked Forrester wonderingly.

"No! Who'd believe you'd keep a promise like that? Anyway, it isn't necessary. What could you do?"

"I don't know."

"Nothing! We've already recircuited most of Central

Computation—no communication anywhere, anymore. Except for the coppers—which are under our direct control—and the DR vehicles. Which I insisted on," he pointed out, "because naturally I'm not going to *hurt* any human beings if I can help it. Sweat! I want to *save* them!"

"What about your friends here?"

"Forget them, Charles," said Taiko easily. "Don't fret yourself, they're just technical advisors. I'm the one that's running this show, and when we finish busting up the machines they're going home."

"How do you know?" Forrester demanded.

"Oh, sweat, Charles," sighed Taiko. He glanced ruefully at the Sirians, shook his head, took Forrester by the arm. He walked him over to a view-wall and pointed.

"The pictures are a little random and fuzzy," he apologized, "because naturally Central Computing isn't monitoring the intercuts any more. But look. You see what the world looks like now?"

Forrester looked. One wall showed a broad hoverway with a single car on it, lying slantwise across the way and motionless; no one was around. The other wall changed as he watched from blank gray to a growing fire that seemed to be consuming most of the central part of a city. It did not look like Shoggo.

"You think the Sirians are going to worry about Earth without Central Computing?" demanded Taiko. "Sweat, no! Once the machine computation facilities are neutralized, they'll be glad to go home. Earth won't be a threat. And they're not naturally warlike."

"How do you know that?"

"Oh, come on, Charles! You have to take *some* things on faith!"

Forrester said carefully, "Are you all that good a judge of Sirian character? Please, I'm not trying to put you down. I want to know. How can you be sure?"

"It stands to reason!" snapped Taiko. "Oh, I know, Charles, you're thinking of the way I've been acting, like a clown, an idiot, pushing an idea that not one human being in a hundred thousand gave a hoot about, warning about dangers most people thought were delights. . . . But I'm not stupid. I moved in fast enough when you gave me the break, right? I showed I was smart enough to grab a chance when it presented itself? So trust me. I'm smart enough to see that there's nothing in it for the Sirians as far as fighting Earth is concerned. Why would they want to do that? They can't live here without suits. There are a thousand planets that would be worth something to them; Earth doesn't happen to be one of them."

There was a sound from the voice-box of one of the Sirians. Taiko jumped. He turned to call out, "All right, just a minute." And, to Forrester, "Well, that's it. I'm a sentimental slob. I'd like to have you with us since you did us a favor—whether you knew it or not. But it's up to you. In or out?"

"I don't know," said Forrester honestly.

"Take your time," grinned Taiko. "The jail's yours. Just remember, there's nothing you can do to hurt us. No communications. No transportation. And damn near no*body*."

Forrester walked back out into the bright, empty corridors of Shoggo's underwater jail. No one stopped him.

There were no green arrows to guide him. As he had come from the left, he turned to the right. He wanted to think. Was Taiko right? Judging from his own experience, this was at least a disconcerting society, filled with unexpected cruelties and cowardices. But who was Taiko to make the world's decisions for it?

He saw a bright light ahead and walked toward it. It was sunlight! Sunlight shining down a shaft, and a white death-reversal car humming quietly to itself as it waited.

There was an attendant, but though it looked human enough it glared into Forrester's eyes and said challengingly, "Man Forrester! Your arrest has been ordered. Do you wish a precis of the charge against you?"

"Machine," he said, "you're a broken record." Then he had a thought. "Take me out of here!" he commanded, climbing into the DR flier.

"Man Forrester! Your arrest has been ordered. Do you wish a precis of the charge against you?"

It was hopeless, of course. He hoped, anyway, and sat there for minutes, while the machine that looked so like a human being glared unmovingly at him and the DR car remained motionless. Then Forrester sighed, got out, walked away.

"I might as well join them," he said aloud.

But he didn't want to. He didn't merely not want to; he actively, passionately wished he could thwart Taiko's plan. As soon as it became clear he had only one choice to make, that choice became abhorrent.

But there was nothing he could do. He considered possibilities, one by one. Nothing would work. His joymaker was mute. There was no way out of the jail. Even the DR car would take him away only if he were dead, not alive. . . .

If he were dead?

He took a deep breath and marched back to the DR car. As he had thought, the side of it was emblazoned with the caduceus of the WEST ANNEX CENTER.

He demanded, "Machine, are you really operating out of the West Annex Center?"

The robot glared into his eyes. "Man Forrester! Your arrest has been ordered. Would you like a precis of the charge against you?"

"What I would like," said Forrester tightly, "is an insurance policy. But I guess I'll have to take a chance this one time without one. Let's hope it's only your speaking circuits that are messed up!"

What he wanted he knew he would find in the flier. He reached into it, fumbled through the nest of first-aid equipment.

The thing he wanted turned up in the first case he opened: a four-inch scalpel, razor sharp. He stared at it glumly, hesitated, searched again until he found a writing stylus and a square of cardboard. Carefully he lettered a sign:

REVIVE ME AT ONCE!
I can tell you what the Sirians are up to.

He pinned it neatly to his shirt front. Then . . .

"Machine!" he cried. "Do your duty!" And with a rapid motion he slit his throat.

The pain was astonishing, but it lasted for only a moment. And then the world roared thinly at him and slipped dizzyingly away.

Chapter Eighteen

"I was dreaming," murmured Forrester into the warm, comfortable darkness, "of committing suicide. Funny I should cut my throat, though. I want to live. . . ."

"You'll live, Chuck," said a familiar voice. Forrester opened his eyes and gazed into the eyes of Hara.

He thrust himself up. "Taiko!" he cried. "The Sirians! I've got to tell you what they're doing!"

Hara pressed him back down on the bed. "You already told us, Chuck. They're taken care of. Don't you remember?"

"Remember?" But then he did remember. He remembered being awake, with a nightmarish pain in his throat, trying by gesture and sign language to communicate something, until at last someone had had the wit to bring stylus and paper and he'd written out a message. He laughed out loud. "Funny! I never thought that with my throat cut it'd be hard to tell you anything."

"But you did, Chuck. The Sirians are under personal human guard, every one of them immobilized and cut off from communication. And Taiko's talking as fast as he can to a computer team, telling them what he did so they can undo it. They've already got all the basic utilities back." Hara stood up, fished in a pocket, proudly produced a pack of cigarettes. "Here," he said. "See how your new throat lining stands up to these."

Forrester gratefully accepted a light. It felt all right as he drew in; he reached up and touched his throat, found it covered with soft plastic film.

"That'll come off today," said Hara. "You're about ready to go back to population. We've already revived close

170

to twenty-five percent of the recent freezees. They'll really be interested in you."

"Oh," said Forrester, dampened. "I guess they will, at that. What's the penalty for letting the Sirian escape?"

"About equal to the reward for letting us know about Taiko," said Hara cheerfully. "Don't worry about it."

"Well, how about if I worry about what the Sirians are going to do?" asked Forrester.

Hara waved a hand. "Be my guest," he said. "Only bear in mind that Taiko's little friends were pretty high when he was dismantling Central Computation, and they're pretty low now. I don't think they'll find us an easy target."

He turned toward the door. "Get yourself checked out," he ordered. "Then I want to talk to you before you leave here."

"About my throat?"

"About your girl," said Hara.

Hours later, Forrester was standing where he had stood before, outside the main entrance to the West Annex Discharge Center. For old time's sake he flipped a cigarette to the ground and watched the tiny bright cleaner robot whisk it up and away.

Clearly, Central Computation was back on the job.

He turned as Hara joined him. "What *about* my girl?" he demanded.

"Well . . ." Hara hesitated. "It's tough to know how to talk to you survivors of the kamikaze era," he said. "You're sensitive about the strangest things. For instance, Adne said she thought you resented the fact that I was the father of one of her kids."

"*One* of them!" Forrester squawked, severely trying his new throat lining. "Holy God! I at least thought they'd have the same father!"

"Why, Chuck?"

"Why? What do you mean, why? The girl's a trollop!"

"What's a trollop?" As Forrester hesitated, Hara pressed on. "In *your* time, maybe that was something bad. I don't know; I'm not a specialist in ancient history. But you aren't in your time any more, Chuck."

Forrester gazed thoughtfully at Hara's patient, weary face. But it was more than he wanted to accept. "I don't care," he said angrily. "I can't help thinking maybe Taiko was right. Somewhere the human race took a wrong turning!"

"Well," said Hara, "actually, that's what I wanted to tell you. Chuck, there's no such thing as a wrong turning. You can't rewrite the history of the race; it happened; this is the result. If you don't like it, there's no reason why you can't try to persuade the world to change again. To something different—anything! Whatever you like. But *you can't go back.*"

He patted Forrester's shoulder. "Think," he advised. "Let your brain decide what's right and wrong, not what's left of your boyhood training. Because all that is dead. . . . And, oh, yes. One other thing," he mentioned. "I checked the schedules. We're reviving them pretty fast now, and it ought to be Adne's turn in about two days."

And he was gone.

Forrester stared after him. It would be hard, he thought, but it would be possible. And, after all, he had very little choice.

So Forrester hailed a flier and ordered it to take him to a suitable dwelling in Shoggo, determined to face the future. Which, as it turned out, was very fortunate, since he had a lot of future to face—not just a few days or years, but, with the help of a few more visits to the freezer, a fair number of millennia, in all of which he was alive, and active, and well.

For he lived happily ever after. And so did they all.

Author's Note

Once upon a time, a quarter of a century or so ago, I was a weatherman for the United States Army Air Force in Italy. It was my first experience in the art of predicting real-time events—that is, in the kind of prediction where money, and lives, are bet on its accuracy.

This was a long time before the advent of the computer and the facsimile machine and TIROS and all the other handy little gadgets that have since come reasonably close to turning meteorology into an exact science. Still, we had our gadgets even then, quite a few of them. Our group weather officer, in my part of the Fifteenth Air Force, was a disheveled captain who smiled and nodded a lot, but rarely spoke. He would hum to himself for an hour or two as he pored over the teletype reports and the synoptic map and the adiabatic charts and the PIREPS. Then he would go out to the instrument shelter and swing the psychrometer and tap the ameroid barograph with his fingernail. And then he would climb on the roof of the station and perhaps he would see, off on the horizon, a cloud no bigger than a man's hand; and he would say, "Ha! Looks like rain," and come back and make a bad-weather forecast for the pilots of the B-24s.

Actually, that's the way to write science fiction. (Well, one kind of science fiction. There are many varieties of the science fiction experience!) First you do your homework with the books and the scientific journals. Then you talk to the astronomers and biochemists and computer people, and if you're lucky perhaps they'll let you play with their machines and look through their lenses. And then you get up on a high place and look at the world around you.

The Age of the Pussyfoot *was constructed to those specifications. Little of it represents invention on my part, barring the personalities and some of the details of settings and events. Almost every aspect of it is visible right now, in July of 1968, as a cloud no bigger than a man's hand; and I too am forecasting rain.*

The joymaker? M.I.T.'s Project MAC was what made me think of the joymaker—well, that's not quite true; I had thought of it before Project MAC ever existed, but certainly MAC is a sort of Jurassic ancestor of my toy. At M.I.T., two big IBM 7094s, plus half a dozen or so servant computers, are available to anyone with a remote-access console in his home or office. The console right now can be anywhere a telephone line will go—including Europe, if you like, or for that matter Antarctica. My only additional assumption is that it will be convenient to do the same thing by radio. The MAC consoles are presently about the size of biggish electric typewriters; my only change involves microminiaturizing them into portability—and, while you're at it, fitting them with a few of such necessities of modern urban life as Miltown, contraceptive pills, aspirin, and the like. I also assume that the pharmacopeia of the next few centuries will be more extensive than our own, but that seems like a reasonably good bet.

Immortality through freezing? Robert C. W. Ettinger has been on a crusade for that for more than five years now. The funny thing about it is that it will probably work. (I offer no money-back guarantees, you understand, only an opinion. But it is an opinion shared by such prestigious men as Jean Rostand, France's most illustrious biochemist.) The other funny thing about it is that there have been very few takers for this offer of immortality in the flesh—as Bob Ettinger says, many are cold, but few are frozen. There are fewer than half a dozen corpses currently in the deep freeze, although there are some hundreds of thousands of persons who would be, except that they haven't yet happened to die. But the facilities are there, including some three competing lines of the man-sized thermos bottles with the liquid gas tanks that are now commercially available for those who would die and live to die again. I mentioned "death-reversal" equipment in the story. Several years ago, I saw an unpublished manuscript that stated, apparently on good authority, that the U.S.S.R. had such vehicles in service then; it implied that one of these had saved the life of the noted Russian scientist Lev Landau. (Who was dead four times, clinically, incontrovertibly dead, before he was brought to life again permanently enough to be released from the hospital.) And, three months ago, parked outside the headquarters of the New York Academy of Sciences, I saw the first American death-reversal machine. The New York DR vehicle is a truck; those in the story are helicopters. Otherwise they are much the same.

It is true, however, that no corpsicle has yet been thawed and returned to life, and there's no firm estimate of when one will be. Yet it could happen tomorrow. The odds appear to be very great that it will happen some time, and according to my personal reading of human psychology, the minute it does we will have a rush to the freezers comparable to no human migration since the opening of the Cherokee Strip. It strikes me that we are all, from birth, so often reminded that we are inevitably going to die that we cannot accept an offer of immortality when it is presented, until and unless it is shown to work. Demonstrate that it works one time, and we'll grab for it as we've grabbed for few things before . . . and then the building of such installations as the West Annex Center will proceed apace.

The economic, social, and cultural "predictions" of the story are perhaps a little less defensible than the hardware. But I think the reason for that is that economics and sociology, et al., are at the present time rather less "scientific" than the hard sciences are. The money part of the story is pretty reliably stated. Obviously we will continue to have both of the two kinds of inflation that have been going on throughout history—both the devaluation of existing currencies (as the Roman solidus, worth several hundred dollars at least, was devalued over two thousand years into the French sou, worth not even a thank you); and the multiplication of things to spend money on, which is the psychological root of a good deal of the "poverty" of our own age and nation. (America's poor usually do have enough money to survive on. It is the fact that they see around them so many desirable things, which they don't have money to buy, that makes them really, miserably, unarguably "poor.")

The notion of being paid a salary for things we might now consider to be properly unpaid, leisure-time activities is not particularly fanciful, either. Witness the proposals of the guaranteed annual wage and the negative income tax; witness institutionalized welfare programs; witness how many "leisure" activities have already become paying professions. Who would have paid a salary to a ski instructor in the Middle Ages? Already in America almost every large volunteer organization has a hard-core paid professional staff. (It is not quite as common in Europe—yet.) I am only suggesting that the memberships as well as the leaderships might as well be paid for what they do.

As to the mating customs, the interpersonal folkways and so on of my twenty-sixth-century characters, I confess I am on shakier ground. I am not sure that things will go exactly this way. But form follows function. There is a need for a family even now, as a sort of nest designed for the raising of children, and there no doubt will be such a need in the foreseeable future. I do not think it will be the same need as in the recent past, however. Then there was enough work at home to keep an able-bodied woman busy from dawn to dark, and enough work involved in earning a living to keep her husband away at the farm or factory almost every waking hour. With the increase in leisure time, in productivity of labor, especially in such external aids to child-rearing as schools and nurseries, the functional need for the family is somewhat different. Our social structure has not yet really caught up with that fact, although the signs are writ large; I am only assuming that in five hundred years it will have done so.

A similar defense could be made for almost every speculation in this novel, including the presence of Sirians. (Or, anyway, extraterrestrial creatures capable of doing the sort of thing that Sirians do in the story. There are more than one hundred billion stars in our own galaxy, and it is a *dead-certain bet that at least some of them have inhabited planets.) But I should confess that there are two areas in which I am defenseless.*

One of these includes the things I have left out. I have not taken into consideration the probabilities of large-scale disaster—through nuclear warfare, or lethal pollution of the air, or a runaway population explosion sufficient to starve us all back to the Neolithic. But there's just so much you can discuss in one story, and I wasn't happening to discuss those possibilities here.

And the other thing I can't defend is the time scale.

If you put together Project MAC and Bob Ettinger's freezers and the negative income tax, you have something that is really quite a lot like The Age of the Pussyfoot *. . . constructed out of materials that are to hand right now. In the novel, the time scale is larger: five centuries. Charles Forrester's revival is as far in one direction along our time scale as Christopher Columbus's voyage is in the other.*

I don't really think it will be that long. Not five centuries.

Perhaps not even five decades.

FREDERIK POHL
Red Bank, New Jersey
July 1968

Drunkard's
Walk

Chapter One

This man's name is Cornut, born in the year 2166 and now thirty. He is a teacher.

Mathematics is his discipline. Number Theory is his specialty. He instructs the Mnemonics of Number, a study which absorbs all his creative thought. But he also thinks about girls a lot; in a detached, remote sort of way.

He is unmarried. He sleeps alone and that is not so good.

If you wander around his small bedroom (it has lilac walls and a cream ceiling, those are the Math Tower colors), you will hear a whispering and a faint whirring sound. These are not the sounds of Cornut's breath, although he is sleeping peacefully. The whispering is a hardly audible *wheep, wheep* from an electric clock. (It was knocked to the floor once. A gear is slightly off axis; it rubs against a rivet.) The whir is another clock. If you look more carefully you will find that there are more clocks.

There are five clocks in this room, all told. They all have alarms, set to ring at the same moment.

Cornut is a good-looking man, even if he is a little pale. If you are a woman (say, one of the girls in his classes), you would like to get him out in the sun. You would like to fatten him up and make him laugh more. He is not aware that he needs sunshine or fattening, but he is very much aware that he needs something.

He knows something is wrong. He has known this for seven weeks, on the best evidence of all.

The five clocks march briskly toward seven-fifteen, the time at which they are set to go off. Cornut has spent a lot of time arranging it so that they will sound at the same moment. He set the alarm dial on each, checked it by revolving the hands of the clocks themselves to make note of the exact second at which the trigger went off, painfully reset and rechecked. They are now guaranteed to ring, clang or buzz within a quarter-minute of each other.

However, one of them has a bad habit. It is the one that Cornut dropped once. It makes a faint click a few moments before the alarm mechanism itself rings.

It clicks now.

The sound is not very loud, but Cornut stirs. His eyes flicker. They close again, but he is not quite asleep.

After a moment he pushes back the covers and sits up. His eyes are still almost closed.

Suppose you are a picture on his wall—perhaps the portrait of Leibniz, taken from Ficquet's old engraving. Out of the eyes under your great curled wig you see this young man stand up and walk slowly toward his window.

His room is eighteen stories up.

If a picture on the wall can remember, you remember that this is not the first time. If a picture on the wall can know things, you know that he has tried to leap out of that window before, and he is about to try again.

He is trying to kill himself. He has tried nine times in the past fifty days.

If a picture on a wall can regret, you regret this. It is a terrible waste for this man to keep trying to kill himself, since he does not at all want to die.

Chapter Two

Cornut was uncomfortable in his sleep. He felt drowsily that he had worked himself into an awkward position, and besides, someone was calling his name. He mumbled, grimaced, opened his eyes.

He was looking straight down, nearly two hundred feet.

At once he was fully awake. He teetered dangerously, but someone behind him had caught him by an arm, someone who was shouting at him. Whoever it was, he pulled Cornut roughly back into the room.

At that moment the five alarm clocks burst into sound, like a well-drilled chorus; a beat later the phone by his bed rang; the room lights sprang into life, controlled by their automatic timer, one reading lamp turned and fitted with a new, brighter tube so that it became a spotlight aimed at the pillow where Cornut's head should have been.

"Are you all right?"

The question had been repeated several times, Cornut realized. He said furiously, "Of course I'm all right!" It had been very close; his veins were suddenly full of adrenalin, and as there was nothing else for it to do it charged him with anger. . . . "I'm sorry. Thanks, Egerd."

The undergraduate let go. He was nineteen years old, with crew-cut red hair and a face that was normally deeply tanned, now almost white. "That's all right." He cautiously backed to the phone, still watching the professor. "Hello. Yes, he's awake now. Thanks for calling."

"They were almost too late," said Cornut. Egerd shrugged.

"I'd better get back, sir. I'll have to— Oh, good morning, Master Carl."

The house master was standing in the doorway, a gaggle

of undergraduates clustered behind him like young geese, staring in to see what all the commotion was. Master Carl was tall, black-haired, with eyes like star sapphires. He stood holding a wet photographic negative that dripped gently onto the rubber tiles. "What the devil is going on here?" he demanded.

Cornut opened his mouth to answer, and then realized how utterly impossible it was for him to answer that question. He didn't know! The terrible thing about the last fifty days was just that. He didn't know what, he didn't know why, all he knew was that this was the ninth time he had very nearly taken his own life. "Answer Master Carl, Egerd," he said.

The undergraduate jumped. Carl was the central figure in his life; every student's hope of passing, of graduating, of avoiding the military draft or forced labor in the Assigned Camps lay in his house master's whim. Egerd said, stammering, "Sir, I—I have been on extra duty for Master Cornut. He asked me to come in each morning five minutes before wake-up time and observe him, because he— That is, that's what he asked me to do. This morning I was a little late."

Carl said coldly, "You were late?"

"Yes, sir. I—"

"And you came into the corridor without *shaving?*"

The undergraduate was struck dumb. The cluster of students behind Carl briskly dissolved. Egerd started to speak, but Cornut cut in. He sat down shakily on the edge of his bed. "Leave the boy alone, will you, Carl? If he had taken time to shave I'd be dead."

Master Carl rapped out, "Very well. You may go to your room, Egerd. Cornut, I want to know what this is all about. I intend to get a full explanation. . . ." He paused, as though remembering something. He glanced down at the wet negative in his hand.

"As soon as we've had breakfast," he said grimly, and stalked majestically back to his own rooms.

Cornut dressed heavily, and began to shave. He had aged a full year every day of the past seven weeks; on that basis, he calculated, he was already pushing eighty and a full decade older than Master Carl himself.

Seven weeks. Nine attempts at suicide.

And no explanation.

He didn't look like a man who had just sleepwalked himself to the narrow edge of suicide. He was young for a professor and built like an athlete, which was according to the facts; he had been captain of the fencing team as an undergraduate, and was its faculty advisor still. His face looked like the face of a husky, healthy youth who for some reason had been cutting himself short on sleep, and that was also according to the facts. His expression was that of a man deeply embarrassed by some incredibly inexcusable act he has just committed. And that fit the facts too.

Cornut *was* embarrassed. His foolishness would be all over the campus by now; undoubtedly there had been whispers before, but this morning's episode had had many witnesses and the whispers woud be quite loud. As the campus was Cornut's whole life, that meant that every living human being whose opinion counted with him at all would soon be aware that he was fecklessly trying to commit suicide—for no reason—and not even succeeding!

He dried his face and got ready to leave his room—which meant facing them, but there was no way out of that. A bundle of letters and memoranda were in the mail hopper by his desk. He paused to look at them: nothing important. He glanced at his notes, which someone had been straightening. Probably Egerd. His scrawled figures on the Wolgren anomalies were neatly stacked on top of the *schema* for this morning's lectures; in the center of the desk, with a paperweight on top of it, was the red-bordered letter from the President's Office, inviting him to go on the Field Expedition. He reminded himself to ask Carl to get him off that. He had too much to do to waste time on purely social trips. The Wolgren study alone would keep him busy for weeks, and Carl was always pressing him to publish. But that was premature. Three months from now . . . maybe . . . if Computer Section allocated enough time, and if the anomalies didn't disappear in someone's ancient error in simple addition.

And if he was still alive, of course.

"Oh, damn it all, anyhow," Cornut said suddenly. He tucked the President's letter into his pocket, picked up his cape and walked irritably out into the hall.

The Math Tower dining room served all thirty-one masters of the department, and most of them were there before him. He walked in with an impassive face, expecting a sudden hush to stop the permanent buzz of conversation in the hall, and getting it. Everyone was looking at him.

"Good morning," he said cheerfully, nodding all around the room.

One of the few women on the staff waved to him, giggling. "Good for you, Cornut! Come sit with us, will you? Janet has an idea to help you stop suiciding!"

Cornut smiled and nodded and turned his back on the two women. They slept in the women's wing, twelve stories below his own dorms, but already the word had spread. Naturally. He stopped at the table where Master Carl sat alone, drinking tea and looking through a sheaf of photographs. "I'm sorry about this morning, Carl," he said.

Master Carl looked vaguely up at him. Dealing with his equals, Carl's eyes were not the brittle star-sapphires that had pierced Egerd; they were the mild, blue eyes of a lean Santa Claus, which was much closer to his true nature. "Oh? Oh. You mean about jumping out of the window, of course. Sit down, boy." He made a space on the table for the student waitress to put down Cornut's place-setting. The whole cloth was covered with photographic prints. He handed one to Cornut. "Tell me," he said apologetically, "does that look like a picture of a star to you?"

"No." Cornut was not very interested in his department head's hobbies. The print looked like a light-struck blob of nothing much at all.

Carl sighed and put it down. "All right. Now, what about this thing this morning?"

Cornut accepted a cup of coffee from one of the student

waitresses and waved away the others. "I wish I could," he said seriously.

Carl waited.

"I mean—it's hard."

Carl waited.

Cornut took a long swallow of coffee and put down his cup. Carl was probably the only man on the faculty who hadn't been listening to the grapevine that morning. It was almost impossible to say to him the simple fact of what had happened. Master Carl was a child of the University, just as Cornut himself was; like Cornut, he had been born in the University's Medical Center and educated in the University's schools. He had no taste for the boiling, bustling Townie world outside. In fact, he had very little taste for human problems at all. Lord knew what Carl, dry as digits, his head crammed with Vinogradoff and Frénicle de Bessy, would make of so non-mathematical a phenomenon as suicide.

"I've tried to kill myself nine times," Cornut said, plunging in, "don't ask me why; I don't know. That's what this morning was all about. It was my ninth try."

Master Carl's expression was fully what Cornut had anticipated.

"Don't look so incredulous," he snapped. *"I* don't know any more about it than that. It's just as much of an annoyance to me as it is to you!"

The house master looked helplessly at the photographic prints by his plate as though some answer might be there. It wasn't. "All right," he said, rubbing the lobes of bone over his eyes. "I understand your statement. Has it occurred to you that you might get help?"

"Help? My God, I've got helpers all over the place. The thing is worst in the morning, you see; just when I'm waking up, not fully alert, that's the bad time. So I've set up a whole complicated system of alarms. I have five clocks set. I got the superintendent's office to rig up the lights on a timed switch. I got the night proctor to call me on the house phone—all of them together, you see, so that when I wake up, I wake up *totally*. It worked for three mornings, and, believe me, the only thing that that experience resembles is being awakened by a pot of ice-water in the face. I even got Egerd to come in early every morning to stand by while I woke, just on the chance that something would go wrong."

"But this morning Egerd was late?"

"He was tardy," Cornut corrected. "A minute more and he would have been late. And so would I."

Carl said, "That's not exactly the sort of help I had in mind."

"Oh. You mean the Med Center." Cornut reached for a cigarette. A student waitress hurried over with a light. He knew her. She was in one of his classes; a girl named Locille. She was pretty and very young. Cornut said absently, following her with his eyes, "I've been there, Carl. They offered me analysis. In fact, they were quite insistent."

Master Carl's face was luminous with interest. Cornut, turning back to look at him, thought that he hadn't seen Carl quite so absorbed in anything since their last discussion about the paper Cornut was doing for him: the analysis of the discrepancies in Wolgren's basic statistical law.

Carl said, "I'll tell you what astonishes me. You don't seem very worried about all this."

Cornut reflected. ". . . I am, though."

"You don't show it. Well, is there anything else that's worrying you?"

"Worrying me enough to kill myself? No. But I suppose there must be, mustn't there?"

Carl stared into the empty air. The eyes were bright blue again; Master Carl was operating with his brain, examining possibilities, considering their relevancy, evolving a theory. "Only in the mornings?"

"Oh no, Carl. I'm much more versatile than that; I can try to kill myself at any hour of the day or night. But it happens when I'm drowsy. Going to sleep, waking up— once in the middle of the night. I found myself walking toward the fire stairs, God knows why. Perhaps something happened to half-wake me, I don't know. So I have Egerd keep me company at night until I'm thoroughly asleep, and again in the morning. My baby-sitter."

Carl said testily, "Surely you can tell me more than this!"

"Well. . . . Yes, I suppose I can. I think I have dreams."

"Dreams?"

"I think so, Carl. I don't remember very well, but it's as though someone were *telling* me to do these things, someone in a position of authority. A father? I don't remember my own father, but that's the feeling I get."

The light went out of Carl's face. He had lost interest. Cornut said curiously, "What's the matter?"

The house master leaned back, shaking his head. "No, you mustn't think anyone is telling you, Cornut. There isn't anyone. I've checked it very thoroughly, believe me. Dreams come from the dreamer."

"But I only said—"

Master Carl held up his hand. "To consider any other possibility," he lectured, in the voice that reached three million viewers every week, "involves one of two possibilities. Let us examine them. First, there might be a physical explanation. That is, someone may actually be speaking to you as you sleep. I assume we can dismiss that. The second possibility is telepathy. And that," he said sadly, "does not exist."

"But I only—"

"Look within yourself, my boy," the old man said wisely. Then, his expression showing dawning interest again, "And what about Wolgren? Any progress with the anomalies?"

Twenty minutes later, on the plea that he was late for an appointment, Cornut made his escape. There were twelve tables in the room, and he was invited to sit down at eight of them for a second cup of coffee . . . and, oh yes, what *is* this story all about, Cornut?

His appointment, although he hadn't said so to Master Carl, was with his analyst. Cornut was anxious to keep it.

He wasn't very confident of analysis as a solution to his problem; despite three centuries, the technique of mental health had never evolved a rigorous proof system, and Cornut was innately skeptical of whatever was not susceptible of mathematical analysis. But there was something else he had neglected to tell Master Carl.

Cornut was not the only one of his kind.

The man at the Med Center had been quite excited. He named five names that Cornut recognized, faculty members who had killed themselves or died in ambiguous circumstances within the past few years. One had made fifteen attempts before he finally succeeded in blowing himself up after an all-night polymerization experiment in the Chem Hall. A couple had succeeded on the first or second try.

What made Cornut exceptional was that he had got through seven weeks of this without even seriously maiming himself. The all-time record was ten weeks. That was the chemist.

The analyst had promised to have all the information about the other suiciders to show him this morning. Cornut could not deny that he was interested. Indeed, it was a matter of considerable concern.

Unless all precedent was wrong, he would succeed as all the others had ultimately succeeded; he would kill himself one way or another, and he probably never would know why he had done it.

And unless precedent was wrong again, it would happen within the next three weeks.

Chapter Three

The University was beginning its day. In the Regents Office a clerk filled a hopper and flipped a switch, and Sticky Dick—sometimes written as S. T.-I. (C.E.), Di. C.—began to grind out grades on the previous day's examinations in English, Sanskrit and the nuclear reactions of the Bethe Phoenix cycle. Student orderlies in Med School wheeled their sectioned cadavers out of the refrigerated filing-drawers, playing the time-honored ribald jokes with the detached parts. In the central tape room, the TV technicians went about their endless arcane ritual of testing circuits and balancing voltages; every lecture was put on tape as a matter of course, even those which were not either broadcast or syndicated.

Thirty thousand undergraduates ran hastily over the probable mood of their various instructors, and came to the conclusion that they would be lucky to live through to evening. But it was better than trying to get along in the outside world, all the same.

And in the kitchen attached to the faculty dining room of Math Tower the student waitress, Locille, helped her C.E. mop the last drops of damp off the stainless steel cooking utensils. She hung up her apron, checked her make-up in the mirror by the door, descended in the service elevator and went out to the hot, loud walks of the Quad.

Locille didn't think them either hot or loud. She had known much worse.

Locille was a scholarship girl; her parents were Town, not Gown. She had only been at the University for two years. She still spent some of her weekends at home. She

knew very clearly what it was like to live in the city across
the bay—or worse, to live on one of the texases off the
coast—with your whole life a rattling, banging clamor day
and night and everyone piled up against everyone else. The
noise in the Quadrangle was only human voices. The
ground did not shake.

Locille had a happy small face, short hair, a forthright
way of walking out. She did not look worried but she was.
He had looked so *tired* this morning! Also he wasn't eating,
and that was not like him. If it wasn't scrambled eggs and
bacon it was a hot cereal with fruit on top, always. Instinctively she approved of a man who ate well. Perhaps, she
planned, smiling at a boy who greeted her without really
seeing his face at all, tomorrow she would just bring the
scrambled eggs and put them in front of him. Probably
he'd eat them.

Of course, that wasn't getting at the real problem.

Locille shivered. She felt quite helpless. It was distressing to care so much what happened to someone, and be so
far outside the situation itself. . . .

Running footsteps came up behind her and slowed.

"Hi," panted her most regular date, Egerd, falling into
step. "Why didn't you wait at the door? What about Satur-
day night?"

"Oh, hello. I don't know yet. They might need me at the
faculty dance."

Egerd said brusquely, "Tell them you can't make it. You
have to go out to the texas. Your brother has, uh, some
disease or other, and your mother needs you to help take
care of him."

Locille laughed.

"Aw, look. I've got Carnegan's boat for the evening! We
can go clear down to the Hook."

Locille cheerfully let him take her hand. She liked
Egerd. He was a good-looking boy, and he was kind. He
reminded her of her brother . . . well, not of her real, living brother; but of the brother she should have had. She
liked Egerd. But she didn't *like* him. The distinction was
quite clear in her mind. Egerd, for example, obviously
liked her.

Egerd said, "Well, you don't have to make up your mind now. I'll ask you again tomorrow." That was a salesman's instinct operating; it was always better to leave the prospect with a "maybe" than a "no." He guided her between two tall buildings toward the back gardens of the campus, where Agronomy had made a little Japanese retreat in the middle of fifteen intensively farmed acres of experimental peas and wheat. "I think I got some demerits from old Carl this morning," he said gloomily, remembering.

"Too bad," Locille said, although that was not an unusual phenomenon. But then he caught her attention.

"I was just trying to do Cornut a favor. Trying? Hell, I saved his life." She was all attention now. He went on, "He was practically out the window. Loopy! You know, I think half of these professors are off their rockers—Anyway, if I hadn't got there when I did he would've been dead. *Splop*. All over the Quad.

"At that," he said cheerfully, "I was kind of late."

"Egerd!"

He stopped and looked at her. "What's the matter?"

She raged, "You shouldn't have been late! Didn't you know Master Cornut was relying on you? Really, you ought to be more careful."

She was actually angry. Egerd studied her thoughtfully, and stopped talking; but some of the pleasure had gone out of the morning for him. Abruptly he caught her arm.

"Locille," he said in a completely serious tone, "please marry me for a while. I know I'm here on a scholarship and my grades are marginal. But I won't go back. Listen, I'm not going to stay with math. I was talking to some of the fellows at Med School. There's a lot of jobs in epidemiology, and that way my math credits will do me some good. I'm not asking for ten years of your life. We can make it month to month, even, and if you don't opt for a renewal I swear I won't hold it against you. But let me try to make you want to stay with me, Locille. Please. Marry me."

He stood looking down at her, his broad, tanned face entirely open, waiting. She didn't meet his eye.

After a moment he nodded composedly.

"All right. I can't compete with Master Cornut, can I?"

She suddenly frowned. "Egerd, I hope you won't feel—I mean, just because you've got the idea I'm interested in Master Cornut, I hope—"

"No," he said, grinning, "I won't let him fall out a window. But you know something? Pretty as you are, Locille, I don't think Cornut knows you're alive."

The analyst followed Cornut to the door. He was furious because he hadn't got his way—not with Cornut, particularly, but furious in general. Cornut said stiffly, "Sorry, but I *won't* put everything else aside."

"You'll have to, if you succeed in killing yourself."

"That's what you're supposed to prevent, isn't it? Or is this whole thing a complete waste of time?"

"It's better than killing yourself."

Cornut shrugged. It was a logically impeccable point. The analyst wheedled. "Won't you even stay overnight? Observation might give us the answer. . . ."

"No."

The analyst hesitated, shrugged, shook hands. "All right. I guess you know that if I had my way I wouldn't be asking you. I'd commit you to Med Center."

"Why, of course you would," Cornut soothed. "But you don't have your way, do you? You've undoubtedly tried to get an order from the President's Office already, haven't you?"

The analyst had the grace to look embarrassed. "Front office interference," he growled, "you'd think they'd understand that Mental Health needs a *little* cooperation once in a while. . . ."

Cornut left him still muttering. As he stepped out onto the Quad the heat and noise struck him like a fist. He didn't mind, either; he was used to it.

He had recovered enough to think of the morning's escape with amusement. The feeling was wry, with a taste of worry to it, but he was able to see the funny side of it. And it was ridiculous, no doubt about it. Suicide! Miserable people committed suicide, not happy ones. Cornut was a perfectly happy man.

Even the analyst had as much as admitted that. It had been a total waste of time, making him dig and dig into his cloudy childhood recollections for some early, abscessed wound of the mind that was pouring poisons out of its secret hiding place. He didn't have any! How could he? He was Gown. His parents had been on the faculty of this very University. Before he could walk, he was given over to the crèches and the playschools, run by the best-trained experts in the world, organized according to the best principles of child guidance. Every child had love and security, every child had what the greatest minds in pediatric psychology prescribed. Trauma? There simply could not be any!

Not only was it impossible on the face of it, but Cornut's whole personality showed no sign of such a thing. He enjoyed his work very much, and although he knew there was something he lacked—a secure, certain love—he also felt that in time he would have it. It did not occur to him to attempt to hurry it along.

"Good morning, good morning," he said civilly to the knots of undergraduates on the walks. He began to whistle one of Carl's mnemonic songs. The undergraduates who nodded to him smiled. Cornut was a popular professor.

He passed the Hall of Humanities, the Lit Building, Pre-Med and the Administration Tower. As he got farther from home ground, the number of students who greeted him became smaller, but they still nodded politely to the master's cloak. Overhead the shriek of distant passing aircraft filled the sky.

The great steel sweep of the Bay Bridge was behind him, but he could still hear the unending rush of cars across it and, farther and louder, the mumble of the city.

Cornut paused at the door of the studio where he was to deliver his first lecture.

He glanced across the narrow strait at the city, where people lived who did not study. There was a mystery. It was, he thought, a problem greater than the silent murderer in his own brain. But it was not a problem he would ever have to solve.

"A good teacher is a good make-up man." That was one of Master Carl's maxims. Cornut sat down at the long table and methodically applied a daub of neutral-colored base to each cheekbone. The camera crew began sighting in on him as he worked the cream into his skin, down from the bone and away.

"Need any help?" Cornut looked up and greeted his producer.

"No, thanks." He brought the corners of his eyebrows down a fraction of an inch.

The clock was ticking off half-seconds. Cornut penciled in age-lines (that was the price you paid for being a full professor at thirty) and brushed on the lip color. He leaned forward to examine himself more closely in the mirror, but the producer stopped him. "Just a minute—Dammit, man, not so much red!"

The cameraman turned a dial; in the monitor, Cornut's image appeared a touch paler, a touch greener.

"That's better. All done, professor?"

Cornut wiped his fingers on a tissue and set the golden wig on his head. "All done," he said, rising just as the minute hand touched the hour of ten.

From a grill at the top of the screen that dominated the front of the studio came the sounds of his theme music, muted for the studio audience. Cornut took his place in front of the class, bowed, nodded, smiled, and kicked at the pedal of the prompter until he found his place.

The class was full. He had more than a hundred students physically present. Cornut liked a large flesh-and-blood enrollment—because he was a traditionalist, but even more because he could tell from their faces how well he was getting across. This class was one of his favorites. They responded to his mood, but without ever overdoing. They didn't laugh too loud when he made a conventional academic joke, they didn't cough or murmur. They never distracted the attention of the huger, wider broadcast audience from himself.

Cornut looked over the class while the announcer was finishing his remarks to the broadcast watchers. He saw Egerd, looking upset and irritable about something, whispering to the girl from the faculty dining room. What was her name? Locille. Lucky fellow, Cornut thought absently to himself, and then the Binomial Theorem entered his mind—it was never far away—and displaced everything else.

"Good morning," he said, "and let's get to work. Today we're going to take up the relationship of Pascal's Triangle to the Binomial Theorem." A sting of organ music rode in under his words. Behind him, on the monitor, the symbols $p+q$ appeared in letters of golden fire. "I presume you all remember what the Binomial Theorem is—unless you've been cutting your classes." Very small laugh—actually a sort of sub-aural grunt, just about what the very small jocularity deserved. "The expansion of p plus q is, of course, its square, cube, fourth power and so on." Behind him an invisible hand began multiplying $p+q$ by itself in bright gold. "P plus q squared is p-squared plus two pq plus q-squared. P plus q cubed—" The writer in gold noted the sum as he spoke: $p^3 + 3p^2q + 3pq^2 + q^3$.

"That's simple enough, isn't it?" He paused; then, deadpan, "Well then, how come Sticky Dick says fifteen per cent of you missed it in the last test?" A warmer giggle, punctuated with a couple of loud, embarrassed hee-haws from the back. Oh, they were a very fine class.

The letters and numbers wiped themselves from the screen and a little red-faced comic cartoon figure of a bricklayer dropped into view and began building a pyramid of bricks:

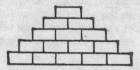

"Now, forget about the theorem for a moment—that won't be hard for some of you." (Small giggle which he rode over.) "Consider Pascal's Triangle. We build it just like a brick wall, only—Hold it a minute there, friend." The cartoon bricklayer paused, and looked curiously out at the audience. "Only we don't start from the bottom. We build it from the top down." The cartoon bricklayer did a comic pratfall in astonishment. Then, shrugging, he got up, erased the old wall with a sweep of his trowel, hung a brick in space and began building a triangle under it.

"And we don't do it with bricks," added Cornut. "We do it with numbers."

The bricklayer straightened up, kicked the wall off the screen and followed after it, pausing just at the rim of visibility to stick his tongue out at Cornut. The monitor went to a film with live models, cartwheeling into view along the banks of seats of the university's football stadium, each model carrying a placard with a number, arranging themselves in a Pascal Triangle:

$$
\begin{array}{ccccccccc}
 & & & & 1 & & 1 & & & \\
 & & & 1 & & 2 & & 1 & & \\
 & & 1 & & 3 & & 3 & & 1 & \\
 & 1 & & 4 & & 6 & & 4 & & 1 \\
1 & & 5 & & 10 & & 10 & & 5 & & 1
\end{array}
$$

Cornut turned to relish the construction Pascal had first written down, centuries before. "You will note," he said, "that each number is the sum of the two terms nearest in the line above it. The Pascal Triangle is more than a pretty pattern. It represents—" He had them. Their faces were rapt. The class was going very well.

Cornut picked up the ivory-tipped pointer that lay on his desk, clustered with the ceremonial desk furnishings of the instructor—paper cutter, shears, pencils; all there for appearance—and with the aid of every audio-visual help possible to man, began explaining to three million viewers the relation between Pascal's Triangle and the binomial distribution.

Every line on Cornut's face, every word, every posturing ballet dancer or animated digit that showed itself on the monitor behind him, was caught in the tubes of the cameras, converted into high-frequency pulses and hurled out at the world.

Cornut had more than a hundred live watchers—the cream; the chosen ones who were allowed to attend University *in person*—but his viewers altogether numbered three million. In the relay tower at Port Monmouth a senior shift engineer named Sam Gensel watched with concentrated attention as across the dimpled tummies of the five girls in the fourth line of the Pascal Triangle electronics superimposed the symbols

$$p^4 + 4p^3q + 6p^2q^2 + 4pq^3 + q^4$$

He was not interested in the astonishing fact that the signs of the five terms in the expansion of $(p + q)^4$ were 1, 4, 6. 4 and 1—the same as the numbers in the fourth line of the triangle—but he cared very much that the image was a trifle fuzzy. He twisted a vernier, scowled, turned it back; threw switches that called in an alternate circuit, and was rewarded by a crisper, clearer image. At some relay point a tube was failing. He picked up the phone to call the maintenance crew.

The crisper, clearer signal was beamed up to the handiest television-relay satellite and showered back down on the world. On the Sandy Hook texas a boy named Roger Hoskins, smelling seriously of fish, paused by the door of his room to watch. He did not care about mathematics, but he was a faithful viewer; his sister was in the class, and Mom was always grateful when he could tell her that he'd caught a glimpse of their very fortunate, very seldom encountered daughter. In a crèche over lower Manhattan three toddlers munched fibrous crackers and watched; the harried nursery teacher had discovered that the moving colors kept them quiet. On the twenty-fifth floor of a tenement on Staten Island a monocar motorman named Frank Moran sat in front of his set while Cornut reviewed Pascal's thesis. Moran did not get much benefit from it. He had just come off the night shift. He was asleep.

There were many of them, the accidental or disinterested dialers-in. But there were more, there were thousands, there were uncounted hundreds of thousands who were following the proceedings with absorption.

For education was something very precious indeed.

The thirty thousand at the University were the lucky

ones; they had passed the tests, stiffer every year. Not one out of a thousand passed those tests; it wasn't only a matter of intelligence, it was a matter of having the talents that could make a University education fruitful—in terms of society. For the world had to work. The world was too big to be idle. The land that had fed three billion people now had to feed twelve billion.

Cornut's television audience could, if it wished, take tests and accumulate credits. That was what Sticky Dick was for; electronically it graded papers, supplied term averages and awarded diplomas for students no professor ever saw. Almost always the credits led nowhere. But to those trapped in dreary production or drearier caretaker jobs for society, the hope was important. There was a young man named Max Steck, for example, who had already made a small contribution to the theory of normed rings. It was not enough. Sticky Dick said he would not justify a career in mathematics. He was trapped as a sexwriter, for Sticky Dick's analyzers had found him prurient-minded and creative. There were thousands of Max Stecks.

Then there was Charles Bingham. He was a reactor hand at the 14th Street generating plant. Mathematics might help him, in time, become a supervising engineer. It also might not—the candidates for that job were already lined up fifty deep. But there were half a million Charles Binghams.

Sue-Ann Flood was the daughter of a farmer. Her father drove a helipopper, skimming the ploughed fields, seeding, spraying, fertilizing, and he knew that the time she put in on college-level studies would not help her gain admittance to the University. Sue-Ann knew it too; Sticky Dick measured abilities and talents, not knowledge. But she was only fourteen years old. She hoped. There were more than two million like Sue-Ann, and every one of them knew that all the others would be disappointed.

Those, the millions of them, were the invisible audience who watched Master Cornut's tiny image on a cathode screen. But there were others. One watched from Bogotà and one from Buenos Aires. One in Saskatchewan said, You goofed this morning, and one flying high over the

Rockies said, Can't we try him now? And one was propped on incredibly soft pillows in front of a set not more than a quarter of a mile from Cornut himself; and he said, It's worth a try. The son of a bitch is getting in my hair.

It was not the easiest task ever given man, to explain the relationship between the Pascal Triangle and the Binomial Distribution, but Cornut was succeeding. Master Carl's little mnemonic jingles helped, and what helped most of all was the utter joy Cornut took in it all. It was, after all, his life. As he led the class, he felt again the wonder he himself had felt, sitting in a class like this one. He hardly heard the buzz from the class as he put his pointer down to gesture, and blindly picked it up again, still talking. Teaching mathematics was a kind of hypnosis for him, an intense, gut-wrenching absorption that had gripped him from the time of his first math class. That was what Sticky Dick had measured, and that was why Cornut was a full professor at thirty. It was a wonder that so strange a thing as a number should exist in the first place, rivalled only by the greater wonder that they should perform so obediently the work of mankind.

The class buzzed and whispered.

It struck Cornut cloudily that they were whispering more than usual.

He looked up, absent-mindedly. There was an itch at the base of his throat. He scratched it with the tip of the pointer, half distracted from the point he was trying to make. But the taped visual aids on the screen were timed just so and he could not falter; he picked up the thread of what he was saying; itch and buzz faded out of his mind. . . .

Then he faltered again.

Something was wrong. The class was buzzing louder. The students in the first row were staring at him with a unanimous, unprecedented expression. The itch returned compellingly. He scratched it; it still itched; he dug at it with the pointer.

—No. Not with the pointer. Funny, he thought, there was the pointer on his desk.

Suddenly his throat hurt very much.

"Master Cornut, stop!" screamed someone—a girl. . . . Tardily he recognized the voice, Locille's voice, as she leaped to her feet, and half the class with her. His throat was a quick deep pain, like fire. A warm tickling thread slipped across his chest—blood! From his throat! He stared at the thing in his hand, and it was not the pointer at all but the letter-opener, steel and sharp. Confused and panicked, he wheeled to gaze at the monitor. There was his own face, over a throat that bore a narrow trickling slash of blood!

Three million viewers gasped. Half the studio class was boiling toward him, Egerd and the girl ahead of the rest. "Easy, sir! Here, let me—" That was Egerd, with a tissue, pressing it against the wound. "You'll be all right, sir! It's only—But it was close!"

Close. . . . He had all but cut his jugular vein in two, right in front of his class and the watching world. The murderer inside his head was getting very strong and sure, to brave the light of day.

Chapter Four

Cornut was literally a marked man now. He had a neat white sterile bandage on his throat, and the medics had cheerfully assured him that when the bandage was gone there would be a handsome scar. They demanded that he stay around for a complete psycho-medical checkup. He said no. They said Would you rather be dead? He said he wasn't going to die. They said How can you be sure? But, as it turned out, the clinic was not going to be free for that sort of thing for a couple of hours, and he fought his way free. He was extremely angry at the medics for annoying him, at himself for being such a fool, at Egerd for staunching the flow of his blood, at Locille for seeing it . . . his patience was exhausted with the world.

Cornut strode like a blinkered cart-horse to the Math Tower gym, looking neither left nor right, though he knew what he would see. Eyes. The eyes of everyone on the campus, looking at him and whispering. He found an undergraduate who was reasonably willing to mind his own business (the boy only looked slightly doubtful when Cornut chose his épée, but one glimpse of Cornut's face made his own turn into opaque stone), and they two fenced for a furious half-hour. The medics had told Cornut to be sure to rest. Winded and muscles aching, he returned to his room to do so.

He spent a long, thoughtful afternoon lying on his bed and looking at the ceiling, but nothing came of it. The whole thing was simply too irritating to be borne.

Medics or not, at a quarter of five he put on a clean shirt to keep his appointment at the faculty tea.

The tea was a sort of official send-off to the University's Field Expedition. Attendance was compulsory, especially for those who, like Cornut, were supposed to make the trip; but that was not why he was there. He considered it to be his last good chance to get off the list.

There were three hundred persons in the huge, vaulted room. The University conspicuously consumed space; it was a tradition, like the marginal pencilings in all the books in the library. Every one of the three hundred glanced once quickly at Cornut as he came in, then away—some with a muffled laugh, some with sympathy, the worst with an unnatural lack of any expression at all. So much for the grapevine. Damn them, Cornut thought bitterly, you'd think no professor ever tried to commit suicide before. He couldn't help overhearing some of the whispers.

"And that's the *seventh* time. It's because he's *desperate* to be department head and old Carl *won't* step down."

"Esmeralda! You know you're making that up!"

His face flaming, Cornut walked briskly past the little knot. It was like a fakir's bed of coals; every step seemed to crisp him. But there were other things to gossip about at the tea, and some of the captured fragments of talk did not concern him at all.

"—want us to get along with a fourteen-year-old trevatron. You know what the Chinas have? Six brand-new ones. *And* coin silver for the windings!"

"Yes, but there's two billion of them. Per capita we stack up pretty—"

Cornut halted in the middle of the drinking, eating, talking, surging mass and looked about for Master Carl. He caught sight of him. The department head was paying his respects to a queer-looking, ancient figure—St. Cyr, the President of the University. Cornut was startled. St. Cyr was an old man and by his appearance a sick one; it was rare to see him at a faculty tea. Still, this one was special—and anyway, that could make it a lot easier to get off the list.

Cornut pushed his way toward them, past a stocky drunk from humanities who was whispering ribaldly to a patient student waitress, and threaded his way through a group of anatomists from the med school.

"Notice what decent cadavers we've been getting lately? It hasn't been this good since the last shooting war. Of course, they're not much good except for geriatrics, but that's selective euthanasia for you."

"Will you watch what you're doing with that Martini?"

Cornut made his way slowly toward Master Carl and President St. Cyr. The closer he got, the easier it was to move. There were fewer people at St. Cyr's end of the room; he was the central figure of the gathering, but the guests did not cluster around him; that's the kind of a man he was.

The kind of a man St. Cyr was was this: He was the ugliest man in the room.

There were others who were in no way handsome—old, or fat, or sick. St. Cyr was something special. His face was an artifact of ugliness. Deep old scars made a net across his face like the flimsy cloth that holds a cheese. Surgery? No one knew. He had always had them. And his skin was a cyanotic blue.

Master Greenlease (physical chem) and Master Wahl (anthropology) were there, Wahl because he was too drunk to care who he spoke to, no doubt; Greenlease because Carl had him by the elbow and would not let him go. St. Cyr nodded four times at Cornut, like a pendulum. "Nice wea-ther," he said, tolling it like a clock.

"Yes, it is, sir. Excuse me. Carl—"

St. Cyr lifted the hand that hung by his side and laid it limply in Cornut's hand—it was his version of a handshake. He opened his seamed mouth and gave the series of unvoiced glottal stops that were his version of a chuckle. "It will be heav-y weath-er for Mas-ter Wahl," he said, spacing out the syllables like an articulate metronome. It was his version of a joke.

Cornut gave him a waxen smile and a small waxen laugh. The reference was to the fact that Wahl, too, was scheduled to go on the Field Expedition. Cornut didn't think that was funny—not as far as he himself was concerned, anyway—not when he had so many other things on his mind.

"Carl," he said, "excuse me." But Master Carl had other things on his mind; he was badgering Greenlease for information about molecular structure, heaven knew why. And also St. Cyr had not released his hand.

Cornut grumbled internally and waited. Wahl was giggling over some involved faculty joke to which St. Cyr was listening like a judge. Cornut spared himself the annoyance of listening to it and thought about St. Cyr. Queer old duck, of course. That was where you started. You could account for some of the queerness by, say, a bad heart. That would be the reason for the blueness. But what would be the reason for not having it operated on?

And then, what about the other things? The deadpan expression. The lifeless voice, with its firmly pronounced terminal "ings" and words without a stress syllable anywhere? St. Cyr talked like a clockwork man. Or a deaf one?

But again, what would be the reason for a man allowing himself to be deaf?

Especially a man who owned a University, *including* an 800-bed teaching hospital.

Wahl at last noticed that Cornut was present and punched his shoulder—cordially, Cornut decided, after thought. "Committed any good suicides lately, boy?" He hiccoughed. "Don't blame you. Your fault, President, you know, dragging him off to Tahiti with us. He doesn't *like* Tahiti."

Cornut said, with control, "The Field Expedition isn't going to Tahiti."

Wahl shrugged. "The way us anthropologists look at it, one gook island is like another gook island." He even made a joke of his specialty! Cornut was appalled.

On the other hand, St. Cyr seemed neither to notice nor to mind. He flopped his hand free of Cornut's and rested it casually on Wahl's weaving shoulder. The other hand held the full highball glass which, Cornut had observed, always remained full. St. Cyr did not drink or smoke (not even tobacco), nor had Cornut ever seen him give a second look to a pretty girl. "Lis-ten," he said in his slow-march voice, turning Wahl to face Carl and the chemist. "This is in-ter-est-ing."

* * *

Carl was oblivious of the President, of Cornut, of every-thing except the fact that the chemist by his side knew something that Carl himself wanted to know. The informa-tion was there; he went after it. "I don't seem to make myself clear. What I want to know, Greenlease, is how I can visualize the exact *structure* of a molecule. Do you fol-low me? For example, what *color* is it?"

The chemist looked uncomfortably at St. Cyr, but St. Cyr was apparently absorbed. "Well," he said. "Uh. The con-cept of color doesn't apply. Light waves are too long."

"Ah! I see." Carl was fascinated. "Well, what about the shape? I've seen those tinker-toy constructions. The atoms are little balls and they're held together with plastic rods— I suppose they represent connecting force. Are they any-thing like the real thing?"

"Not much. The connecting force is real enough, but you can't see it—or maybe you could, at that" (Greenlease, like most of the faculty members present, had had a bit more than enough; he was not of a temper to try to inter-pret molecular forces in tinker-toy terms for professors who, whatever their status in Number Theory, were physical-chemical idiots) "if, that is, you could see the atoms in the first place. One is no more impossible than the other. But the connecting force would not look like a rod, any more than the gravitation that holds the moon to the earth would look like a rod. . . . Let's see. . . . Do you know what I mean by the word 'valence'? No. Well, do you know enough atomic theory to know what part is played by the number of electrons in— Or, look at it a different way." He paused. By his expression, he was getting seri-ously annoyed, in a way he considered unjust—like an ivory hunter who, carrying a .400 Express in his crooked arm, cannot quite see how to cope with the attack of a hungry mosquito. He seemed on the point of reviewing atomic structure back through Bohr and well on the way to Democritus. "I'll tell you what," he said at last, "stop around tomorrow if you can. I have some plates made un-der the electron microscope."

"Oh, thank you!" cried Carl with enthusiasm. "Tomorrow—but tomorrow I'll be off on this con—" he smiled at St. Cyr—"tomorrow I'll be with the Field Expedition. Well, as soon as I get back, Greenlease. Don't forget." He warmly shook hands as the chemist took his leave.

Cornut hissed angrily, "That's what I want to talk to you about."

Carl looked startled but pleased. "I didn't know you were interested in my little experiments, Cornut. That was quite fascinating. I've always thought of a molecule of silver nitrate, for example, as being black or silvery. Perhaps that's where my work has gone wrong. Greenlease says—"

"No, I'm not talking about that. I mean the Field Expedition. I *can't* go."

An observer a yard away would have thought that all of St. Cyr's attention was on Wahl; he had lost interest in the dialogue between Carl and Greenlease minutes before. But the old head turned like a parabolic mirror. The faded blue eyes radared in on Cornut. The slow metronome ticked, "You must go, Cor-nut."

"Must go? Of course you must go. Good heavens, Cornut—Don't mind him, President. Certainly he'll go."

"But I have all the Wolgren to get through—"

"And then a su-i-cide to com-mit." The muscles at the corner of the mouth tried to twitch the blue lips upward, to show that it was a pleasantry.

But Cornut was nettled. "Sir, I don't intend to—"

"You did not in-tend to this morn-ing."

Carl interrupted. "Cornut, be quiet. President, that was distressing, of course. I've had a full report on it, and I believe we can pass it off as an accident. Perhaps it was an accident. I don't know. It would have been quite easy to pick up the paper-knife in error."

Cornut said, "But—"

"In an-y case, he must go."

"Naturally, President. You understand that, don't you, Cornut?"

"But—"

"You will take the ad-vance plane, please. I want you to be there when I ar-rive."

"Very well. It's settled, then."

"But—" said Cornut, but he was destined never to get a word deeper into that thought; through the mill of faculty came a man and a woman with the tense, nervous bearing of Townies. The woman carried a photo-taper; the man was a reporter from one of the nets.

"President St. Cyr? Yes, of course. Thanks for inviting us. Naturally, we'll have a whole crew here when your expedition gets back, but I wonder if we can't get a few photographs now. As I understand it, you've located seven aboriginals. Seven? I see. It's a whole tribe, then, but seven are being brought back here. And who is the head of the expedition? Oh, naturally. Millie, will you be sure to get President St. Cyr?"

The reporter's thumb was on the trigger of his voice-taper, getting down the fact that nine faculty members were going to bring back the seven aborigines, that the expedition would leave, in two planes, at nine o'clock that night, so as to arrive at their destination in early morning, local time; and that the benefits to anthropological research would surely be beyond calculation.

Cornut drew Master Carl aside. "I don't want to go! What the hell does this have to do with mathematics, anyhow?"

"Now, please, Cornut. You heard the President. It has nothing to do with mathematics, no, but it is purely a ceremonial function and a good deal of an honor. At the present time, you should not refuse it. You can see that some rumors of your, uh, accidents have reached him. Don't cause friction."

"What about the Wolgren? What about my, uh, accidents? Even here I nearly kill myself, and I'm all set up. What will I do without Egerd?"

"I'll be with you."

"No, Carl!"

Carl said, speaking very clearly, "You are going." The eyes were star-sapphires.

Cornut studied the eyes for a moment, and then gave up. When Carl got that expression and that tone of voice, it meant that argument served no further useful purpose.

Since Cornut loved the old man, he always stopped arguing at that point.

"I'm going," he said. But the expression on his face would have soured wine.

Cornut packed—it took five minutes—and went back to the clinic to see if diagnostic space was free. It was not. He was cutting his time very close—take-off for the first plane was in less than an hour—but mulishly he took a seat in the reception room. Stolidly he did not look at the clock.

When the examination room was available things went briskly. His vital statistics were machine-measured and machine-studied, his blood spectrum was machine-chromatographed, automatically the examining table was tipped so that he could step off, and as he dressed a photoelectric eye behind his hanging garments glanced at him, opened the door to the outside corridor and said, "Thank you. Wait in the outer office, please," from a machine-operated tape.

Master Carl, in a fluster, found him waiting.

"Good God, boy! Do you know the plane's about to take off? And the President *specially* said we were to go in the first plane. Come on! I've a scooter waiting. . . ."

"Sorry."

"Sorry? What the devil do you mean, sorry? Come!"

Cornut said flatly, "I agreed to go. I will go. But, as there is some feeling, shared by yourself, that the medics can help keep me from killing myself, I do not intend to leave this building until they tell me what I must do. I am waiting for the results of my examination now."

Master Carl said, "Oh." He glanced at the clock on the wall. "I see," he said. He sat down beside Cornut thoughtfully.

Suddenly he grinned. "All right, boy. The President can't argue with that."

Cornut relaxed. He said, "Well, you go ahead, Carl. No reason for both of us to get in trouble—"

"Trouble!" Master Carl seemed quite gay. Cornut realized that it had finally occurred to the house master that this trip was a sort of vacation; he was practicing for a holiday mood. "Why should there be any trouble? You have a good reason for being tardy. I, too, have a good reason for waiting for you. After all, the President urged me to bring the Wolgren analysis along. He's quite interested, you know. And as I did not see it in your room, I suppose it is in your bags; therefore I will wait for your bags."

Cornut protested, "But it isn't anywhere near finished!"

Carl actually winked. "Now, do you suppose he'll know the difference? Be flattered that he is interested enough to pretend to look at it!"

Cornut said grudgingly, "Well, all right. How the devil did he hear about it in the first place?"

"I told him, of course. I—I've had occasion to discuss you with him a good deal, these past few days." Carl's expression lost some of its glow. "Cornut," he said severely, "we can't let this go on, can we? You must regularize your life. Take a woman."

Cornut exploded, "Master Carl! You have no *right* to interfere in my personal affairs!"

"Trust me, boy," the old man wheedled. "This thing with Egerd is only a makeshift. A thirty-day marriage would surely see you through the worst of it, wouldn't it?"

Three weeks, thought Cornut, diverted.

"And, truly, you need a wife. It is bad for a man to go through life alone," he explained.

Cornut snapped, "How about you?"

"I'm older. You're young. How long is it since you've had a wife."

Cornut was obstinately silent.

"You see? There are many lovely young girls in the University. They would be proud. Any of them."

Cornut did not want his mind to roam the corridors that had just been opened for it, but it did.

"Besides, you will have her with you at all the dangerous times. You won't need Egerd."

Cornut's mind ran back quickly and began to trace a more familiar, less attractive maze. "I'll think about it," he said at last, just as the medic came in with his report, a couple of boxes of pills and a sheaf of papers. The report was negative, all down the line. The pills? They were just in case, said the medic; they couldn't hurt, they might help.

And the sheaf of papers. . . . The top one said: *Confidential. Tentative. Studies of Suicidal Tendencies in Faculty Members.*

Cornut covered it with his hand, interrupted the medic as he was about to explain the delay in getting the dossiers for him and cried, "Let's get a move on, Carl! We can still make that plane."

But, as it turned out, they couldn't.

As fast as the scooter would go, they got to the aircraft park just in time to see the first section of the Field Expedition lift itself off the ground with a great whistling roar on its VTO jets.

Much to Cornut's surprise, Master Carl was not upset. "Oh, well," he said, "we had our reasons. It isn't as though we were *arbitrarily* late. And anyway——" he allowed himself another wink, the second in a quarter of an hour—— "this gives us a chance to ride in the President's private plane, eh? Real living for us of the underprivileged class!" He even opened his mouth to chuckle, but he didn't do it, or if he did the sound was not heard. Overhead there was a gruff giant's cough and a bright spray of flame. They looked up. Flame, flame all over the heavens, falling in great white droplets to the earth.

"My God," said Cornut softly, "and that was our plane."

Chapter Five

"Nothing loath," said Master Carl thoughtfully, "I kissed your concubine." He squinted out the window of the jet, savoring the sentence. It was good. Yes. But was it perfect?

A towering cumulo-nimbus, far below, caught his attention and distracted him. He sighed. He didn't feel like working. Apparently everyone else in the jet was asleep. Or pretending to be. Only St. Cyr, way up front, propped on pneumatic pillows in the semicircular lounge, looked as much awake as he ever did. But it was better not to talk to St. Cyr. Carl was aware that most conversations involving himself turned, sooner or later, to either his private researches or to Number Theory. As he knew more about either than anyone else alive, they wound up as lectures. That was no good with St. Cyr. He had made it clear long ago that he was not interested in being instructed by the instructors he hired.

Also he was in a bad mood.

It was odd, thought Master Carl, less in resentment than in a spirit of scientific inquiry, but St. Cyr had been quite furious with Cornut and himself for no good reason. It could not have been for missing the first plane—if they'd caught it, they would have died, just like its crew and the four graduate students it carried. But St. Cyr had been furious, the tick-tock voice hoarse and breathless, the hairless eyebrows almost scowling. Master Carl took his eyes away from the window and abandoned the question of St. Cyr. Let him sulk. Carl didn't like problems that had no solution. *Nothing loath, I kissed your concubine.* But mightn't it be better to stick to songwriting?

He became conscious of a beery breath on the back of his neck.

"I'm glad you're awake, Wahl," he said, turning, his face inches away from the hung-over face of the anthropologist. "Let me have your opinion, please. Which is easier to remember: 'Nothing loath, I kissed your concubine.' Or, 'Last digit? O, a potential square!' "

Wahl shuddered. "For God's sake. I just woke up."

"Why, I don't think that matters. It might help. The whole idea is to present the mnemonic in a form that is available under any conditions—including," he said delicately, "a digestive upset." He rotated his chair to face Wahl, flipping through his notebook to display a scribbled page. "Can you read that? The idea, you see, is to provide a handy recognition feature for quick factoring of aliquot numbers. Now, you know, of course, that all squares can end in only one of six digits. No square can end in two, three, seven or eight. So my first idea—I'm still not sure that I wasn't on the right track—was to use, 'No, quantity not squared.' You see the utility, I'm sure. Two letters in the first word, 'no.' Eight letters in 'quantity,' three in 'not' and seven in 'squared.' It's easy to remember, I think, and it's self-defining. I consider that a major advantage."

"Oh, it is," said Wahl.

"But," Carl went on, "it's negative. Also there is the chance that 'no' can be misread for 'nought' or 'nothing'— meaning zero. So I tried the reverse approach. A square *can* end in zero, one, four, five, six or nine. Letting the ejaculative 'O' stand for 'zero,' I then wrote: 'Last digit? O, a potential square.' Four, five, zero, one, nine and six—you see that. Excuse me. I'm so used to lecturing to undergraduates that sometimes I tend to overexplain. But, although that has a lot to recommend it, it doesn't have—well— *yumph*." He smiled with a touch of embarrassment. "So, just on an inspiration, I came up with 'Nothing loath, I kissed your concubine.' Rather mnemonic, at least?"

"It's all of that, Carl," agreed Wahl, rubbing his temples. "Say, where's Cornut?"

"You realize that the 'nothing,' again, is 'zero.' "

"Oh, there he is. Hey, Cornut!"

"Be quiet! Let the boy sleep!" Carl was jolted out of his concentration. He leaned forward to see into the wing-backed seat ahead of him and was gratified to see that Cornut was still snoring faintly.

Wahl burst into a laugh, stopped abruptly with a look of surprise and clutched his head. After a moment he said, "You take care of him like he was your baby."

"There is no need to take that sort of—"

"Some baby! I've heard of accident-prones, but this one's fantastic. Not even Joe Btfsk wrecks planes that he ought to be in but isn't!"

Master Carl bit back his instinctive rejoinder, paused to regain his temper and pondered an appropriate remark. He was saved the trouble. The jet lurched slightly and the distant thunderheads began to wheel toward the horizon. It wasn't the clouds, of course. It was the jet swinging in for a landing, vectored by unseen radar. It was only a very small motion, but it sent Wahl lurching frantically to the washroom and it woke Master Cornut. Carl leaped up as soon as he saw the younger man move, standing over him until his eyes were open. "Are you all right?" he demanded at once.

Cornut blinked, yawned and stretched his muscles.

"—I guess so. Yes."

"We're about to land." There was relief in Carl's voice. He had not expected anything to happen. Why should it? But there had been the chance that something might. . . . "I can get you a cup of coffee from the galley."

"All right—no. Never mind. We'll be down in a minute."

Below them the island was slipping back and forth slant-wise, like a falling leaf—a leaf that was falling upward, at least in their eyes, because it was growing enormously fast. Wahl came out of the washroom and stared at the houses.

"Dirty hovels," he growled. It was raining beneath their plane—no, around them—no, over. They were through the patchy cloud layer, and the "hovels" Wahl had glimpsed were clear beneath. Out of the patches of clouds rain was falling.

"Cum-u-lus of or-o-graph-ic or-i-gin," said St. Cyr's un-

inflected voice, next to Master Carl's ear. "There is always cloud at the is-land. I hope the storm does not dis-
turb you."

Master Wahl said, "It disturbs *me*."

They landed, the jet's wheels screaming thinly as they
touched the wet concrete runway. A short, dark man with
an umbrella ran out and, holding it protectively over St.
Cyr's head, escorted them to the administration building,
though the rain had nearly stopped.

It was evident that St. Cyr's reputation and standing
were working for them. The whole party was passed
through customs under seal; the brown-skinned inspectors
didn't even touch the bags. One of them prowled briefly
around the stack of the Field Expedition's luggage, carrying a portable voice-taper. "Research instruments," he
chanted, singsong, and the machine clacked out its entry.
"Research instruments. . . . Research instruments."

Master Carl interrupted, "That's my personal bag! There
aren't any research instruments in it."

"Excuse," said the inspector politely; but he went right
on with calling every bag "research instruments"; the only
concession he made to Carl's correction was to lower his
voice.

It was, to Master Carl, an offensive performance, and
he had it in his mind to speak to someone in authority
about it, too. Research instruments! They had nothing resembling a research instrument to their names, unless you
counted the collection of handcuffs Master Wahl had
brought along, just in case the aboriginals were obstinate
about coming along. He thought of bringing it up to St.
Cyr, but the President was talking to Cornut. Carl didn't
want to interrupt. He had no objection to interrupting Cornut, of course, but interrupting the President of the University was something else again.

Wahl said, "What's that over there? Looks like a bar,
doesn't it? How about a drink?"

Carl shook his head frostily and stomped out into the
street. He was not enjoying his trip, and it was a pity, he
thought, because he realized that he had been rather look-

ing forward to it. One needed a change of scene from the Halls of Academe every once in a while. Otherwise one tended to become stuffy and provincial, to lose contact with the mass of humanity outside the University walls. For that reason Carl had made it a practice, through the thirty-odd years since he began to teach, at least once in every year to accept or invent some task that would bring him in contact with the non-academic world. . . . They had all been quite as distasteful as this one, but since Master Carl had never realized this before it hadn't mattered.

He stood in a doorway, out of the fresh hot sun, looking down a broad street. The "filthy hovels" were not filthy at all; it was only Wahl's bad temper that had said that, not his reason. Why, they were quite clean, Master Carl marveled. Not *attractive.* And not *large.* But they did have a quaint and not too repulsive appearance. They were clumsy prefabs of some sort of pressed fiber, plastic bonded—a local product most likely, Master Carl diagnosed; pulp from palm trees had gone into the making of them.

A roadable helipopper whirred, dipped, settled in the street before him, folded its vanes and rolled up to the entrance of the building where Carl was standing. The driver jumped out, ran around the side of the craft and opened the door.

Now, that was odd.

The driver acted as though the Empress Catherine was about to set foot on the soil she ruled, and yet what came out of the popper was no great lady but what seemed, at least at first glance, like a fourteen-year-old blonde. Carl pursed his thin lips and squinted into the bright sun. Curious, he marveled, the creature was waving at him!

The creature said, in the brassy voice of no fourteen-year-old, "You're Carl. Come on, get in. I've been waiting for you people for an hour and a half, and I've got to get clear back to Rio de Janeiro tonight. And hurry up that old goat St. Cyr, will you?"

To Carl's surprise, St. Cyr didn't strike the child dead. He came out and greeted her as affably as his corpse's voice could be made to sound, and he sat beside her in the front seat of the popper in the wordless association of old friends. But it wasn't the only surprising thing. Looking a little more closely at the "girl" was a kind of surprise too, because a girl she was not. She was a painted grandmother with a face-lift, Bermuda shorts and a blonde bob! Why couldn't the woman grow old gracefully, like St. Cyr, or for that matter like Master Carl himself?

All the same, if St. Cyr knew her she couldn't be *all* bad, and anyway Carl had something else bothering him. Cornut was missing.

The helipopper was already on the bounce. Carl stood up. "Wait! We're missing someone." No one was listening. The grandmother in shorts was chattering away in St. Cyr's ear, her voice queer and muffled under the sound of the sequenced rockets that whirled the vanes. "President St. Cyr! Please have this pilot turn back." But St. Cyr didn't even turn his head.

Master Carl was worried. He pressed his face to the window, looking back toward the native town, but already it was too far to see anything.

Of course, he told himself, there was no danger. There were no hostile natives anywhere in the world. Lightning would not strike. Cornut was as safe as if he were in his own bed.

—Exactly as safe, his own mind assured him sternly, but no safer.

But the fact of the matter was that Cornut was drinking a glass of beer at a dusty sidewalk table. For the first time in—was it forever?—his mind was at rest.

He was not thinking of the anomalies a statistical census had discovered in Wolgren's Distributive Law. He was not thinking of Master Carl's suggestion about term marriage, or even about the annoying interruption that this expedition represented. It did not seem quite as much of an annoyance, now that he was here. It was so *quiet*. It was like the fragrance of a new flower. He tested it experimentally with his ears and decided that, though odd, it was pleasant. A few hundred yards away some aircraft chugged into the sky, destroying the quiet, but the odd thing was that the quiet returned.

Cornut now had the chance he had been looking for since leaving the clinic, the night before and ten thousand miles away. He ordered another beer from the sallow waitress and reached into his pocket for the sheaf of reports that medic had handed him.

There were more of them than he had expected.

How many cases had the analyst said had occurred at their own University? Fifteen or so. But here were more than a hundred case histories. He scanned the summaries quickly and discovered that the problem extended beyond the University—cases from other schools, cases from outside university circles entirely. There seemed to have been a rash of them among Government employees. There was a concentration of twelve on the staff of a single television network.

He read the meaningless names and studied the almost as meaningless facts. One of the TV men had succeeded in short-circuiting a supposedly foolproof electric mattress eight times before he managed to die of it. He was happily married and about to be promoted.

"Ancora birra?" Cornut jumped, but it was only the waitress.

"All right—wait." There was no sense in these continual interruptions. "Bring me a couple of bottles and leave them."

The sun was setting, the clouds overhead powerless to shield the island from its heat, as the horizon was bare blue. It was hot, and the beer was making him sleepy.

It occurred to him that he really ought to be making an effort to catch up with the rest of the party. It was only chance that they had gone off without him, probably Master Carl would be furious.

It also occurred to him that it was comfortable here.

On an island as small as this, he would have no trouble finding them when he wanted them. Meanwhile he still had some beer, and he had all these reports, and it did not seem particularly disturbing to him that, though he read

them all from beginning to end, he still found none where
the course of the syndrome had taken more than ten weeks
to reach its climax. Ten weeks. He had twenty days left.

Master Carl demanded, "Turn back! You can't leave the
poor boy to die!"

St. Cyr whinnied surprisingly. The woman shrilled,
"He'll be all right. What's the matter, you want to spoil his
fun? Give the kid a chance to kill himself, will you?"

Carl took a deep breath. Then he started again, but it
was no use, they insisted on treating the matter lightly. He
slumped back in his seat and stared out the window.

The helipopper came down in front of a building larger
than most of the prefabs. It had glass in the windows, and
bars over the glass. The blonde leaped up like a stick doll
and shrilled, "Everybody out! Hop to it, now, I haven't got
all day."

Carl morosely followed her into the building. He wondered how, even for a moment and at a distance, he had
taken her for a child. Bright blue eyes under blonde hair,
yes; but the eyes were bloodshot, the hair a yellow mop
draped on a skull. Loathing her, and worrying about Cornut, he climbed a flight of steps, went through a barred
door and looked into a double-barred room.

"The aborigines," St. Cyr said in his toneless voice.

It was the local jail, and it had only one cell. And that
cell was packed with a dozen or more short, olive-skinned,
ragged men and women. There were no children. No children, thought Master Carl petulantly, but they had been
promised an entire population to select from! These were
all *old*. The youngest of them seemed at least a hundred. . . .

"Ob-serve them care-ful-ly," came St. Cyr's slow voice.
"There is not a per-son there more than fif-ty years old."

Master Carl jumped. Mind-reading again! He thought
with a touch of envy how wonderful it must be to be so
wise, so experienced, so all-understanding that one could
know, as St. Cyr knew, what another person was thinking
before he spoke it aloud. It was the sort of wisdom he
hoped his subordinates would attribute to him, and they
didn't; and it hurt to see that in St. Cyr it existed.

Master Carl roamed fretfully down the corridor, looking through electrified bars at the aborigines. A sallow fat man in flowered shorts came in through the door, bowed to the blonde woman, bowed to St. Cyr, offered a slight inclination of the head to Master Carl, staring contemptuously through the others. It was an instructive demonstration of how a really adept person could single out the categories of importance of a group of strangers on first contact. "I," he announced, "am your translator. You wish to speak to your aborigines, sir. Do so. The short one there, he speaks some English."

"Thank you," said Master Carl. The short one was a surly-looking fellow wearing much the same costume as the others. All of them were basically clad in ragged shorts and a short-sleeved jacket with an incongruous, tight-fitting collar. The clothes looked very, very old; not merely worn, but *old*. Men and women dressed alike. Only in the collars and shoulders-bars of the jackets were there any particular variations. They seemed to have military insigne to mark their ranks. One woman's collar, for example, bore a red cloth patch with a gold stripe running through it; the red was faded, the gold was soiled, but once they had been bright. Across the gold stripe was a five-pointed star of yellow cloth. The shortest of the men, the one who looked up when the translator spoke, had a red patch with much more gold on it, and with three stars of greenish, tarnished metal. Another man had a plain red patch with three cloth stars.

These three, the two men and the woman, stepped forward, placed their palms on their knees and bowed jerkily. The one with the metal stars spoke breathily, "Tai-i Masatura-san. I captain, sir. These are of my command: Heicho Ikuri, Joto-hei Shokuto."

Master Carl stepped back fastidiously. They *smelled!* They didn't look dirty, exactly, but their complexions were all bad—scarred and pitted and seamed, as well as sallow; and they did have a distinct sour aura of sweat hanging over them. He glanced at the interpreter. "Captain? Is that an Army rank?"

The interpreter grinned. "No Army now," he said reassuringly. "Oh, no. Long gone. But they keep military titles, you see? Father to son, father to son, like that. This fellow here, the tai-i, he tells me they are all part of Imperial Japanese Expeditionary Force which presently will make assault landing in Washington, D.C. Tai-i is captain; he is in charge of all of them, I believe. The heicho—that's the woman—is, the captain tells, a sort of junior corporal. More important than the other fellow, who is what they call a superior private."

"I don't know what a corporal or a private is."

"Oh, no. Who does? But to them it is important, it seems." The translator hesitated, grinned, and wheezed: "Also, they are related. The tai-i is daddy, the heicho is mommy, the joto-hei is son. All named Masatura-san."

"Dirty-looking things," Master Carl commented. "Thank heaven I don't have to go near them."

"Oh," said a grave, slow voice behind him, "but you do. Yes, you do. It is your re-spon-si-bi-li-ty, Carl. You must su-per-vise their tests by the med-ics."

Master Carl frowned and complained, but there was no way out of it. St. Cyr gave the orders, and that was the order he gave.

The medics looked over the aborigines as thoroughly as any dissecting cadavers. Medics, thought Master Carl in disgust. How can they! But they did. They had the men and women strip—flaccid breasts, sagging bellies, a terminator of deepening olive showing the transition from shade to sun at the lines marked by collars and cuffs and the hem of their shorts. Carl took as much of it as he could, and then he walked out—leaving them nakedly proud beside their rags, while the medics fussed and muttered over them like stock judges.

It was not only that he was tired of the natives—whose interest to a mathematician was not zero, no, but a quantity vanishingly small. More than that, he wanted to find Cornut.

There was a huge moon.

Carl retraced his steps to where the helipopper was casting a black silhouette on the silver dust. The pilot was half asleep on the seat, and Carl, with a force and determination previously reserved for critical letters in *Math. Trans.*, said sharply, "Up, you. I haven't all night." The startled pilot was airborne with his passenger before he realized that it was neither his employer, the young-old blonde, nor her equal partner, the old, old St. Cyr.

By then it did not much matter. In for a penny, in for a pound; when Carl ordered him back to the town where the jet had landed, the pilot grumbled to himself but complied.

It was not hard to find where Cornut had gone. The police scooter told Carl about the sidewalk cafe, the cashier told him about the native cafeteria, the counterman had watched Cornut, failing to finish his sandwich and coffee, stagger back to—the airport again. There the traffic tower had seen him come in, try to get transportation to follow the others, fail and mulishly stagger off into the jungle on the level truck road.

He had been hardly able to keep his eyes open, the towerman added.

Carl pressed the police into service. He was frightened.

The little scooter bounced along the road, twin spotlights scanning the growth on both sides. Please don't find him, begged Carl silently. I *promised* him. . . .

The brakes squealed and the scooter skidded to a halt.

The police were small, thin, young and agile, but Master Carl was first off the scooter and first to the side of the huddled figure under the breadfruit tree.

For the first time in weeks, Cornut had fallen asleep—passed out, in fact—without a guardian angel. The moment of helplessness between waking and sleeping, the moment that had almost killed him a dozen times, had caught him by the side of a deserted road, in the middle of an uninhabited sink of smelly soft vegetation.

Carl gently lifted the limp head.

". . . My God," he said, a prayer instead of an oath, "he's only drunk. Come on, you! Help me get him to bed."

Cornut woke up with a sick mouth and a banging head,

very cheerful. Master Carl was seated at a field desk, a shaded light over his head. "Oh, you're up. Good. I had the porter call me a few minutes early, in case—"

"Yes. Thanks." Cornut waggled his jaw experimentally, but that was not a very good experiment. Still, he felt very good. He had not been drunk in a long, long time, and a hangover was strange enough to him to be interesting in itself. He sat on the side of the bed. The porter had evidently had other orders from Master Carl, because there was coffee in a pewter pot, and a thick pottery cup. He drank some.

Carl watched him for a while, then browsed back to his desk. He had a jar of some faintly greenish liquid and the usual stack of photographic prints. "How about this one?" he demanded. "Does it look like a star to you?"

"No."

Carl dropped it back on the heap. "Becquerel's was no better," he said cryptically.

"I'm sorry, Carl," Cornut said cheerfully. "You know I don't take much interest in psion—"

"Cornut!"

"Oh, sorry. In your researches into paranormal kinetics, then."

Carl said doubtfully, having already forgotten what Cornut had said, "I thought Greenlease had put me on the track of something. You know I've been trying to manipulate single molecules by P.K.—using photographic film, on the principle that as the molecules are just about to flip over into another state, not much energy should be needed to trigger them—Yes. Well, Greenlease told me about Brownian Movement. Like this." He held the jar of soap solution to the light. "See?"

Cornut got up and took the quart jar from Master Carl's hand. In the light he could see that the greenish color was the sum of a myriad wandering points of light, looking more gold than green. "Brownian Movement? I remember something about it."

"The actual motion of molecules," Carl said solemnly. "One molecule impinging on another, knocking it into a third, the third knocking it into a fourth. There's a term for it in—"

"In math, of course. Why, certainly. The Drunkard's Walk." Cornut remembered the concept with clarity and affection. He had been a second-year student, and the house master was old Wayne; the audio-visual had been a marionette drunkard, lurching away from a doll-sized lamppost with random drunken steps in random drunken directions. He smiled at the jar.

"Well, what I want to do is sober him up. Watch!" Carl puffed and thought; he was a model of concentration; Rodin had only sketched the rough outlines, compared to Master Carl. Then he panted. "Well?"

Apparently, Cornut thought, what Carl had been trying to do was to make the molecules move in straight lines. "I don't think I see a thing," he admitted.

"No. Neither do I. . . . Well," said Master Carl, retrieving his jar, "even a negative answer is an answer. But I haven't given up yet. I have a few more thoughts on photographs—if Greenlease can give me a little help." He sat down next to Cornut. "And you?"

"You saw."

Carl nodded seriously. "I saw that you were still alive. Was it because you were on your own drunkard's walk?"

Cornut shook his head. He didn't mean No, he meant, How can I tell?

"And my idea about finding a wife?"

"I don't know."

"That girl in the dining hall," Carl said with some acuteness. "How about her?"

"Locille? Oh, good God, Carl, how do I know about her? I—I hardly know her name. Anyway, she seems to be pretty close to Egerd."

Carl got up and wandered to the window. "Might as well have breakfast. The aborigines ought to be ready now." He stared at the crimson morning. "Madam Sant' Anna has asked for a helper to get her aborigines to Valparaiso," he said thoughtfully. "I think I'll help her out."

Chapter Six

Ten thousand miles away, in the early afternoon, Locille was not very close to Egerd at all. "Sorry," she said. "I *would* like to. But—"

Egerd stood huffily up. "What's the record?" he said angrily. "Ten weeks? Good enough. I'll be around to see you again along about the first of the month." He stalked out of the girls' dayroom.

Locille sighed, but as she did not know what to do about Egerd's jealousy, she did nothing. It was rather difficult to be a girl sometimes.

For here's Locille, a girl, pretty enough, full of a girl's problems. It is a girl's business to keep her problems to herself. It is a girl's business to look poised and lovely. And available.

It is not true that girls are made of sugar and spice. These mysterious creatures, enameled of complexion, faintly scented with distant flower-fields and musk, constricted *here* and enlarged *there*—they are animals, as men are animals, sustained by the same sludgy trickle of partly fermented organic matter; and indeed with a host of earthy problems men need never know, the oestral flow, the burgeoning cells that replenish the race. Womanhood has always been a triumph of artifice over the animal within.

And here, as we say, is Locille. Twenty years old, student, child of a retired subway engineer and his retired social-worker wife. She is young, she is nubile. The state of her health is a plowmare's. What can she know of mysteries?

But she knew.

On the night the Field Expedition was due to return,

Locille was excused from all of her evening classes. She took advantage of an hour of freedom to telephone her parents, out on the texas. She discovered as she had discovered a hundred times before that there was nothing to say between them; and returned to the kitchens of the Faculty Mess in time to take up her duties for the evening.

The occasion was the return of the Field Expedition. It promised to be a monstrous feast.

More than two hundred visiting notables would be present, as well as most of the upper faculty of the University itself. The kitchens were buzzing with activity. All six C. E.s were on duty, all busy; the culinary engineer in charge of sauces and gravies spied Locille first and drafted her to help him, but there was a struggle; the engineer whose charge was pastries knew her and wanted her too. Sauces and gravies won out, and Locille found herself emulsifying caked steer blood and powdered spices in a huge metal vat; the sonic whine of the emulsifier and the staccato hiss of the steam as she valved it expertly into the mixture drowned out the settling roar of the jet; the party had returned without her knowing it; the first clue she had was when there was a commotion at one end of the kitchens, and she turned, and there was Egerd, dourly shepherding three short, sallow persons she didn't recognize.

He saw her. "Locille! Come on over and meet the aborigines!"

She hesitated and glanced at her C. E., who pantomimed take-ten-if-it-won't-spoil-the-gravy. Locille slipped off her gauntlets, set the automatic timers and thermostats and ducked past the kneading, baking, pressure-cooking machines of the Faculty Kitchen toward Egerd and his trophies.

"They're Japanese," he said proudly. "You've heard of War Two? They were abandoned on an island, and their descendants have been there ever since. Say, Locille—"

She took her eyes off the aborigines to look at Egerd. He seemed both angry and proud. "I have to go to Valparaiso," he said. "There are six other aborigines who are going to South America, and Master Carl picked me to go along."

She started to answer, but Cornut was wandering into the room, looking thoughtful.

Egerd looked thoughtfully back at him.

"I wondered why Carl picked me for this," he said, not bitterly but with comprehension. "All right." He turned to leave through another door. "He can have his chance—for the next sixteen days," he said.

Thoughtful Cornut was. He had never proposed marriage before. "Hello, Locille," he said formally.

She said, "Hello, Master Cornut."

He said, "I, uh, want to ask you something."

She said nothing. He looked around the kitchen as though he had never been in it before, which was probably so. He said, "Would you like to—ah, would you like to meet me on Overlook Tower tomorrow?"

"Certainly, Master Cornut."

"That's fine," he said politely, nodding, and was halfway into the dining room before he realized he hadn't told her when. Maybe she thought he expected her to stand there all day long! He hurried back. "At noon?"

"All right."

"And don't make any plans for the evening," he commanded, hurrying away. It was embarrassing. He had never proposed marriage before, and had not succeeded in proposing now, he thought. But he was wrong. He had. He didn't know it, but Locille did.

The rest of the evening passed very rapidly for Cornut. The dinner was a great success. The aborigines were a howl. They passed among the guests, smoking their pipe of peace with everyone who cared to try it, which was everyone, and as the guests got drunker the aborigines, responding to every toast with a loud *Banzai!*, then a hoarse one, then a simper—the aborigines got drunker still.

Cornut had a ball. He caught glimpses of Locille from time to time at first, then not. He asked after her, asked the waitresses, asked the aborigines, finally found himself asking—or telling—about Locille with his arm around the flaccid shoulders of Master Wahl. He was quite drunk early, and he kept on drinking. He had moments of clarity:

Master Carl listened patiently while Cornut tried to demonstrate Brownian motion in a rye-and-ginger-ale; a queer, alone moment when he realized he was staggering around the empty kitchen, calling Locille's name to the cold copper caldrons. Somehow, God knows how, he found himself in the elevators of Math Tower, when it must have been very late, and Egerd in a cream-colored robe was trying to help him into his room. He knew he said something to Egerd that must have been either coarse or cruel, because the boy turned away from him and did not protest when Cornut locked his door, but he did not know what. Had he mentioned Locille? When had he not! He fell sprawled on his bed, giggling. He had mentioned Locille a thousand times, he knew, and stroked the pillow beside him.

He drifted off to sleep.

He drifted off to sleep and halted, for a moment sober, for a moment terrified, knowing that he was on the verge of sleep, again alone. But he could not stop.

He could not stop because he was a molecule in a sea of soapy soup and Master Carl was hurling him into the arms of Locille.

Master Carl was hurling him away because Egerd had hurled him at Master Carl; Locille thrust him at St. Cyr and St. Cyr, voicelessly chuckling, hurled him clear out of the jar, and he could not stop.

He could not stop because St. Cyr told him: You are a molecule, drunken molecule, you are a molecule, drunk and random, without path, you are a drunken molecule and you cannot stop.

He could not stop though the greatest voice in the world was shouting at him: YOU CAN ONLY DIE, DRUNKEN MOLECULE, YOU CAN DIE, YOU CANNOT STOP.

He could not stop because the world was reeling, reeling, he tried to open his eyes to halt it but it would not stop.

He was a molecule.

He saw that he was a molecule and he saw he could not stop.

Then—

the molecule

—stopped.

Chapter Seven

Egerd tried pounding on the locked door for nearly five minutes and then went away. He could have stayed longer, but he didn't want to; he thought it out carefully and concluded, first, that he had done what he undertook to do— in spite of the fact that Cornut's choosing to marry Locille upset the undertaking; and second, that if he was too late he was already too late.

Nearly an hour later Cornut woke up.

He was alive, he noticed with interest.

It had been a most peculiar dream. It did not seem like a dream. His afternoon lecture, with Pogo Possum drawling hickory-bark rules for factoring large integers, was much more fantasy in his mind than the dream-scene of himself contemplating himself, staggering drunk and with a bottle in his hand, trapped in the ceaseless Brownian zigzag. He knew that the only way a molecule could stop was to die, but curiously he had not died.

He got up, dressed and went out.

He was remarkably hung over, but it was much, much better outside. It was bright morning and, he remembered very clearly, he had an engagement with Locille for that morning.

He was on tape for the A.M. lecture; it gave him the morning off. He walked about the campus aimlessly, past the green steel and glass of the Stadium, past the broad lawns of the lower campus to the Bridge. The Med School lay huddled under the Bridge itself. He liked the Bridge, liked its sweep across the Bay, liked the way it condescended to drop one pylon to the island where the Univer-

228

sity had been built. He very much liked that pylon; that was Overlook Tower.

On impulse, thinking that this was a good time to be quite sober, he stopped at the Clinic to get a refill on his wake-up pills. The clinic was not manned at that hour, except for emergencies, but as Cornut was a returnee he was admitted to the automatic diagnosis machines. It was very much the same as the experience of three nights before, except that there was no human doctor at all. A mechanical finger inserted a hair-thin tendril into his arm and tasted his blood, compared it with the recent chromatograph, and whirred thoughtfully while it considered if there had been changes. In a moment the *Solution* light winked pink, there was a click and clatter, and in a hopper by his hand there dropped a plastic box of his pills.

He took one. Ah, fine! They were working. It was a strange and rewarding sensation. Whatever the pills contained, they fought fatigue at first encounter. He could trace the course of that first pill clear down his throat and into his abdomen. The path tingled with well-being. He felt pretty good. No, he felt *very* good. He walked out into the fresh air again, humming to himself.

It was a long climb up the pylon to Overlook Landing, but he did it on foot, feeling comfortable all the way. He popped another pill into his mouth and waited in patient good humor for Locille.

She came promptly from her class.

From the base of the pylon she glanced up at the Overlook Landing, nearly two hundred feet over her head. If Cornut was there she couldn't see him. She rode up on the outside escalators, twining round the huge hexagonal tower, for the sake of the air and the view. It *was* a lovely view—the clean white rectahedron of the biologicals factory, the dome-shaped Clinic under the spreading feet of the pylon itself, the bright University buildings, the green of the lawns, the two dissimilar blues of water and sky. Lovely. . . .

But she was nervous. She stepped off the escalator,

turned around the bulk of the pylon and bowed. "Master Cornut," she said.

The wind caught at her blouse and hair. Cornut stood dreaming over the rail, his own short hair blown carelessly around his forehead. He turned idly and smiled with sleepy eyes. "Ah," he said. "Locille." He nodded as though she had answered—she had not. "Locille," he said, "I need a wife. You will do."

"Thank you, Master Cornut."

He waved a gentle hand. "You aren't engaged, I understand?"

"No." Unless you counted Egerd—but *she* didn't count Egerd.

"Not pregnant, I presume?"

"No. I have never been pregnant."

"Oh, no matter, no matter," he said hastily. "I don't mind that. It isn't any sort of physical problem, I suppose?"

"No." She didn't meet his eye that time, though. For there *was* a sort of physical problem, in a way. There couldn't have been a pregnancy without a man. She had avoided that.

She stood waiting for him to say something else, but he was a long time in getting around to it. Out of the corner of her eye she noted that he was taking pills out of that little box as though they were candy. She wondered if he knew he was taking them. She remembered the knife-edge at his throat in class; she remembered the stories Egerd had told. Silly business; why would anyone try to kill himself?

He collected himself and cleared his throat, taking another pill. "Let me see," he mused. "No engagements of record, no physical bars, no consanguinity, of course—I'm an only child, you see. Well, I think that's everything, Locille. Shall we say tonight, after late class?" He looked suddenly concerned. "Oh, that is—you have no objection, do you?"

"I have no objection."

"Good." He nodded, but his face remained clouded. "Locille," he began, "perhaps you've heard stories about me. I—I have had a number of accidents lately. And one reason why I wish to take a wife is to guard against any more accidents. Do you understand?"

"I understand that, Master Cornut."

"Very good. Very good." He took another pill out of the box, hesitated, glanced at it.

His eyes widened.

Not understanding, Locille stood motionless; she didn't know that a sudden realization had come to Master Cornut.

It was the last pill in the box. But there had been twenty at least! Twenty, not more than three-quarters of an hour before—twenty!

He cried hoarsely, "Another accident!"

It was as if the realization released the storm of the pills. Cornut's pulse began to pound. His head throbbed in a new and faster tempo. The world spun scarlet around him. A rush of bile clogged his throat.

"Master Cornut!"

But it was already too late for the girl to cry out—he knew; he had acted. He hurled the box out into space, stared at her, crimson, then without ceremony leaped to the rail.

Locille screamed.

She was after him, clutching at him, but impatiently he shrugged her off, and then she saw that he was not climbing to hurl himself to death; he had his finger down his throat; without romance or manners, Master Cornut was getting the poison out of him quickly, efficiently—

And all by himself.

Locille stood by silently, waiting.

After a few minutes his shoulders stopped heaving, but he leaned on the rail, staring, for minutes after that. When he turned his face was the racked face of a damned soul.

"I'm sorry. Thanks."

Locille said softly, "But I didn't do anything."

"Of course you did. You woke me up—"

She shook her head. "You did it by yourself, you know. You did."

He looked at her with irritation, then with doubt. And then at last, he looked at her with the beginning of hope.

Chapter Eight

The ceremony was very simple. Master Carl officiated. There was a friendly meal, and then they were left alone, Locille and Cornut, by the grace of the magisterial power inherent in housemasters man and wife.

They went to his room.

"You'd better rest," said Locille.

"All right." He sprawled on the bed to watch her. He was very much aware of her, now studying, now doing womanlike tasks around his room—no. *Their* room. She was as inconspicuous as a flesh-and-blood person could be, moving quickly when she moved. But she might have been neon-lit and blaring with sirens for the way she kept distracting him.

He stood up and dressed himself, not looking at her. She said questioningly: "It's time for sleep, isn't it?"

He fumbled. "Is it?" But the clock said yes; it was; he had slept the day through. "All right," he said, as though it were some trivial thing and not world-shaking at all. "Yes, it's time for—sleep. But I think I will take a walk around the campus, Locille. I need it."

"Certainly." She nodded and waited, polite and calm.

"Perhaps I shall be back before you are asleep," he went on. "Perhaps not. Perhaps I—" He was rambling. He nodded, cleared his throat, picked up his cloak and left.

No one was in the corridor outside, no one in sight in the hall.

There was a thin electronic *peep* from the robot night-proctors, but that was all right. Master Cornut was no undergraduate, to wriggle under the sweep of the scanning

232

beams on his belly. It was his privilege to come and go as he chose.

He chose to go.

He walked out onto the campus, quiet under a yellow moon, the bridge overhead ghostly silver. There was no *reason* why he should be so emotionally on edge. Locille was only a student.

The fact remained, he was on edge.

But why should he be? Student marriage was good for the students, good for the masters; custom sanctioned it; and Master Carl, from the majesty of his house-master's post, had suggested it in the first place.

Queerly, he kept thinking of Egerd.

There had been a look on young Egerd's face, and maybe it was that which bothered him. Master Cornut was not so many years past his sheepskin that he could quite dismiss the possible emotions of an undergraduate. Custom, privilege and law to one side, the fact remained that a student quite often did feel jealous of a master's prerogatives. While a student, Cornut himself had contracted no liaisons to be interfered with. But other students had. And there was no doubt that, in Egerd's immature, undergraduate way, he might well be jealous.

But what did that matter? His jealousy could harm only himself. No serf, raging inwardly against his lord's *jus primae noctis,* was less able to make his anger felt than Egerd. But somehow Cornut was feeling it.

He felt almost guilty.

He was no logician, his field was Mathematics. But this whole concept of *right,* he thought as he paced along the riverbank, needed some study. What the world sanctioned was clear: The rights of the higher displaced the rights of the lower, as an atom of fluorine will drive oxygen out of a compound. But *should* it be that way?

It *was* that way—if that was an answer.

And all of class, all of privilege, all of law, seemed to be working to produce one single commodity—a product which, of all world's goods, is unique in that it has never been in short supply, never quite satisfied its demand

and never failed to find a market: Babies. Wherever you looked, babies. In the crèches in the women's dorms, in the playrooms attached to the rooms of the masters—babies. It was almost as though it had been planned that way; custom and law determined the fact that as many adult humans as possible spend as much of their time as possible in performing the acts that made babies arrive. Why? What was the drive that produced so many *babies?*

It wasn't a matter of sex alone—it was *babies.* Sex was perfectly possible and joyous under conditions that made the occurrence of *babies* utterly impossible; science had arranged that decades, even centuries, before. But contraception was—well, *wrong.* And so, all over the world, this uncomplicated and unaided practice of baby-making added a clear two per cent to the world's population every time the earth sailed around the sun.

Two per cent per year!

There were now something over twelve billion persons alive. Next year's census would show four hundred million more than that.

And why?

What made babies so popular?

Crazy as it was, the conclusion forced itself on Master Cornut: It was *planned* that way.

By whom, he wondered, settling down to a long night's thoughtful ramble and pursuing of the line of thought to its last extreme—

But not tonight; because he looked up and there was his own dorm. His feet had known more clearly than he the ultimate answer to the question: *Babies?*

He was back at the entrance of Math Tower where the girl, Locille, was waiting.

The thing was, the bed.

She had had a bed of her own moved into the room, for that was the way it was done; but of course there was his bed already there, much larger, so that—

Well, which bed would she be in?

He took a deep breath, nodded blindly to the unseeing

electronic night proctor, and opened the door of his room.

A riotous alarm bell shattered the stillness.

Master Cornut stood staring, stupidly, while the flesh-and-blood undergraduate charged with supervising the corridors came peering worriedly around the corner, drawn by the sound; and the bell continued to ring. Then he realized it was connected with the door; it was his automatic alarm bell, rigged by himself. But he had not connected it this night, he knew.

He stepped in quickly, threw a scowl back at the undergraduate, and closed the door. The ringing stopped.

Locille was rising from the bed—*his* bed.

Her hair was soft about her head and her eyes were downcast but bright. She had not been asleep. She said, "You must be tired. Would you like me to fetch you something to eat?"

He said in a tremblingly stern voice: "Locille, why did you bug the door?"

She looked at him. "Why, to wake me up when you came in. The bell was there; I only had to turn it on."

"And why?"

"Why," she said, "I wanted to." And she yawned, rather prettily; and excused herself with a smile; and turned to straighten the covers on the bed.

Cornut, watching her from behind as he had never watched her from the front, made note of two incredible facts.

The first was that this girl, Locille, was beautiful. She was wearing very little, only a sleeping skirt and a sleeping yoke, and there was no doubt of her figure; and she was wearing no make-up that the eye could see, and there was no doubt about her face. Beautiful. Amazing, Cornut told himself, conscious of commotions inside himself, amazing, but I want this girl very much.

And that led him to the other fact, which was more incredible still.

Cornut had picked her out as a shopper might select one roast over another. Cornut had told her what to do; Cornut had, as far as he possibly could, arranged to destroy, with method and plan, everything of eagerness and spontaneous joy there might have been. It was his peculiar fortune that he had failed.

He looked at her and knew what had never entered into his calculations. It had never occurred to him that she might be eager for *him*.

Rap, tap.

The girl shook him awake—fully awake. "What do you want?" Cornut cried crossly at the door. Beside him, Locille made a face, a sweet, a mock-arrogant face, that was a tender caricature of his own; so that by the time the morning proctor opened the door a crack and peered around it, Cornut was smiling at him. Wonders never-ceasing, thought the proctor, and said timidly, "Master Cornut, it is eight o'clock."

Cornut drew the covers over Locille's bare shoulder. "Go away," he said.

The door closed, and one of Locille's pink slippers slapped lightly against it. She raised the other to toss after the first. Cornut caught her arm, laughing very softly; and she turned to him, not quite laughing, and kissed him, and sprang away.

"And *stay* awake," she warned. "I have to go to class."

Cornut leaned back against the pillowcase.

Why, it was a pleasant morning, he thought, and maybe in a way a pleasant world! It was perfectly amazing what hues and brightnesses there were in the world, that he had either never suspected or long forgot. He watched the girl, miraculously a part of his life, a segment joined on without a trace or seam where he had never suspected a segment was missing. She moved lightly around the room, and she looked at him from time to time; and if she wasn't asmile like a grinning ape it was because there wasn't any need for smiles just then, of course.

Cornut was a well satisfied man that morning.

Quick-quick, she was dressed; much too quickly. "You," said Cornut, "are in much too much of a hurry to be gone from here."

Locille came and sat on the edge of the bed. Even in the

uniform she was beautiful now. That was another amazing thing. It was like knowing that a chalice was purest gold under the enamel; the colors were the same, the design was the same; but suddenly what had been a factory product was become a work of art, simply through knowing what graces lay underneath. She said, "That is because I am in a hurry to return." She looked at him again and said questioningly, "You won't go back to sleep?"

"Of course not." She was frowning slightly, he saw with fondness; reminding him of the reason he had sought a companion in the first place; *that* old reason.

"All right." She kissed him, rose, found her carry-all where she had left it on a chair, and her books. She caroled softly to herself. "Strike the Twos and strike the Threes, the Sieve of Eratosthenes. When the multiples—Cornut, you're *sure* you won't go back to sleep?"

"Sure."

She nodded, hesitating with one hand on the door. She said doubtfully, "Maybe you'd better take a wake-up pill. Will you?"

"I will," he said, rejoicing in being nagged.

"And you'd better start dressing yourself in a few minutes. It's only half an hour until your first class—"

"I know."

"All right." She blew him a kiss, and a smile; and she was gone.

And the room was very empty. But not as empty as it had been all the days and nights before.

Cornut dutifully got up, found himself the pillbox with the red and green sleeping regulators, took one and returned to bed; he had never felt better in his life.

He lay back against the pillow, utterly relaxed and at peace. He had bought himself an alarm clock and it turned out to be a wife. He smiled at the low cream-colored ceiling, and stretched and yawned. What a perfectly fine bargain! What a super-perfect alarm clock!

And that reminded him; and he glanced at his watch; but he'd taken it off and the wall clock was out of his angle of vision. Well, no matter; the wake-up pill would keep him from going back to sleep again. It was common knowledge that the wake-up pill made time run short. It felt as though he had been lying here half an hour; well, it couldn't be more than five minutes; that was how they worked.

Still. . . .

He fumbled in the little divided box. Fortunate that they were handy; another pill would make doubly sure.

He swallowed it, leaned back again and yawned. There was something about the pillow, he thought. . . .

He turned his head, sniffed, breathed deeply. Yes. There was Locille about the pillow; that was what it was. Locille, who left a fragrance behind her. Beautiful fragrance of Locille, beautiful name. Beautiful girl. He caught himself yawning again—

Yawning?

Yawning!

He blinked the eyes that were much too heavy, and tried to turn the very weary head. Yawning! But after two wake-up pills—or was it three, or six?

History was repeating!

Red pills for wake-up, green for sleep. The green pills, he sobbed in his thoughts, he'd been taking the *green* ones! He was caught.

Oh, Lord, he whimpered soundlessly—oh, Lord, why this time? Why did you wait to catch me until I *cared?*

Chapter Nine

The assistant audio engineer, staring bemused through the glass at the filling studio, was humming to himself. It irritated Master Carl. He could not help fitting words to the tune:

> Strike the Twos and strike the Threes:
> The Sieve of Eratosthenes!
> When the multiples sublime,
> The numbers that are left, are prime.

It did not alleviate his annoyance that the song was one of his own. Classic Prime-Number Exposition was not the subject of the morning's class; it was Set Theory; he snapped, "Be still, man! Don't you like your work here?" The assistant audio engineer paled. He had been brought up on a texas and never forgot that he might some day have to go back to one.

It was not really true that the humming distracted him. At Master Carl's age, you either know what you are doing or you don't, and he knew. He went out at the precise moment his theme began and spoke the words he always spoke, while his mind was on Cornut, on the Wolgren anomaly, on his private investigation of the paranormal, on—especially on—the responses and behavior of each individual undergraduate in his in-studio audience. He noted every yawn of a drowsy nucleonics major in the far corner; he observed with particular care the furtive passage of notes from the boy, Egerd, to his protégé's new wife, Locille. He did not intend to do anything about it. He was grateful to Locille. As a good watchdog, she might very well save the life of the only man on the faculty Carl considered to have any chance of ever replacing himself.

In five minutes he had concluded the live portion of his lecture and, indulging his own harmless desires, left the studio. Taped figures danced on the screen behind him, singing *The Ballad of Sets*.

> Let "S" be a number set, then progress:
> If, of any two numbers (a and b) in S,
> Their sum is also in the set,
> The set is *closed!* And so we get
> A *reproductive set* with this definition:
> "The number set S is closed by addition!"

He put the class out of his mind and eagerly drew a sheaf of photographic prints out of his briefcase. He had slept only restlessly the night before and had risen early to work at his newest hobby. He had had many. He needed many. Carl was in no way dissatisfied, could not have conceived a world in which he would not have been a mathematician, but it wasn't all pleasure to be a towering elder statesman in a young man's game. It was a queer fact of mathematics that nearly every great mathematician had done his best work before he was thirty. And most of them, like Carl, had turned to other curiosities in their later years.

Someone opened the door and the choral voices from the studio surged in on him:

> If number set M is closed by subtraction,
> A *modul* is the term for this transaction!

Master Carl turned, frowning like ice. Egerd! He demanded terribly, "What is a number set closed by multiplication?"

Egerd quailed but said, "It's a ray, Master Carl. It's in the fourth canto. Sir, I want to—"

"Closed to addition and subtraction as well?"

"A ring, sir. Can I speak to you a moment?"

Carl grunted.

"I did study the lesson, Master Carl. As you can see."

He would have said more, but Carl had not finished being stern. "There is no excuse, Egerd, for leaving a class without permission. You must know that. It may seem to you that you are able to grasp set theory by studying from books, no doubt. You are wrong. A mathematician must know these simple classical facts and definition as well as he knows that February has twenty-eight days, and in the same way. By mnemonics! I assure you that you will never become a first-rate mathematician by cutting classes."

"Yes, sir. That's it. I want to transfer out. As soon as I get back from South America, if it's all right with you, sir."

Master Carl was purely horrified.

This was not a case for discipline, he saw at once. Carl did not consider that the separation of Egerd from mathematics would be a loss to mathematics. It was compassion for the boy himself that gave him concern. "Well. What is it you want to transfer to?"

"Med School, sir. I've made up my mind." He added, "You can understand why, Master Carl. I don't have much talent for this stuff."

Carl didn't understand; he would never understand. He had, however, some long time before that made up his mind that there were things about his students that didn't much need understanding. His students had many facets; only one concerned him. They were like those paper patterns the soft-headed undergraduates in Topology played with, hexihexiflexagons, constructions that turned up new sides in bewildering variety each time they were flexed. He said mournfully, "All right. I'll sign your release." He scowled when he saw that Egerd already had it filled out and ready for him; the boy was *too* eager.

The door opened again.

Master Carl halted with the pen in his hand. "Now what?" He recognized the man—vaguely—it was that hanger-on of the Department of Liberal Arts. The name escaped him, but he was a sexwriter. He was also agitated.

The man said, "Excuse me. I'm sorry. Name's Farley. I'm Master Cornut's—"

"You're a sexwriter. I have no objection to that. I do object to having my privacy disturbed." Although that was not quite true either. Master Carl was prude enough (perhaps because he was woman-shy enough) to feel that the private affairs of men and women should not be inspired by scripts provided by sexwriters or, as they were once called, marriage counselors. *He* would never have employed one, and he was irked with Cornut.

As it turned out, neither would Cornut. "I was a wedding present," Farley explained, "and so I went to see Cornut this morning with a rough thirty-day draft. I don't use standard forms; I believe in personalized counseling. So I thought I'd better interview the male subject right away because, as you know—"

Egerd interrupted desperately, "Master Carl. Please sign my transfer."

The expression in his eyes said more than his words. The flexagon turned up another side, and this time Carl was able to read its design. He nodded and wrote his name. It was entirely clear that Egerd's reasons for transferring away from Locille and Master Cornut had nothing much to do with his talent for mathematics.

But the sexwriter would not be stopped. "Then where is the female subject, Master Carl?" he demanded. "They said she would be here. . . ."

"Locille? Of course." A terrible thought entered Carl's mind. "You mean that something happened—*again?* When you went to see Cornut he was—"

"Out cold, yes. Almost dead. He's having his stomach pumped now, though; they think he'll be all right."

When they reached Cornut's room, the medic was scanning a spectrum elaborated for him by a portable diagnosticon. Cornut himself was unconscious. The medic reassured them. "Close, but he missed this time. What was it, his fifteenth? And the record is—"

Carl interrupted frostily. "Can you wake him up? Good. Then do."

The medic shrugged and fished for a hypodermic. He slipped the piston of the needle into the barrel; the faint spray appeared, hovering over Cornut's unbroken skin. The tiny droplets found their way through dermis and epidermis and subcutaneous fat and, in a moment, Cornut sat up.

He said clearly, "I had the most ridiculous dream."

And then he saw Locille; and his face was alight. That at least was no dream. Master Carl had little tact, but he had enough to take the medic and leave the two of them there.

The experience of having one's stomach pumped is not attractive. This was Cornut's third time, but he had not come to like it; he tasted bile and foulness, his esophagus had been painfully scraped; the sleeping pills had left him with a headache.

"I'm sorry," he said.

Locille brought him a glass and one of the capsules the medic had left. He swallowed it and began to chuckle. "Lucky Wahl," he said. "You know, if I'd been awake when that fellow came in I'd have gone over and punched Wahl in the head; it was his idea; he got half of Anthropology to chip in to buy us Farley's services for a year. As it is. . . . I guess Wahl saved my life." He got up and began to wander around. In spite of the taste and the head, he was feeling rather cheerful, in an unanalyzed way. Even the dream, though queer, had not been unpleasant. Master Carl had been in it, and so had St. Cyr and the woman from South America; but so had Locille.

He paused by his desk. "What's this?" It was a neat sheaf of papers clipped in a folder on which was printed: *S. R. Farley, Consultant.* That was all. Just *Consultant.* He opened it and found the first page a cleanly typed set of what seemed to be equations. The symbols $\male$ and $\female$ occurred frequently, along with strokes, daggers and congruencies which he vaguely remembered from an undergraduate course in symbolic logic. "That's almost a Boolean notation," he said interestedly. "I wonder—Say, look at this, Locille. Line three. If you substitute these three terms from the expansion in line four, and—"

He stopped. She was blushing. But he hadn't noticed; he was suddenly scowling at his desk. "My Wolgren! Where is it?"

"If you mean the report on distributive anomalies you were preparing for Master Carl, he took it as he went out."

"But it isn't finished!"

"But he didn't want you working on it. Or anything. He wants you to take the day off—get off the campus—and he wants me to stay with you."

"Huh." He stared glumly at the window. "Hum." He made tasting motions with his lips and tongue and made a face. "Well. All right. Where is there to go, off campus? Do you have any ideas?"

Locille looked a little worried. "As a matter of fact," she said diffidently, "I do. . . ."

At sundown they boarded the one-a-day ferry to the texas; there was traffic enough from the city to the texas, and even from the University to the city; but between the texas and the University there was almost none. They leaned against the rail as the ferry rose, looking down at the University's island, the city and the bay. The almost silent blades overhead chopped the scarlet sunset sky into dots and dashes; all they could hear inside the domed deck of the ferry was a bass flutter of blades and a more-than-soprano hiss of the blade-tip jets.

Locille said abruptly, "I didn't tell you about Roger. My brother," she said swiftly.

Cornut stopped an emotion before it had quite got started. "What about him?" he asked, relieved.

She said flatly, "He isn't University caliber. He might have been, but— When Roger was about five years old—he was swimming off the texas—there was another boy in the water, and he dove. They collided. The other boy drowned." She paused, turning to look at him. "Roger fractured his skull. Ever since then, he's been—well, his intelligence never developed much past that point."

Cornut received the information, frowning.

It was not that he minded a stupid brother-in-law; it was only that he had never thought of there being any brother-in-law at all. It had never occurred to Cornut that marriage involved more than two people.

"He isn't insane," Locille said worriedly, "just not intelligent."

Cornut hardly heard her. He was busy trying to cope with the thought that there was more here than watchdog or love; there was something here that he had never counted on. It took twenty minutes to fly the rest of the way to the texas, and it took all of that time for Cornut to puzzle out the fact that he had taken on more than a convenience or a pleasure, he had assumed a sort of obligation as well.

The texas stood in ninety feet of water, just over the horizon from Sandy Hook. It was fifteen acres of steel decks, twelve levels high, the lowest of the levels forty feet above mean high water. It was not the fault of the designers of the texas that "mean high water" was an abstraction, the average distance between trough and peak of the great swells of the ocean. The texas crouched on hundreds of metal legs that sank into the ooze to the bedrock beneath, and it was a target. In storms the whitecaps slapped demandingly at its underbelly. If there was lightning, it was sure to strike at the radar beacon on its tower.

Time was when those radars had been the reason for the existence of texas towers. That time was past; satellite eyes and ionosphere-scatter search methods had ended their importance. But the world had found other uses for them. They guided the whale-backed submersibles of the world's cargo fleets as they surfaced over the continental shelf to find harbor; they served as mother "ships" for the ranging fishery fleets in shallow seas. They provided living room for some tens of millions on the American seaboard alone. They provided work space for nuisance industries—the ones that smelled, or were loud, or were dangerous.

Power was free, nearly, on a texas. Each hollow leg was slotted in its lower stretch. The waves that came crashing by compressed the air in the columns, valved through a one-way exhaust into a pressure tank; pneumatic turbines whirred at the release vents of the tanks, and the texas' lights and industries drew current from those turbines. In "good" weather—when the waves roared and pounded—there was power to smelt aluminum; the ore boats that unloaded the raw materials carried away the slag, dumping it within sight of the texas itself in the inexhaustible disposal pit of the ocean. When weather was "bad"—when the Atlantic was glassy smooth—aluminum making stopped for a while. But weather was never really "bad" for long.

Locille's parents lived with her brother, in a three-room apartment in the residential area of the texas. It was leeward of the fisheries, across the texas from the aluminum refinery, six levels above the generators. Cornut thought it horrible. It smelled and it was noisy.

Locille had brought presents. A sash for her father, something cosmetic for her mother and, Cornut saw with astonishment, one of the flags the aborigines had brought with them as a gift for her brother Roger. It had not occurred to Cornut that there should be gifts, much less gifts as expensive as any aboriginal artifact; the things were in great demand as conversation pieces. But he was grateful. The flag was a conversation piece here, too, and he needed one. Locille's mother brought out coffee and cakes, and Cornut entertained them with his trip to the South Seas.

He did not, however, mention his blackout by the side of the road; and he could not keep his eyes off Roger.

Locille's brother was a huge young man, taller than Cornut, with a pleasant expression and dull eyes. He was not offered coffee and refused cake; he sat there, watching Cornut, fingering the worn fabric of his gift, even smelling it, rubbing it against his face. Cornut found him disconcerting. Barring the aborigines and a handful of clinical cases under study, there was not one human being on the campus with an I.Q. under a hundred and forty, and Cornut had no experience of the simple-minded. The boy could talk— but mostly did not—and though he seemed to understand what Cornut was saying, he never changed expression.

The fact of the matter was that Roger didn't much care what Cornut was saying. His whole attention was taken up with his gift. As soon as he thought it was proper to do so, he excused himself and carried it to his room.

Roger was aware that it was very old and came from very far away; but that could have been something of last week's, from the city just below the horizon; he had little memory. What Roger thought principally about the flag was that it was a pretty color.

He tacked it with magnetic grips to the wall of his room, stood back thoughtfully, removed the grips and replaced it closer to his bed. He stood there looking at it, because somehow it satisfied him to stand and look at it.

It was bright moonlight outside, but there was a fair wind sweeping across the long reach from Portugal. The waves were high; and the pneumatic hammer-hammer and the rattle-slam of the valves opening and closing pounded through the texas, one noise reinforcing the other. It made it hard for anyone to talk in the other room. (Cornut was growing more and more uneasy.) But it didn't bother Roger. Since the day his own crushed skull had minced a corner of his brain, nothing had really *bothered* Roger.

But he liked the flag. After ten minutes of staring at it, he took off the magnets that held it, folded it and put it under his pillow. Smiling with pleasure, he went back into the other room to say good night to his sister's new husband.

Chapter Ten

Master Carl lighted a do-not-disturb sign on his door and opened the folding screen that hid his little darkroom from the casual eyes of the student housekeepers. He was not ashamed of the hobby that made him operate a darkroom; it was simply none of their business. Carl was not ashamed of anything he did. His room attested to that; it bore the marks of all his interests.

Three boards held chess problems half worked out and forgotten, the pieces lifted, dusted and replaced by a dozen generations of student maids. On the cream-and-lilac walls were framed prints of Minoan scenes and inscriptions, the ten-year-old relics of his statistical examination into the grammar of Linear B. A carton that had once contained two dozen decks of Rhine cards (and still contained five unopened packs) showed the two years he had spent in demonstrating to his own satisfaction, once for all, that telepathy was not possible.

The proof rested on an analogy, but Master Carl had satisfied himself that the analogy was valid. If, he supposed, telepathic communication could be subsumed under the general equations of Unified Field Law, it had to fall into one of the two possible categories therein. It could be tunable, like the electromagnetic spectrum; or it could be purely quantitative, like the kinetogravitic realms. He eliminated the second possibility at once: it implied that every thought would be received by every person within range, and observation denied that on the face of it.

Telepathy, then, if it existed at all, had to be tunable. Carl then applied his analogy. Crystals identical in structure resonate at the same frequency. Humans identical in structure do exist: They are called identical twins. For two years Master Carl had spent most of his free time locating, persuading and testing pairs of identical twins. It took two years, and no more, because that was how long it took him to find three hundred and twenty-six pairs; and three hundred and twenty-six was the number the chi-square law gave as the minimum universe in which a statistical sampling could be regarded as conclusive. When the three hundred and twenty-sixth twin had failed to secure significantly more than chance correlation with the card symbols viewed by his sibling, Carl had closed out the experiment at once.

When the two-year job was ended Carl was not angry, but he was also not hopeful. It did not occur to him to go on to a three hundred and twenty-seventh set. He did, however, permit himself to turn at once to investigating other aspects of what had once been called psionics.

Precognition he eliminated on logical grounds; clairvoyance he pondered over for several months before deciding that, like the conjecture that flying saucers were of extraterrestrial origin, it offered too few opportunities for experimental verification to be an attractive study. Hexing he ruled out as necessarily involving either telepathy or clairvoyance. It was not the cases in which the sufferer knew he was hexed that offered a problem; simple suggestion could account for most of those; a man who saw the wax doll with the pins in it, or was told by the ju-ju man that his toenails were being roasted, might very easily sicken and die out of fear. But if the victim did not learn of his hex through physical means, he could learn only by either telepathy or clairvoyance; and Carl had eliminated them.

The traditional list of paranormal powers included only two other phenomena: fire-sending and telekinesis.

Carl elected to consider the first as only a subdivision of the second. Speeding the Brownian Movement of molecules (i.e., heating them) to the point of flame was surely no different in kind than gross manipulation of groups of molecules (i.e., moving material objects).

His first attempts at telekinesis involved a weary time of attempting to shift bits of matter, papers first, then balanced pins, hanging threads, finally grains of dust on a microbalance. There was no result. Co-opting some help from Classical Physics, Carl then began a series of tests involving photographic film. It was, the drafted physicists assured him, the medium in which the least physical force produced the greatest measurable effect. A photon, a free electron, almost any particle containing energy could shift the unstable molecules in the film emulsion.

Carl worked with higher and higher speed emulsions, learning tricks to make the film still more sensitive—special developers, close temperature control, pre-exposing the film to "soak up" part of the energy necessary to produce an image. With each new batch of film he then sat for hours, attempting to paint circles, crosses and stars on the emulsion with his mind, visualizing the molecules and willing the change-over. He scissored out stencils and held them over the wrapped filmpacks, considering it possible that the psionic "radiation" might show only as a point source. He had one temporary, and illusive, success: a plate of particularly trigger-happy film, wrapped under his pillow all one night, developed the next morning into a ghostly, wavering "X." Master Florian of Photo-chemistry disillusioned him. Carl had only succeeded in so sensitizing the film that it reacted to the tiny infrared produced by his own body heat.

Master Carl's project for this night involved preexposing a specially manufactured batch of X-ray film, by means of contact with a sheet of luminescent paper; the faint gamma radiation from the paper needed hours to affect the emulsion, but those hours had to be accurately timed.

To fill the space of those hours, Master Carl had another pleasant task. He sent a student courier to his office for the unfinished draft he had abstracted from Cornut's room. It was headed:

A Reconciliation
Of Certain Apparent Anomalies
In Wolgren's Distributive Law

Carl drew a stiff-backed chair up to his desk and began to read, enjoying himself very much.

Wolgren's Law, which had to do with the distribution of non-uniform elements in random populations, was purely a mathematician's rule. It did not deal with material objects; it did not even deal with numerical quantities as such. Yet Wolgren's Law had found applications in every sort of sampling technique known to man, from setting parameters for rejecting inferior batches of canned sardines to predicting election results. It was a general law, but the specific rules that could be drawn from it had proved themselves in nearly every practical test.

In every test but one. One of Carl's graduate students had attempted to reconcile the Wolgren rule with census data for his doctoral thesis—queerly, the subject seemed never to have been covered. The boy had failed. He had found another subject, got his degree and was now happily designing communications systems for the TV syndicates, but in failing he had produced a problem worth the attention of a first-rate mathematician; and Carl had offered it to Cornut.

Cornut had worked on it, in his own after-hours time, for six months. Incomplete as it was, the report gave Master Carl three hours of intensive enjoyment. Trust Cornut to do a beautiful job! Carl followed every step, mumbling to himself; cocking an eyebrow at the use of chi-squared until it was proved by a daring extension of Gibbs' phase-analysis rule. It was the mathematical statement that concerned him, not the subject of census figures themselves. It was only when he had finished the report and sat back, glowing, that he wondered why Cornut had thought it was not finished. But it was! Every equation checked! The constants were standard and correct, the variables were pinned down and identified with page after page of expansions.

"Very queer," said Carl to himself, staring vacantly at the bench where his X-ray film was quietly soaking up electrons. "I wonder—"

He shrugged, and attempted to dismiss the problem. It would not be dismissed. He thought for a moment of calling in Cornut, but stopped himself; the boy would not be back from his visit to Locille's family, and even if he were it was no longer feasible to burst in on him.

Dissatisfied, Master Carl read again the last page of the report. The math was correct; this time he allowed the sense of it to penetrate: "Of n births, the attained age of the oldest member of the population shall equal n times a constant e-log q." Well? Why not?

Carl was irritated. He glanced at his clock. It was only ten.

Frowning, he buttoned his jacket and went out, leaving lights on, door open, report open on the desk . . . and the X-ray film still firmly taped to its gamma-emitting paper.

No one answered his knock on Cornut's door, so Carl, after a moment's thought, pushed it open. The room was empty; they had not returned from the texas.

Carl grumbled at the night proctor and dropped in the elevator to the campus. He thought a stroll might help. It was chilly, but he scarcely noticed. The q quantity, was there something wrong with that? But its expansions were all in order. He recalled, as clearly as though they were imprinted on the wall of the Administration Building ahead of him, the equations defining q; he even remembered what quantities those equations involved. Public health, warfare, food supply, a trickily derived value for the state of the public mind . . . they had all been in the accompanying tabulations.

"Good night, Carl-san."

He stopped, blinking through the woven iron fence. He had reached the small encampment where the aborigines were housed; the captain, whatever his name was, had greeted him. "I thought you people were off—ah, lecturing," he finished lamely. "On exhibition," he had been about to say.

"Tomorrow, Carl-san," said the waffle-faced man, offering Carl a long, feathered pipe. That had been in the briefing; it was a peace pipe, a quaint and for some reason, to the anthropologist a surprising, custom of the islanders. Carl shook his head. The man—Carl remembered his name; it was Masatura-san—said apologetically, "You softspeak hard, sir. I smell you coming long way yester-day."

"Really," said Carl, not hearing a word. He was thinking about *e*-log and the validity of applying it; but that was all right too.

"Softspeak brownie not smell good," the man explained seriously.

"No, of course not." Carl was wondering about the values for *a*, the age factor in the final equation.

Tai-i Masatura-san said, growing agitated, "Cornut-san smell bad also, St. Cyr-san speak. Carl-san! Not speak brownie!"

Master Carl glanced at him. "Certainly," he said. "Good night." After him the tai-i called beseechingly, but Carl still did not hear; he had realized what it was that was unfinished about Cornut's report. The numerical values had been given for every quantity but one. It was still early; he did not intend to sleep until he had that one remaining value. . . .

Cornut, with his arm around Locille, yawned into the face of the red moon that hung over the horizon. It was growing very late.

They had had to take the ferry to the city and wait to transfer; the only direct popper from the texas to the city was in mid-morning, and Locille's family had no place to put them up. Nor, if they had, would Cornut have stayed. He needed time to become accustomed to domesticity; it was too many things at once; bad enough that he should have to interrupt his routine to accommodate Locille's presence in his room.

But it was, on the whole, worth while.

The University was under them now, the cables of the Bridge lacing the red moon, the lights from the Administration Building bright in the dark mass of towers.

It was odd that the Administration Building should be lighted.

Drowsily Cornut looked, out of the corner of his eye, at the neat, sleepy head of his wife. He did not know if he liked her better or worse as a member of a family. The parents—dull. Amiable, he supposed, but he was used to brilliance. And her brother was an unfortunate accident, of course, but he had been so enchanted with the rag Locille had brought him, like a child, like an animal. Cornut was not quite pleased to be related to him. Of course, you couldn't choose your relatives. His own children, for example, might be quite disappointing. . . .

His own children! The thought had come quite naturally; but he had never had that particular thought before. Involuntarily he shivered, and looked again at Locille.

She said sleepily, "What's the matter?" And then, "Oh. Why, I wonder what they want."

The ferry was coming in close, and on the hardstand several men were standing patiently, behind them a police popper, its blades still but its official-business light winking red. In the floodlights that revealed the landing X to the pilot, Cornut vaguely recognized one of the men, an administration staffer; the others all wore police uniforms.

"I wonder," he said, glad that he didn't have to explain the shudder. "Well, I'll sleep well tonight." He took her hand and helped her, unnecessarily but pleasurably, down the steps.

A squat uniformed man stepped forward. "Master Cornut? Sergeant Rhame. You won't remember me, but—"

Cornut said, "But I do. Rhame. You were in one of my classes, six or seven years ago. Master Carl recommended you; in fact, he was your advocate at the orals for your thesis."

There was a pause. "Yes, that's right," said Rhame. "He wanted me to apply for the faculty, but I'd majored in Forensic Probabilistics and the Force had already accepted me, and— Well, that's a long time ago."

Cornut nodded pleasantly. "Good to see you again, Rhame. Good night." But Rhame shook his head.

Cornut stopped, a quick, vague fear beginning to pulse in his mind. No one enjoys the sudden knowledge that the policeman in front of him wants to discuss official business; Rhame's expression told Cornut that that was so. He said sharply, "What is it?"

Rhame was not enjoying himself. "I've been waiting for

you. It's about Master Carl; you're his closest friend, you know. There are some questions—"

Cornut hardly noticed Locille's sudden, frightened clutching at his arm. He stated, "Something's happened to Carl."

Rhame spread his hands. "I'm sorry. I thought you knew. The lieutenant sent word to have you called from the texas; probably you'd left before the message got there." He was trying to be kind, Cornut saw. He said, "It happened about an hour ago—around twelve o'clock. The President had gone to bed—St. Cyr, I mean. Master Carl came storming into his residence—very angry, the house-keeper said."

"Angry about what?" shouted Cornut.

"I was hoping you could tell us that. It must have been something pretty serious. He tried to kill St. Cyr with an axe. Fortunately—" He hesitated, but could find no way to withdraw the word. "As it happened, that is, the President's bodyguard was nearby. He couldn't stop Master Carl any other way; he shot him to death."

Chapter Eleven

Cornut went through that night and the next day in a dream. It was all very simple, everything was made easy for him, but it was impossibly hard to take. Carl dead! The old man shot down—attempting to commit a murder! It was more than unbelievable, it was simply fantastic. He could not admit its possibility for a second.

But he could not deny.

Locille was with him almost every moment, closer than a wife need be, even closer than a watchdog. He didn't notice she was there. He would have noticed if she were missing. It was as though she had always been there, all his life, because his life was now something radically new, different, something that had begun at one o'clock in a morning, stepping out of a ferry popper to see Sergeant Rhame.

Rhame had asked him all the necessary questions in a quarter of an hour, but he had not left him then. It was charity, not duty, that kept him. A policeman, even a forensic probabilistician detailed to Homicide at his own personal request, is used to violence and unlikely murderers, and can sometimes help to explain difficult facts to the innocent bystanders. He tried. Cornut was not grateful. He was only dazed.

He canceled his classes for the next day—tapes would do—and accompanied Rhame on a laborious retracing of Carl's last moves. First they visited St. Cyr's residence and found the President awake and icy. He did not seem shaken by his experience; but then, he never did. He gave them only a moment of his time. "Carl a kill-er. It is a great shock, Cor-nut. Ge-ni-us, we can not ex-pect it to be sta-ble, I sup-pose." Cornut did not want to linger. St. Cyr's presence was never attractive, but the thing that repelled him about the interview was the sight of the fifteenth-century halberd replaced on the floor where, they said, Master Carl had dropped it as the gunman shot him down. The pile of the carpet there was crisper, cleaner than the rest. Cornut was sickly aware that it had been cleaned, and aware what stain had been so quickly dissolved away.

He was glad to be out of the President's richly furnished residence, though the rest of the day was also no joy. Their first stop was the night proctor on Carl's floor, who confirmed that the house master had left at about ten o'clock, seeming disturbed about something but, in his natural custom, giving no clue as to its nature to an undergraduate. As it did not occur to them to question the aborigines, they did not learn of his brief and entirely one-sided conversation, but they picked up his trail at the next point.

Master Carl had turned up at the stacks at twenty-five minutes past ten, demanding instant service from the night librarian.

The librarian was a student, working off part of his tuition, as most students did. He was embarrassed, and Cornut quickly deduced why. "You were asleep, weren't you?"

The student nodded, hanging his head. He was very nearly asleep talking to them; the news of Master Carl's death had reached every night clerk on the campus, and the boy had been unable to get to sleep. "He gave me five demerits, and—" He stopped, suddenly angry with himself.

Cornut deduced the reason. "Consider them canceled," he said kindly. "You're quite right in telling us about them. Sergeant Rhame needs all the information."

"Thank you, Master Cornut. I—uh—I also didn't have a chance to get the ashtray off my desk, and he noticed it. But he just said he wanted to use the stacks." The undergraduate waved toward the great air-conditioned hall where the taped and microfilmed University Library was kept. The library computer was served by some of the same circuits as the Student Test-Indices (College Examinations) Digital Computer on the level above it; all the larger computers on the campus were cross-hooked to some degree.

Rhame was staring at the layout. "It's got more compli-

cated since I was here," he said. "Did Master Carl know
how to use it?"

The student grinned. "He thought he did. Then he came
storming back to me. He couldn't get the data he wanted.
So I tried to help him—but it was classified data. Census
figures."

"Oh," said Cornut.

Sergeant Rhame turned and looked at him. "Well?"

Cornut said, "I think I know what he was after, that's
all. It was the Wolgren."

Rhame understood what he was talking about—
fortunately, as it had not occurred to Cornut that anyone
would fail to be aware of Wolgren's Distributive Law.
Rhame said, "I only use come special Wolgren functions; I
don't see exactly what it has to do with census figures."

Cornut sat down, beginning to lecture. Without looking
he put out his hand and Locille, still with him, took it. "It's
not important to what you're looking for. Anyway, I don't
think it is. We had a question up for study—some anomalies in the Wolgren distribution of the census figures—
and, naturally, there shouldn't be any anomalies. So I took
it as a part-time project." He frowned. "I thought I had it
beaten, but I ran into trouble. Some of the values derived
from my equations turned out to be . . . ridiculous. I tried
to get the real values, but I got the same answer as Master
Carl, they were classified. Silly, of course."

The student librarian chimed in, "*He* said moronic. He
said he was going to take it up with the Saint—" He
stopped, blushing.

Rhame said, "Well, I guess he did. What were the values
that bothered you?"

Cornut shook his head. "Not important; they're wrong.
Only I couldn't find my mistake. So I kept going over the
math. I suppose Carl went through the same thing, and
then decided to take a look at the real values in the hope
that they'd give some clue, just as I did."

"Let's take a look," said Rhame. The student librarian
led them to the library computer, but Cornut nodded him
away. He set up the integrals himself.

"Age values," he explained. "Nothing of any great importance, of course. No reason it should be a secret. But—"

He finished with the keyboard, and indicated the viewer of the screen. It flickered, and then bloomed with a scarlet legend:

Classified Information

Rhame stared at the words. He said, "I don't know."

Cornut understood. "I can't believe it, either. True, Carl was a house master. He felt he had certain rights. . . ."

The policeman nodded. "What about it, son? Did he act peculiar? Agitated?"

"He was mad as hell," said the student librarian with satisfaction. "He said he was going right over to the Sa—to the President's residence and get clearance to receive the data. Said it was moronic—let's see—'moronic, incompetent bureaucracy,' " he finished with satisfaction.

Sergeant Rhame looked at Cornut. "Well, the inquest will have to decide," he said after a moment.

"Do you think he would try to *kill* a man?" Cornut demanded harshly.

"Master Cornut," said the policeman slowly, "I don't think anybody ever really wants to kill anybody. But he blew his top. If he was angry enough, who knows?" He didn't give Cornut a chance to debate the matter. "I guess that's all," he said, turning back to the night librarian. "Unless he said anything else?"

The student hesitated, then grinned faintly. "Just one other thing. As he was leaving, he gave me ten more demerits for smoking on duty."

The following morning Cornut was summoned to the Chancellor's office to hear the reading of Carl's will.

Cornut was only mildly surprised to find that he was Master Carl's sole heir. He was touched, however. And he was saddened, for Master Carl's own voice told him about it.

That was the approved way of recording the most important documents, and it was like Master Carl to believe that the disposition of his tiny estate was of great importance. It was a tape of his image that recited the sonorous phrases: "Being of sound and disposing mind, I devise and bequeath unto my dear friend, Master Cornut—" Cornut sat blinking at the image. It was entirely lifelike. That, of course, was the point; papers could be forged and sound tapes could be altered, but there was no artisan in the world who could quite succeed in making a change in a video tape without leaving a trace. The voice was the voice that had boomed out of a million student television sets for decades. Cornut, watching, hardly listened to the words but found himself trying to tell when it was that Carl had made the decision to leave him all his worldly goods. The cloak, he recalled vaguely, was an old one; but when was it Carl had stopped wearing it?

It didn't matter. Nothing mattered about Master Carl, not any more; the tape rattled and flapped off the reel, and the picture of Master Carl vanished from the screen.

Locille's hand touched his shoulder.

The chancellor said cheerfully, "Well, that's it. All yours. Here's the inventory."

Cornut glanced over it rapidly. Books, more than a thousand of them, value fixed by the appraisers (they must have been working day and night!) at five hundred dollars and a bit. Clothing and personal effects—Cornut involuntarily grinned—an arbitrary value of $1. Cash on hand, a shade over a thousand dollars; including the coins in his pocket when he died. Equity in the University pension plan, $8,460; monthly salary due, calculated to the hour of death, $271; residuals accruing from future use of taped lectures, estimated, $500. Cornut winced. Carl would have been hurt by that, but it was true; there was less and less need for his old tapes, with newer professors adopting newer techniques. And there was an estimate of future royalties to be earned by his mnemonic songs, and that was unkindest of all: $50.

Cornut did not bother to read the itemized liabilities—inheritance tax, income tax due, a few miscellaneous bills. He only noted the net balance was a shade over $8,000.

The funeral director walked silently from the back of the room and suggested, rather handsomely, "Call it eight thousand even. Satisfactory? Then sign here, Master Cornut."

"Here" was at the bottom of a standard mortuary agreement, with the usual fifty-fifty split between the heirs and the mortician. Cornut signed quickly, with a feeling of slight relief. He was getting off very lightly. The statutory minimum fee for a basic funeral was $2500; if the estate had been less than $5 000, he would have inherited only the balance above $2500; if it had been under $2500, he would have had to make up the difference. That was the law. More than one beneficiary, legally responsible for the funeral expenses, had regretted the generous remembering of the deceased. (In fact, there were paupers in the world who sold their wills as an instrument of revenge on occasion. For a hundred dollars' worth of liquor they would bequeath their paltry all to the drink-supplier's worst enemy, who would then, sooner or later, find himself unexpectedly saddled with an inescapable $2500 cost.)

Sergeant Rhame was waiting for them outside the Chancellor's office. "Do you mind?" he asked politely, holding out his hand. Cornut handed over the mortuary agreement, containing the inventory of Carl's estate. The policeman studied it thoughtfully, then shook his head. "Not much money, but he didn't need much, did he? It doesn't help explain anything." He glanced at his watch. "All right," he said. "I'll walk over with you. We're due at the inquest."

As a tribute to the University, the state medical examiner had impaneled a dozen faculty members as his jury. Only one was from the Mathematics Department, a woman professor named Janet, but Cornut recognized several of the others, vaguely, from faculty teas and walks on the campus.

St. Cyr testified, briefly and in his customary uninflected pendulum-tick, that Master Carl had shown no previous signs of insanity but had been wild and threatening indeed the night of his death.

St. Cyr's housekeeper testified the same, adding that she had feared for her own life.

The bodyguard who killed Carl took the stand. Cornut

felt Locille shrink in the seat beside him; he understood; he felt the same revulsion. The man did not seem much different from other men, though; he was middle-aged, husky, with a speech impediment that faintly echoed St. Cyr's own. He explained that he had been on President St. Cyr's payroll for nearly ten years; that he had once been a policeman and that it was not uncommon for very wealthy men to hire ex-policemen as bodyguards; and that he had never before had to kill anyone in defense of St. Cyr's life. "But this one. He was dangerous. He was . . . going to kill . . . somebody." He got the words out slowly, but without appearing particularly agitated.

Then there were a few others—Cornut himself, the night proctor, the student librarian, even the sexwriter, Farley, who said that Master Carl had indeed seemed upset on his one personal contact with him but, of course, the occasion had been a disturbing one; he had told him of Master Cornut's most recent suicide attempt. Cornut attempted to ignore the faces that turned toward him.

The verdict took five minutes: "Killed in self-defense, in the course of attempting to commit murder."

For days after that Cornut kept away from St. Cyr's residence, for the sake of avoiding Carl's executioner. He had never seen the man before Carl was killed, and never wanted to see him again.

But as time passed, Carl's death dwindled in his mind; his own troubles, more and more, filled it.

As day followed day, he began to approach, then reached, finally passed the all-time record for suiciders. And he was still alive.

He was still alive because of the endless patience and watchfulness of Locille. Every night she watched him asleep, every morning she was up before him. She began to look pale, and he found her taking catnaps in the dressing room while he was lecturing to his classes; but she did not complain. She also did not tell him, until he found the marks and guessed, that twice in one week, even with her alert beside him, he had nearly severed his wrists, first on a letter opener, second on a broken drinking tumbler.

When he chided her for not telling him, she kissed him. That was all.

He was having dreams, too, queer ones; he remembered them sharply when he woke, and for a while told them to Locille, and then stopped. They were very peculiar. They had to do with being watched, being watched by some gruff, irritated warden, or by a hostile Roman crowd waiting for his blood in the arena. They were unpleasant; and he tried to explain them to himself. It was because he was subconsciously aware of Locille watching him, he told himself; and in the next breath said, *Paranoia.* He did not believe it. . . . But what then? He considered returning to his analyst, but when he broached it to Locille she only looked paler and more strained. Some of the sudden joy had gone out of their love; and that worried Cornut; and it did not occur to him that the growing trust and solidarity between them was perhaps worth more.

But not all the joy had gone. Apart from interludes of passion, somewhat constrained by Locille's ironclad determination to stay awake until he was quite asleep, apart from the trust and closeness, there were other things. There was the interest of work shared, for as Cornut's wife Locille became more his pupil than ever before in one of his classes; together they rechecked the Wolgren, found it free of gross error, reluctantly shelved it for lack of confirming data and began a new study of prime distribution in very large numbers. They were walking back to the Math Tower one warm day, planning a new approach through analytic use of the laws of congruence, when Locille stopped and caught his arm.

Egerd was coming toward them.

He was tanned, but he did not look well. Part of it was for reasons Cornut had only slowly come to know; he was uncomfortable in the presence of the girl he loved and the man she had married. But there was something else. He looked sick. Locille was direct: "What in the world's the matter with you?"

Egerd grinned. "Don't you know about Med School? It's traditional, hazing freshmen. The usual treatment is a skin fungus that turns sweat rancid, so you stink, or a few drops of something that makes you break out in orange blotches, or—well, never mind. Some of the jokes are kind of, uh, personal."

Locille said angrily, "That's terrible. You don't look very funny to me, Egerd."

Cornut said to her, after Egerd had left, "Boys will be boys." She looked at him swiftly. He knew his tone had been callous. He didn't know that she understood why; he thought his sudden sharp stab of jealousy had been perfectly concealed.

A little over two weeks after Master Carl's death, the proctor knocked on Cornut's door to say that he had a visitor. It was Sergeant Rhame, with a suitcase full of odds and ends. "Master Carl's personal effects," he explained. "They belong to you now. Naturally, we had to borrow them for examination."

Cornut shrugged. The stuff was of no great value. He poked through the suitcase; some shabby toilet articles, a book marked *Diary*—he flipped it open eagerly, but it recorded only demerits and class attendances—an envelope containing photographic film.

Sergeant Rhame said, "That's what I wanted to ask you about. He had a lot of photographic equipment. We found several packs of film, unopened, which Master Carl had pressed against some kind of radiation-emitting paint on a paper base. The lab spent a lot of time trying to figure it out. They guessed he was trying to get the gamma radiation from the paint to register on the film, but we don't know why."

Cornut said, "Neither do I, but I can make a guess." He explained about Carl's off-duty interests, and the endless laborious work that he had been willing to put into them. "I'm not sure what his present line was, but I know it had something to do with trying to get prints of geometrical figures—stars, circles, that sort of thing. Why? Do you mean he finally succeeded in getting one?"

"Not exactly." Sergeant Rhame opened the package and handed Cornut a glossy print. "All the negatives were blank except one. This one. Make anything of it?"

Cornut studied it. It seemed to be a photograph of a sign, or a printer's proof. It was not very well defined, but there was no doubt what it said. He puzzled over it for a while, then shook his head.

The lettering on the print said simply:

YOU DAMN OLD FOOL

Chapter Twelve

The wind was brisk, and the stretched cables under the texas made a bull-roarer sound as they vibrated. The pneumatic generators rattled, whined and crashed. Locille's brother was too used to them to notice.

He wasn't feeling very well, but it was his custom to do what his parents expected him to do, and they expected that he would watch the University broadcasts of his sister's classes. The present class was Cornut's, and Roger eyed with polite ignorance the professor's closely-reasoned exposition of Wilson's Theorem. He watched the dancing girls and the animated figures with more interest, but it was, on the whole, a disappointing show. The camera panned the studio audience only twice, and in neither case was he able to catch a glimpse of Locille.

He reported to his mother, took his last look at the flag Locille had brought him, and went to work.

As the day wore on, Roger felt worse. First it was his head pounding, then his bones aching, then an irresistible sudden nausea. Roger's job was conducive to that; he spent the whole day standing thigh deep in a smelly fluid composed of salt water, fish lymph and blood.

Ordinarily it didn't bother him (as nothing much bothered him, anyhow). Today was different. He steadied himself with one hand against a steel-topped table, shook his head violently to clear it. He had just come back from a hasty trip to the washroom, where he had vomited profusely. Now it seemed he was close to having to race out there again.

Down the table the sorter called, "Roger! *Hey!* You're holding up the works."

Roger rubbed the back of his neck and mumbled something that was not intelligible, even to himself. He got back to work because he had to; the fish were piling up.

It was the sorter's job to separate the females of the stocked Atlantic salmon run from the males. The male fish were thrust down a chute to a quick and undistinguished death. But the females, in breeding season, contained something too valuable to be wasted on the mash of entrails and bony parts that made dry fish meal. That was Roger's job—Roger's and a few dozen others who stood at tables just like his. The first step was to grasp the flopping female by the tail with one hand and club her brains out, or as nearly as possible out, with the other. The second was to hold her with both hands, exposing her belly to his partner across the table, whose long, fat knife ripped open the egg sac inside. (Quite often the knife missed. Roger's job was not sought after.) A quick wringing motion; the eggs poured one way, the gutted body slid another; and he was ready for the next fish. Sometimes the fish struggled terribly, which was unpleasant for a man with imagination; even the dullest grew to dislike the work. Roger had held the same job for four years.

"Come on, Roger!" The sorter was yelling at him again. Roger stared at him woozily. For the first time he became suddenly aware of the constant *slam*, bang, rattle, *roar* that permeated the low-level fishery plant. He opened his mouth to say something; and then he ran. He made it to the washroom, but with nothing at all to spare.

An hour later, his mother was astonished to see him home. "What happened?"

He tried to explain everything that had happened, but it involved some complicated words. He settled for "I didn't feel good."

She was worried. Roger was always healthy. He didn't look good, ever, but that was because the part of his brain that was damaged had something to do with his muscle tone; in fact, he had been sick hardly a week's total in his life. She said doubtfully, "Your father will be home in an hour or so, but maybe I ought to call him. I wonder. What do you think, Roger?"

That was rhetoric; she had long since reconciled herself to the fact that her son did not think. He stumbled and straightened up, scowling. The back of his neck was beginning to pain badly. He was in no mood to contemplate hard questions. What he wanted was to go to bed, with Locille's flag by his pillow, so that he could fondle it drowsily before he slept. That was what he liked. He told his mother as much.

She was seriously concerned now. "You *are* sick. I'd better call the clinic. You lie down."

"No. No, you don't have to. They called over at the place." He swallowed with some pain; he was beginning to shiver. "Mr. Garney took me to the dia—the dia—"

"The diagnosticon at the clinic, Roger!"

"Yes, and I got some pills." He reached in his pocket and held up a little box. "I already took one and I have to take some more later."

His mother was not satisfied, but she was no longer very worried; the diagnostic equipment did not often fail. "It's that cold water you stand in," she mourned, helping him to his room. "I've told you, Roger. You ought to have a better job. Slicer, maybe even sorter. Or maybe you can get out of that part of it altogether. You've worked there four years now. . . ."

"Good night," Roger said inappropriately—it was early afternoon. He began to get ready for bed, feeling a little better, at least psychologically, in the familiar, comfortable room with his familiar, comfortable bed and the little old Japanese flag wadded up by the pillow. "I'm going to sleep now," he told her, and got rid of her at last.

He huddled under the warming covers—set as high as the rheostat would go, but still not high enough to warm his shaking body. The pain in his head was almost blinding now.

At the clinic, Mr. Garney had been painfully careful to explain what the pills were for. They would take away the pain, stop the throbbing, make him comfortable, let him sleep. Feverishly Roger shook another one out of the box and swallowed it.

It worked, of course. The clinic's pills always performed as advertised. The pain dwindled to a bearable ache, then to a memory; the throbbing stopped; he began to fall asleep.

Roger felt drowsily peaceful. He could not see his face, and therefore did not know how flushed it was becoming; he had no idea that his temperature was climbing rapidly. He went quite happily to sleep . . . with the old, frayed flag against his cheek . . . just as he had done for nearly three weeks now, and as he would never in this life do again.

The reason Roger hadn't seen his sister in the audience was that she wasn't there; she was waiting in Cornut's little dressing room. Cornut suggested it. "You need the rest," he said solicitously, and promised to review the lesson with her later.

Actually he had another motive entirely. As soon as he was off the air, he wrote a note for Locille and gave it to a student to deliver:

There's something I have to do. I'll be gone for a couple of hours. I promise I'll be all right. Don't worry.

Before the note reached her, Cornut was at the bridge, in the elevator, on his way to the city.

He did have something to do, and he did not want to talk to Locille about it. The odd dreams had been worsening, and there had been other things. He nearly always had a hangover now, for instance. He had found that a few drinks at night made him sleep better and he had come to rely on them.

And there was something else, about which he could not talk to Locille at all because she would not talk.

The monotrack let him out far downtown, in a bright, noisy, stuffy underground station. He paused at a phone booth to check the address of the sexwriter, Farley, and hurried up to street level, anxious to get away from the smell and noise. That was a mistake. In the open the noise pounded more furiously, the air was even more foul. Great cubical blocks of buildings rose over him; small three-wheeled cars and large commercial vehicles pounded on two levels around him. It was only a minute's walk to Farley's office, but the minute was an ordeal.

The sign on the door was the same as the lettering on his folder:

S. R. Farley
Consultant

The sexwriter's secretary looked very doubtful, but finally reported that Mr. Farley would be able to see Master Cornut, even without an appointment. Cornut sat across the desk, refused a cigarette and said directly, "I've studied the sample scripts you left for us, Farley. They're interesting, though I don't believe I'll require your services in future. I think I've grasped the notation, and I note that there is one page of constants which seems to describe the personality traits of my wife and myself."

"Oh, yes. Very important," said Farley. "Yours is incomplete, of course, as I had no real opportunity to interview you, but I secured your personnel-file data, the profile from the Med Center and so on."

"Good. Now I have a question to ask you."

Cornut hesitated. The proper way to ask the question was to say: I suspect, from a hazy, sleepy recollection, that the other morning I made a rather odd suggestion to my wife. That was the proper way, but it was embarrassing; and it also involved a probability of having to explain how many rather odd things he had done, some of them nearly fatal, in those half-waking moments. . . . "Let me borrow a piece of paper," he said instead, and rapidly sketched in a line of symbols. Stating the problem in terms of δ and $\female$ made it vastly less embarrassing; he only hoped he had remembered the terms correctly. He shoved it across the desk to the sexwriter. "What would you say to this? Does it fit in with your profile of our personalities?"

Farley studied the line and raised his eyebrows. "Absolutely not," he said promptly. "You wouldn't think of it; she wouldn't accept it."

"You could say it was an objectionable thing?"

"*Mas*ter *Cor*nut! Don't use moralistic terms! A couple's sex life is entirely a private matter; what is customary and moral in one place is—"

"Please, Mr. Farley. In terms of our own morals—you have them sketched out on the profile—this would be objectionable?"

The sexwriter laughed. "More than that, Master Cornut. It would be absolutely impossible. I know my data weren't complete, but this sort of thing is out of the question."

Cornut took a deep breath. "But suppose," he said after a moment, "I told you that I had proposed this to my wife."

Farley drummed his fingers on the desk. "I can only say that other factors are involved," he said.

"Like what?"

Farley said seriously, "You must be trying to drive her away from you."

In the two blocks between Farley's office and the monotrack station entrance, Cornut saw three men killed; a turbotruck on the upper traffic level seemed to stagger, grazed another vehicle and shot through the guard rail, killing its driver and two pedestrians.

It was a shocking interpolation of violence into Cornut's academic life, but it seemed quite in keeping with the rest of his day. His own life was rapidly going as badly out of control as the truck.

You must be trying to drive her away from you.

Cornut boarded his train, hardly noticing, thinking hard. He didn't *want* to drive Locille away!

But he also did not *want* to kill himself, and yet there was no doubt that he had kept trying. It was all part of a pattern, there could be no doubt of its sum: He was trying to destroy himself in every way. Failing to end his life, that destroyer inside himself was trying to end the part of his life that had suddenly grown to mean most to him, his love for Locille. And yet it was the same thing really, he thought, for with Locille gone, Carl dead, Egerd transferred, he would have no one close to him to help him through the dangerous half-awake moments that came at least twice in every twenty-four hours.

He would not last a day.

He slumped back into his seat, with the first sensation of despair he had ever felt. One part of his mind said judgmentally: It's too bad.

Another part entirely was taking in his surroundings; even in his depression, the novelty of being among so many non-University men and women made an impression. They seemed so tired and angry, he thought abstractedly; one or two even looked sick. He wondered if any of them had ever known the helplessness of being under siege from the most insidious enemy of all, himself.

But suppose Master Carl was right after all, said Cornut to himself, quite unexpectedly.

The thought startled him. It came through without preamble, and if there had been a train of rumination that caused it, he had forgotten its existence. Right? Right about what?

The P.A. system murmured that the next stop was his. Cornut got up absently, thinking. Right?

He had doubted that Master Carl had really tried to kill St. Cyr. But the evidence was against him; the police lab had verified his fingerprints on the axe, and they could not have been deceived.

So suppose Carl really had picked up the weapon to split the old man's skull. Incredible! But *if* he had . . . And *if* Carl had not merely gone into an aberrated senile rage. . . .

Why then, said Cornut to himself, emerging from the elevator at the base of the Bridge pier and blinking at the familiar campus, why then perhaps he had a reason. Perhaps St. Cyr needed killing.

Chapter Thirteen

Entering the room was like being plunged under the surface of the sea. The lights were blue-green, concealed and reflecting from blue-green walls. A spidery mural of blue and green lines covered one wall like a wave pattern; from boxes along the floor grating rose curving branches of pale plants from the hybridization farms, resembling the kelp of the mermaid forests.

The pelagic motif was not a matter of design, it was only that these shapes and these colors were those that most pleased and comforted President St. Cyr. This was his room. Not his study, with its oak panels and ancient armor; not even the "private" drawing room where he sometimes entertained members of the faculty. This was the room he reserved for a very, very few.

Four of these few were present now. A fat man, gross arms quivering, turned himself around and said, "When?" He said, "Do you want us all?" He said, "That's Jillson's job." St. Cyr grinned and, after a moment, his bodyguard said, "No, I don't. Really. You enjoy it more than I do." A woman in a preposterously young frock opened her thin-lipped mouth and cackled hilariously, as there was a knock on the door.

Jillson, the bodyguard, opened it and revealed St. Cyr's thin, silent housekeeper with Master Cornut.

St. Cyr, on a turquoise wing chair, raised a hand. Jillson took Master Cornut by the arm and led him in, the door behind him closing on the housekeeper. "Mas-ter Cor-nut," said St. Cyr in his odd, uninflected voice. "I have been wait-ing for you." The old woman in the young dress

273

laughed shrilly for no visible reason; the bodyguard smiled; the fat man chuckled.

Cornut could not help, even then, looking around this room where he had never been. It was cool—the air was kept a full dozen degrees under the usual room temperature Cornut liked. There was a muted muttering of music in the background, too low to distinguish a tune. And these people—were odd.

He ignored Jillson, the assassin of Master Carl, whom he remembered from the inquest. The fat man blinked at him. "Sen-a-tor Dane," said St. Cyr. "And Miss May Kerbs."

Miss May Kerbs was the one who had laughed. She swayed over to Cornut, looking like a teen-age girl in her first party formal. "We were talking about you," she said shrilly and Cornut, with a physical shock, recognized that this was no teen-ager. She suddenly resembled the woman from South America whom he had met on the Field Expedition; the features were not much alike, but their state of repair was identical. The face was a skull's face under the make-up. She was fifty if she was a day—no, seventy-five—no; she was older than that; she was older than he liked to think, for a woman who dressed like a brash virgin.

Cornut found himself grotesquely acknowledging the introductions. He could not take his eyes off the woman. Talking about him? What had they been saying.

"We knew you'd be here, pal," said the assassin, Jillson, kindly. "You think we murdered the kid."

"The kid?"

"Master Carl," explained Jillson. *He had a reason*, said a thought in Cornut's mind. Queerly, it came in the half-stammering accent of Jillson.

"But sit down, Mas-ter Cor-nut." St. Cyr gestured. Politely the woman plumped cushions of aqua and turquoise on a divan.

"I don't want to sit down!"

"No. But please do." St. Cyr's blue-tinged face was only polite.

The fat man wheezed, "Too bad, youngster. We didn't want to goose him along. I mean, why bother? But he was a nuisance. Every year," he explained sunnily, "we get maybe half a dozen who really make nuisances of themselves, mostly like you, some like him. His trouble was going after the classified material in the stacks. Well," he said severely, waving a fat finger, "that material is classified for a reason."

Cornut sat down at last because he couldn't help himself. It was not going at all as he had expected; they were not denying a thing. But to admit that they killed Carl to protect some unimportant statistic in the census figures? It made no sense!

The blonde floozie laughed shrilly.

"Forgive Miss Kerbs," said the fat man. "She thinks you are funny for presuming to judge whether or not our actions are sensible. Believe me, young man, they are."

Cornut found that he was grinding his teeth. These one-sided conversations, the answers coming before the questions were spoken, these queer half-understood remarks. . . .

It was as though they were reading his mind.

It was as though they knew every thought he had.

It was as though they were—but that's impossible! He thought, no, it can't be! Carl proved it!

The damn old fool.

Cornut jumped. The thought was in the tones of the fat man's wheeze, and he remembered where he had seen words like that before.

The fat man nodded, his chins pulsing like a floating jellyfish. "We exposed his plate for him," he chuckled. "Oh, yes. It was only a joke, but we knew he would not live to make trouble over it. Once he had the Wolgren analysis, he would have to be helped along." He said politely, "Too bad, because we wanted him to publish his proof that telepathy was impossible. It is; quite true. For him. But not for us. And unfortunately, my young friend, not for you."

Locille woke shivering, reaching out at once to Cornut's side of the bed; but he was not in it.

She turned on the room lights and scanned the nearest of the battery of clocks; one o'clock in the morning.

She got up, looked out the window, listened at the hall door, turned on the broadcast radio, shook the speaker-mike of the University annunciator to make sure it was working, checked the telephone to see that it was not unhooked, sat down on the side of the bed and, finally, began silently to weep. She was frightened.

Whatever compulsion drove Cornut to try suicide had never before stricken him when he was wide-awake and in possession of his thoughts. Was that no longer true? But if it was still true, *why* had he gone off like that?

The radio was whispering persuasively its stream of news-bulletins: Strikes in Gary, Indiana, a wreck of a cargo rocket, three hundred cases of Virus Gamma in one twelve-hour period, a catastrophic accident between a nuclear trawler and a texas (she listened briefly, then relaxed) off the coast of Haiti. As it did not mention Cornut's name, she heard very little. Where could he be?

When the telephone sounded she answered it at once.

It was not Cornut; it was the rough, quick voice of a busy man. "—asked me to call. She is with your brother. Can you come?"

"My mother asked you to call?"

Impatiently: "That's what I said. Your brother is seriously ill." The voice did not hesitate. "It is likely that he will die within the next few hours. Good-by."

Love said, No, stay, wait for Cornut; but it was her mother who had sent for her. Locille dressed swiftly.

She left urgent instructions with the night proctor on what to do when—not if; *when*—Cornut returned. Watch him asleep; keep the door open; check him every half hour; be with him when he wakes. "Yes, ma'am," said the student, and then, with gentleness, "He'll be all right."

But would he? Locille hurried across the campus, closing her mind to that question. It was too late for a ferry from the island. She would have to go to the Bridge, ride to the city, hope for a helipopper ferry to the texas from there. The Med Center was bright with lights from many rooms; curious, she thought, and hurried by. In their wired enclosure, the aborigines were murmuring, not asleep. Curious again.

But suppose the proctor forgot?

Locille reassured herself that he would not forget; he was one of Cornut's own students. In any case, she had to take the chance. She was almost grateful that something had happened to take her away, for the waiting had been unbearable.

She walked by the President's residence without a glance; it did not occur to her that the fact that it, too, was lighted, was of any relevance to her own problems. In this she was wrong.

It was not until she was actually boarding the slow-arriving monotrack that realization of where she was going and why finally struck her. Roger! He was *dying*.

She began to weep, for Roger, for the missing Cornut, for herself; but there was no one else on the car to see.

At that moment, Cornut, sore-eyed, was picking himself up from the floor.

Over him stood Jillson, patient and jolly, holding a club wrapped with a wet cloth. Cornut was aching as he had never imagined he could. He mumbled, "You don't have to hit me any more."

"Per-haps we do," said St. Cyr from his blue-green throne. "We do not like this, you know. But we must."

"Speak for yourself," said Jillson cheerfully, and the ancient blonde screeched with laughter. They were talking among themselves, Cornut realized; he could hear only the audible part, but they were joking, commenting . . . they were having a fine old time, while this methodical maniac bludgeoned him black and blue.

The fat senator wheezed, "Understand our position, Cornut. We aren't cruel. We don't kill you shorties for nothing. But we aren't human, and we can't be judged by human laws. . . . All right, Jillson."

The bodyguard brought the club around, and Cornut sank against the cushions the thoughtful old blonde kept re-piling for him. What made it particularly bad was that the senator held a gun. The first time he was beaten he had fought, but then the senator had held him at gunpoint while Jillson methodically battered him unconscious. And all the time they kept talking!

St. Cyr said mildly, "Stop."

It was time for another break. That had been the fifth beating in six or seven hours, and in between they had interrogated him. "Tell us what you un-der-stand, Cornut."

The club had taught him obedience. "You are a world-wide organization," he said obediently, "of the next species after humanity. I understand that. You need to survive, and it doesn't matter if the rest of us don't. Through your telepathic abilities you can suggest suicide to some persons who have the power in a latent form——" *Thud*.

"An a-bort-ed form," corrected St. Cyr as Cornut struggled erect again after the blow.

He coughed, and saw blood on the back of his hand. But he only said, "An aborted form. Like myself."

"Abortions of mutations," chuckled the senator. "Unsuccessful attempts on the part of nature to create ourselves."

"Yes. Abortions of mutations, unsuccessful attempts. That is what I am," Cornut parroted. "And——and you are able to suggest many things, as long as the subject has the——the abortive talent, and as long as you are able to reach his mind when it is not fully awake."

The blonde said, "Very good! You're a good learner, Cornut. But telepathy is only a fringe benefit. Do you know what it is that makes us *really* different?"

He cringed away from Jillson as he shook his head.

The bodyguard glanced at the woman, shrugged and said, "All right, I won't hit him. Go ahead."

"What it is that makes us different is our age, my dear boy." She giggled shrilly. "For example, I am two hundred and eighty-three years old."

They fed him after a while and let him rest.

Although he ached in every cell, there was hardly a mark on him; that was the reason for the padding in the club. And that had a meaning too, Cornut thought painfully. If they didn't intend to mark him, then they realized that he would be seen. Which meant that, at least, they weren't going to kill him out of hand and dump his body in the sea.

Two hundred and eighty-three years old.

And yet she was not the oldest of the four of them; only Jillson was younger, a child of a century or so. The senator had been born while America was still a British colony. St. Cyr had been born in de Gaulle's France.

The whole key had been in the restricted areas of the stacks, if he had only seen it; for the anomaly in the Wolgren application was not Wolgren's fault at all. What the data would have shown was a failure of some people to die. Statistically insignificant for thousands of years, that fraction had grown and grown in the last two or three centuries—since Lister, since Pasteur, since Fleming. They were immortal—not because they could not become diseased or succumb to a wound, but because they would not otherwise die.

And with the growth of preventive medicine, they had begun to assert their power. They had really very little. They were not wiser than the rest of humanity or stronger. Even their telepathy was, it seemed, only unique because the short-lived human had not the time to develop it; it depended on intricate and slow-forming neuronic hookups; it was a sign of maturity, like puberty or facial hair. Everything that made them powerful was only the gift of time. They had money. (But who, given a century or two of compound interest, could not be as rich as he chose?) They had a tight-held closed corporation devoted to their mutual interests—which was only sensible. They had furthered many a war, for what greater boon than war is there to medical science? They had endowed countless foundations, for the surgery of the short-lived could help preserve their own infinitely more valuable lives. And they had only contempt for the short-lived who fed them, served them and made their lives possible.

They *had* to be a closed corporation. Even an immortal needs friends, and the ordinary humans could for them be nothing more than weekend guests.

Contempt . . . and fear. There were, they told him, the

Cornuts, who had a rudimentary telepathic sense, who could not be allowed to live to develop it. Suggest killing, and the short-lived one died; it was that easy. The sleeping mind can build a dream out of a closing door, a distant truck's exhaust. The half-awake mind can convert that dream into action. . . .

He heard a shrill laugh and the door opened. Jillson came in first, beaming. "No!" cried Cornut instinctively, bracing himself against the club.

Chapter Fourteen

Locille sat next to her mother in the hospital's cafeteria, grateful that at last they had found a place to sit down. The hospital on the texas was unusually busy, worried visitors occupying every inch of space in the waiting room, the halls outside the reception area, even the glassed-in sundeck that hung over the angry waves and was normally used for the comfort of the patients during the day. It was very late, and the cafeteria should have been closed; but the hospital had opened it for coffee and very little else. Her mother said something, but Locille only nodded. She hadn't heard. It was not easy to hear, with the loud bullroarer *twangg* of the suspended cables from the texas droning at them. And she had, besides, been thinking mostly of Cornut.

There had been no fresh news from the night proctor on the phone; Cornut had not returned.

"He ate so well," her mother said suddenly. Locille patted her hand. The coffee was cold, but she drank it anyhow. The doctor knew where to find her, she thought, though of course he would be busy. . . .

"He was the best of my babies," said her mother.

Locille knew that it was very close to ending for her brother. The rash that baffled the medics, the fever that glazed his eyes—they were only the outward indicators of a terrible battle inside his motionless body; they were headlines on a newspaper a thousand miles away, saying *800 Marines Die Storming Iwo;* they represented the fact of blood and pain and death, but they were not the fact itself. Roger was dying. The outward indicators had been controlled, but salve could only dry up the pustulant sores, pills could only ease his breathing, shots could only soothe the pain in his head.

"He ate so well," said her mother, dreaming aloud, "and he talked at eighteen months. He had a little elephant with a music box and he could wind it up."

"Don't worry," whispered Locille falsely.

"But we let him go swimming," sighed her mother, looking around the crowded room. It was she, not Locille, who first saw the nurse coming toward them through the crowd, and she must have known as soon as Locille, from the look on the nurse's face, what the message was that she had for them.

"He was the tenth in my ward today," whispered the nurse, looking for a private place to tell them and not finding it. "He never regained consciousness."

Cornut walked out of the residence, blinking. It was morning. "Nice day," he said politely to Jillson, beside him. Jillson nodded. He was pleased with Cornut. The kid wasn't going to give them any trouble.

As they walked Jillson "shouted" in Cornut's mind. It was hard with these half-baked telepaths, he sighed; but it was part of his job. He was the executioner. He took Cornut's elbow—bodily contact helped a little, not much—and reminded him what he was supposed to do. *You need to die. You'll kill yourself.*

"Oh, yes," said Cornut aloud. He was surprised. He'd promised, hadn't he? He bore no resentment for the beating. He understood that it had a purpose; the more dazed, the more exhausted he was, the surer their control of him. He had no objection at all to being under the control of four ancient immortals, since—he was.

You die, Cornut, but what difference does it make? Today, tomorrow, fifty years from now. It's all the same.

"That's right," Cornut agreed politely. He was not very interested, the subject had been thoroughly covered, all night long. He noticed absently that there was a considerable crowd around the Med Center. The whole campus seemed somehow uneasy.

They crossed under the shadow of the Administration Building and circled around it, toward Math Tower.

You will die, you know, "shouted" Jillson. *One day the world will wake up and no Cornut. Put a stethoscope to his poor chest, no heart beats. The sound of a beating heart that you have heard every day of your life will never be heard again.* Cornut was embarrassed. These things were true; he did not mind being told them; but it was certainly rather immature of Jillson to take such evident pleasure in them. His thoughts came with a sort of smirk, like an adolescent gloating over a dirty picture.

The brain turns into jelly, chanted Jillson gleefully. *The body turns into slime.* He licked his lips, hot-eyed.

Cornut looked about him, anxious to change the subject. "Oh, look," he said. "Isn't that Sergeant Rhame?"

Jillson pounded on: *The hangnail on your thumb that hurts now will dissolve and rot and molder. Not even the pain will ever be thought of by any living human again. Your bedgirl, is there anything you put off telling her? You put it off too long, Cornut.*

"It is Sergeant Rhame. Sergeant!"

Damn, crashed a thought in Cornut's mind; but Jillson was smiling, smiling. "Hello, Sergeant," he said with his voice, his mind raging.

Cornut would have helped Jillson along if he had known how, but his half-dazed condition robbed him of enterprise. Too bad, he thought consolingly, hoping that Jillson would pick up the thought. *I know St. Cyr ordered you to stay with me until I was dead, but don't worry. I'll kill myself. I promise.*

Sergeant Rhame was talking gruffly to Jillson about the mob at Med Center. Cornut wished Rhame would go away. He understood that Rhame was a danger to the immortals; they could not be involved, with the same people, in too many violent deaths. Rhame had investigated the death of Master Carl at Jillson's hands; he could not now be allowed to investigate even the suicide of Master Cornut, when he had seen Jillson with him going to his death. Jillson would have to leave him now. Too bad. It was so *right*, Cornut thought, that he should die for the sake of preserving the safety of the immortals, as they were the future of humanity. He knew this; they had told him so themselves.

A word caught his attention: "—since the sickness began they've been mobbing every hospital," said Sergeant Rhame to Jillson, waving at the mob before Med Center.

"Sickness?" asked Cornut, diverted. He stared at the policeman. It was as though he had said, I've got to get some garlic, there are vampires loose tonight. Sickness was a relic of the dark ages. You had a headache or a queasy stomach, yes, but you went to the clinic and the diagnosticon did the rest.

Rhame grumbled, "Where've you been, Master Cornut? Nearly a thousand deaths in this area alone. Mobs seeking immunization. What they were calling Virus Gamma. It's really smallpox, they think."

"Smallpox?" Even more fantastic! Cornut knew the word only as an archeological relic.

"Accidents all over the city," said Rhame, and Cornut thought suddenly of the crash he had seen. "Fever and rash and—oh, I don't know the symptoms. But it's fatal. The medics don't seem to have a cure."

"Me disfella smellim," said a voice from behind Rhame. "Him spoilim fes distime. Plantim manyfella pox." It was one of the aboriginals, quietly observing while Rhame's police erected barricades in front of their enclosure. "Plantim mefella Mary," he added sadly.

Rhame said: "Understand any of it? It's English, if you listen close. Pidgin. He says they know about smallpox. I think he said his wife died of it."

"Plantim mefella Mary," agreed the aboriginal.

Rhame said, "Unfortunately, I think he's right. Looks like your Field Expedition brought a lot of trouble back with it; the focus of infection seems to vector from these people. Look at their faces." Cornut looked; the broad, dark cheeks were waffled with old pitted scars. "So we're trying to keep the mob from making trouble here," said Sergeant Rhame, "by putting a fence around them."

Cornut was even more incredulous than before. Mob violence?

It was not really his problem . . . since he would have no more problems in the world. He nodded politely to Rhame, conspiratorially to Jillson, and moved on toward Math Tower. The aborigine yelled something after him— "Waitimup mefella Masatura-san, he speak you!"—it sounded like. Cornut paid no attention.

Jillson "yelled" after him too. *Don't forget! You must die!* Cornut turned and nodded. Of course he had to die. It was only right. . . .

But it was difficult, all the same.

Fortunately Locille was not in the room. Cornut felt, and quelled, a swift reeling sense of horror at the thought of losing her. It was only an emotion, and he was its master.

Probably the pithecanthropus had had similar emotions he thought, casting about for a convenient way to die. It was not as easy as it looked.

He made sure his door was locked, thought for a moment, and decided to treat himself to a farewell drink. He found a bottle, poured, toasted the air and said aloud, "To the next species." Then he buckled down to work.

The idea of dying is never far from the mind of any mortal, but Cornut had never viewed it as anything up close in the foreground of his future. It was curiously alarming. Everybody did it, he reassured himself. (Well, almost everybody.) Babies did it. Old men fouled themselves, sighed and did it. Neurotics did it because of an imagined insult, or because of fear. Brave men did it in war. Virgins did it as the less undesirable alternative to a sultan's seraglio, so said the old stories. Why did it seem so hard?

As Cornut was a methodical man, he sat down at his desk and began to make a list, headed:

MEANS OF DEATH

1. Poison.
2. Slashed wrists.

3. Jumping from window. (Or bridge.)
4. Electrocution. . . .

He paused. Electrocution? It didn't sound so bad, especially considering that he had already tried most of the others, nearly. It would be nice to try something new. He poured himself another drink to think about it, and began to hum. He was feeling quite peaceful.

"It's only right that I should die," he said comfortably. "Naturally. Are you listening, Jillson?" He couldn't tell, of course. But probably they were.

And maybe they were worried. That was a saddening thought; he didn't want the immortals to worry about him. "I understand perfectly," he said out loud. "I hope you hear me. I'm in your way." He paused, not aware that he had raised a lectorial finger. "It is," he said, "like this. Suppose I had terminal cancer. Suppose St. Cyr and I were in a shipwreck, and there was only one lifebelt. He has a life ahead of him, I have at best a week of pain. Who gets the lifebelt?" He shook the finger. "St. Cyr does!" he thundered. "And this is the same case. I have a mortal disease, humanity. And it's their lives or mine!"

He poured another drink and decided that the truths that had been whipped into him were too great to lose. The sheet of paper with suicide possibilities fell unheeded to the floor; humming, he wrote:

We are children and the immortals are fully grown. Like children, we need their knowledge. They lead us, they direct our universities and plan our affairs; they have the wisdom of centuries and without them we would be lost, random particles, statistical chaos. But we are dangerous children, so they must remain secret and those who guess must die. . . .

He crumpled the piece of paper angrily. He had nearly spoiled everything! His own vanity had almost revealed the secret he was about to die to protect. He scrambled on the floor for the list of possibilities, but stopped himself, bent over, staring at the floor.

The truth was that he didn't really like any of them.

He sat up and poured a drink sadly. He couldn't rely on himself to do a good job, he said to himself. Slashing his wrists, for example. Someone might come; and what could be more embarrassing than waking up on an operating table with sutures in his veins and the whole damned thing to do over again?

He noticed that his glass was again empty, but didn't bother to refill it. He was feeling quite sufficiently alcoholic already. If it weren't for his own confounded ineptitude he could be feeling pretty good, in fact, for it was nice to know that in a very short time he would be serving the best interests of the world by dying. Very nice. . . . He got up and wandered to the window, beaming. Outside the mobs were still swarming, trying to get immunization at the Med Center; poor fools; he was *so* much better off than they! "Strike the Twos and strike the Threes," he sang. "The Sieve of— Say!"

He had an idea. How fine it was, he thought gratefully, to have the wise helping hand of an elder friend in a time like this. He didn't have to worry about how to die, or whether he'd make a mess of it. He needed only to give St. Cyr and the others a chance. Just relax . . . let himself get drowsy . . . even more drunk, perhaps. They would do the rest.

"The Sieve of Eratosthenes," he sang cheerfully. "When the multiples sublime, the numbers that are left, are prime!" He stumbled over to his bed and sprawled. . . .

After a moment he got up, angrily. He wasn't being a bit fair. If it was difficult for him to find a convenient way of dying in his room, why should he impose that difficulty on his good liege, St. Cyr?

He was extremely irritated with himself over that; but, picking up the bottle, marching out into the hall, singing as he looked for a conveniently fatal spot, he gradually began to feel very good again.

Sergeant Rhame tested the barricades in front of the aborigines' enclosure and let his men go back to trying to control the mobs at Med Center. All the time his men were

working, the aborigines had been trying to talk to them in
their odd pidgin, but the police were too busy. The one who
spoke English at all well, Masatura-san, was in his hut; the
others were almost incomprehensible. Rhame glanced at
his watch and decided that he had time for a quick cup of
coffee before going over to help his men with the crowd.
Although, he thought, it might be kinder to leave the crowd
alone to crush half its members to death. At least it would
be quick. And the private information of the police department surgeon was that the inoculations were not effective. . . . He turned, startled, as a girl's voice called him.

It was Locille, weeping. "Please, can you help me? Cornut's gone, and my brother's dead, and—I found this." She
held out the sheet with Cornut's carefully lettered list of
suicide possibilities.

The fact that Rhame had been taken from his computer
studies to help hold a mob down was evidence enough that
he really belonged there; but he hesitated and was lost. Individual misery was that much more persuasive than mass
panic. He began with the essentials: "Where is he? No idea
at all? No note? Any witnesses who might have seen him
go? . . . You didn't ask? *Why*—" But he had no time to
ask why she had failed to question witnesses; he knew that
every moment Cornut was off by himself was very possibly
the moment in which he would die.

They found the student proctor, jumpy and distracted
but still somewhere near his post. And he had seen Cornut!

"He was kind of crazy, I thought. I tried to tell him
something—you know Egerd, used to be in his class?" (He
knew perfectly just how well Locille had known Egerd.)
"He died this morning. I thought Master Cornut would be
interested, but he didn't even hear."

Rhame observed the expression on Locille's face, but
there was no time to worry about her feeling for a dead
undergraduate. "Which way? When?"

He had gone down the corridor more than half an hour
before. They followed.

Locille said miserably, "It's a miracle he's alive at all!
But if he lasted this long . . . and I was just a few minutes late. . . ."

"Shut up," the policeman said harshly, and called out to another undergraduate.

Following him was easy; he had been conspicuous by his wild behavior, even on that day. A few yards from the faculty refectory they heard raucous singing.

"It's Cornut!" cried Locille, and raced ahead. Rhame caught her at the door of the kitchens where she had worked so many months.

He was staggering about, singing in a sloppy howl one of Master Carl's favorite tunes:

> Add ray to modul, close th' set
> To adding, subtracting—

He stumbled against a cutting table and swore goodnaturedly.

> Produce a new system, an' this goddam thing
> Is gen'rally termed a (hic) ring!

In one hand he had a sharp knife, filched from the meat-cutter's drawer; he waved it, marking time.

"Come on, damn it!" he cried, laughing. "Goose me along!"

"Save him!" cried Locille, and started to run to him; but Rhame caught her arm. "Let go of me! He might cut his throat!"

He held her, staring hard. Cornut didn't even hear them; he was singing again. Rhame said at last, "But he isn't doing it, you see. And he's had plenty of time, by the look of the place. Suicidal? Maybe I'm wrong, Locille, but it looks to me as if he's just blind drunk."

Chapter Fifteen

Throughout the city and the world there were scenes like the one in front of Med Center, as a populace panicked by the apparition of pestilence—vanished these centuries!—scrambled for the amulet that would guard them against it. Hardly one man in a hundred was seriously ill, but that was enough. One per cent of twelve billion is a hundred and twenty million—a hundred and twenty million cases of the most deadly, most contagious . . . and least excusable . . . disease in medicine. For smallpox can infallibly be prevented, and only a world which had forgotten Jenner could have been taken by it unaware . . . or a world in which the memory of Jenner's centuries-old prophylaxis had been systematically removed.

In the highest tower of Port Monmouth the eight major television networks shared joint transmitter-repeater facilities. Equatorially mounted wire saucers scanned the sky for the repeater satellites. As each satellite in its orbit broke free of the horizon, a saucer hunted and found it. That saucer clung to it as it traversed the sky, breaking free and commencing the search pattern for a new one as the old one dipped beneath the curve of the earth again. There were more than sixty satellites circling the earth which the repeaters could use, each one specially launched and instrumented to receive, clean, amplify and rebroadcast the networks' programs.

Sam Gensel was senior shift engineer for the all-network technical crew at Port Monmouth.

It was not up to him to go out and get the pictures, to stage the shows or to decide what image went out on the air. Lecturing math professors, dimple-kneed dancers, sobbing soap-opera heroines—he saw all of them on the banked row of monitors in his booth. He saw all of them; he saw none of them. They were only pictures. What he really liked was test patterns, as they showed more of what he wanted to see. He watched for ripples of poor phasing, drifts off center, the electronic snowstorm of line failure. If the picture was clear, he hardly noticed what it represented . . . except tonight.

Tonight he was white-faced.

"Chief," moaned the rabbity junior engineer from Net Five, "it's all over the country! Sacramento just came in. And the relay from Rio has a local collect that shows trouble all over South America."

"Watch your monitor," Gensel ordered, turning away. It was very important that he keep a clear head, he told himself. Unfortunately the head that he had to keep clear was aching fiercely.

"I'm going to get an aspirin," he growled to his line man, a thirty-year veteran whose hands, tonight, were trembling. Gensel filled a paper cup of water and swallowed two aspirins, sighed and sat down at the coffee-ringed desk in the office he seldom had time to use.

One of the monitors showed an announcer whose smile was desperate as he read a newscast: "—disease fails to respond to any of the known antibiotics. All persons are cautioned to stay indoors as much as possible. Large gatherings are forbidden. All schools are closed until further notice. It is strongly urged that even within families personal contact be avoided as much as possible. And, above all, the Department of Public Health urges that everyone wait until an orderly program of immunization can be completed. . . ."

Gensel turned his back on the monitor and picked up the phone.

He dialed the front office. "Mr. Tremonte, please. Gensel here. Operational emergency priority."

The girl was businesslike and efficient (but did her

voice have a faint hysterical tremor?). "Yes, sir. Mr. Tremonte is at his home. I will relay." Click, click. The picture whirred, blurred, went to black.

Then it came on again. Old man Tremonte was slouched
at ease in a great leather chair, staring out at him irritably;
the flickering light on his face showed that he was sitting
by his fireplace. "Well? What's up, Gensel?"

That queer, thin voice. Gensel had always, as a matter
of employee discipline, stepped down hard on the little
jokes about the Old Man—he had transistors instead of
tonsils; his wife didn't put him to bed at night, she turned
him off. But there was something definitely creepy about
the slow, mechanical way he talked; and that old, lined
face!

Gensel said rapidly, "Sir, every net is carrying interrupt
news bulletins. The situation is getting bad. Net Five canceled the sports roundup, Seven ran an old tape of Bubbles
Brinkhouse—the word is he's dying. I want to go over to
emergency procedure. Cancel all shows, pool the nets for
news and civil-defense instructions."

Old man Tremonte rubbed his thin, long nose and abruptly laughed, like a store-window Santa. "Gensel, boy,"
he rasped. "Don't get upset over a few sniffly noses.
You're dealing with an essential public service."

"Sir, there are *millions* sick, maybe dying!"

Tremonte said slowly, "That leaves a lot who aren't.
We'll continue with our regular programs, and Gensel. I'm
going away for a few days; I expect you to be in charge. I
do not expect you to go over to emergency procedure."

I never got a chance to tell him about the remote from
Philadelphia, thought Gensel despairingly, thinking of the
trampled hundreds at the Municipal Clinic.

He felt his warm forehead and decided cloudily that
what he really needed was a couple more aspirin . . .
although the last two, for some reason, hadn't agreed with
him. Not at all. In fact, he felt rather queasy.

Definitely queasy.

At the console the line man saw his chief gallop clumsily
toward the men's washroom, one hand pressed to his
mouth.

The line man grinned. Fifteen minutes later, though, he was not grinning at all. That was when the Net Three audio man came running in to report that the chief was passed out cold, breathing like a broken-down steam boiler, on the washroom floor.

Cornut, with black coffee in him, was beginning to come back to something resembling normal functioning. He wasn't sober; but he was able to grasp what was going on. He heard Rhame talking to Locille: "What he really needs is massive vitamin injections. That would snap him right around—but you've seen what the Med Center looks like. We'll have to wait until he sobers up."

"I am sober," said Cornut feebly, but he knew it was untrue. "What happened?"

He listened while they told him what had been going on in the past twenty-four hours. Locille's brother dead, Egerd dead, plague loose in the land . . . the world had become a different place. He heard and was affected, but there was enough liquor still in him and enough of the high-pressure compulsion exercised by the immortals so that he was able to view this new world objectively. Too bad. But—he felt shame—*why* had he failed to kill himself?

Locille's hand was in his, and Cornut, looking at her, knew that he never wanted to let it go again. He had not died when he should have. Now . . . now he wanted to live! It was shameful, but he could not deny it.

He still felt the liquor in him, and it gave the world a warm, fresh appearance. He was ashamed, but the feeling was remote; it was a failure of his childhood, bad, but so long ago. Meanwhile he was warm and comfortable. "Please drink some more coffee," said Locille, and he was happy to oblige her. All the stimuli of twenty-four full hours were working on him at once, the beating, the strain, the compulsion of the immortals. The liquor. He caught a glimpse of Locille's expression and realized he had been humming.

"Sorry," he said, and held out his cup for more coffee.

* * *

Around the texas the waves were growing higher. The black barges tossed like chips.

Locille's parents braved the wind-blown rain topside to witness the solemn lowering of their son's casket into the black-decked funeral barge. They were not alone—there were dozens of mourners with them, strangers—and it was not quiet. *Dwang-g-g* went the bullroarer vibration of the steel cables. Hutch-*chumpf*, hutch-*chumpf* the pneumatic pens in the tower's legs caught trapped air from the waves and valved it into the pressure tanks for the generators. The noise nearly drowned out the music.

It was the custom to play solemn music at funerals, from tapes kept in the library for the purpose. The bereft were privileged to choose the program—hymns for the religious, Bach chorales for the classicists, largos for the merely mourning. Today there was no choice. The audio speakers played without end, a continuous random selection of dirges. There were too many mourners watching their children, parents or wives being awkwardly winched onto the tossing barges, on their way to the deep-sea funerary drop.

Six, seven . . . Locille's father carefully counted eight barges lying along the texas, waiting to be loaded. Each one held a dozen bodies. It was a bad sickness, he thought with detachment, realizing that the mourners were so few because, often enough, whole families were going to the barge together. He rubbed the back of his neck, which had begun to hurt. The mother standing beside him neither thought nor counted, only wept.

As Cornut sobered, he began to view his world and his past day in harsher, clearer perspective. Rhame helped. The policeman had the scraps of paper Cornut had left and he was remorseless in questioning. *"Why* must you die? *Who* are the immortals? *How* did they make you try to kill yourself—and why didn't you just now, with every chance in the world?"

Cornut tried to explain. To die, he said, remembering the lesson that had come with the beating, that is nothing; all of us do it. It is a victory in a way, because it makes death come to us on our terms. St. Cyr and the others, however—

"St. Cyr's gone," rasped the policeman. "Did you know that? He's gone and so is his bodyguard. Master Finloe from Biochemistry is gone; and his secretary says he left with Jillson and that old blonde. Where?"

Cornut frowned. It was not in keeping with his concept of immortality that they should flee in the face of a plague. Supermen should be heroic, should they not? He tried to explain that, but Rhame pounced on him. "Super-murderer, you mean! Where did they go?"

Cornut said apologetically, "I don't know. But I assure you that they had reasons."

Rhame nodded. His voice was suddenly softer. "Yes, they did. Would you like to know what those reasons were? The aborigines brought that disease. They came off their island carrying active smallpox, nearly every one of them; did you know that? The worst active cases were brought, the well ones were left on the island. Did you know that? They were given injections—to cure them, they thought, but the surgeon says they were only cosmetic cures, the disease was still contagious. And they were flown to every major city in the world, meeting thousands of people, eating with them, in close contact. They were coached," said Rhame, his face working, "in the proper behavior in civilized society. For example, the pipe of peace isn't their custom; they were told it would please us. Does that add up to anything for you?"

Cornut leaned forward, his head buzzing, his eyes on Rhame. Add up? It added up; the sum was inescapable. The disease was deliberately spread. The immortals had, in their self-oriented wisdom, determined to move against the short-lived human race, in a way that had nearly destroyed it more than once in ancient days: They had spread a fearsome plague.

Locille screamed.

Cornut realized tardily that she had been drowsing against his shoulder, unable to sleep, unable, after the sleepless night, to stay fully awake. Now she was sitting bolt upright, staring at the tiny glittering manicure scissors in her hand. "Cornut!" she cried, "I was going to stab you in the throat!"

It was night, and outside the high arch of the Bridge was a line of color, the lights of the speedy monotracks and private vehicles making a moving row of dots.

On one of the monotracks the motorman was half listening to a news broadcast: "The situation in the midwest is not as yet critical, but a wave of fear has spread through all the major cities of Iowa, Kansas and Nebraska. In Omaha more than sixty persons were killed when three heli-buses bearing emigrants collided in a bizarre midair accident, apparently caused by pilot error in one of the chartered planes. Here in Des Moines all transportation came to a halt for nearly ninety minutes this morning as air-control personnel joined the fleeing throngs, leaving their posts unattended. In a statement released—"

The motorman blinked and concentrated on his controls. He was fifty years old, had held this job and almost this run for more than half his life. He rubbed the sensor collar irritably; he had worn it nearly thirty years, but tonight it bothered him.

The collar was like a dead-man's switch, designed to monitor temperature and pulse, electronically linked to cut the monotrack's power and apply the brakes in the event of death or serious illness to the motorman. He was quite used to wearing these collars and appreciated the need for them; but tonight, climbing the approach ramp to the Bridge in third speed, his throat began to feel constricted.

Also his head ached. Also his eyes itched and burned. He reached for the radiomike that connected him to the dispatcher's office, and croaked, "Charley, I think I'm going to black out. I—" That was all. No more. He fell forward. The sensors around his neck had marked his abnormal pulse and respiration for minutes, and reacted as he collapsed. The monotrack stopped dead.

Behind it another one drove catastrophically into its tail.

The motorman of the second unit had been feeling queasy for more than an hour and was anxious to get to the end of his run; he had been overriding the automatic slowdown controls all the way across the Bridge. As he passed the critical parameters of sensor monitoring, his own collar switched off the power in his drive wheels; but by then it was too late; the wheels raced crazily against air. Even the sensor collars had not been designed to cope with two motorman-failures in the same second. White sparks flew from Bridge to water and died—great white sparks that were destroyed metal. The pile-up began. The sound of crashing battered at the campus of the University below. The Bridge stopped, its moving lights becoming a row of colored dots with one great hideous flare of color in the middle.

After a few moments distant ambulance sirens began to wail.

Cornut held the weeping woman, his face incredulous, his mind working. Locille trying to kill him? Quite insane!

But like the other insane factors in his own life, it was not inexplicable. He became conscious, rather late, of faint whispering thoughts in his own mind. He said to Rhame, "They couldn't reach me! They tried to work with her."

"Why couldn't they reach you?"

Cornut shrugged and patted her shoulder. Locille sat up, saw the scissors and hurled them away. "Don't worry, I understand," he said to her, and to the policeman, "I don't know why. Sometimes they can't. Like in the refectory kitchen, just now; they could have killed me. I even wanted them to; but they didn't. And once on the island, when I was blind drunk. And once—remember, Locille?—on the Bridge. Each time I was wide open to them, and on the Bridge they almost made it. But I stopped in time. Each time I was fuddled. I'd been drinking," he said, "and they should have been able to walk right in and take possession. . . ." His voice trailed thoughtfully off.

Rhame said sharply, "What's the matter with Locille?"

The girl blinked and sat up again. "I guess I'm sleepy," she said apologetically. "Funny. . . ."

Cornut was looking at her with great interest, not as a wife but as a specimen. "What's funny?"

"I keep hearing someone talking to me," she said, rubbing her face fretfully. She was exhausted, Cornut saw; she could not stay awake much longer, not even if she thought herself a murderer, not even if he died before her eyes. Not even if the world came to an end.

He said sharply, "Talking to you? Saying what?"

"I don't know. Funny. 'Me softspeak you-fella.' Like that."

Rhame said immediately, "Pidgin. You've been with the aborigines." He dismissed the matter and returned to Cornut, "You were on the point of something, remember? You said sometimes they could get at you, sometimes not. Why? What was the reason?"

Cornut said flatly; "Drinking. Each of those times I had been drinking!"

It was true! Three times he had been where death should have found him, and each time it had missed.

And each time he had been drinking! The alcohol in his brain, the selective poison that struck first at the uppermost level of the brain, reducing visual discrimination, slowing responses . . . it had deafened him to the mind voices that willed him to death!

"Smellim olefella bagarimop allfella," Locille said clearly, and smiled. "Sorry. That's what I wanted to say."

Cornut sat frozen for a second.

Then he moved. The bottle he had carried with him, Rhame had thriftily brought back to the room. Cornut grabbed it, opened it, took a deep swallow and passed it to Locille. "Drink! Don't argue, take a good stiff drink!" He coughed and wiped tears from his eyes. The liquor tasted foul; it would take little to make him drunk again.

But that little might save his life . . . Locille's life . . . it might save the world's!

Chapter Sixteen

Tai-i Masatura-san got up from his bed and walked to the strong new fence.

The crazy white people had not come up with dinner for them. It was getting very late, he judged, though the position of the stars was confusing. A few weeks ago, on his island, the Southern Cross, wheeling about the sky, was all the clock a man needed. These strange northern constellations were cold and unpleasant. They told him nothing he wanted to know, neither time nor direction.

His broad nostrils wrinkled angrily.

In order to become a tai-i he had had to become skilled in the art of reading the stars, among many other arts. Now that art was of no value, rendered useless by the stronger art of the white man. His gift of deepsmell, the reaching out with a part of his mind to detect truth or falsehood that made him a tribal magistrate, it had been voided by the old ones, who smelled so strongly and yet could baffle his inner nose.

He should never have trusted the softspeaking white man of great age, he thought, and spat on the ground.

His second in command moaned at the door of the hut.

In the creolized speech which served them better than the tribe's pidgin or Masatura-san's painful English, the man whimpered: "I have asked them to come, but they do not hear."

"One hears," said Masatura-san.

"The old ones are softspeaking endlessly," whined the sick man.

"I hear," said Masatura-san, closing his mind. He squatted, looking at the stars and the fence. Outside the campus was still noisy, voices, vehicles, even so late at night.

He thought very carefully what he wanted to do.

Masatura-san was a tai-i because of strength and learning, but also because of heredity. When the Japanese off the torpedoed destroyer had managed to reach his island in 1944 they had found a flourishing community. The Japanese strain in Masatura-san's ancestry came only from that generation. Before that his forebears were already partly exotic. The twelve Japanese were not the first sailors to wash ashore. Once "Masatura-san" had been "Master-son." English fathers and Melanesian mothers had produced a sturdy race—once the objecting male Malanesians had been killed off. The Japanese repeated the process with the hybirds they found, as the English had done before them, except for a few.

One of those few was the great-grandfather of Tai-i Masatura-san. He had been spared for exactly one reason: He was the chief priest in the community, and had been for nearly a century; the islanders would have died for him. Many of them did.

Three hundred years later, his third-generation offspring had inherited some of his talents. One was "deep smelling"—no sniff of the nostrils, but a different sense entirely. Another was age. Masatura-san himself was nearly a century old. It was the only thing he had managed to conceal from the owners of the strange softspeak voice who had found him on his island, and promised him much if he would help them.

The "deep smell" of the world beyond the barricade was very bad.

Tai-i Masatura-san thought carefully and made a decision. He moved over to the hut and poked his second in command with his foot. "Speak along him-fella two-time again," he ordered in pidgin. "Me help."

Cornut left his wife smiling laxly and sound asleep. "I'll be back," he whispered, and with Sergeant Rhame hurried out onto the campus. The wind was rising, and stars broke through scudding clouds. The campus was busy. Around the Med Center hundreds of people still waited, not because they had hope of immunization—the fact that the vaccine was ineffective had been announced—but because they had nowhere else to go. Inside the Clinic, medics with white faces and red eyes labored endlessly, repeating the same tasks because they knew no others. In the first hour they had discovered that the reference stacks had been looted of three centuries of epidemiology; they could not hope to replace them in finite time, but they could not help but try. Half the medics were themselves sick, ambulatory but doomed.

Cornut was worried, not for himself but for Locille. Thinking back to the Field Expedition, he remembered the shots that St. Cyr himself had taken and felt it more than likely that everyone receiving them had been rendered immune to the smallpox. But what of Locille? She had had nothing.

He had already told Rhame about the shots, and Rhame had instantly reported to the police headquarters; they would radio the island, try to locate the medics who had administered the vaccine. Neither of them was hopeful. The immortals would surely have removed all traces of what might halt their attack against the short-lived bulk of humanity.

But that thought had a corollary too: If the immortals had removed it, the immortals had it now.

They found the aborigines waiting for them. "You called us," said Cornut—it was a question; he still could not really believe in it—and Masatura-san nodded and reached for his hand.

Rhame blinked at them dizzily. Cornut had made him take three large drinks too—not because Rhame had shown any signs of being telepathic, only because Cornut was not sure. It seemed like a drunken vision, the math teacher linking hands with the squat brown man, wordless. But it was no vision.

After a moment Cornut released the islander's hand. Masatura-san nodded and, without a word, took the bottle from Cornut, drank deep, and passed it to his second in command, barely conscious on the ground behind him.

"Let's go," said Cornut thickly, his eyes glazed. (It was hard to be just drunk enough!) "We need a popper. Can you get one?"

Rhame reached into his pocket automatically and spoke briefly into his police radio before he asked questions. "What happened?"

Cornut wavered and caught his arm. "Sorry. It's all the immortals. You were right; they imported the smallpox carriers—went to a lot of trouble. But this fellow here, he's a lot older than he looks. He can read minds too."

The police radio squawked faintly. "They'll meet us over near Med Center," Rhame said, putting it back in his pocket. "Let's go." He was already moving before he asked, "But where are we going?"

Cornut was having difficulty walking. Everything was moving so slowly, so slowly; his feet were like sausage-shaped balloons, he was wading through gelatine. He measured his movements carefully, in a drunken, painstaking effort at clarity; he did not dare get too drunk, he did not dare become sober. He said; "I know where the immortal are. He told me. Not words—holding my hand, mind to mind; bodily contact helps. He didn't know the name of the place, but I can find it in the popper." He stopped and looked astonished. He said, "God, I *am* drunk. We'll need some help."

Rhame said, stumbling over the words, "I'm drunk too, but I figured that out for myself. The whole Emergency Squad is meeting us."

The cleared space near the Med Center was ideal for landing helipoppers, even though it was dotted now with prostrate figures, sick or merely exhausted. Rhame and Cornut heard the staccato bark and flutter of the helipoppers and stood at the edge of the clear space, waiting. There were twelve police poppers settling toward them; eleven poised themselves in air, waiting; the twelfth blossomed with searchlights and came on down.

In the harsh landing light, one of the recumbent figures near them pushed himself up on an elbow, mumbling. His eyes were wide, even in the blinding light. He stared at Cornut, his lips moving, and he cried faintly; "Carriers!"

Rhame first realized the danger. "Come on!" he cried, beginning to trot, lurching, toward the landing popper. Cornut followed, but others were waking feverishly. "Carriers!" they cried, ten of them and then a dozen. It was like the birth of a lynch mob. "Carriers! They did it to us! Get them!" Sick figures pushed themselves to their knees, hands clutched at them. Half a dozen men, standing in a knot, whirled and ran toward them. "Carriers!"

Cornut began to run. Carriers? Of course they were not carriers; he knew what it was. It was St. Cyr perhaps, or one of the others, unable to break through the barrier of alcohol to reach his own mind, working with the half-waking minds of the hopeless hundreds on the grass to attack and destroy them. It was quite astonishing, meditated one part of his mind with drunken gravity, that there were so many partial telepaths in this random crowd; but the other part of his mind cried Run, run!

Stones began to fly, and from fifty yards away, across the green, Cornut heard a sound that might have been a shot. But the popper was whirling its blades above them now; they boarded it and it lifted, leaving the sudden mob, wakened to fury, milling about below.

The popper rose to join the rest of the squad. "That was just in time," breathed Cornut to the pilot. "Thanks. Now head east until—"

The co-pilot was turning toward him, and something in his eyes stopped Cornut. Rhame saw it as fast as he. As the co-pilot was reaching for his gun the police sergeant brought up his fist. Co-pilot went one way, the gun another. Sitting on the co-pilot, Cornut and Rhame stared at each other. They didn't have to speak; the communication that passed between them was not telepathic; they both came to the same conclusion at once. Cornut jumped for the gun, pointed it at the only other man in the popper, the pilot. "This is an emergency popper, right? With medical supplies."

Rhame understood at once. He leaped for the locker and

broke out a half-liter of brandy in a sealed flask. He handed it to the pilot. "Drink!" he ordered. Then: "Get on the radio! Tell every man in the squad to take at least two ounces of brandy!"

It was, thought Cornut dizzily, a hell of a way to fight a war.

Chapter Seventeen

Rhame was only a sergeant, but the pilot of the lead popper was a deputy inspector. Once he had enough alcohol in his bloodstream to blot out the nagging drive of the immortals he took command. The other helipoppers questioned his orders, all right. But they obeyed.

The fleet sailed out over the bay, over the city, up toward the mountains.

Underneath them the city lay helpless. It was flat and quiet from above, but at ground level it was a giant killing-pen where blind mobs roamed in terror. A thousand feet over the terrified streets, Cornut could see the fires of wrecked vehicles, the little heaps of motionless bodies, the utter confusion that the plague had wrought. Worse than plague was the panic. The deputy inspector had told him that there were by now more than ten thousand reported deaths in the city, but only a fraction of them were from smallpox. Terror had slain the rest.

Cornut knew that that was what the immortals wanted.

They had kept their herd of contented, helpless, short-lived cattle long enough. The herd had prospered until it competed with its unseen owners for food and space. Like any good husbandmen, the immortals had decided to thin the herd out.

What could be more painless, for them, than a biological thinner? As myxamotosis had rid Australia of the rabbit pest, so smallpox could control the swarming human vermin that was dangerous to the immortals.

Sergeant Rhame said thickly, "Bad weather up there. I don't suppose we can go around." Behind them the poppers

305

trailed in clear air, but ahead, over the mountains, were towering clouds.

Cornut shook his head. He only knew the way St. Cyr had gone, as St. Cyr had seen it with his own eyes and the old islander had relayed it to him. They would have to fight through the storm.

Cornut closed his eyes briefly. It was war to the death now, and he wondered what it would be like to kill a man. He could understand well enough the motives of St. Cyr and the others, waging a jealous battle against every threat, striking down those who like himself might learn of their existence, defeating research that might give them away by concealing it. It was a constant defensive action, and he could understand, he could even in a way forgive, their need to remove the threat. He could forgive their attempts on his own life, he could forgive their try at destroying most of a world.

He could not forgive the threat to Locille. For she was exposed. A few would survive the plague in any event—a few always did—but Cornut was a mathematician, and he did not accept one chance in a million as a sporting gamble against odds.

All these years, he dreamed, and all the while immortals were directing humanity in directions they chose. No wonder the great strides in medicine, no wonder the constant grinding competition between manufacturers for luxuries and comforts. How would it be if the immortals were destroyed?

And yet, he thought, beginning to sober up, and yet wasn't there something in Wolgren about that? No, not Wolgren. But somewhere in statistical theory. Something about random movements. The Brownian Movement of molecules? That had been on Master Carl's mind, he remembered. The drunkard's walk—the undirected progress that moved from a dead center ever more slowly, asymptotically, yet never stopped. Straight-line progress was always to an end; if the immortals directed it, it could go only so far as they could conceive.

They were not the future, he realized with sharp clarity.

No super-potent force was the future; a kennelman could breed dogs only to his own specifications, he could not give the species the chance at free growth that could go on and on and endlessly on; and—*Cornut,* said a shrill, angry whine in his brain.

Panicky, he grabbed for the flask of medical brandy and blotted out the voice with a choking swallow.

The flask was getting low. They would have to hurry. They dared not get more sober.

Senator Dane stirred angrily and crackled an oath with his mind that sent ripples of laughter through the party. *Don't laugh, you damned fools!* he thought. *I've lost them again.*

"Sweety-heart," caroled the ancient bobbysoxer from South America, Madam Sant'Anna, "san fairy-ann. Don't cry." A mental image of a fat weeping baby with Dane's face.

Pistols firing, Madam Sant'Anna skewered with a thousand swords, thought the senator.

Not me. "What, me worry?" A giggle.

You'll laugh out of the other side of your face. An image of an unmarked grave. An obscene gesture from the senator; but, in truth, he wasn't really worried either. He cast out for Cornut's mind again, but not more than half-heartedly, and when he could not find it he projected a mental picture of a staggering, vomiting drunk that made them smile. The senator hurled a painful thought at one of the dark servants and cheerfully awaited the bringing of his candies.

Senator Dane never drank, but he had observed the shorties drinking, he knew what drinking could do. Sometimes the immortals got the same sort of selective release from alkaloids. Enough alcohol to blot out control, he was confident, would blot out the motor reflexes. They would pile up against a hill, they would crash into each other. Certainly they would never find this place—although Masatura-san's mind had been powerfully clear, and possibly there had been a leak, and—no. St. Cyr himself had selected Masatura-san's tribe for the job of extermination. No one could conceal anything from St. Cyr. And the place was quite unfindable.

It very nearly was. It had been a resort hotel at one time, used for conventions of the sort that are not meant to be public, pre-empted from a gangster who had in turn pre-empted it from its (more or less) legitimate builders. The gangster had been a nuisance, and the immortal who killed him had felt rather virtuous as he murdered a murderer.

The hotel no longer had roads leading to it, and there was no other habitation within twenty miles. *That* had been expensive; but the immortals had known this storm was brewing half a century before and expense was the least important factor in any of their plans. There was room for all of them, seventy-five immortals from all over the world, "children" of sixty or sixty-five, the oldest of all a man who had been born in the reign of Caligula. (There were very few born before the twentieth century, because of the public-health contribution to their longevity; but those few seemed unwilling ever to die at all.) There were women who, with repeated plastic surgery, had managed to keep themselves in the general appearance, from a distance, of youth. There were visible ancients, like St. Cyr with his cyanosis and his scars, the squat old Roman with his great recurring keloids, the hairless, fat black man who had been born in slavery on the estate of the king's governor of Virginia. Color made no difference to them, nor race nor age; the factor that counted was power. They were the strongest in the world, as they insured by killing off the weak.

They were, however, cowards. They flocked like wild geese to favorable climates, away from Europe in the early twentieth century, away from the Pacific during the bomb tests of the 1950's. They left North Africa well before the Israeli-Arab clashes, and none of them had visited China since the days of the Dowager Empress. Not one had seen an earthquake or a volcano at close range—or at any rate, not after realizing what they were; and every one had, for all of his prolonged life, surrounded himself with walls and with guards. They were cowards. They had the avarice of the very rich. There were drawbacks to their lives, but not such a drawback as dying.

In the great hotel, staffed by Sudanese flown in a decade earlier, completely out of touch with the world around them and guarded from even chance contact with a wanderer by a totally unfamiliar tongue, they prepared to sit out the plague. Senator Dane wandered among them, jovial but faintly worried. He annoyed them. The undertone of worry was like a constant mumble to them, irritating. They chaffed him about it, in words of fifty languages (they knew them all) or in thoughts, with gesture and tone. But he infected them all.

Fear is a relative thing. The man who is starving does not fear the sudden early frost that may destroy the crops. It is too late for that; he can only worry about what is close at hand. The well-fed man can worry years ahead.

The immortals could worry a full century ahead. They were Rockefellers of life, dispensing hours and days to the short-lived like dimes; they looked far into the future, and every distant pebble in their path was a mountain. Dane's worry was small and remote, but it was a worry. Suppose, mumbled the fear behind the jolly mask, that they do find our place here. True, they can't do much to us—we can destroy them with their minds, as we always have—but that is a nuisance. We would want to flee. This is our best place, but we have others.

Shut up, thought (or said, or gestured) the others.

He was interfering with their fun. The Roman was demonstrating a delicate balance of a feather on a soap-bubble (he was the strongest of them; it was hard to move physical objects with the mind, but with age it became possible). But the fear said: We have lost them. They might be anywhere. (The bubble collapsed.) The fear said; Even if we flee, they are not stupid; they might search the house and find our own medics. And then—look then! Then they can end the plague and, with only a few of them dead, some five billion people will be looking for us seventy-five! (The feather floated to the ground. The immortals shouted at him peevishly.)

I'm sorry.

"Don't be sorry, you damn old fool," cried Madam Sant'Anna, petulantly picturing him in an embarrassingly private blunder. The Roman picked up the image and added a third-century refinement.

But suppose they do get through, sobbed Dane.

"Go," said St. Cyr in his clock-tick voice, angry enough to speak aloud, "de-stroy the ser-um. Do not spoil our day!"

Unwillingly Dane went, his mumbling worry diminishing in their minds with distance. It stopped abruptly, and cheerfully the immortals returned to their pleasures. . . .

It stopped abruptly for Dane too.

He was in the downstairs hall, searching for one of the Sudanese servants, when he heard a sound behind him. He started to turn. But he was fat and he was, in spite of everything, very old.

The blow caught him and he fell heavily, like a bladder filled with lard. He was only vaguely conscious of the hands that rolled him over, the acrid taste of the something—was it liquor? But he *never* drank liquor!—they were forcing down his throat.

"Got one," said one of the helicops thickly, staggering slightly.

Senator Dane did not know, but there were a dozen reeling figures around him, and more coming in. As he began to recover consciousness he knew, but then it was too late. It was so *still.* The voices in his mind were silent!

The alcohol was a barrier. It deafened him, blinded him, marooned him. He had only eyes and mouth and ears, and for one whose life has been illuminated by the rapid flash of the mind itself, that is blindness. He began to sob.

Cornut passed the kitchen where the servants huddled under guard and Senator Dane lay on the floor, and hurried after the helicops. He heard gunfire and felt a queasy panic. This was the moment of truth; in a few seconds now the world would change its complexion forever, a pastured herd with immortals fattening on its bounty or a brawl of leaderless billions— *No.* He had not thought that! And in a flash he was in another mind; it was a seepage from the cranky petulance of St. Cyr that had touched him then, so close and so strong that even battle and alcohol could not quite subdue it; what he had felt was what St. Cyr felt.

Cornut began to run. It was like being in two places at once; he saw the police coming in, shooting; he ran behind them.

The immortals resisted as best they could, but their weapons were no longer appropriate. They were like billionaires trying to buy off a charging rhino or a Hitler attempting to sway an earthquake to his will. They could not prevail against this naked force, they could only die or be taken; and the blurred fury of their minds was like a shout or a stench.

He caught one last clear thought from St. Cyr: *We lose.* There was no other. St. Cyr was dead; and all about him police were overpowering the survivors.

Chapter Eighteen

Cornut passed out completely on the way back, and slept soddenly for hours. Rhame let him sleep. There was time enough for everything now, even for sleep. The medics, with the restored tapes for the stacks, had already begun the task of preparing vaccine; the hundred liters of serum was already being rationed among the already ill. The mobs were quieted—it took only hope to end their rage— and the danger, for most, was past. Not for all. The serum would never reach South Africa in time for some, for instance; and there were many already dead. But the dead were only in the millions. . . .

Cornut woke up like an explosion.

His head was pounding; he staggered to his feet, ready to fight. Rhame, full of wake-up pills but obviously fading, reassured him quickly. "It's all right. Look!" They were back in the city, in a hastily cleared penal wing of one of the hospitals. Along a corridor, in room after room, there were couples of old, old men and women, sleeping or staggering. "Twenty of them," said Rhame proudly, "and everyone guaranteed to have one point five per cent of alcohol in the blood or better. We'll keep them that way until we decide what to do next."

"Only twenty?" demanded Cornut, suddenly alarmed. "What about the others?" Rhame smiled like a shark. I see, said Cornut, visioning that queer contradiction, a dead immortal. . . . Better, he told himself, than a dead planet.

He did not linger. He had to see Locille. Rhame had already phoned the campus and reported that she was well but still asleep; but Cornut needed first-hand assurance.

A police popper took him to the campus in a pelting

rainstorm and he ran through the wet grass, looking around. The grass was stained and littered; the windows of the Med Center showed where the mob had nearly smashed its way in. He hurried past, past the aborigines' camp, now deserted, past the Administration Building; past the memory of Master Carl and the Clinic where Egerd had died. The rain clouds stank of fumes from fires in the city; across the river there still lay thousands of unburied dead.

But the clouds were thin, and radiance began to shine through.

In his room, Locille stirred and woke. She was quite calm, and she smiled.

"I knew you'd be back," she said. He took her in his arms, but even in that moment he could not forget what Rhame had told him, what they had already learned from the drunken, babbling immortals. The number of incipient telepaths was great indeed, as he had begun to suspect; but they were not "abortions" of immortals, not at all.

They were the real thing. The mutation that had produced a St. Cyr had produced many, many millions; it was not short-lived humans they had killed or driven to death, it was young immortals. The gene was a dominant, and now that it had shown so often it would soon fill the race. What the immortals had done was not to preserve themselves at the expense of a race that should have become extinct. They had only protected their own power against the Cornuts, the Locilles, the others with whom they did not wish to share.

"I knew you'd be back," she whispered again.

"I told you I would," he said. "I'll always be back . . ." and he wondered how to tell her what "always" had suddenly come to mean for them.

About the Author

Frederik Pohl has been about everything one man can be in the world of science fiction: fan (a founder of the fabled Futurians), book and magazine editor, agent, and, above all, writer. As editor of *Galaxy* in the 1950s, he helped set the tone for a decade of SF—including his own memorable stories such as *The Space Merchants* (in collaboration with Cyril Kornbluth). His latest novel is *The Cool War*. He has also written *Beyond the Blue Event Horizon*, a sequel to the Hugo and Nebula Award-winning novel, *Gateway*, and *The Way the Future Was*, a memoir of his forty-five years in science fiction. Frederik Pohl was born in Brooklyn, New York, in 1919, and now divides his time between Red Bank, New Jersey, and New York City.